WHISKEY CHARM

A Foster House Novel

WALKER ROSE

LE Publishing

I came to Huckleberry Springs to regroup—not to flash a cowboy while rescuing some strays from a ditch.

Haven Hennessy is everything I don't want anyway: A man who puts himself first. A man who'd rather have fun than face commitment. A man who can charm a girl right out of a good decision. So he can kiss my red lace panties goodbye the moment I figure out how to ditch this town.

Yet he takes in the puppy and three kittens I rescue from the side of the road. He's loyal to his brothers and his company. And he makes it his mission to give me new experiences, like fly-fishing, horseback rides, and getting naked in a tack room.

My stay in this small Montana town is only supposed to be temporary until I can launch a new career. Am I as wrong about that as I am about Haven? Because he makes me feel something no one else ever has: wanted.

But the more I get to know Haven, the more I realize I was right all along. Haven doesn't let people in. Not fully. Not when he's spent his whole life being left behind. So when my dream opportunity finally manifests, I have to leave before I break all my rules and my own heart in the process. I don't dare fall for his whiskey charm.

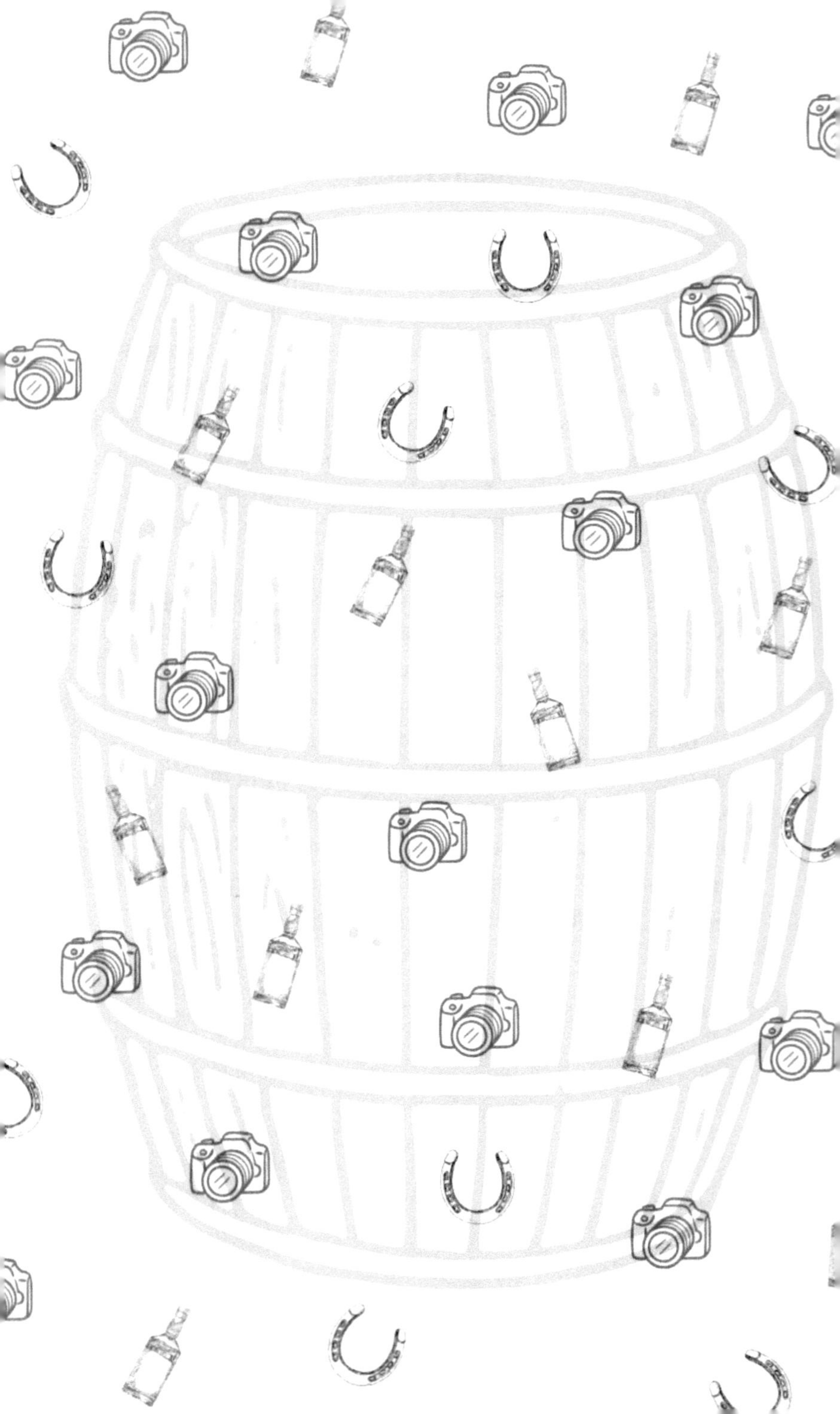

CHAPTER ONE

Prescott

Outside my car, there is nothing but sweeping pastures, rolling hills, and peaked mountains in the background. Not a dive bar in sight. "I think I'm lost, Papa."

His raspy grunt echoes through my speakers, accompanied by the tink of glassware. He must be working at the bar already. "Where are you?"

"Montana," I say wryly, but I don't have much more information than that. My map app insists I've reached my destination, but my destination should have people and buildings instead of cattle.

"You in Huckleberry Springs?" he asks, oblivious that I wouldn't be lost if I were in town already. From what I recall, it's too small for me to get lost in, even in the middle of the night under the new moon. Right now, the sun is high in the afternoon sky, and all I see is a gorgeous Montana view.

"Maybe? I took the back roads from Gillette." I split

my trip from Chicago over two days, staying in Spearfish, South Dakota, last night. The last several hours have been nothing but gorgeous, rugged land dotted with dark trees. The only clue that I'm close to Huckleberry Springs is the Beartooth Mountains in the distance. "I turned off the interstate after Billings, and now I'm surrounded by cows."

"Black? Brown?"

What does that matter? "Black."

"Solid? Or baldies?"

I slow before I go off the road. The highway doesn't have much for a shoulder, and I'm distracted. A couple of houses line the valley, but other than a sign for fishing access, I don't have much else for landmarks. "They're solid black cows. Lots of calves."

"Black Angus," Papa mutters. "Could be anywhere."

I snort. Not even the cattle can help me. I pull over as much as I can and stop before I end up back in Wyoming or something. Instead of smacking my head against the wheel, I pull up my photos and gaze at Buford. Like Pavlov's dog, I exhale my stress. Stern, lovable, fluffy, orange Buford.

Buford the boss cat, may he rest in peace.

A pang snaps against my heart. I could use his cuddles now, but he's gone, and I'm in the middle of nowhere, Montana, getting almost as much help from my dad as I have my whole life. Why'd I expect this to be different?

Maybe because I'm lost on my way to go live with him. Definitely a new development in our father-daughter relationship.

"You see signs for the ski resort, Pressie?" he asks. Once, my ex tried to call me by the same nickname. I don't have much from Papa that makes me feel special, so I put a stop to that. *Be more inventive. Give me my own special nickname*. But that was one of the many things Milo couldn't put himself out for.

"I didn't accidentally go to Red Lodge, Papa." I did accidentally go to Red Lodge at my map app's insistence.

"What else is around you? A lot of trees?"

I scan the valley full of trees along the Stillwater River. Then to the blanketed mountains. "Yes to trees."

"The old Hennessy mine?"

I crane my head around. A mine? "What's that look like?"

"It's an old gold mine."

"I've never seen an old gold mine." Or a new one.

"Didn't I take you to one?" He makes a clicking sound. "In Colorado, when I had that ride—"

"Oh, I see a sign. I'll call you back." I hang up on him, squeeze my eyes shut, and blow out a breath. Did I make the right decision? I'm going to be living with Papa and hearing his beloved rodeo stories. Hearing him talk about memories he thinks we made together.

No, he never took me anywhere, but yes. Now I remember that I have been to a former gold mine. If something didn't include a rodeo or the animals in the rodeo, he wasn't interested. I toured a mine turned museum with Mom once in Colorado. Papa had been on the rodeo circuit, we'd followed, and he'd had the time of his life while Mom and I had done our own thing. While Mom quietly cried about how her husband seemed to spend time with everyone but her.

This dismal trip down memory lane is not going to get me to Huckleberry Springs, nor will it aid me in figuring out my next phase in life while living with Papa. Sighing, I throw the car into gear. I've just started pulling back onto the highway when a kitten darts in front of me and disappears into the grass.

I gasp and flip the car into park. There are no homes close enough for such a small kitty to have roamed from. Grabbing my phone, I scramble out of the car. I'm alone on the road, and the wind flutters my hair. It's not as windy as Chicago, but the breeze licks at the hem of my skirt.

I should've thrown on shorts, but the weather forecast this morning for Huckleberry Springs was a pleasant seventy-two degrees with light wind and full sunshine. I didn't think I'd be heading into a ditch full of weeds in my skirt and hiking sandals.

I'm doing all sorts of things I didn't think I'd be doing today, like moving to Montana to live with my absentee dad. But it's only for a little while. Until I figure out what I want to be when I grow up. Again. And until I have the money to do so.

"Here, kitty, kitty." I inspect the grass like I have x-ray vision. It was a cat, right? An orange kitten. Not many other wild animals are orange.

Nostalgia explodes in my chest. Once upon a time, an orange kitten changed my life. The warm little memory bursts. He changed it again when he was gone too.

A tiny mew reaches me. I spin around. "Kitty?"

Another sound reaches me. A meow?

"Kitty, kitty?" I start slowly. If it's that far ahead, it's a fast runner.

Should I lock my car? It's full of my life's belongings. I sold all my photography equipment except my camera before I moved.

A pang of regret hits me square in the chest.

I look around. Still no other vehicles. My car is fine.

I creep forward. "Kitty?"

A little mew sounds in the distance. I pull up the camera on my phone and switch to video before I realize what I'm doing. Really? Haven't I learned that no one wants to see what I post without Buford? I switch my phone off and stuff it into my bra. This dress has no pockets.

I high-step through the grass and wildflowers. The leaves scrape against my calves, tickling my skin as I try to keep from crushing the blossoms of the wildflowers. Just as I'm about to put my foot down, a blur of orange springs up and disappears again. I windmill my arms, struggling for balance. Once I'm stable, I bend down.

I look through the late spring growth. "Hello? Kitty?"

Little green eyes blink at me before dashing away into thicker weeds.

I lean over farther, my ass in the air. A gust of wind comes up, blowing my skirt high. I distractedly bat it down, but the material catches again, lifting higher until a cool breeze gusts across my butt cheeks.

An engine drones. Right *behind me*. I close my eyes, my cheeks—both sets—warming. Damn.

Whoever it is had better spare my dignity and keep driving. *Please, no dashcam.*

The wind blows stronger for a second as the truck continues past me.

Thank Go—

The truck comes to a stop.

Fuck.

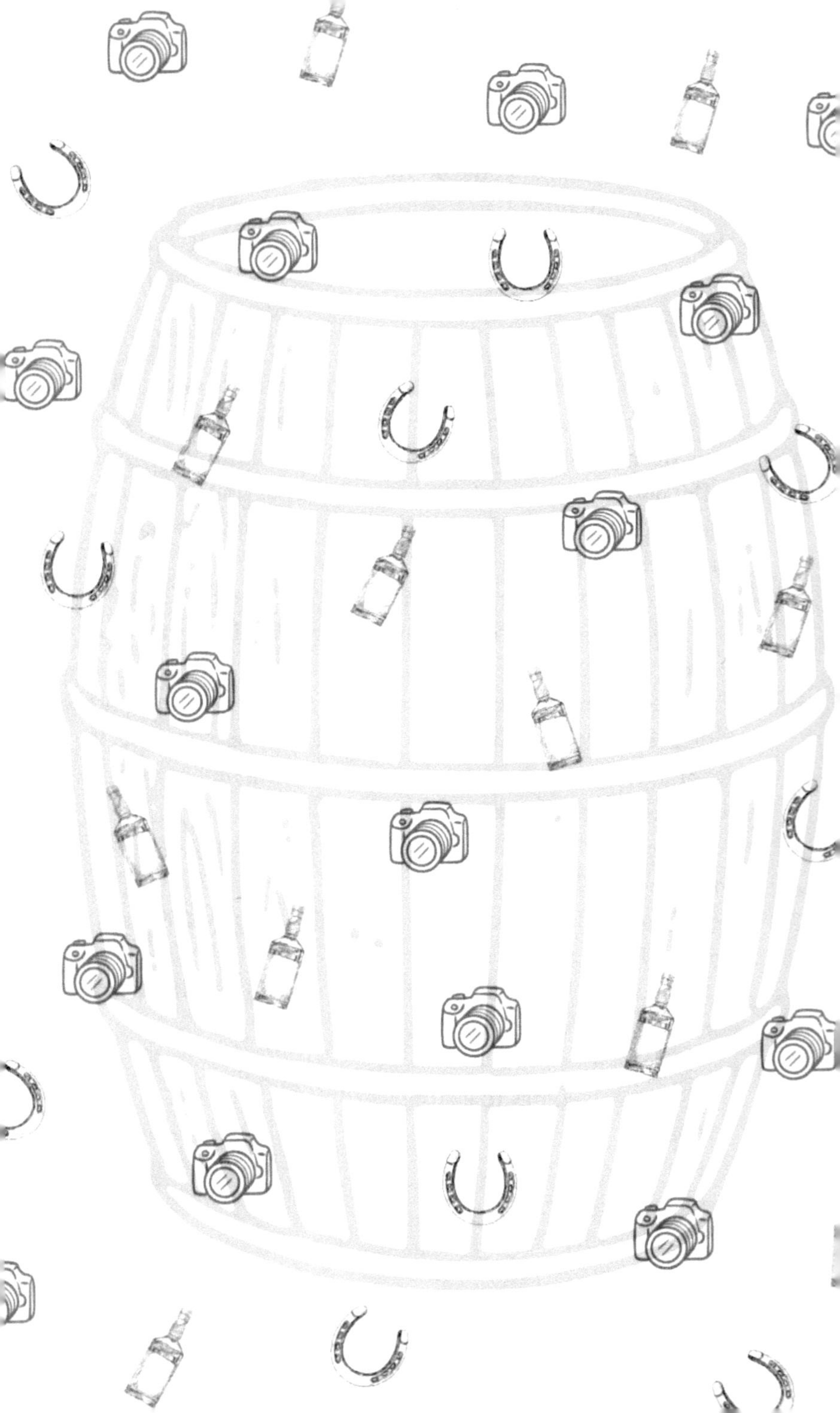

CHAPTER TWO

Haven

It's the middle of the day, but there's the ripest, juiciest full moon in the ditch. And it's encased in the skimpiest pair of lacy red underwear. I pull to the side of the road and let my brain come online when my dick so badly wants to take over.

I consider the sight in the rearview mirror. A small blue car takes up half the lane and all of the narrow shoulder. A woman is in the weeds in the ditch, looking around.

Did something fly off her car? Out the window? Can the wind blow her skirt up again?

I should check on her. I can't drive by someone possibly stranded on the side of the road and go about business as usual. Shutting the radio off in the middle of the weather report, I back my pickup closer to the car.

I don't recognize the vehicle or the woman, though I haven't seen much other than long, creamy legs, a full ass, and that unforgettable lacy red underwear. What does the rest of her look like?

After I flip my pickup into park, I grab my cowboy hat off the passenger seat and climb out. I stuff the hat on and cock my head at the sound of her voice. Who is she talking to?

"Here, kitty, kitty." Her soothing tone rolls over me, a caress along my skin.

The closer I get, the clearer the woman becomes. She's tall. The grasses in the ditch don't reach to her knees, but it's early in the season. A mop of coppery hair glows almost orange under the sun and swirls over her head in a large bun. Strands that frame her face flutter in the breeze.

"Kitty? Come here, hon."

I could record her cooing and replay it all night and day long.

She turns, and a cry rips from her. She cartwheels her arms, and I rush to the edge of the road. Her eyes go wider. Blue. Clear, like the sky above us.

I pull to a stop at the edge of the ditch to keep from scaring her even more, and she recovers her balance.

Planting her bare legs wide, she looks ready to sprint in either direction. "Who are you? What do you want?"

I raise my hands like I'm getting mugged. "Sorry, ma'am. I stopped to see if you need any help."

She blinks at me. "Ma'am," she whispers to herself. "Isn't that just the cherry on the day?" Giving herself a shake, she lifts her chin. "Did you, um... Did you just drive by?"

I nod while carefully reining in my expression. Nice and neutral. I can't lie to her. I'm better than that, but she won't know how the sight affected me. I was unmoved. My pulse did not beat through my dick.

Her "figures" is inaudible but still clear from her lips. Mine twitch as I hold back a smile. Better she doesn't know for certain that I can describe the exact shade of her panties. Ruby red, like a precious jewel that should be thoroughly inspected.

She looks around her feet. "I swear I saw a kitten out here. And where there's one, there might be more."

It is prime dumping season for spring batches of kittens. "You got something to put them in?"

She lifts the green material of her skirt. Paired with her brilliant hair and matching top, she looks like just another wildflower mixed into the ditch weeds. "I can make a pouch out of this."

Depends how many there are, how big they are, and how dirty she wants to get that outfit. "Let me see what I have." I start for my pickup.

An "oh my god!" spins me right back around. My boots scrape on the pavement as I rush through the grasses.

"I found them," she says in a loud hiss. "A puppy too!"

My stomach drops. Kittens *and* a puppy? Just tossed on the side of the road? It's more of a wonder that I'm still shocked it happens.

I peer over her shoulder. A pleasing floral scent amplifies the other smells coming from the grasses around us. I catch myself leaning into her to sniff. Damn. *Don't be creepy.*

In front of her is a puddle of fur. One of the two gray tabby kittens lets out a halfhearted hiss, and a little black Lab puppy thumps its tail.

She squats. Her skirt catches on some of the grasses, but that doesn't stop her. Her soft words fill the air. "Look at you. And you're all tame, aren't you?" The little tabby hisses again. "Oh, I know. You're a tough one. You're the protector." She scratches its head, and the whole guardian role goes out the window. The kitten's eyes roll back, and a second one bumps its head into her hand, wanting its own pets.

When she reaches the puppy, it rolls to bare a round little belly. To be fair, if this girl put her fingers on me, I'd bare a lot more if she wanted me to.

She looks back at me. I'm pinned in place by shrewd sapphire gems. "Did you find a box?"

Shit. I forgot about that. I'm not usually so useless. I make a point of it. "No, you called out, and I thought something was wrong."

"Oh." A tiny frown passes over her bow-shaped mouth, like she isn't sure what to think about me checking on her.

Meanwhile, I have too much to think about. Like how her top lip is a little thinner, making her bottom lip perfect to nibble on. Her figure is full of curves, but what's the boxy outline by one of her breasts?

"There're only two gray tabbies and the puppy here." She rips me out of my inappropriate perusal. "The one I saw looked like an orange kitten, about the same size as these. They've got to be together."

I squint at the strays, struggling to concentrate. I'm not usually this distracted by a woman. It's the range of emotions she's put me through, that's all. First, I got flashed. Unintentionally, but my libido doesn't care about the motivation, just that it happened. Then I thought she was stranded and inadvertently scared her. Now I'm ready to do whatever bidding she needs from me.

She lifts a kitten and inspects it all over while giving it some love. "I can carry them all. I'll put them in my car and look for the other one."

She'd get that pretty dress dirty. "No need. Hand them

here." The animals look fairly healthy. There's no matted fur or watery eyes, and their sides haven't sunken in. They've been recently unhoused. "Then I can look for the third."

"You don't mind?"

"Why would I?"

"Do you have somewhere to be?" She adopts that slight frown again.

"Not at the moment." Is it my willingness to help that's throwing her? Hasn't she experienced a hand-up from a passerby? Is she a city girl?

She considers my answer for a heartbeat, then gives me the wiggly cats. The velvety black puppy gets cradled in her arms. "I think it's a Lab." She checks the backside. "A little girl."

"Good huntin' dog."

She arches a manicured brow, and I steel myself to get berated by a girl who thinks hunting is cruel when it's how my dad fed me and my two brothers for years. "She'll come in handy for all that hunting I do."

The dry sarcasm in her voice somehow fits the strong vibe she puts off. "Duck hunting can be addictive."

"I'm afraid I haven't had the pleasure." She scratches the puppy under the chin, and there's barely a smile despite the faint trace of humor.

Hell, she's pretty. Her cheeks are flushed, and her eyes sparkle. Her breasts are more than a handful, and thanks to the view I got earlier, I can picture her naked too easily.

There goes my blood flow. *Control yourself, dammit!* I'm better than this base reaction. I never get in over my head with a girl, and I don't even know her name. I tip the brim of my hat instead of laughing with her, and her smile falters. "Where do you want them?"

The humor's gone from her eyes, and the loss is acute. "In the trunk, I think. Just so they're a little contained while I move everything around and make space for them."

I get a better look at her car. Plastic bins are stacked high in the back seat. Is that bedding in her back window?

"Got it." I climb out of the ditch, and she's right behind me.

I should be sidled up to a bar by now, helping my brother Durban with his wedding prep. Since wedding planning is his future wife's thing, I know exactly what I'm in for, and it's not much. But just because I don't have many tasks doesn't mean I'm going to slack. Durban and Campbell deserve a dream wedding.

The woman's reassuring tone reaches me where I search. The cattle in the field watch me like they're not sure why I'm out here at this time of day. They're in their summer pastures farther away from home, and they don't see me as often as during the winter months.

A tiny mew reaches me, and I find the third kitten hiding by a fence post. "You're coming with me, bud."

It tries to get away, but I'm too quick. It quiets down when I cradle it to my chest. She's bent over the trunk of her car where the critters must be. The wind is fluttering the hem of her skirt. I lift my gaze skyward, just in case. My mama didn't raise me better than that, but my brothers did.

As I come up behind her, she's taking pictures. Her trunk is full of plastic totes, and she has the kittens nestled between them. The puppy is at the edge, tail wagging so hard it could concuss one of the kittens. "Look at you. So photogenic. You were made for the big screen."

"Are you going to get them an agent?"

She jumps. "How are you so quiet in cowboy boots?"

"I'm usually on a horse."

Instead of looking impressed, her lips turn down. She rakes her eyes down my body like she's just registering how I'm dressed—boots, jeans, and a plain black T-shirt. Distaste curls the corner of her mouth. "You're a cowboy. Rodeo?"

My ego isn't inflated, but it shrivels at her flat tone. Not the usual reaction from women, and perhaps I'm a little spoiled from working the tasting room. And from the dive bar in town. And from getting groceries... Women don't look at me with distaste. Usually, I'm trying not to earn too much of their attention.

"No to the rodeo. Sometimes a cowboy, yes. I was exaggerating. I'm not always on a horse." I lift my chin toward the cattle. Some are still watching us, their smaller calves at their sides growing nicely. "Those are mine and my brothers'."

Her shoulders loosen only slightly. "Oh, this is your land. These are yours?"

It takes a second before it dawns on me that she's talking about the fresh strays. "Uh, no." I hold out the orange kitten. He lets out a big meow. "Finders keepers."

Her expression falls. "My dad isn't going to let me keep them at his place. He's horribly allergic, and his garage is full of all his—well." She looks around. "Is there a shelter nearby?"

"Billings has the closest rescue. I think someone in town helps out with finding local foster homes, but you'd have to go through the main office anyway."

The blue in her eyes darkens. "Oh, no. Crap. Where am I going to keep them?" She pokes at the screen of her phone. "Is there really nothing?"

I pet the orange kitten she didn't take from me. It starts purring. *Don't do that.* "People around here either just keep them, or as you can see, a lot of people dump them. My brothers each have litters they rescued."

"What about you?" she asks, too interested.

I don't need more animals. Well, I do, but I don't need pets. I'm used to the tragic things that can happen to cattle and chickens. The fate of working dogs that fend off creatures with fangs and claws bigger than theirs or just decide to eat the wrong thing on the wrong day. And cats. Barn cats can have a short life expectancy. They can also be extra cuddly and friendly, and then they're gone.

Am I going to end up with three kittens and a dog by the end of this conversation? With the hem of her dress fluttering in the breeze, it's lucky I can think at all. "I had a barn cat, but she disappeared last winter."

Sympathy fills her luminous eyes. "I'm sorry."

"Happens." She doesn't ask for details, and I don't have them. Without the cats, I have a lot more mice and pocket gophers though.

A sad sigh escapes her. "It does happen." She holds up her hands, tipped with manicured nails. "I'll figure out what to do."

I don't hand my furry bundle over. It's still purring, but passed out. A quick look over the woman's shoulder shows the others all in some sort of napping phase. What is she going to do with them? Her car's packed full. Is she moving? Where is she heading? Whatever the case, she has plans and stopped to help, and now she's stuck with four little bellies to feed.

Hell. I can't just drive away and let her figure it out. "Do you have somewhere to keep them until you find help?"

She shakes her head. "I'm staying with my dad, and trust me—that's harrowing enough without animals, which he won't tolerate." She licks her bottom lip, and suddenly, I'm a hawk circling overhead, my focus on the ripe little mouse in front of me. "Is there a vet in town?"

I don't have to check the time. I've already put in a full day for a Saturday. "Dr. Small is closed. She'll do after hours, but she charges extra."

"Oh."

Her disappointment worms through the walls of my chest. "How about you keep them in my barn until you find them a home?"

"How secure is your barn?"

I didn't expect her to jump into my arms, but the question still catches me off guard. "How many other options do you have?"

"I'm not tossing them from the frying pan into the fire." She stands like a wall between me and the critters, except for the one in my arms.

Frustration builds like a thundercloud on the horizon. She's not impressed that I'm a cowboy, and she doesn't trust me with baby animals. Ouch. Though I did just tell her I lost my last barn cat. "I wouldn't do that to them either."

"Sorry," she says. "It's just that I don't want them getting under hooves or anything."

I'm mollified by her unnecessary apology. "Everything's out to pasture, including the bottle calves. Though I do have horses."

"Where do you live?"

I point down the way I came. "Straight down that way. Where you probably turned off, you take the highway around to the other side of Huckleberry Springs. By the Foster House Distillery."

"Just how far is Huckleberry Springs?"

"Only a few miles. Straight that way."

Her red lips turn down. "So close. And the old something mine?"

"Old Hennessy mine." Pride fills my chest. "That's the distillery now."

"Oh, right. I think I heard about that."

If my ego was recovering, it's kicked back down again. I've come a long way since being the hired help at the Hawthorne ranch. Now I am Haven Hennessy, part owner of Foster House Gold and of a ranch with my brothers. Being a distiller and a rancher is all I do, yet neither impresses her.

I've got to get over myself. I'm not special. "Want to follow me?"

She nibbles on her bottom lip, indecision scrawled across her face. Her gaze darts around, and some of her flush leeches from her cheeks. "I don't know if that's a good idea."

Right. She's alone with some guy, and that guy just asked her to seclude herself even more. "I can call a sister-in-law and see if she can meet us at our place," I offer. "Or they can meet us here, and we'll convoy in."

She nods like she's pondering it. "I should call my dad and make sure you're a stand-up guy."

"Who's your dad?"

"Silas Young."

Shock propels through me, and I take a step back. "Silas?"

"You know him?"

"Bootleg's Silas?" The dive bar owner who only talks

about his rodeo days and the price of cattle? The wiry man with shock-white hair and a handlebar-mustache-and-goatee combo who is maybe the same height as this girl? A guy I've known for years, and he never once mentioned he had a kid?

"Bootleg Tavern?" Her tone is devoid of emotion. "Yeah. That Silas."

"Holy shit." There's no resemblance. Is there? Was Silas a redhead back in the day? The eyes maybe?

"So if I call him, he can vouch for you?" She is clueless to my astonishment.

"He'd better. I've been his patron for years."

Her brows notch up, but her mouth turns down again. "Years, huh?"

Yeah, that sounds bad. "Go ahead. Ask him whatever you want."

She taps her phone and puts it to her ear. "Hi, it's me— Yeah. No. Papa. *Papa*. I found some strays— I know. Yes, I know. *Papa*. I'm with a guy who said he can house them until— That's why I'm calling."

I bite my tongue to keep from smiling. I've heard Silas read plenty of guys the riot act, but never a young woman. He indulges them, but never in a creepy way. Now I know why. He's a dad. That doesn't stop a lot of guys, but despite Silas's very rusty exterior, he's a good person.

"What's your name?" She ignores Silas's raised voice coming through the phone.

"Haven Hennessy."

"I knew a girl named Haven once," she says.

"Not the first time I've heard that. Five-year-olds everywhere are stealing my name."

"It's a pretty one."

"Sure is, Red."

She gives me a look like I could've tried harder for a nickname. Only she doesn't know that I'm not referring to her hair. I'm talking about the vibrant shade of her red panties.

Prescott

Red is such a low-hanging fruit of a nickname, but there's something about the glint in his warm brown eyes that makes it different. Suddenly, Red gives me tingles.

"Give him the phone," Papa growls.

I don't want to hand Haven my phone. He's got big hands to go with that big body. It takes a lot to make me feel petite, but this guy's shadow on the pavement has muscles. Not to mention, I just had this thing in my bra. Thankfully, I dug it out when he was looking for the orange kitten.

"Pressie," Papa prompts.

I roll my eyes. Everything but my full name is getting used right now. To be fair, the hot cowboy doesn't know my name. To be even more transparent, I'm allergic to giving any information to men just like him. Men who remind me of my dad in his prime.

"He wants to talk to you," I mumble.

Haven's lips quirk, and he takes the phone without touching my fingers.

Why am I disappointed? He's not my type. My ex wore slacks to work and probably thought chocolate milk came from brown cows. But he'd been around. Until he wasn't.

I'm not Haven's type either. He's probably got leggy

cowgirls all over him, with their bronzed, shiny skin and slender muscles. I can heft some strays around, but I have little interest in living my life around horses and cowboys again—to my dad's eternal disappointment.

"Silas," Haven says smoothly. Surprise lights his face. "Absolutely not. Yes. No, of course. Not a finger. Promise. You know I'm— That was a long time ago. She's *married*, Silas."

Well, that one's not about me. Not only am I not married, despite all my well-laid plans, I'm also unerringly, publicly single.

"You know I won't. Not one hair, got it." He grimaces and hands the phone back. It's warm from his touch, and I hold it closer to my ear than normal. A faint sandalwood scent clings to it.

"You can trust him," Papa says with a grumble. "But don't fall for that pretty face of his."

I wouldn't call Haven pretty. His name, yes. The man, though, has long, dark lashes, and his scruff is just shy of a beard. His mustache is a little longer, and his rich-brown hair is crushed behind his ears thanks to his cowboy hat. He's rugged. Handsome. Appealing. He could melt panties right—

Oh no. The exact pair of underwear I put on this morning flashes through my head. Red lace. A little uncomfortable, but I needed the pick-me-up as a thirty-two-year-old woman going to live with her dad because she's single and broke.

Red. Surely, he didn't mean... No. It's my hair. It's like a rite of passage to get called that nickname at least once with this shade.

My face burns as I hang up with my dad. "He vouched for you."

"He threatened to hunt me down in the middle of the night and cut my balls off."

I make a choking sound. "Did he really?"

"I hear him threaten that at least once a week."

"Who's married?" I'm nosy. I shouldn't have asked. I don't care. Yet I'm hanging on his answer.

"A woman I used to, uh, go out with. She wasn't married at the time," he rushes to add.

Sure. The strength with which I want to believe him catches me off guard. Have I learned nothing?

He rubs the back of his neck. "Anyway, she doesn't even live in the state anymore. Hooked up with a tourist and kept the fling going five years now."

Does he sound wistful? For her, or for her life? Or is the latter my wishful thinking?

He drops his arm. "I never got your name. He called you Pressie?"

"Only Papa calls me Pressie. It's Prescott Keys." His gaze flicks down to my left hand, and it might be because of the different last name. I was never a Young. "Should I just follow you? I need to put these guys in my front seat in case my tubs shift around."

"Put them in my back seat in case the puppy wants to roam. I know where I'm going."

Makes sense. I shouldn't risk the distraction. He helps me transfer the sleepy animals. Haven wandered all over looking for the fluffy orange cat, so I'm confident we found the whole group.

Minutes later, I'm in my car and following a nice but dusty black pickup down the highway. Eventually, he turns onto a winding dirt road that disappears into a mature copse of trees.

An old white ranch house comes into view. The yard

looks cleaned up, and the fence around it is tidy. A lot of new houses have popped up since I was last in Huckleberry Springs, and my memory is only fuzzy at best, but this place has been here a while.

Haven drives past that, farther down to a brown barn. To the left, chickens in a mobile pen peck in the grass around a small shed. The doors are open and blocked by scaffolding. Has Haven been here long? How much of the obvious care in this property is from him?

I park next to his pickup. When I hop out, the smell of the barn surrounds me—dry straw, dust, and a hint of manure. Two bay quarter horses watch us from a pasture next to the barn, their tails swishing.

The smell brings back memories I'd rather stay trapped in my head.

"I've got a little tack room that can be their home base. Come take a look and see what you think." He walks with a swagger that's mesmerizing. Long, powerful legs eat up the ground. The way that shirt hugs him is obscene. "I have some cat food left over. Think they're old enough for some kibble?"

"Yeah, it'll be fine. I can pick up some wet food in town and bring it by tomorrow." Is that a weird offer? To just stop by a hot cowboy's house? For the animals. That's the only reason. And maybe to ogle those chickens darting across the yard.

"Stop in whenever. I keep the doors open."

"Just like that?"

He shrugs his brawny shoulders. "Why not? I can give you my number, but if you need to get ahold of me, I'm around here somewhere or at the distillery."

"You hang out at the distillery a lot too?" I'm not a fan of cowboys who are only interested in a good time.

His eyes narrow slightly. "You could say that."

"Why?" I have to hear it. Why spend so much time at Bootleg and the distillery? It's probably nicer than my dad's bar, but still, why not spend time with his family or friends?

"I own it."

Oh. Shame fills me. I didn't even think of that option. Haven's done nothing but help me, and I assumed he had no life outside of a glass or bottle. Technically, he doesn't, since he's the owner, but it's not the same. "Congrats."

A hint of a smile crosses his lips. "Thanks. Co-owner, actually. I run it with my brothers and the Foster brothers." The pride in his voice is unmistakable.

Well. One of us has our life together. "Papa mentioned an old mine getting renovated into a new place. He was worried he'd be out of a job." I let out a nervous laugh. "In a weird and previously unheard of twist, he might've moved in with me instead."

Haven's gaze sharpens. "You're living with Silas?"

"Temporarily. I'm...between jobs." Not for lack of trying. Tears sting the backs of my eyes, but I turn away before he can tell I'm on the verge of crying and head to his pickup. "I can help you get them settled. I'll make calls tomorrow."

"You might not have a lot of luck until Monday."

Of course not. Why would anything be easy this year? "I'll keep trying. Eventually, I should get these little guys out of your hair."

He opens the door, and the puppy launches herself at me. I catch her and enjoy the deep chuckle behind me. "Looks like you got yourself a friend. What should we call her while she's here?"

The name comes to me immediately. "Meadow, since that's where I found her."

"Meadow the black Lab. Think she's purebred?"

"Maybe from a backyard breeder, but why not sell her?"

"They don't always have buyers. Or someone had buyer's remorse." He collects all the kittens, and my various hormones peak at the same time. A big man with an armload of baby animals? I'm flushed, but I'm cold. I'm breathless, but my chest is heavy. I'm turned on, and I'm terrified. The sight of Haven Hennessy with kittens is insisting he's very much my type.

"I can put these guys in the tack room." He juggles them as they try to squirm out of his hold. "There's an old saddle blanket I don't use anymore that they can all lie on."

"Let me see if Meadow needs to potty." I set her down on the edge of the gravel that abuts the grassy area by the barn. She sniffs around, her velvety ears barely lifting. Then she trots to the grass and starts peeing.

"Good call, Red," Haven says as he strolls past. His shadow falls over me as he goes, and I almost lean into it.

No, that's just the breeze. It's upsetting my balance...or something. I straighten my skirt. It shouldn't blow up again, but I can't take any chances.

What are the odds he saw when it did? It was like two seconds, if that. I was quick to right my clothing, and then I heard the engine. It was just my luck that the hottest guy I've ever seen had to drive by, *and* that he's everything I don't want in a man.

I don't want any man right now.

He owns his own business. Figures it's a bar of sorts, though. If he ever did rodeo, I'd take all four strays and hide them in my room until Papa started sneezing. This is just temptation. A wall to force me in a different direction, as if Huckleberry Springs isn't everything I've been avoiding since I gave up on being a daddy's girl. And here I am, living with the dad who never wanted to be with Mom and me.

When Meadow's done, I pick her up to go to the tack room. The door is closed. I crack it open to find a neat little arrangement. Haven's spread out an Aztec-patterned saddle blanket on the ground. The kittens are inspecting all the edges and corners. Their little claws shouldn't hurt anything in the room that they can reach or climb on.

It's better than a ditch. They have food and shelter and a handsome man who's doting on them.

Lucky cats.

"I was thinking," Haven says, still squatting by the blanket in a way that highlights the power in his thighs, "that Meadow should stay in my mudroom. She'll need to be taken outside for the bathroom, and it'll help her get used to people. It'll make it easier to find her a home."

"I appreciate it."

"Don't mention it." He rises, and wow, the man is taller up close, but not intimidatingly so. I'm five-ten and not at all used to looking up at people. My ex is my height, and looking back, he was resentful about it.

I overlooked so much.

"I was also thinking that I could get my niece down here to help acclimatize the kittens to people. She'll get them good and desensitized quickly."

"They're not feral, but I'm sure a kid handling them will only help to find homes for them." One of the gray tabbies stalks the orange one, the short fur along her back standing up in a razor line.

I take out my phone and open the camera. Smiling, I

take several action shots and two videos, moving all over and contorting myself as much as I can without baring my butt again.

Meadow's inspecting everything too, her nose working overtime. As she explores, I take more pictures. Haven stays quiet the whole time. He probably thinks I'm absurd, some wannabe wildlife photographer who thinks she isn't a talentless hack.

Or is that me superimposing how I felt trying to make a go of influencing without Buford?

"You seem more serious than the usual animal lover," he finally says.

The observation is free of the judgment I have been heaping on him. It's not like I don't have a reason to be wary of guys like him, but a little bit of guilt slips in. Being jaded is exhausting, and I had to humble myself when I called Papa to see if I could stay with him for a while. Still, tension creeps in as I prepare my answer. "I used to do this for a living."

"Pet photography?" He actually sounds interested.

"People first. Then one cat specifically. It morphed into an influencer career." I can't help but cringe, waiting for the surprised looks. The judgment. The questions about when I'll get a real job.

A dark brow arches, but he remains quiet.

I tuck a rogue strand of hair behind my ear. The need to explain is ever-present. I didn't fail because I'm bad. "The big drawback of blowing up big with one cat is that the money dries up when he gets sick and dies."

"Shit, I'm sorry."

My heart constricts. I miss Buford way more than the money, but unfortunately, the world doesn't care that I miss him. I'm now broke. "Thank you. He got me through losing my mom, and then he was gone. Anyway, when the star of the show passes, the sponsorships vanish, and poof. I've lost my companion *and* my job."

"Damn."

That's not the worst of it. It was only the beginning. Or the middle? It doesn't matter.

I go to tuck my phone into my pocket, but I graze my thighs instead. Right. I drove across the state all gussied up to help myself feel better. Didn't help. "So I'll be slinging drinks at Bootleg for a while." I shrug, clinging to my phone. "It'll help me support these guys until I find a home." For them and me.

"Don't worry about it. Come out and see them whenever it works for you. A little pet food won't break me."

No, it won't. The man has a house, property, a job—two jobs. I'd have to check my car seats for loose change to buy the rescues food. So as much as I'd like to argue, I can't. I went from being an independent woman, globe-trotting with my hopefully-soon-to-be fiancé, to being a homeless woman, couch surfing with my dad and working in his bar.

All I need is time. I'll save up tip money. I'll figure out what I'm going to do for a career that doesn't include returning to wedding shoots or getting rejected over and over again by social media algorithms because no one's interested in me. And I'll leave town. As soon as possible.

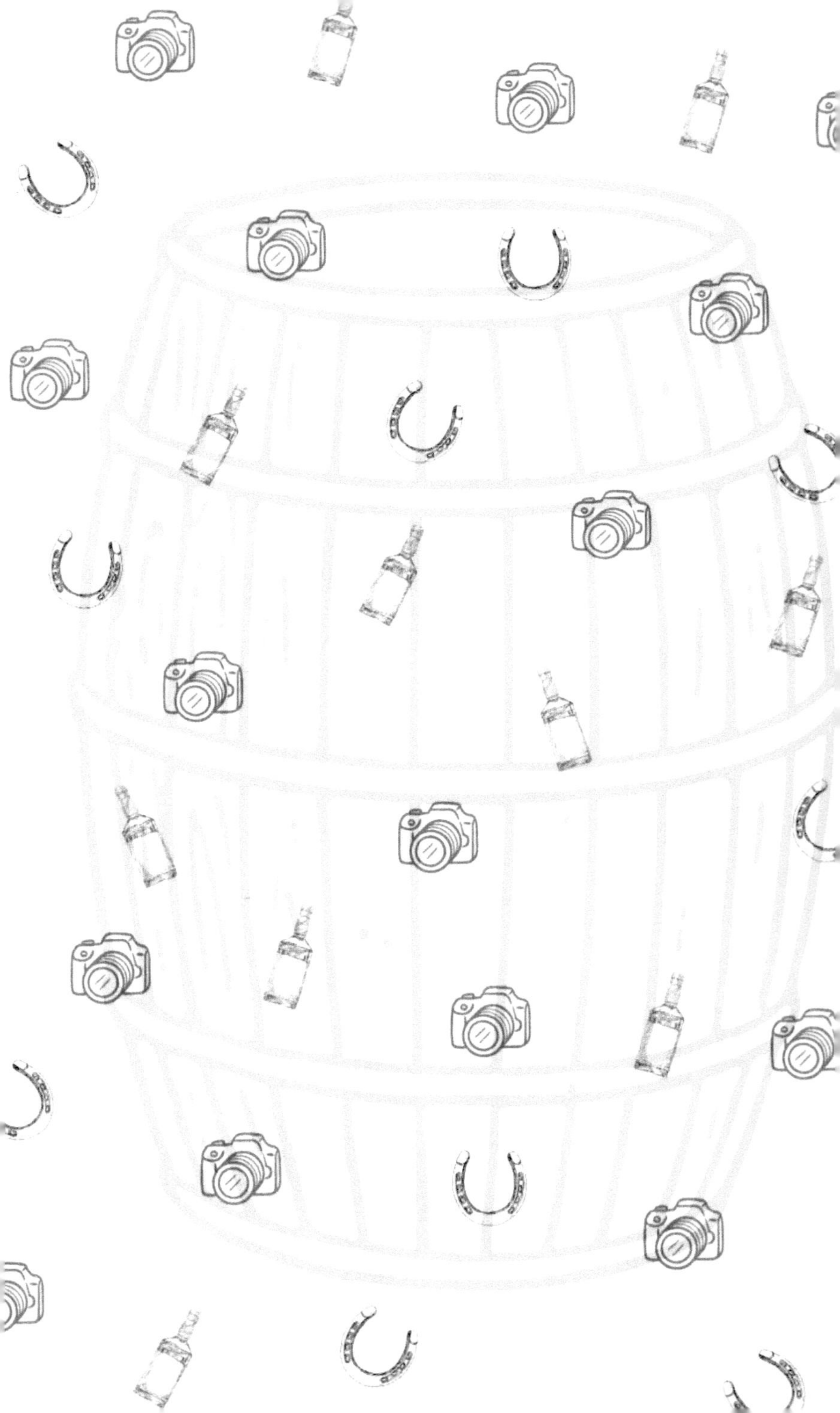

CHAPTER THREE

Haven

The tasting room at the distillery is quiet, but it's ten minutes before closing. One couple is finishing their cocktails, and once they go, I can close the place up and head to town.

Lane's in his office upstairs, but other than popping his head in to let me know he's there, I haven't seen him. I check the time again. Almost ready to flip the sign. The couple is laughing together, and usually, I don't care how long past closing they stay, but today, I do. Damn the consumption hour. I could've been outta here an hour ago and at a different bar.

Prescott is serving drinks at Bootleg Tavern tonight.

I missed her earlier when she stopped by to see the rescues. I was doing chores, then came home to clean up before going to the distillery, and I found a flat of canned kitten food by the tack room and fresh water in their bowls. They had all survived the night.

I barely had. Meadow whined and had to pee three times before I woke up for good. Then she was passed out when I left for chores. By the time I came back, I'd missed the photographer turned pet influencer turned bartender.

What color underwear is she wearing tonight?

I'm not going to find out if this couple doesn't leave.

Lane pushes through the door from the distillery. He nods toward the couple and weaves through the tables and behind the bar. Coming to a stop next to me, he leans against the counter.

"How was tonight?" He crosses his arms. He was in Denver at Foster House's main headquarters last week, and as usual, his hair is freshly trimmed. His oldest brother, Myles, started the distillery and grew it into one of the dominant whiskey producers in the nation. He's been married with kids for years and lives a couple of hours west of us now, but Lane tries to emulate him while slowly taking over at the Denver site.

"There was a busy run a couple of hours ago." I face away from the couple who will not leave. "Just waiting for them to go."

He glances at me. "You're not usually in a hurry to leave."

I haven't told anyone about Prescott Keys and the strays. I'd sound like I'm talking about a girlie pop band. Yet a part of me is bursting to tell someone. Only because she's new in town, sort of, and I'm a small-town guy. The urge to gossip is strong. That's all. "I ran across this girl in the ditch by the curve to town."

Surprise passes through his features. He grabs a rocks glass and the nearest bottle of apple whiskey. It was produced two years ago and aged until we dumped and bottled it two months ago. After pouring a finger, he lifts the glass. "Tell me about this ditch girl."

The description doesn't fit her. She was the most vibrant wildflower out there. And apparently I'm a fucking poet now. "She's actually Silas's daughter."

His eyes fly wide. "Silas has kids?"

"He even yelled at me on the phone not to mess with her. I'm helping her with some strays she found, and he told me he'd hack my balls off if I touch her."

"He says that all the time. We need to invite him out for castration. I think he misses it." Lane takes another sip, his jaw moving as he rolls the whiskey around on his tongue.

"She's working for him tonight, and I wanted to check in with her. Let her know the animals are doing okay." As if she wasn't at my place this morning.

"What's her name?"

"Prescott Keys."

His brows lift again. "I honestly thought he'd name a kid Mustang Sally or something like that."

"I thought he'd name his kid after the bull who shattered his leg."

"Maybe it's her middle name. You wanna go see her?"

Yes. "I have to talk to her. That's all."

"Sure."

I don't react to his dubious response.

He gestures to the front door with his glass. "Go check it out. I can close."

A thrill courses through me. "Yeah?"

"Dude, you've never wanted to leave early for a girl."

I've never needed to. "It's not like that. I've got three kittens and a puppy that she's trying to find a home for."

He groans. "'Tis the season." Shaking his head, he sets the glass down and smirks. "Go on. Git."

I do just that. Within fifteen minutes, I'm parking in the dirt lot outside Bootleg. The run-down wooden building has stood the test of time. It looks like it should be condemned, but underneath the worn grime, it's got good bones.

I step inside and give my eyes time to adjust to the darker interior. Outside, the sun is setting, but the sky is still blue. In here, the only light is from fluorescent brand signs and low-hanging lamps over the pool tables. By one of those tables is Prescott.

Her pale-green blouse stands out against the wood veneer of the walls. It's not paired with a skirt today, but brown slacks that hug her heart-shaped ass. Her bright hair is pulled back in a thick French braid, the kind that sits above her hair instead of being woven in. The style has a name, and I never cared to know it before now. She's still a wildflower, but no longer in a ditch.

Two guys flank her on either side, and one keeps side-stepping her as she tries to get around him.

That motherfucker.

I storm toward them, and when I'm a few steps away, one asshole tries to grab a stray curl. She clamps her hand on his and twists so quick and hard his arm bends at an unnatural angle. He nearly drops to his knees, catching himself on the edge of the pool table with his free arm.

"Shit, lady," he cries. "Sorry. I'm sorry."

Nice. I slow, but linger in case she needs a hand that she doesn't have to twist.

"That's right," she coos. "I am a lady, and I'm working." She releases him.

He shakes his arm, but I don't sense rage coming from him. "Damn. What about when you're not working?"

She sighs. "If you've got cowboy boots on, you're off-limits."

I look down at my clean pair of Tecovas. They're the pair I wear when I'm in the tasting room. Damn.

"Because of boots?" The guy's voice cracks.

"Because of all the lies that come with them." She sidles around the man and stops when she sees me. "Haven."

"Oh, hey. That's my niece's name," the second man says.

"It's a good one," I reply without taking my attention from a flushed Prescott. "Hey."

"Hey," she says lightly and continues to the bar.

"I thought I was going to have to step in there."

She rounds the counter and spares a glance at the two guys who probably stared at her butt just like me. "When I was younger, my mom trailed after Papa to all his rodeos. Being surrounded by so many men, she insisted I learn how to take care of myself. Ironically, there were plenty of guys around to teach me. Came in handy when I bartended through my college years." She props her hands on her generous hips. "What can I get you?"

I slide onto a stool when what I really want to do is take a moment and thank Silas for teaching his girl some skills. Not only is she new in town, but her brand of loveliness will make her a bigger target as the night goes on and the alcohol flows. "Surprise me."

Without missing a beat, she grabs the closest bottle. It happens to be a Foster House whiskey. The one I named.

"Nice choice."

She holds it up and studies the label. "Foster House

Gold," she says flatly and slants her gaze toward me. "Haven's Rye."

"Foster House Gold is what we call the Huckleberry Springs facility. We make all the fun stuff. Foster House is in Denver, and they make the tried-and-true whiskey that lines the shelves." My chest puffs out a little. "Haven's Rye is one of mine."

"I don't like rye." She gives me an almost apologetic smile. "I don't like whiskey."

"I can change that. If you want."

She thinks for a moment, then presses her hands onto the counter and leans in. "Why would I want that?"

A smile twitches at my lips. "Because it can be quite enjoyable—as long as it's not overdone."

"Have you ever overdone your whiskey, Hennessy?" Her voice is almost a purr.

"Before I really knew about it, yeah. Now I respect it. It's an art."

"It's whiskey," she says flatly, but she can't hide the interested light in her blue eyes.

"It's an experience." I bite back my grin. Prescott hasn't responded to boasting, but I'm just giving her facts.

Unimpressed, she retrieves two glasses, giving them both a dubious once-over. "I told Papa he needs a dishwasher."

"The dirty glassware only adds to the flavor."

She throws her head back and laughs. My mouth goes dry. Her unrestrained reaction just makes me a hungry man. I want more—of her, of this chatting, and of that broad smile that lights up a dim bar.

She ends with a sigh. "It's crazy how everyone lets Papa get away with doing whatever he wants."

Is she happy the town has embraced the cantankerous

former rodeo star since he moved back years ago? Or is she bitter? "He's just Silas to us. A fixture in town."

"Yeah. Exactly. Not all of us can make a living just being ourselves," she mutters and splashes some rye whiskey into one glass and fills the other one nearly halfway. Then she purses her lips and eyes me before grabbing two small cubes of ice to plop in. She slides the fuller glass to me.

"How do you know I don't like it neat?" I swirl my drink to get the ice melted a little.

"Oh, I think you do, Mr. Hennessy." Fuck, that throaty voice goes straight to my dick. I take a drink just to pry my mind off the sultry sound. "But I also think you like it on the rocks."

"I do. I'm not picky." When she gets that detached expression again, the need to explain rises up. "Doesn't mean I'm a big drinker."

"I didn't say you were."

"Your expressions say a lot, Red, and that one said that you don't like people who drink too much."

"Most people have drunk too much a time or two. I don't like people who choose a good time over their loved ones."

That statement digs into me and takes root. "I don't like people who choose themselves over people they should be caring for. So I guess we're agreed." I lift my drink in a mock toast.

She does the same and tries a sip of the rye, grimacing.

The distiller in me dies just a bit. "That's not a proper tasting."

She pushes the glass away, distaste curling her lips. "I put some on my tongue. That's a taste."

I shake my head and shove her drink closer to her. "It's

not the best glass, but it'll do. Swirl, sniff, and sip. It's an experience, not something to endure."

She presses her lips together like she's trying not to smile. Slowly, she swirls the glass. "Isn't this what you do with wine?"

"It opens up the aromas and adds oxidation for the flavor."

She delicately sniffs at the edge of the glass. Her eyelids flutter, and I lean forward. Is that what happens when she feels pleasure?

"I smell whiskey."

I sit back, fighting disappointment. She doesn't like it? "You aren't getting notes of smoke and leather?"

"Ew, no." But she smells it again. "Maybe?"

Good girl. "Now see if you can taste them."

"I don't want my drink to taste like smoke and leather."

"You don't want your Coke to taste like smoke and leather. Or your lemonade. Whiskey is supposed to be full of pleasant notes of all sorts that come from the grain we use, the wood of the barrel we age it in—every part of the process."

She tilts her head like she's studying me. "You really get into this."

"I love it." It's my place. "If you don't like whiskey, Foster House Gold also produces vodka and gin. Come out to the tasting room, I can give you samples of our infused vodka."

She takes another drink and lets it sit on her tongue a moment before smacking her lips together. "I'll be damned. It's not terrible," she says grudgingly. Pushing the glass aside, she flattens her hands on the counter. "Why more than whiskey?"

The story is part of the Foster House brand. Most people don't know the details, but I don't mind sharing if Prescott is willing to listen. "When Myles Foster learned he had two younger brothers—Lane and Cruz—he wanted to bring them into the fold. But Foster House is in Denver, and they all have roots in Montana. So he bought the old mine from me and my brothers, and we reinvested the money into Foster House Gold."

"Ah. The old Hennessy mine. Haven Hennessy." She snaps her fingers. "I forget that small towns can be so intertwined."

"You don't make that sound like a good thing."

"It's not bad. Unless you're stuck in one." She lifts her hands as if to point out that she's, in fact, stuck here.

A small part of me deflates. I love this town. All my best memories are here.

"Gold?" she asks. "Because it's an old gold mine?"

"And platinum and palladium."

"Your family owned it?"

"My grandparents bought it from the mine company. They were so proud to have a piece of Montana back in their family name, but they went broke trying to milk the land dry."

She gives me a little smile. "Do the Hennessys go back for generations around here?"

"Some do. I don't know much, and everything got lost, but I remember my dad talking about how proud his parents were to reclaim a part of their history." I swirl the glass again. My brothers and I held out against Myles's offer to buy. We all remembered the proud stories Dad would tell of his parents. But we had no future without it. "We sold the mine and some acreage. The land we live and ranch on is still ours. Foster House Gold is where we play and experiment. We make the infusions, tinker with aging times and barrels, and use local products, and we decided right away to branch out into vodka and gin."

"Gin? Is that still around?"

"A gin and tonic never goes away. You should come try some."

She lifts a shoulder like she couldn't care less if that happened. This girl is hell on my pride, but it doesn't matter. I promised her dad I wouldn't touch her. She makes me want to, and that's another problem.

Prescott gets called away, and I stare into my Haven's Rye. She doesn't like my drink, and she doesn't seem to like me, yet my ass stays planted on the stool. I'm not usually one to hang around women when I'm not wanted—or even when I am. But if any more guys try to accost her, I can be her backup. She'll probably put them in their place, but just in case, I'm here.

Familiar perfume wafts around me, but it doesn't make me think of wildflowers and kittens.

"Hey, Haven. Fancy meeting you here." Allison Johnson plops onto the stool next to me. In the process, she scoots it closer.

"Hi." I grind my molars together. I like Allison, but she got a lot serious a little fast. She'd play her antics off like she was joking, but I wasn't sure, so I quit going out with her.

"What are you doing tonight?" Her knee brushes against mine. I angle my legs toward the other side.

"I came here to talk to Prescott."

"Who?"

Prescott returns behind the bar counter, her gaze touching on me, then Allison's arm bumping against mine. "What can I get you?" she asks the new arrival.

"What do you recommend, Haven?" Allison leans closer. "You always have such good suggestions."

"It's my job, but I'm not here professionally. Allison, this is Prescott. She's in town for a while and helping her dad out." They murmur *nice to meet you*s to each other, and I slip off the stool and dig my wallet out. I don't string women along, and staying here would give Allison the wrong idea. Usually, that bothers me, but I also don't like the thought that Prescott would get the wrong impression too. I toss down twice the amount of my drink and Allison's. "I'm not at work tomorrow, so I'll keep an eye out for you."

Prescott's lips are in a confused line. She's probably wondering why I'm running off. She already thinks I'm a party boy or something, and that sits on my skin and stings. I shouldn't care. I should welcome it—I'm not under the spell of the new girl in town. The forbidden one.

But in this moment, I want the dream that's not mine. The cozy, calm home. The two point five kids. The picket fence.

It doesn't matter. I have *my* home. The one where the only good memories in my life were made. I'm not fucking it up, and the only way I can keep my present from colliding with certain parts of my past is to give Prescott Keys and all the mixed feelings she gives me a wide berth.

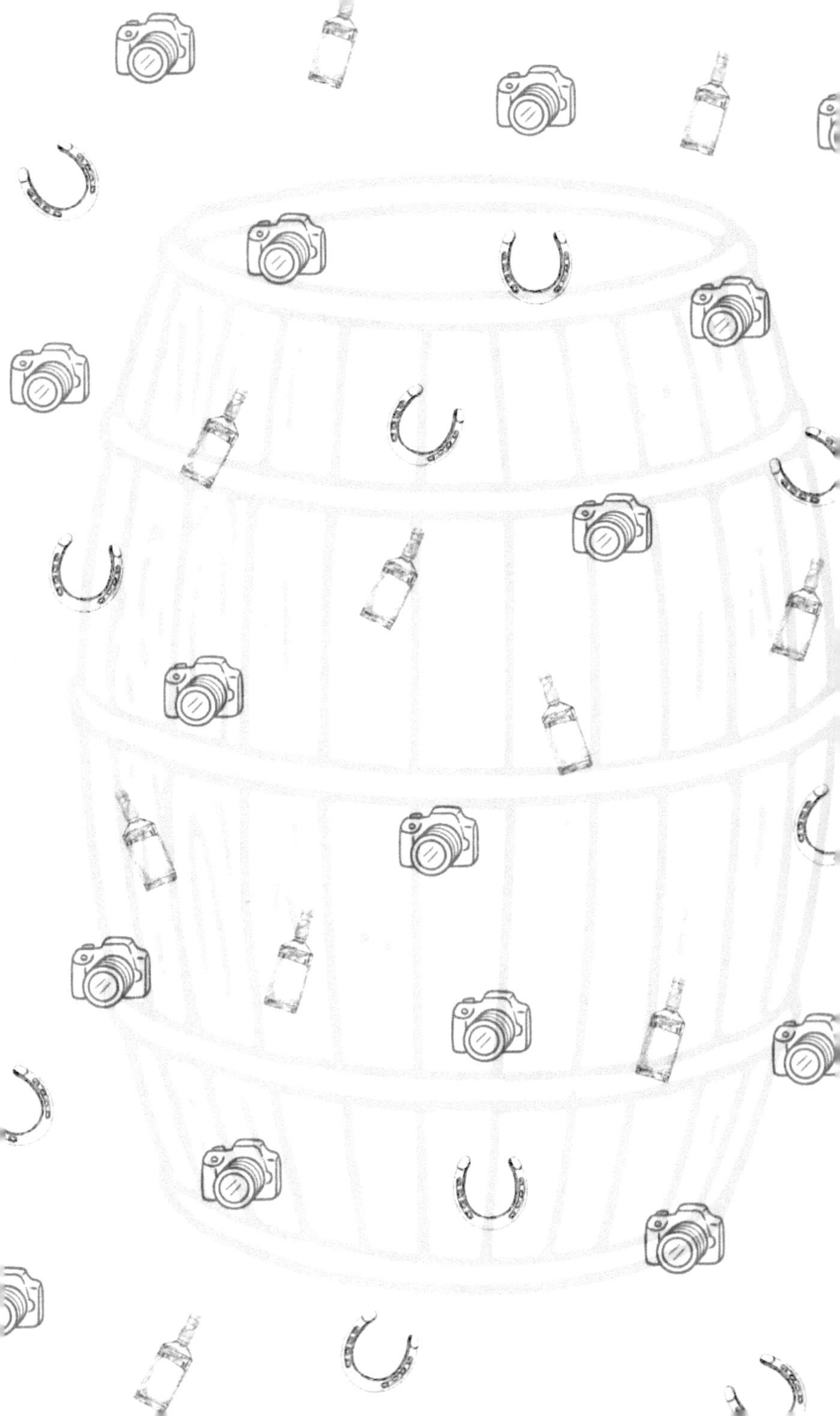

CHAPTER FOUR

Prescott

I hope he's gone. I amble down the long drive, past the quiet house. His pickup is parked in front of the garage, but it was also there yesterday, and I didn't see him.

I had a revealing chat with Allison last night after Haven ditched Bootleg.

The chickens dart around inside their pen, which is in a different spot in the yard. Haven must move it every day. I park on the edge of the drive close to the chicken shed. Taking the tote on my passenger seat with me, I start for the barn.

The soles of my sandals crunch against the gravel. "Hey, kitty, kitty."

The orange fluffy one sprints inside the barn, but a gray tabby trots toward me, its little exclamation point tail pointing high into the air.

"Hey there, Thistle." I crouch, hoping he'll run right into my arms.

He starts to when a large shadow emerges from the barn. "Thistle?"

Meadow sprints out from behind him and careens toward me. Thistle skitters to the side, his back arched, watching both the dog and me.

My heart leaps into my throat—first, from being startled. Next, from the handsome, looming cowboy with a fur ball in his arms. "A ditch weed." I gesture to the orange fluff ball before I give Meadow a bunch of scratches. "That's Tansy, or Tan for short, and the girl tabby is Daisy."

Thistle stumbles toward me and bats at the tip of my sandal. The puppy changes direction back to Haven.

Haven sets Tan down, and the kitten spins to dive back into the barn. He's a skittish one. Can't say the same about the cowboy, although... "I had a nice talk with Allison. She's interesting."

His shoulders go stiff. "Oh?"

"I didn't realize you two were so serious."

He blanches and panic fills his eyes. "We're not. We hardly even dated, and she was joking that I was her future husband—to other people in front of me."

"I gathered that." Chuckling, I rise. He's so scandalized, I can't keep the ruse going. "She was very intent on letting me know how close you two are. A little too intent, you could say."

He blows out a breath and scratches the back of his neck. "I gotta say, I'm glad you could see through that."

"She's a lonely girl, and you're what? The most wanted bachelor in town?"

He snorts. "No. If anyone thinks that, they don't know me."

That's odd. Most guys would wear the title with pride.

"Huckleberry Springs can't be filled with a lot of options." In Chicago, Haven would still top the list. My luck that I found him when I first arrived in town. Or he found me. "It probably sucks for her to think she fumbled it, and then to think she still has a chance."

"She'll meet someone else."

"In the metropolis of Huckleberry Springs? In the robust crowd at Bootleg?"

"You don't think it can happen, city girl?"

"I'm not all city." I dig around in my tote. My tips the last few nights have been good, and it's likely due to the news that I'm Silas Young's mystery daughter. "I have some deworming medicine and stuff for fleas and ticks."

"How?"

"Um, I think they're both topical. Let me check."

"No, how did you know that Allison was exaggerating? And how are you not all city?"

I quit rooting around my bag of goodies and adjust the strap on my arm. "Oh." That's my life history right there. How much do I want to share? "Well, I bartended through college, and you get to know people and see trends in behavior. I hate to say it, but desperation is pretty clear in everyone. Then, as a photographer, I got to see behind the smiles to all the things a gorgeous photo is supposed to hide. As for the city stuff, I moved to one as soon as I could."

"Where did you live before this?"

"Chicago." His interest is endearing, but I'm not here to play get to know you with the hot cowboy. "I've traveled enough and bartended enough to know that Allison might meet a nice guy passing through town, and they'll hit it off and start a good relationship, and then she'll find out he has a girl in each town he stops in."

"Ouch."

"It sucks." I swallow the lump in my throat. "Or so I've heard. Mind giving me a hand to treat these guys?"

If he catches any subtext there, he doesn't say anything. For the next half hour, Haven brings me each animal one by one for the deworming. They've grown in the few days since I found them, and I should probably tell Haven my dirty secret.

"I haven't called any rescues yet." I gather all the extra supplies and stuff them all back into my tote. "I know I should've called or messaged or at least searched for who to call or message, but I haven't."

"Okay."

"I'm just not used to the late nights at the bar. When I ran the Buford account, I kept banker's hours after years of working evenings and weekends doing photography. When I wake up, Papa talks my ear off, and then I'm back at Bootleg."

"Red, it's not a problem."

Is he really that chill? "The longer they stay, the harder it will be to get them into a rescue."

Indecision flickers in his expression a second before it vanishes. "I'll take the risk. You just moved to town."

"I'm *not* moving here."

He recoils, and yes, I might've nearly shouted it. "Sorry. I remember. Are you going to wait until after these guys find a home?"

"They'll find one before I do." I wish they could live here. The kittens are happy, and Meadow is in heaven. I know that it's not fair to shove strays on people who aren't ready or willing for whatever reason, but it's like this place was made for them. I can't ask for more. Haven's helping me out more than he wanted to. An engine sounds in the distance. "Are you expecting someone?"

"It's probably one of the guys."

A door slams. "Yoo-hoo, Haven?" a woman's voice calls out.

"You're popular." Lead lines my stomach and sinks. Why am I even surprised? Of course Haven's got women everywhere. Look at him and those abs visible through that shirt. The way he removed himself when Allison arrived to keep from leading her on was more attractive than I care to admit, but it doesn't change that he's exactly what I've been staying away from all my dating life.

My ex, Milo, broke my heart, and he had less than half of Haven's charm.

"Not always, but that's Jamison."

"Uncle Haven?" a younger girl calls in a singsong voice.

Haven's grin goes straight to my heart, and if I could get a snapshot in this moment, I'd frame it. His eyes crinkle at the corner, and his white teeth have the perfect asymmetry to make him real, almost attainable, to make a girl think she has a chance at his undying loyalty.

I might still be a photographer at heart, so I do know that pictures can lie.

"That's Kacey. My niece." He pops his head out of the tack room. "In here."

Rapid footsteps slap the ground, and a small girl with rich-brown hair throws herself into her uncle's arms. He swoops her up and squeezes her tight.

"It's like I haven't seen you for three whole days, buckaroo."

She giggles and kicks her feet. The kid's cowboy boots she wears with her purple shorts and gray T-shirt send nostalgia swirling through me. Her fashion used to be mine, once upon a time.

He sets her down, and she looks around.

"Where are they?" Her wide gaze lands on me. "Who are you?"

"Kacey, my word." This must be Jamison. She stands in the doorway, holding a little boy who can't be much older than a year. He reaches for Haven. As if my ovaries haven't endured enough hormonal turmoil in the last few minutes, Haven lifts him from Jamison's arms.

The boy immediately grabs for the brim of his hat. Haven takes it off and plops it on the kid's head. Only the baby's chin is visible, and his giggles are muffled.

Haven plucks the hat off and sets it back on his head. "Jamison, this is Prescott Keys."

Jamison's amber eyes brighten. "Silas's daughter?" She sticks her hand out. "I've been waiting to meet you."

I've only been here two days. No one's been that thrilled to meet me, ever. I shake her hand. "Nice to meet you. I hear you have kids who can make these cats perfect for families."

Jamison smirks. "They'll definitely do that. Kacey tamed a litter before she was allowed to touch them."

"That's what they need." It'll be easier to find them homes if they can mouse *and* give cuddles.

Kacey sneaks around her mom and returns five seconds later with the two gray tabbies.

Haven chuckles, pride shining in his eyes. "She's on the job. Can I get you two anything to drink?"

"Lemonade," Kacey says, putting the grays down to stalk Tan. The orange cat runs off.

"I should get going." Yet I don't want to leave. "I don't want to intrude."

"Don't let me chase you off." Disappointment rings in Jamison's words. "I don't get to Bootleg much these days, and I've got enough of my dad in me to want to chat up a new face."

I could've used a million Jamisons months ago when I was trying to be Prescott the Influencer instead of the human behind Buford. I won't mistake her interest as genuine. For everyone in town, their curiosity begins and ends with my relationship to my dad. My relationship with him doesn't go much farther than that either. "It's okay. You're not chasing me off. I told Papa I was going to clean Bootleg today before it opens."

"The grime is part of its charm," Haven says.

"It's going to attract the health department if something's not done." At the risk of being selfish, I can't get on my feet if Papa loses his income stream. "I'll let you know what I hear," I say to Haven.

"You coming out again tomorrow?" he asks.

Understanding fills me. He doesn't want to be responsible for feeding and watering, and he's training Meadow. I shouldn't foist everything onto him. "Yes, I can."

His grin is hotter than the late June sun. "I'll be waiting for you."

Haven

It's Saturday, and I'm packaging the last of the barrel I dumped this afternoon when Iverson appears at my side, an expectant look on his face. I put the lid on the last box

I filled, marking off my progress for the day in the computer, ignoring him the whole time.

"You've been dogging me for days," I say with a growl when I'm done.

"And you've been avoiding me for days."

I have. After Jamison and Kacey met Prescott, my brothers all wanted answers. I don't have any. Prescott has shown up each day this week and managed to avoid me every single one. She left me a note to say no one has openings to foster the strays. Our furry wildflowers are wait-listed. As for me, I've got a black Lab who follows me everywhere and is fascinated with chickens.

Having a dog follow me around again is kind of nice. The house isn't so empty when she's skidding across the floor.

My reply to Prescott's note was to run into the house for a pen and leave my phone number on it. She hasn't replied. Or texted. Why didn't I think to get her number in the first place?

Probably because I usually avoid that step. Things can end easier that way.

"What's with Silas's daughter?" he asks.

I scowl at him. "I don't know anything you don't know."

"Hell, Haven. You haven't talked to me all week."

"You have a job and a family." Tavis has been extra fussy with teething, and Iverson stayed home the last two days so Jamison could go to work. I could've stopped in during morning chores or when I fixed some fence last Wednesday, but yeah, I kept clear.

"You picked up a dog, three cats, and a woman on the side of the road, and you didn't say a thing."

His hurt tone is exactly why I've been a lone wolf all

week. Lane knew the story and didn't pry. Cruz is the same. My brothers? Nosy fuckers. Both of them. They have their own lives now, and I can stand on my own. "There's nothing to say. She's only landing in Huckleberry Springs for a little while."

"Jamison said she's pretty."

Pretty is too weak a description. Stunning. Enthralling. Mesmerizing. It's not just her loveliness. She has a body a guy could get lost in for days, and she keeps me on my toes in conversation. "She is, but I heard her tell a guy in Bootleg that she doesn't date men in cowboy boots."

Iverson snorts. "I imagine Silas was a hellion back in his day."

"Enough to scare his girl away from them forever." My fondness for the cantankerous bar owner dips. "He never talked about a daughter. Doesn't that seem weird?"

"Because he's too busy reliving his glory days. That's where his head probably was then and now." He levels me with a stare. "You aren't talking about her either."

"Why would I?"

"Haven, you don't let a woman keep a toothbrush at your place, much less four animals."

The back of my neck prickles. Accurate statement, but it makes me sound callous instead of prudent. "I never wanted to lead anyone on. Toothbrushes and overnights do that."

"You don't even *bring* them to your house."

Now it's like sandpaper across my nape. I'm cautious. "This is different. She's not staying at my place, and she's only out there for the rescues—not me." A sour taste hits my tongue. "It's only while she's trying to find a home for them."

"You rushing to get them off your property?"

Do I think about handing Meadow off to someone who doesn't know that she loves hanging out by the chickens, but she won't bother them? Or that she makes a mess drinking water, so make sure to have a mat for all the drops that splatter off her tongue? Don't smother Tan. He loves getting loved, but his drive to hunt is stronger. Turn those cuddles toward Daisy and Thistle. They'll soak it all up.

Yeah, I'm banking all the information, and there's a protectiveness I can't run from. But I'll give them up for a good home. The right home. The perfect home. "I'll ask around once they're ready for a family."

"Sunny said the dog followed you into the house." Only Iverson calls his wife Sunny. It's behind the story of how they hooked up. It's special between them.

Does anyone else call Prescott Red? "I've been working on training her. She's a good dog."

His scrutiny increases. "And Silas's girl? She follow you into the house too?"

I scowl at him. "No. Besides, Silas said he'd cut off my balls."

"Who hasn't he said that to?"

I smirk but shake my head. "You didn't hear him. He's really protective of her."

"So protective he doesn't talk about her?" Iverson squints across the packaging room to the large stills on the other side. He finally shrugs. "I guess if I worked around a bunch of horny, drunk men, I wouldn't talk about Kacey either."

Suddenly my perspective changes. It's probably the best decision Silas ever made. "She's working for him now. I don't know what Prescott and Silas's relationship is like, but she's turned to him when she's down. That's something."

"Campbell wants to meet her. Durban and I are curious as hell."

I bristle for no damn reason. Prescott isn't mine, and I can't control who has access to her. I wouldn't anyway. I get enough of that dealing with my mom and brothers.

I could stay here jaw-jacking about how Prescott isn't interested in me, but there's work to do. "I'm gonna go to the rickhouse and pull Monday's barrel."

"I'll go with."

I don't move. He doesn't either.

"Fuck, man." I take off my ball cap and run my hand through my hair. "It's nothing."

"It could be."

"I told you, she's not interested."

"Not her, but with someone."

I shake my head and start for the back door. How did this turn to my dating life? "I'm not interested either."

"Sure about that?"

I shoot him a glare over my shoulder. "Why wouldn't I be?"

"Because you still get doses of Mom's nonsense."

Defensiveness heats the back of my neck. I push out the back door and start across the corner of the parking lot to the rickhouse. "It's not that. Just because you found marital bliss doesn't mean I'm dying to."

"Durban's almost in marital bliss too."

As if I need to be reminded. "Yup."

He follows me inside, and I stop at the first row of double-stacked barrels. The one I need is on the second shelf. I hit the button for the big overhead door. The forklift is parked in a shed attached to the rickhouse.

His attention bores into my back. He's not dropping this, dammit. I'm almost forty, and they haven't bugged me about my single status until now. Until they both found the loves of their lives. "I'm not sitting at home all lonely."

Not most nights anyway. Maybe I have worked more and gone to Bootleg more since Durban and Campbell attached themselves to each other.

"You don't have to be either. You can let someone in. Besides her."

Irritation sweeps through me. The back-and-forth about our mother gets old after a while. "You mean Mom?"

"She was never a mom."

"She did her best, but she has issues. You know that. The difference is, I don't blame her for them." I go down the row, looking for the whiskey from six months ago, aging in an old pinot noir barrel. We're going to call it Foster Noir.

He stays on my heels. "I don't blame her for that. I blame her for everything else. She'll ruin your life and blame you for it."

"She just wants some connection." I find the barrel and bypass it, heading for the door to the shed.

"And some money."

A knot forms between my shoulders. Sometimes. She's been asking for more lately.

"Is she taking her meds?" he presses.

"I don't know. I don't ask." I don't want to know the answer. Mom thinks she knows best.

"You haven't told her about Durban and Campbell, have you?"

I spin on him, frustrated with myself more than him. "It was a mistake. I was happy for you and got too excited."

I let slip that Iverson was married and had a kid. Mom showed up, and when I wasn't home, she made a scene at the Hawthorne ranch. It's the first and only time she's met Jamison. She hasn't met the kids, and I've been able to keep Tavis a secret.

I'm trying not to reveal that Durban's wedding is four weeks away.

"I know, Haven," he says quietly. "We were nothing but puppets for her. She'll want you to cater to her when she wants, and when you need her, she won't be there."

I know that. But she's my mom, and she didn't die on a hike like our dad. It's not a bad thing to want to get to know her. To want a connection of some sort.

"I've got to get this done before the distillery locks up." As if I can't open it back up. Each owner has a code.

"You going to Bootleg tonight?"

Why? Is he waiting to bug me about going to see Prescott? "No."

"Too bad." The hair on my arms stands on end. There's something in his tone. "You could've said hi to Sunny and Campbell while you were there."

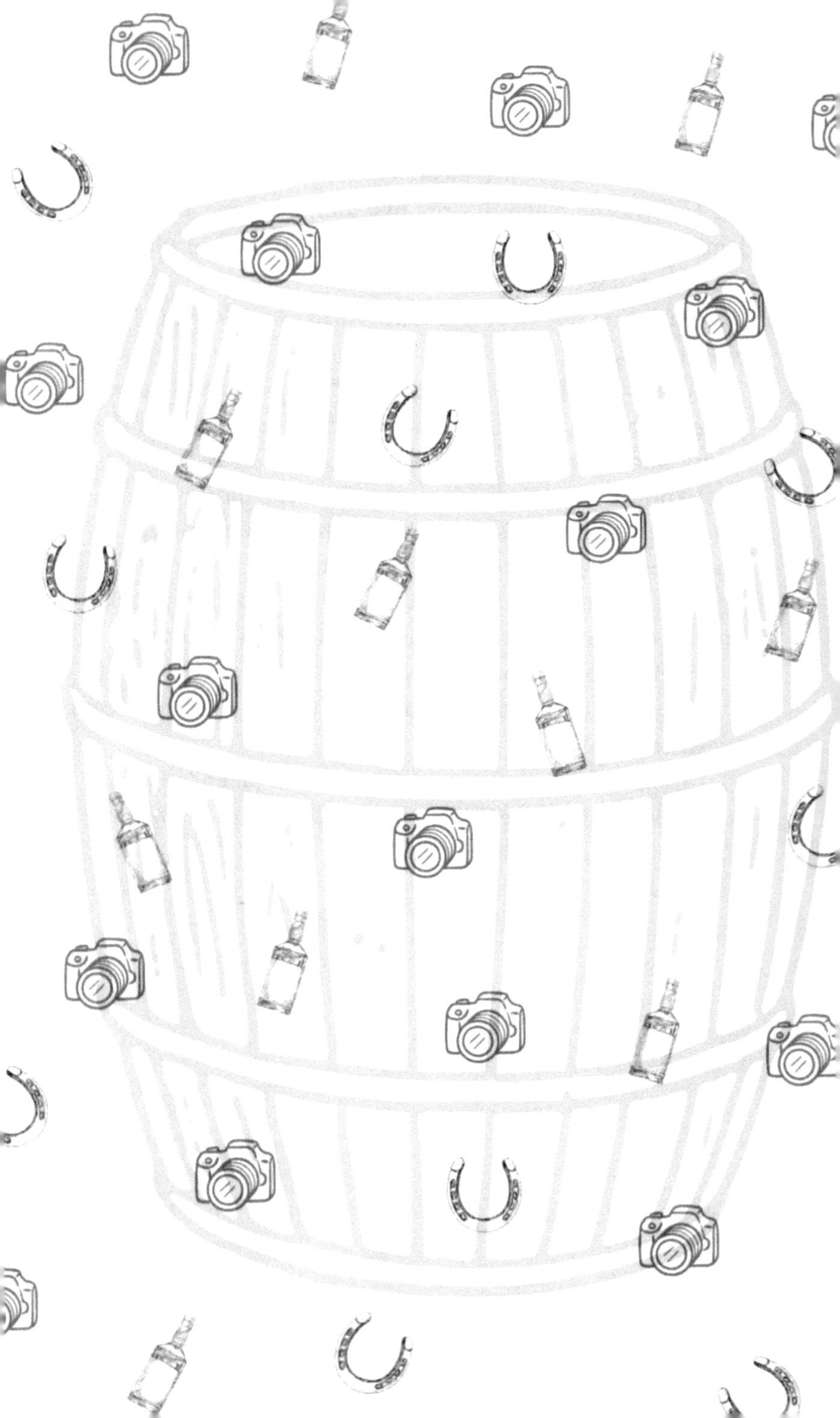

CHAPTER FIVE

Prescott

A big group filters into Bootleg. It's a mix of men and women. There are a lot of guys here already. Many are seasonal workers in town as hiking and river guides, some run the trail rides outside of town, and a few are on construction crews. Then there are the locals, and they have all been very interested in me because of Papa.

I don't know what stories they've concocted, but I've been hit on more in the last week than I have all my life. None of them interest me, and none of them are truly interested *in* me. I'm new and convenient. Besides, one guy keeps holding up space in my brain, and I haven't seen him since last Tuesday.

I do not keep hoping to see him walk through when the front door opens.

Silas dips some empty glasses into a sink of old dishwater I haven't been able to refresh.

Ew. "Papa, I can get that."

He waves me off, but I ignore him. The water is cold and gross.

"I'll do it. I need a breather," I lie. "Did you see how many people just entered?"

"They're the loan officers from the bank. They each order one drink and nurse the damn thing the whole night." He gets closer and mutters in his not-so-quiet growl, "Between you and me, I think they don't want to go home to their families."

I bite the inside of my cheek. I'm mostly sure the group didn't hear him. He could be right, but they're here to spend money, no matter how little, and from my first impression of the bar, it needs every dime. "They might just like to socialize without it being about work."

He gives me an incredulous look but shakes his head. "Take your breather, Pressie."

I'm washing the dishes in soapy, warm water when awareness brushes across my back. Someone's watching me. I finish my task, but there's no friendly cowboy who rescues strays sitting at the corner of the bar.

Jamison and another woman with similar long dark hair are there instead.

"Hey, Prescott." Jamison nudges the other girl. "This is my sister Campbell. She's marrying the middle Hennessy brother next month."

The pretty brunette's smile is wide, and she sticks her hand over the bar. "Nice to finally meet you."

I shake her hand. Once again, I want to run and hide. When I first started helping out with school photos, I had to be over the top to get kids to smile. But when I transitioned to larger groups and wedding photography, I strived to be invisible. I was the shadow at weddings and family reunions. I stayed subdued so families weren't so self-conscious. After that, it was Buford, my rescue Norwegian Forest cat, who drew people to my account. Then my foray in front of the camera showed me exactly why I should have stayed behind it.

"What can I get you?" Do they expect small talk out of me? They seem nice, but I won't be here that long.

Longing tugs at my chest. I've done fine without a ton of friends. This is just another transition period like all the ones before.

"Anything Foster House," Campbell says. "They really do make the best spirits around."

The pride in her voice isn't for the distillery, but for the guys behind it. Another pull on my heart.

I find a rosemary-and-cherry-infused vodka that hasn't been opened. I frown at the bottle. Rosemary?

"It's really good," Jamison says like she read my mind. "One of my favorites, and I'm not usually a fan of rosemary."

"The cherries are local," Campbell adds. "Durban gifted a bottle to Silas shortly after the distillery first opened." Her gaze dips to the unbroken seal, and her lips quirk. "That was almost five years ago."

"Fancy infused vodka isn't Papa's style." I'm not defending him. I just don't want to offend these two.

"Papa." Jamison puts her chin in her hand. "I like that."

"Well, he wasn't a dad." I say it bluntly enough that surprise fills the women's faces. Why did that slip out? The old pang in my chest hasn't dulled over the years. "What would you like with it? I know you said anything Foster House, but my bartending years didn't include infused vodkas."

Campbell wipes the sympathy from her expression like she can tell I don't want it. "Oh no. I became that customer, didn't I? 'Surprise me.' And now you're worried I'm going to complain about whatever you concoct when I asked for it." She presses her fingers to her forehead. A big diamond twinkles on her ring finger. "I'm so sorry."

I laugh at her chagrin. "No, it's fine. I used to try to guess what people liked, and then that got boring, so I'd try to surprise them with the most obscure combination. If I made it strong, they usually didn't care."

"No need to make mine extra strength." Campbell scans the labels on the soda guns. "Can I get it with Sprite? They call it the Seasoned Virgin at the tasting room."

My snicker comes out like I'm in middle school. "That's a good one."

"I'll have the same," Jamison says.

I make their mixed drinks and slide them over. Papa's still at the table of bankers, chatting away. He even pulled up a stool.

"I'll be right back." Someone's got to fill the big group's order. On my way there and back, I get peppered with refill requests. I should've brought a notepad with me.

I return with an armful of empty glasses, but I keep them to help me remember what the refills are.

Jamison and Campbell chat with each other while I prepare drinks. A guy wanders up to the bar, his gaze boring into Jamison's back. No surprise there. Her long, glossy hair hangs from a ponytail, and she can pull off a brown sundress like no one's business. She's country and classy. Campbell's the same, but she has her brown locks in a fishtail braid. Her bare legs in her jean shorts are drawing their own share of attention from some of the seasonal workers.

I start filling drinks as the man sidles up to the bar

next to Jamison, but instead of hitting on her, he aims a grin my way.

"I'm almost done with your Morgan Coke."

"I'm in no rush."

Then why was he—oh. I could've used this at some point during the last six months. Some attention that didn't make me feel like a warty toad would've been a nice boost. I could've told myself they weren't just single guys working in a small town with an even tinier dating pool. But he's just an opportunist, and I want to be more than convenient.

"I never caught your name," he says.

Jamison arches a delicate brow, looking from him to me. Her eyes narrow like she'll step in if I say the word. I've got inches on her, but she might fight dirtier.

I won't need her help. He's not *really* interested. This lesson goes back to my bartending days.

"Here ya go." I slide his order toward him.

"Thanks." He doesn't look at it. "I still don't know what to call you."

"Miss will be fine." Haven's "ma'am" from the other day singed my ego. What was that one comment under my first solo post? *Let the young, pretty ones play this game.*

Shit like that gave me more to cry about than missing my cat and my mom.

"When do you get off work, *miss*?"

The guy isn't bad-looking. He's handsome in a summer-rafting-guide way—the athletic type who likes to have a good time. Sucks for him that I have a strict no-picking-men-up-from-bars rule. I don't even pick guys up who frequent bars. I have everything against cheating assholes, and the risk is too high when liquor is involved.

Campbell swirls her thin green straw, her avid gaze on the interaction.

"It's going to be a late night" is all I say.

"How about tomorrow night?" He grins, undaunted.

My ex picked me up like this. Persistent when it suited him. The commitment part never came. It never does.

A tall form behind the man dominates my attention. Haven's dark gaze lights a spark in places that should stay ice cold.

"Excuse me." He shoulders the guy out of the way and takes the stool next to his sister-in-law. "How's it going, Red?"

A giant part of me, much bigger than it should be, jumps for joy at his obvious use of my nickname in front of the stranger. The smaller part reprimands my giddy reaction. Haven's off-limits, and I'm not interested.

I'm not *supposed* to be interested.

I move the Morgan Coke to the side, but I keep my attention on Haven. "I think you need a Seasoned Virgin."

Haven coughs but recovers quickly when the guy gives up and takes his drink back to his table.

I cross my arms. "Did you think I needed saving?"

"No," he says easily. "I saw that arm-twist thing you do. He was in my spot."

And the Red add-on?

He drums his hands on the counter. "Can I have an extra cherry in my Seasoned Virgin?"

I've said the name of the drink before, and I've heard way worse, yet my cheeks grow warm. "Bold of you to think Papa has ever bought a jar of cherries."

He clicks his tongue against his teeth. "You're right. I should've known better."

I laugh. How do I enjoy every interaction with him so much?

He chats with Jamison and Campbell while I make his drink. I hand it over and deliver all the others.

Several minutes later, I'm back behind the bar. Campbell and Jamison push off their stools.

"You should come out sometime and do a tasting." Jamison runs her hand down the length of her ponytail. "We'll make sure we're there if you go. You know what? Can I give you my number?"

"Ooh, me too." Campbell takes her phone out.

"I don't know how long I'll be in town." Yet I dig out my phone and exchange numbers, thankful that Haven can't see that I have him in my phone as Haven Hennessy, Hot Cowboy.

"When don't you work this week?" Campbell asks.

"I'm not sure yet." Papa doesn't like to have employees, so he does it all himself. I can pick and choose when I work, but he can't afford to pay me, so I'm working for tips. I get free room and sort of free board, but it's going to take time to earn enough to get my own place.

I'm going to have to find something to bring in money, and photography is the obvious choice. Do I want to go back?

"Thursday." Campbell nods like it's a done deal. She snaps her fingers. "Oh, and if you're in town through August, there's the Taste of Springs fair. All the local food vendors show off their goods. Foster House will have a booth."

"Oh, right." Jamison slips her phone back into her purse. "Have you been to the local bakery?"

"No, not yet." I've been eyeing it, but working late

means sleeping late, and then I have my daily stop out to Haven's place. I eye the cute little place each time I pass it, but I've spent so much on the strays already. I'm supposed to be saving money, not buying deworming medicine and muffins.

"Elodie will be there, and she makes stuff with Foster House products."

My interest is officially piqued, and it's growing to see this Foster House I keep hearing about. So far, all the people I've met who are involved with the distillery have been nice and accommodating. "I'll make sure to get there before I leave."

"See you Thursday," Campbell says brightly, and they take off.

"I never agreed to Thursday," I say to myself.

"They can be like that," Haven says wryly and takes a drink.

Is that a good thing or a bad thing? I don't make friends easily, and it's like they're not giving me a choice. Do I want any roots here? The lure of a small town usually leads to loneliness.

Haven slides over to the stool on the corner that Campbell had been in. "Every time I come in, you're getting hit on."

I clean up the empties the girls left behind. "It doesn't mean anything. It's the nature of the beast."

His lips form a perplexed line. "In that metaphor, who's the beast?"

"Not who, the scenario." I smother a giggle. "But Beast is my other nickname."

"Weird that both of us have the same one."

My laugh bursts out of me. "Coincidence, right?"

Papa makes his way over, a glare firmly fixed on Haven. "My daughter's trying to get some work done, Hennessy."

Haven ducks his chin down. "Sorry, Silas."

Haven could've argued with my dad or been flippant, but he wasn't. My respect for him notches even higher. The rebellious teenager inside me wants to rear up and flirt with Haven just to aggravate my papa, to get his attention, but I did not move here to regress.

My mind has to stay on work. The large group left, and a few more tables have emptied. While I clean those, Haven gets up and tosses some money on the bar top.

"Have a good night, Prescott."

I smirk at him. Too chicken to say Red in front of Papa?

He flashes me the smallest of smiles before turning to Papa. "Night, Silas."

Papa scowls at him but tips his head. Haven leaves, and I only sneak one peek at his fine ass. Papa watches me.

"You can't let that boy get to you," he says as I arrange the glasses by the sink.

"Is Haven Hennessy that bad of a guy?"

"No." He hastily dumps out the ice and leftover liquid. "The Hennessys are all good, stand-up guys."

"You'd rather I date a bad boy?"

"No, I'd rather you go out there and live life."

"I don't quite know what that is." My gaze strays to the door as it opens. Is Haven coming back?

A woman my age walks in and waves to one of the seasonal workers.

Why'd I get my hopes up?

"What do you want to do?"

Cuddle cats and take pictures of them. I've actually enjoyed my shifts at Bootleg too. Papa's giving me flexibility, and that's probably what I'll lose when I embark on my next career. He's waiting for me to say something. "I don't know. Probably go back to photography. Maybe start my own studio. I could do other people's animals this time."

"See? You've got a plan. No need for a Hennessy to interfere."

"You're afraid he's going to dickmatize me into the trad-wife life?"

Papa stiffens, his sharp inhale loud. "I don't know what any of that means, but I don't like the sound of it."

Chuckling, I shake my head. "Haven does seem like a good guy." Thoughtful, responsible, and handsome. He would be the guy to make me go back on all the promises I made myself after my ex left. Technically, I kicked him out. "But I'm not on the market."

Papa grunts. "Does he know that?"

"I'm not his type."

"That boy doesn't have a type, other than women who want everything. But as soon as they say so, he dumps them. I've had more than one of the ladies in here sobbing into their vodka tonic."

My heart drops to the floor and flops. Gah, I should've known. I did know, yet my hopes rose without me noticing. "He avoids commitment?" Seems ironic to say that to a guy who's only ever committed to this bar.

Papa runs his fingers along his mustache. "Accidentally poured one of those girls a Foster House vodka too and made her cry harder."

"Papa!"

He shrugs, pulls out two shot glasses, and fills them with the rosemary-and-cherry-infused vodka. "Been meaning to see what this piss tastes like."

I take one and shoot it back, grateful for the burn.

Damn, that's bad news about the best man I've ever met.

And damn, that's good vodka.

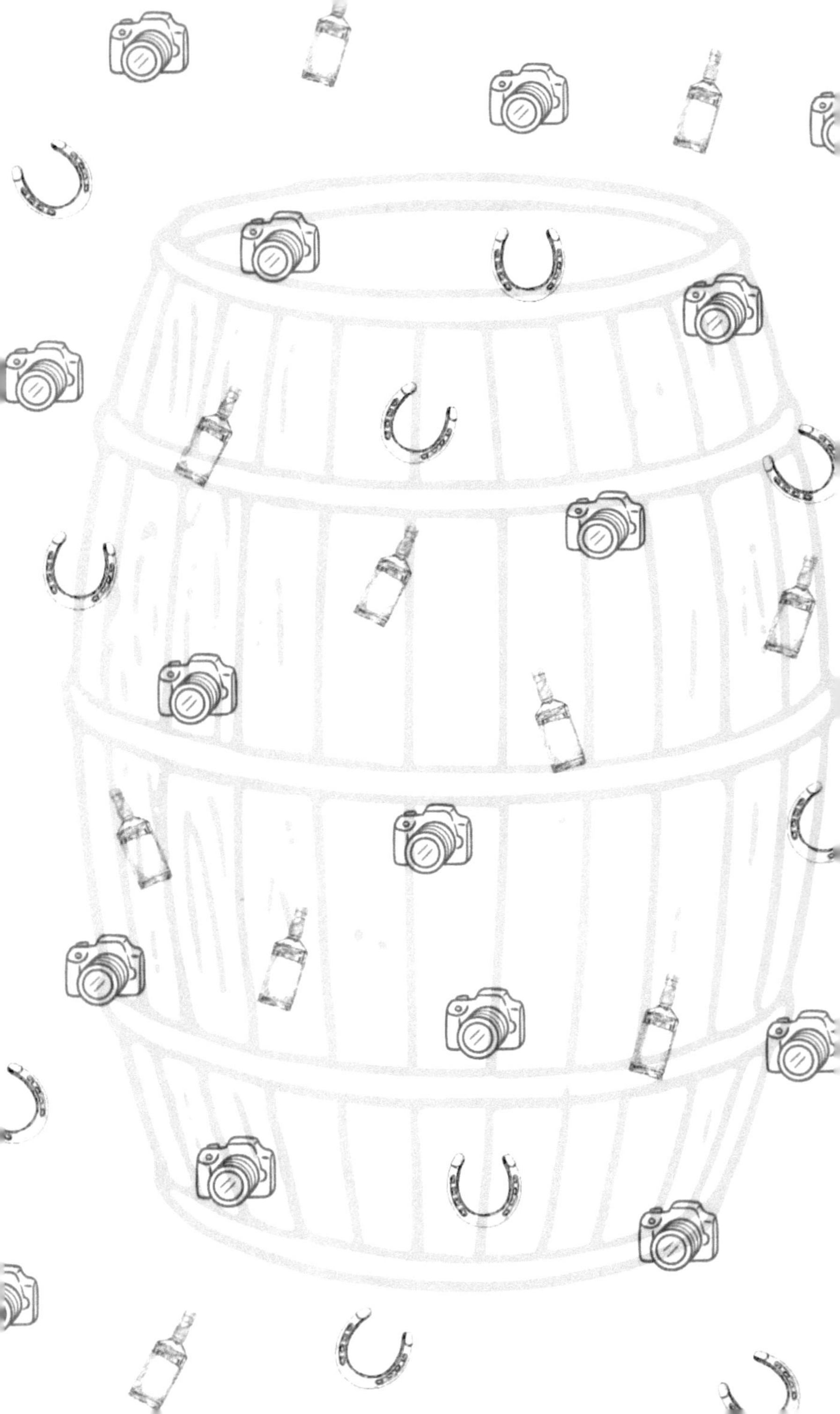

CHAPTER SIX

Haven

As soon as it's time for my shift in the tasting room, I veer out of my office and tear down the stairs. Lane's at the table of screens in the distilling room, where we log all our data for the day.

I toss him a wave and enter the tasting room through the side door outside of the merch store. I flip the open sign on by the front door and light the inside up. Trying to see the space from a new person's point of view, I stand by the large front windows.

The timber and steel aesthetic of the distillery carries into the tasting room, especially with the old pictures I rescued from the basement of my house. The mine's heyday is spread out in black and white, along with a few shots of the surrounding land—before my brothers moved in cattle—and an aerial of the Stillwater River cutting through our property.

Satisfied the appearance won't scare away Prescott, I

go behind the bar. I usually pour through inventory sheets during the slow parts of a tasting room shift and do some ordering, but today, I make sure everything is stocked. I sift through bottles and glasses, anticipating anything anyone might want, especially Prescott.

Did she try the rosemary-and-cherry-infused vodka? Did she like it? I pull three bottles of my favorite vodkas, two gins, and the most popular whiskey.

The door to the distillery cracks open, and I look up. My hopes nose-dive when Durban enters.

He frowns and glances behind him. "Disappointed?"

"Yes." Hopefully, an honest answer will throw him off.

He slides onto a stool. "Campbell told me she's coming tonight with Jamison. This Prescott I've heard a lot about —not from you—is supposed to join them. Any chance she's behind your hound-dog expression when I walked in?"

Sometimes having astute siblings sucks. "You're crashing their party?"

"No, I'm here to ask you about wedding stuff before they arrive."

"You want me to lie during my speech?"

"You don't want to do a speech."

Now's the time to have an astute sibling. "Nope, but I will."

"I don't need one. I just want to marry her." Before the sappiness can make me heave, he continues. "Campbell would like a trail ride when Avery and Thea are here."

"I'm in."

"Can you and Iverson pick out a flavor of whiskey for our wedding favors?"

"Want me to make one?" Not that I've thought about

it—but I have. I was just waiting for the go-ahead. "I can make party favors."

Neither of my brothers ever shows a lot of emotion, but Durban is both pleased and touched. "Yeah, I'd like that. I should've asked earlier, but she's basically planned this wedding once already."

That was a fun night. "Whatever you want, Durban." I check the time on the clock behind the counter. "Is Campbell coming this early?"

He doesn't answer right away, and tension creeps into my bones.

He rubs a thumb and forefinger along his lower lip. "Iverson said he talked to you about Mom."

I crunch my teeth together. "I haven't told her yet, so why are you worried I will?"

"She has a sixth sense for when something's up, and she can read you. If she thinks you're not telling her something, she's going to be a dog with a bone."

I drop my chin down. He's right, of course. She calls me, and I tell her about my life. My life is entwined with theirs—not so much these days—so she does sense what I'm not saying. "I'm careful when she calls."

"She's going to keep calling. You don't deserve that."

She's Mom. I'm all she has. My brothers don't talk to her. Men don't give her the time of day anymore. She's been holding down a job, but she's lonely. I can't just cut her off like she did to us. "You know how she is. Something else will always grab her attention sooner or later."

He grunts. "I know, and it's never good. But you know the real reason she made a scene here?"

"She had to make it all about herself?"

"She wanted to drive a wedge between us." He pins me with a frank stare. "She's using you."

What if she's not? What if I need to be better than her? "Look, my lips are sealed, and I'm well aware of what she's like."

His gaze is steady on me. "Has she tried calling lately?"

"Last month." When she was short on grocery money because she'd gotten pneumonia. The guys wouldn't believe her story, so I didn't tell them. I don't tell them a lot when it comes to her.

"She still in Casper?"

"Gillette. Desk clerk at a hotel."

He nods.

A windshield flashes out the front window. Excitement that it might be Prescott rises with the relief that we're done with the topic of our mother. "They're here."

Two cars pull in. Campbell's and Prescott's. Jamison's with Campbell.

Durban drums his fingers on the countertop. "It's your time to shine."

I scowl at him. "She's just a friend." The back of my neck grows hot. She's not even that.

"Do her friends call her Red?"

My sisters-in-law have big mouths. I give him an impatient look before my gaze lifts above his shoulder. Prescott has her head down. Her vibrant hair is pulled back and curls fan behind her head. Her tan pants fall to above her ankles, and she's wearing flat sandals. It's her snug top that captures me. Her full hourglass figure won't leave my brain.

"You should invite your friend to the wedding."

Shock fills me, and I want to hide in a corner. Inviting someone to a wedding is more serious than sidling up to a bar. "You don't know her."

"Campbell won't mind. She might do it herself. But I

bet Prescott would think about it if you asked." Durban's smirk digs under my collar and chafes.

There's no reason to ask. So it's not an issue.

Jamison throws the door open. "Hey, guys." She waves and beelines into the main distillery. Probably to find Iverson.

Campbell holds the door for Prescott. "Welcome to Foster House Gold. Haven can give you a tour later."

Hell yes, I will. When Prescott lifts her gaze to me, a coppery brow arches, and I grin. "Come on in and make yourself comfortable."

She slides onto a stool close to the wall. "Aren't you going to be surprised when I change into pajamas and put my feet up."

I laugh, grateful to put aside my earlier conversation with Durban. As for him, he spins around in time to catch Campbell as she throws herself into his arms. Prescott's gaze slips away, avoiding me and the couple next to us.

Yeah, this could get awkward. "This time I get to ask what I can get you."

Her attention lifts back to me, just where I want it. "I don't even know where to start. I'm not usually the customer."

I give her a laminated menu. "These are our cocktails, but you can also sample our spirits with a tasting flight."

Interest lightens the blue in her eyes, but she shakes her head. "I don't like getting wasted."

"Legally, we're limited in how much we can serve in a tasting room. I can splash just enough for a sip so you get to taste more than drink."

"Okay. You pick what you think I should try."

"No Seasoned Virgin?"

Pink dusts her cheeks. "No, something new."

From the corner of my eye, Durban gives Campbell a questioning look. She whispers in his ear, but she doesn't have to strain to do so since she's practically sitting on his lap.

I dig out two Glencairn glasses, then I retrieve several small plastic medicine cups. "We'll do two official tastes of whiskey, and then I'll give you some vodkas to sample."

After filling a glass of water for her, I find the Butter Barrel and Haven's Rye.

Prescott cranes her neck to see the bottles. "I've already tried Haven's Rye, or do you just like to give that to everyone and casually drop that it's named after you?"

My brother snickers.

I ignore him. "No, that's the Haven Is Awesome whiskey."

Her laugh rings through the tasting room. Durban gives Campbell an indulgent look.

Campbell moves to a stool next to Prescott. "Durban's going to make my drink so you can go through the tasting routine."

My brother uses the jalapeño-infused vodka to make his fiancée a jalapeño orange cream spritzer.

When he sets it in front of Campbell, she steals two straws out of our holder. "Here." She holds the cup out to Prescott. "This is weak enough it shouldn't interfere with your tasting."

She takes a sip, her pink lips wrapping around the straw. I lean forward until Durban clears his throat. I shoot him a look, and he returns it with a knowing one of his own. Was I staring?

She pulls away and licks her lips. "Mm. That's different. Good, but different."

The ever-present heat in my gut when I'm around her

curls through me. It's a strange affliction that started when her skirt blew up.

Campbell's smile is pleased. "Durban came up with that one."

"It's not unique, but we try to put our own spin on cocktails," Durban says.

"Now try the Butter." Campbell pushes the Glencairn glass closer to Prescott. "It's a lower proof than Haven's Rye, and you should work your way up." She glances at me and puts her hands up. "I'm taking over. Sorry."

"It's no problem." She's putting Prescott at ease. I don't do that as well. "You and Jamison practically work here." I switch my attention back to the redhead. "Remember how to taste?"

Prescott swirls the glass and sniffs it. "Oh." She sniffs again. "That's really rich."

"It's one of our favorites, and the town loves when Elodie works it into her baking." I don't say why, since she hasn't tasted it yet. I want to witness her discovering the flavor. "Take a small sip and let it coat your tongue. Then take a bigger one."

She does as I say, and fuck, I like the idea of that. "Oh my gosh, that's buttery." She takes another sip. "I could almost like whiskey with this."

I'll get her to appreciate whiskey. All I need is time. If she never likes the drink, I'll just buy everything Elodie makes with our whiskey products. Either way, I'll get the satisfaction of watching something I made slide past her lips.

I walk her through tasting the rye. She doesn't dislike it as much as last time. I line up three different vodkas, and she chats with Campbell and Durban.

Jamison breezes in, and Iverson's hot on her heels. Her

face is flushed, her eyes bright. Neither of them appears guilty, despite what they were likely up to. That's why I never look too hard for where my brothers are when their women are around.

Fingers of envy wrap around my throat.

Campbell lifts her drink in a salute. "To Iverson and Jamison, the one-night stand that started it all."

"I don't need to hear about my brother's sex life," Durban grumbles.

"It's a good thing we were in here," Campbell says, "or we would've heard it."

"Campbell!" Jamison plants her hands on her hips, but she can't hold her admonishing look. "You totally would've."

Iverson's satisfied grin helps me get over myself. My brothers have found their partners, and they're happy. Guys like us weren't raised to know what a solid marriage, or even a relationship, is supposed to look like. Iverson might've figured it out eventually, Durban too, but Jamison and Campbell come from a good family. Their parents are ambitious and supportive. Christine and William Hawthorne might also be critical and smothering, but they provided a stable home.

How long will it last? Jamison hasn't up and left Iverson after two kids, but my mom didn't leave until after I was born. Isn't he concerned? He's the one who remembers it all. I was too young to recall more than the emotions of the time, but I've heard the stories.

A small group wanders in, dressed in loose hiking pants and trail shoes. I ditch the counter to take their order, and while I do, more people arrive. My time with Prescott is up. I'm a Hennessy first, and this distillery is my priority.

The pull to the bar counter is strong.

Durban tells Prescott about the vodka I poured for her to taste.

When I'm done making the cocktails and tasting flights and delivering them, Durban comes around the bar. "Give Prescott a tour. I got this."

Any one of us could give her a tour, and I'm officially on duty, but I'll take him up on his offer.

Prescott stacks her little empty vodka cups.

I clear them from in front of her. "Want a look around?"

Jamison spins toward Prescott, delighted. "You have to see the rest of the place. They kept so much of the mine's character. It's just gorgeous."

"I might as well," Prescott says almost shyly. "Since I'm here."

Yes. "Follow me."

The chatter from the tasting room dies down once we're in the merch store.

"This is cute." She dances her fingers along the brim of a charcoal-gray hat with a faded yellow Foster House logo. She snatches her hand back. "Sorry."

"Why?"

"Touching the merchandise."

"I'll tell you what you can't touch, and it's not that long of a list," I say with a grin.

No reaction. "So. The tour?"

Shit. Right. She's not here to date anyone. But now she's in front of me, and my gaze drops right to her ass. Firm and round. Fuck. The way her hips flare? Nothing but a tease.

"Where are we going?" She twists to look at me over her shoulder.

I jerk my stare up. "Straight ahead. If you find yourself next to a boiling tank, you're exactly where I want you."

"That sounds sinister. I like your whiskey charm better."

I bite back a smile and trot to fall in step beside her. "This is where the magic happens. From the bags of grain stacked along the far wall to the big round tanks—our mash tuns—to the tall stills."

"And that's the magic bubbling inside?" She doesn't get close to the edge, but rises on her tiptoes.

"You know the old saying—when the yeast is farting, the money's pouring in."

She smiles. "That doesn't have a smooth ring."

"Probably why Myles didn't have it put on a hat. Go ahead. Have a sniff."

She creeps closer and inhales. "It's a little bready. Definitely yeasty." She tips her head like she's concentrating. "A little fruity."

"Yep. It's almost ready for the next phase, which is what we're all about. Distillation."

"And the stills?" She cranes her head up, following the tall still closest to the pipes lining the space over our heads. "They're really pretty. It's like someone picked them to match the rock on the exterior so well."

Pride fills me. Of course I want people who tour Foster House Gold to be in awe, but it means more that *she* is. "This is my favorite spot. It seems like it should be loud, but when no one's in here, it's quiet. Everything's working hard, product is being made, but it's not a loud process. Just the noise of a big room."

"I don't like the quiet," she says softly, her gaze stroking across the piping above us.

"Why not?" I ask just as gently.

"Home was quiet, and I could hear Mom crying."

"Oh, shit. I'm sorry."

She gives her head a shake, forcing a smile. "No, it's nothing. I shouldn't have brought it up."

"Mine's the opposite," I say gruffly, giving her something in return. A part of me I've never told anyone. "I was young when my dad died, but a house with three boys isn't quiet. Still, it was normal." Her focus is on me, but I can't meet her eyes and talk about this. "Then he died, and we were sent to a foster home. It's how we met Myles."

"Myles Foster? The guy behind Foster House?" she asks, surprised.

I nod. "We were only there a little over two months before the social workers tracked our mom down, but we lucked out. The Bailey home was a damn good place to be a foster kid." I pause as the memory passes through me, carrying all the emotions with it—fear. Awareness from all those faces looking at me. Uncertainty. Overwhelming sadness. "Then we went to live with our mom, and when it wasn't quiet, it was..." How do I explain it? Uncertain? Scary? Unstable?

Her warm fingers twine with mine. "Haven."

I give myself a shake, but I clutch her hand tighter. "I like the quiet, and you like the noise."

"Utterly incompatible."

"Totally. Too bad we share three cats and a dog."

She laughs and extracts her hand from mine. "What's behind these monsters?"

My fingers tingle where she touched them. "The production line. We bring in a barrel from the rickhouse, dump it, and it gets filtered before getting bottled."

"It's...small."

I clutch my chest. "Ouch. Red."

I'm rewarded with more laughter. "It doesn't need much to get the job done."

I wink at her. "It goes as fast or slow as needed."

She rolls her eyes. "I hate to cut the tour short, but I promised Papa that I'd work a shift tonight. This is the busiest summer he's ever had." She snaps her fingers. "I forgot to tell you—I saved enough tip money to get a vet checkup for them all."

"Bootleg is really coming through for you."

"Papa gives me his tips." She shrugs. "I shouldn't take it, but he insists, and I like thinking he cares about me."

"He does. He almost ran me out the other night."

The corner of her mouth tips up. "He has his moments, and I guess I'm not used to that."

"Can I ask you something?" My curiosity about her chews away at me. Why is it never enough when I'm around her?

"Can't promise I'll answer."

This girl is guarded. "Did something happen between you and him?"

She drags in a deep breath. "I'm inclined to say nothing happened. When he was around, I felt like I had to compete for his attention, but it was nothing like what my mom went through with him. And I guess it's been hard to forgive him for that."

"They're divorced?"

"That's two questions, Hennessy." She falls quiet for a moment. "No. They never married. After years of Mom trying to get him to choose her over riding bulls, she gave up. She kept hoping that he'd come back for her. He never did. I didn't see him much after that."

"The quiet?" The crying.

"Yeah." She forces a bright smile. "He didn't have to let

me come live with him or work at the bar. Amazingly, I make more than a lot of other part-time jobs I've had. Besides, it's amusing to watch him meticulously count out the ones for me at the end of the night."

Again, since she's sharing, I'll give her something. A good memory. "My dad used to love breaking a five-dollar bill into five ones and splitting it with all of us. We felt like kings." I suck in a breath and hold it. I haven't thought about that since I was a kid.

"That's really sweet." She wets her lower lip, and the simmering desire surges inside of me. "I think you're really sweet too."

She said it almost sadly, like it's an unfortunate finding.

I don't want to end on a down note. "And smooth like Butter Barrel?"

"You're definitely smooth, Hennessy, but I think you might burn my palate."

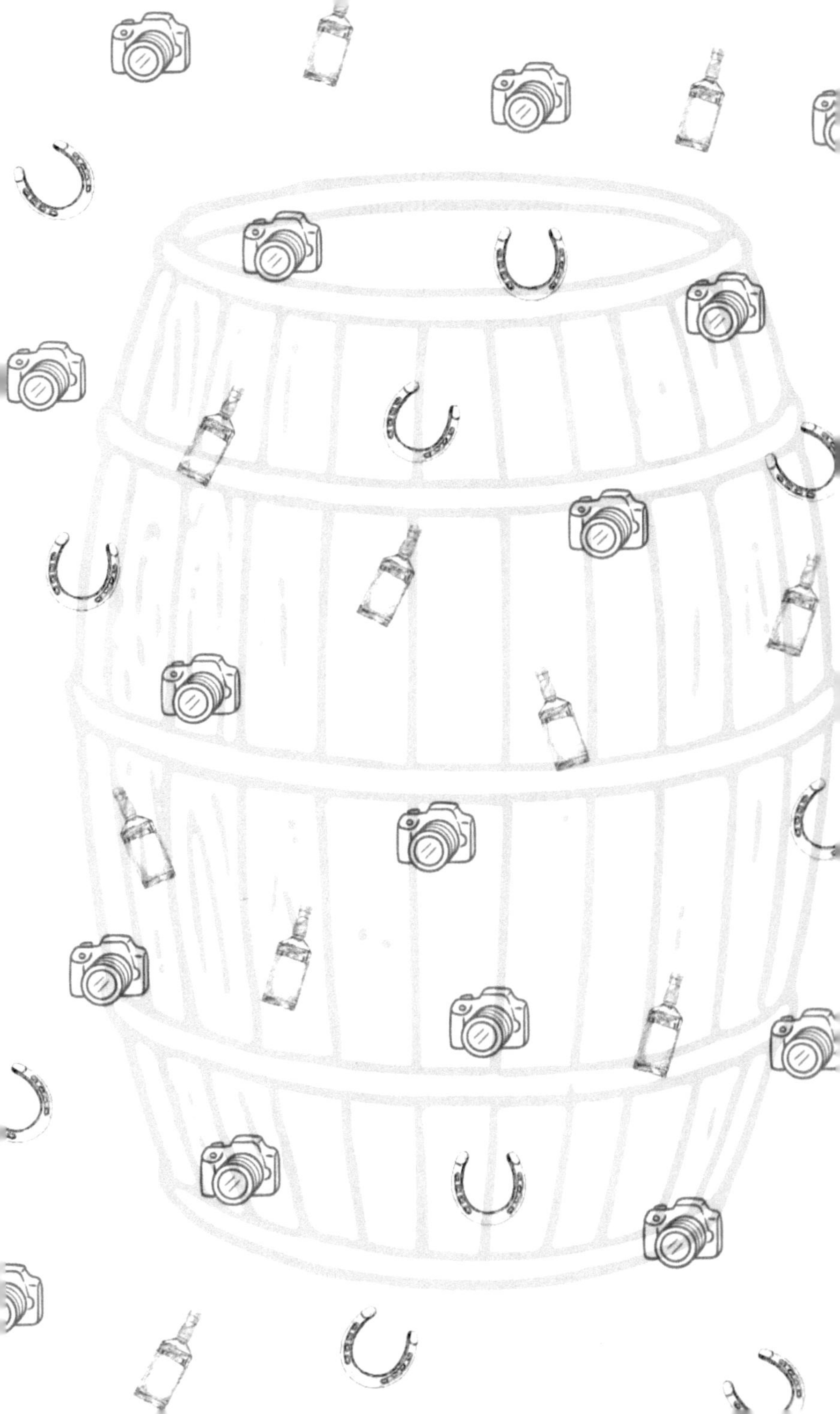

CHAPTER SEVEN

Prescott

It's Saturday morning, and Dr. Small, the vet, has agreed to meet me at Haven's place, and Haven okayed it. I have to get out there early before he returns from doing chores or whatever ranchers do. If he's there too, then I'll be hanging out with him, and the idea of that sends too many thrills through my belly.

I pull into my normal parking spot by the barn and get out. It's another gorgeous summer day with a few clouds and a slight breeze. The faint smell of cattle and manure doesn't bother me like it normally does. I've been out here enough that some memories stay in the background.

Haven has Meadow with him on a leash by the fenced-off pasture next to the barn.

My traitorous belly clenches.

A horse stands in front of them, its tail swishing. The puppy runs back and forth, then she stops and sits. Haven digs in a pouch he's hooked to his belt and gives Meadow a treat.

My heart turns into a puddle. He's done a lot of training with Meadow if she's listening so well around such a large creature. I've seen her around the chickens, and she's curious, but she doesn't chase around the pen. Tan didn't get that memo yet, but he got pecked and has since laid off.

Haven scratches the horse's neck and turns when I approach. "Morning, Red."

His words warm me faster than the sun shining overhead. "Good morning." Meadow's tail is going wild, and I stoop to pet her. When I rise, Haven's scratching under the horse's chin. Great. I'm jealous of these things again.

"Who's this?" I can be polite. The man is housing my rescues, training the dog, still caring for his livestock, and working a full-time job.

"Gravy." The gelding snuffles and stretches his neck out like he thinks I have goodies for him. "No treats for you, Gravy Train," Haven murmurs to him, "or Dr. Small is going to think she's here for you." He pats Gravy's neck. "This guy likes his goodies, but goodies don't like him."

Gravy's still trying to sniff me, and I'm a sucker, so I move in closer. Large nostrils puff my hair, and I pat his neck. "I'm a sucker for goodies too."

Haven smiles. "You like horses?"

"I've always loved horses. I just also resented them." Why do I get diarrhea of the childhood trauma around him?

"Silas rode bulls."

I snort. Rumor has it he rode anything.

"Some other reason?"

"No," I say on a sigh. "It's basically that. The life.

Horses. Bulls. Steers. Even the mutton-busting sheep. He loved it all so damn much."

Here I go, spilling more. And he's listening. His understanding reactions only make me want to say more. At the distillery, he shared a part of himself instead of getting irritated that I contradicted his love of silence with my love of noise. My heart has been hammered the last five years, and he just healed a part of it.

After this vet visit, it's going to take at least a week to convince myself I don't want to find out what Huckleberry Springs has to offer.

Yet I can't force the words back into the recesses of my mind. I want to talk about it. I scratch up and down Gravy's slender neck. He's also a sucker for attention.

Same, Gravy. Same. "When I was little, it felt like I either had to go riding to talk to him, or do all the chores the guys were too hungover to do in the morning. I hauled bales around and fed and watered the pickup horses and groomed them, and I'd do it just to have some time with Papa."

"And you hardly saw him if you weren't on the road with him or at one of his rodeos."

The back of my throat burns, but I swallow past it. "Easy conclusion to make, isn't it?"

"All too common, from what I've heard over the years. A lot of guys that I cowboyed with told the same stories. I only heard their side." He squints into the sun. "Never did much agree with it."

Is that why he does the opposite? Rather than hurt someone, he keeps his distance? If what Papa says is to be believed. But I've given guys too much credit before.

His warm gaze brushes across me, licking along my skin. "Have you ever gone horseback riding for fun?"

I frown. "Yeah. I mean, it was fun."

"But you were always left disappointed because the real outcome you wanted was time with your dad. What about riding for the sake of riding?"

I shrug, trying to recall all the times I've been out on trail rides or circling the arena for fun. I was trying to get my dad's attention. Nothing more. "Not really, I guess. I think I was last on a horse when I was twelve? So, twenty years ago."

His grin is instant. "Then let's go today. After Doc is done, we'll take Gravy here and his buddy Biscuits out—"

"Biscuits and Gravy? Are you serious?"

As if he heard his name, the other bay lifts his head from where he's been grazing.

Haven scratches up and down Gravy's neck again. "Would you believe it's a coincidence? I got them separately."

I giggle, lighter than I've been for...years. "No, I wouldn't, but Biscuits and Gravy sounds good for two working horses."

He leans on the fence post. "I don't work 'em too hard. I was just thinking I needed to get them saddled up for more than rounding up cattle."

"For them or you?"

"No wrong answer." The grin he flashes blazes right to my stomach, and the swirl of awareness is as inconvenient as always. I should be used to it after as much Haven exposure as I've had.

A dusty pickup rumbles down the drive, and a dark-haired woman a little younger than my dad waves her hand out the window.

"That's the doc. So whaddya say, Red? Up for a ride?"

Haven

"Do you think Meadow's doing okay?" Coppery curls flutter around her head. The horses are walking through the pasture side by side. The swish of the grass against their legs is the loudest sound out here, mingling with the horses' breathing and occasional nickers.

"She's just fine." She's secured in my entryway so she doesn't chase after us and get tired, or get under a hoof. The dog is smart and learning fast, but she's still less than three months old.

"Do you really run home and let her out for bathroom breaks?"

"What's the perk of being my own boss if I can't have puppy visits in the middle of the day?"

"You like her."

"It'd be weird if I hated cute puppies."

"Sure." Her smile is pure daylight. When she wiggles in the saddle, I repress a groan. I'd love to ride a few feet behind her and enjoy the flare her hips make when her legs are spread, but that's for another time. Or a never time, since fucking with the gorgeous redhead is only asking for regrets.

Given when she said she last rode, she's now thirty-two. Six years younger than me. Prickly Miss Prescott Keys has a lot of reasons to resent being in Huckleberry Springs, but she didn't run away after Dr. Small finished with all the immunizations and exams.

"You should've let me pay." She doesn't look at me when she says it.

I took a risk, knowing that she'd get upset when she learned I'd asked the vet to charge me. "It's a ranch expense."

"But they're rescues."

"They're working." My brothers won't care, but they might give me shit about doing it for Prescott. It'd be wrong not to.

"Well, thank you." She said it before, and it's still just as begrudging now. She keeps her attention straight ahead. "It really is beautiful."

"Yes, it is. I've seen this view a million times, and I want to see it a million more. There was a time I thought I'd never lay eyes on it again." And it's infinitely better with her in it.

"You grew up in town, right?"

"In the house I'm living in."

She twists to squint at me. "The *same* house?"

"Mom ran off right after I was born. Three young boys? She couldn't do it." Prescott frowns, but I keep going. "So it was us and my dad, and it was nice."

"Yeah?"

"Yeah," I say gruffly. "We'd hunt and fish, and then at night, Dad would watch old movies with us."

"I haven't done any of that."

"Seriously?" When she nods, my chest gets tight. I had a great childhood. My brothers made sure of it. She was let down in hers. The experiences I listed were simple. What if I did them with her? "Red, we're going to have to change that while you're in town."

"Old movies?"

All of it. "We'll make a rule. They have to be from before we were born."

A smile plays along her lips. "Fishing?"

I've hooked her. "The Stillwater is right over there." I tip the brim of my hat toward where the land slopes down into the valley, a copse of trees filling the distance. "Be a shame not to use it when I know some good spots. The best one is by the distillery."

"And hunting?"

"That one might be a little harder."

"I don't like killing things." She holds up a hand, but I wasn't going to argue. "I get the idea of hunting. For food. I know it helps keep local wildlife populations healthy. I even like the idea of tromping through the woods. I just don't want to kill something."

"I have to admit dragging a kill back to the pickup is a pain in the ass too." I'm not going to leave any opportunity to spend time with her on the table. My brothers say I'm like Mom sometimes. Here I am, making bad decisions for myself. "Old movies and fishing. What are you doing tomorrow?"

"I..."

I'm pushing too fast. "The weather's supposed to be perfect for some fly-fishing. I was planning to go anyway, and I have an extra set of waders."

I planned to start cutting hay, but it's not supposed to rain all week. Haying can wait. Prescott won't.

She chews the inside of her cheek. "Doesn't seem fair that you're showing me stuff I've never done, and I'm not doing the same for you."

So she's willing, but she doesn't want to feel like she's only taking. I can work with that.

Why is this so important to me?

I'm enjoying my morning. My days since I've met Prescott have been lighter. Brighter. I go to work and do all the same things I've done, but...there's something to look forward to now. Not just figuring out what's going into the whiskey bottle wedding favors or joking around with the guys.

I like coming home to Meadow. And being greeted in the barn with sleepy yawns and loud purrs. And I like getting to know the girl I found in the ditch. Prescott and her sharp wit. She quickly relaxed into her saddle. She's looking around at the rolling pastures and the mountains in the distance rather than fiddling with the reins and watching each step Biscuits takes. She's moving with him now, naturally, and not questioning her every breath. She clearly has experience, but now she's enjoying the ride. I'm sharing this with her.

Can we do it again with fishing? Maybe, but she'd like a tit for tat. What is there that I haven't done that she could help me with?

I've done a lot of things that would make her blush. Finding out how far down her creamy skin that blush goes could easily become another obsession, but I'm playing this safe. What wouldn't make her run and hide from me?

She rescues strays, and she's a photographer. An idea sparks. "I've never had professional photos taken. Like a photo shoot."

"Never?"

"Other than school photos and Iverson's wedding? No. None with just me. Our mom wasn't the portrait type." She never even ordered those school photos.

She'd laugh and say, *I know what you look like. I don't need to pay for it.*

Her brows draw together, and those plump lips purse. The swish of Gravy's tail fills the silence. "Not even senior pictures?"

"We were lucky to graduate. My brothers and I mostly

worked so we could move as soon as I was done with school."

She considers me, holding the reins loosely. I didn't have to correct one thing about how she saddled Biscuits or her seat, nor did I have to make any suggestions. Her dad taught her right, and those skills have been lying dormant, just waiting to be used. Is that what photography is like?

"How long has it been since you did photography?" I ask.

"Five years. Right after my mom died, I decided to move with my ex when he got a job in Chicago. I used the transition to rescue a cat. Buford the Boss Cat." She chuckles, and the loss is loud and clear—of both her mom and cat. "He was a photogenic little bugger. One of a kind."

"The ex?"

She barks out a laugh. Biscuits huffs. "No, he was not." She purses her lips. "Actually, he was. After Buford died, I tried to keep posting. A lifestyle account with photography lessons. I used him a lot as a model to show techniques. So when another influencer posted and got the back of him sitting on her bed, he was recognized. I had a big enough following for that," she says bitterly.

"What a fucking asshole."

She grunts. "The *fucking* part was more accurate than I thought. Two more influencers called him out for playing them. He traveled for work and used Buford to connect with them."

"Ah, hell, Red. No man should've treated you like that. Was he at least good to the cat?"

She nods. "You know, that's the only thing that might've opened my eyes. I trailed that idiot to Chicago, and then I stayed. Getting strung along. Anyway, yes, he was decent to Buford."

"You going to post the kittens or Meadow?"

"No."

I draw back at her quick answer. Does she realize how much she lights up when she talks about them? The way she wielded her camera was natural, and I could watch and listen to her all day. I could do that without the camera.

"I deleted it all," she explains. "I don't have the will to start up again."

"But you have all that footage. I bet it's good."

"It is." When I smile at her confidence, she matches my grin. "With Buford, it just happened naturally. His account grew organically, and then I started getting cat food and supply companies hitting me up for sponsorships. Even a pet DNA company. My Prescott Photog endeavor failed, and I don't want to feel like I'm using the animals."

Her social influencer adventure failed when her ex betrayed her. Was the drama all anyone cared about afterward? All public and impersonal, when to her it was very much personal. My private life is speculated on enough. It was like that growing up, and it's like that now. I go on a date, and people are wondering if she's the one. But there's no one. I'm not stringing a girl along the way Prescott's ex did to her.

"So I stay offline," she says. "But I enjoy taking pictures. How about a senior photo shoot after fishing?"

If she wants to change the subject, I'll let her. I'm soaking up everything she tells me and storing it away in a part of my memory that's filling up with all things Prescott Keys. Starting with her red underwear. "Red, I need time to prepare. I've gotta get a haircut. I have to pick my clothes."

She bites back a grin. "You need at least two outfit changes. I used to charge per location too."

"How much will I owe you?"

She looks aghast. "Are you charging me for the ride?"

"Hundred bucks an hour."

"What a coincidence. My rate is a hundred an hour too."

Her quick wit keeps me on my toes. "An even trade. Horseback riding for a senior photo shoot. I'll let you know what we can trade for the fishing tomorrow." I'll have to think of it first. Something that takes a lot of time.

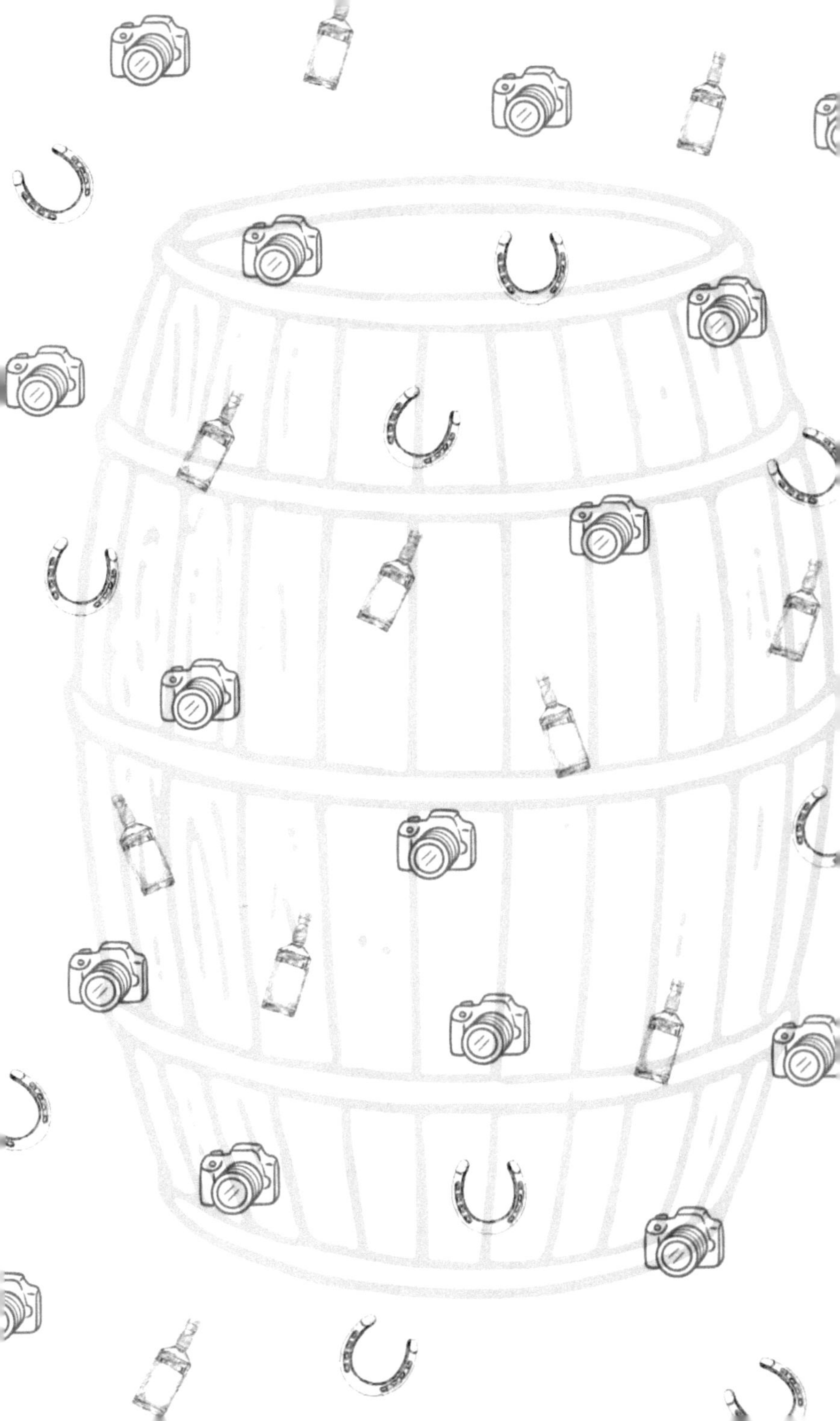

CHAPTER EIGHT

Prescott

Before I leave the small guest room that's nothing but an old futon with a record player doubling as my nightstand, I dig my camera case out and hook it over a shoulder. Might as well blow the dust off and practice during my fishing trip today.

Senior pictures. For a guy who's twenty years or so past his senior year. Still, I smile. Haven's been a go-with-the-flow type since I met him, but a photo shoot?

My excitement's building, and I thought the days of being revved up for a session were over.

I find Papa at the square kitchen table, sipping what's gotta be his fifth cup of coffee. The smell has seeped into every fiber of the house, and it's become my new perfume. There are worse smells, but I'll be glad to get my own place. Someday.

"Need anything before I go, Papa?"

He scrutinizes my camera. "You working again?"

He sounds so hopeful, I don't have the heart to tell him I'm doing a shoot for free. "I've got to keep my skills sharp."

Making a show of looking at his watch, he sucks his teeth against his lips. "You going to that Hennessy boy's place?"

The Hennessy boy whose strong thighs grip his horse just right? The Hennessy boy whose biceps flex when he's holding the reins? Or the Hennessy boy who has a nice, deep laugh and a smoldering gaze under the brim of his hat?

"I'm going to get some images of the cats. I'm thinking of starting a new account." The first part's not a lie.

Papa takes a slurping sip. "That social media stuff is just gambling."

But it made me happy. "Isn't that sort of what you did with rodeo?"

Instead of getting disgruntled, he shrugs. "The social media stuff has guarantees. How about that?"

"Agreed."

"That all you're doing there?" His eyes glint over his mug, taking in my long-sleeved, moisture-wicking top and leggings. "Taking pictures?"

I tug at my hem. I might've looked up what to wear fly-fishing and dressed as best I could with what I have. "I'm socializing the cats."

He sniffs and pooches his lips out, giving his mustache a little lift. "Just the cats?"

I'm a grown woman. I don't have to answer to him even if I'm staying in his place. Yet blowing him off will only make him suspect something is going on, and nothing is.

I'm not laughing on horseback when Haven's riding

next to me. Nor am I admiring how sexy he is when he's training a puppy. Definitely not making plans to do more things with him that don't include the rescues he's caring for.

"Haven's been nothing but friendly, and *only* friendly."

Papa grunts and takes another drink, interrupting the flow of steam. "Haven's friendly, all right."

"Don't worry, Papa. I've developed a severe allergy to charming men who can't commit." I should thank Haven. I don't have to worry about getting seduced into staying in this small town, only to cry myself asleep when Haven spends his nights everywhere else. "I'll be back to help you out at the bar tonight."

His muttered, "You better be," has nothing to do with me covering a shift. He's used to working alone. I'm going to go ahead and take my time today.

Haven told me to meet him in the distillery parking lot. Before I get into my car, I spray myself off with sunscreen. I'm not turning into a beet in front of him. Then I slip on my sunglasses and hit the road.

Each time I'm out this way, the beauty of the Beartooth Mountains captivates me. Papa only brought me here once when I was a kid, but he talked about returning home all the time. It was one of his many campfire stories. After he had his last ride, he'd go home.

My chest tightens for that little girl. I can't believe I told Haven the story of my parents. He's one of Bootleg's customers, but he didn't get hung up on how cool my dad's life must've been, or what a whiner I am. What I experienced is nothing compared to him. But he listened.

A girl could get used to that.

Soon, I pull into the parking lot. Haven's pacing behind his pickup. His head is bent, and he's on the phone, brows pinched together. He stops, looks at his phone, and angrily stuffs it into his back pocket.

I park a spot away from him, and his scowl automatically turns into a welcoming grin. Butterflies explode in my stomach. Other than my mom, no one's ever been that excited to see me. If my ex looked at me like that, I might've believed his lies.

When I get out, a warm grain smell surrounds me. He's waiting behind his pickup, his stance easy, relaxed, the phone call forgotten.

Is my presence enough to wipe away whatever angst the call gave him? Wishful thinking? "Hey."

"Ready to cast a line?"

The wings of the butterflies in my stomach droop a little. Did I expect him to unload all his problems on me? I barely know him. I'm drawn to him. I can't deny that. It's like the more a guy doesn't want to settle down, the more attracted I get.

Whoever he was talking to and whatever they were talking about is none of my business. I'm just spoiled. He's opened up so much, and now I'm feeling shut out.

None of this day is about us. It's about fly-fishing.

"I'll need help with my casting stroke." Now I'm flirting. I shouldn't do this. But I get my hat out of the passenger seat, hook my camera bag over my shoulder, and lock my car.

His gaze drops to my feet and lazily climbs all the way up, leaving streaks of heat where it touches. "You came outfitted for the occasion."

"All I had were hiking sandals."

"We'll make it work. You gonna do my senior shoot?"

"You said you needed a haircut first." The edges of the hair he pushes off his face stick out from the bottom of his hat. Is he going to trim so much that a girl can't run her fingers through the strands?

What about those whiskers? It'd be a shame to shave those clean off. I want to catch the real Haven Hennessy.

My curiosity continues pushing out at the seams. It's the most animated I've seen him since I arrived. Which isn't long, but still. "Did I interrupt your call?"

He flinches. "No. It was winding up."

That's all I get. The day grows a little dimmer. "Oh. Guess we're ready, then."

"Got anything else to bring? It's not a long hike."

"No. I can help carry whatever you have."

I get another smile, but there's a heaviness in his eyes that isn't usually there. From the bed of his truck, he digs out a couple of poles, a boxy backpack that he slings across his shoulders, a small cooler, and another backpack.

"Is that bait?" I point to the cooler. Does fly-fishing need bait? I didn't read as much as I should've about it.

"Close. Snacks." He lifts the second backpack. "This is a cooler for anything we catch. I just fillet them on the riverbank instead of setting up a stringer. The bears don't usually bother us here."

"Bears?"

"Never seen a mountain lion either." He smirks. "Bet they've seen me, though."

"That's not funny!" I laugh anyway. If he's not worried, I'll try not to be jumpy. "I'll carry the cooler." I hold my hand out. "I should've thought about packing food. I could've contributed."

"Nope. I've got my fishing snacks. No problem adding more."

"Let me guess—beef sticks and cheese?"

He laughs and starts for a break in the trees around the parking lot. "Oh, the city girl thinks she has me pegged."

"Compared to Huckleberry Springs, everywhere I've lived is a metropolis. Although I lived in Phoenix for a while."

"Are you from Arizona?" He moves to the edge of the trail to give me room to walk next to him.

"I spent most of my time in Colorado. It's where Mom met Papa. She moved where he did, and when they broke up, we went to Phoenix, but it was too expensive. Back to Colorado we went." I trace the map in my head. "After I graduated, I went back to Arizona for college, got a job in Tucson, and I traveled around and did school photos. That's how I picked up some clients for senior pictures." The gentle trickle of the river grows louder. "And some wedding and family portraits."

"You don't sound excited about those."

"They were a lot of work," I lie. "Juggling so many people. Photographing kids and cats is easier."

He chuckles, but his gaze lingers on me longer, like he knows I'm not telling the total truth. Weddings used to be some of my favorite shoots. Until they weren't.

I wanted him to open up to me, and here I am shutting him down. But exploring why I don't like working weddings or family sessions would sound unhinged. Or so I've been told.

Time for a subject change. "Fun fact, I'm named after Prescott, Arizona."

"Don't tell me that's where you were conceived."

"Please don't make me think about that." I shudder. "I could've been, but the bull ride of Papa's life is more significant to him."

"Oh, damn."

Yep. "How about you? What are you named after?" Hopefully, his name won't hold as much baggage as mine.

"We're all last names. Iverson is my mom's maiden name. Her mom's maiden name was Durban, and my great-grandma's was Haven."

"That's sweet. You all have some family history."

His jaw goes rock hard, and the glint in his eyes is bright enough for me to see from the side. Ah. So there is baggage. "She wanted to have all the names for herself. Not my dad's name. Not his middle name. Not his parents' or grandparents' names."

"So that's how she played it?"

"That's how she's still playing it." He contemplates the trail in front of us. "It was her on the phone."

I gently squeeze his forearm. "I didn't want to pry, but it didn't seem like it was going well."

"It wasn't."

We continue walking. I won't ask more. The slightly fishy odor of mud and the faint scent of wildflowers and grasses calm the air between us.

"She wants to know about the guys and their families, but they don't want me to tell her."

"They don't talk to her?"

He barks out a laugh, and a bird scatters from a tree next to us. "Not since we left and barely before that. Iverson was almost fourteen when we went to live with her. I had just turned eight. They both think I should be the one with zero contact." His brows pull together like they were when he was on the phone. "She left because of me."

His admission rips right through my ribs like a sharp, narrow blade. He's saying it like it's a fact. "Haven. I don't know what happened, but I know that's not true. You were just a kid."

"I was a baby. Three young boys, and she said I was the last straw."

I don't like his mom. Not at all. "Your brothers are trying to protect you."

He shrugs. "She's my mom, and she took us in when it was critical. I won't forget that. Not after going into the foster system. Like I said, we got lucky with the Baileys, but it was a stressful time."

Stressful, says the grown man. To a kid who was seven and had just lost his dad? Terrifying. So his mom swoops in like a savior, but she's someone his brothers don't want to have in their lives.

I can't imagine what that's like. Mom and I only had each other, but she was the best mother I could've asked for. "You get caught between her and your brothers."

"I don't recommend it."

"I'll keep your secret, but I can't argue with your brothers' concerns. They care about you." A little scared Haven burrows right in next to my heart. I want to hug the younger and older versions of him closer. His mom had a life that I dream about, and she abandoned it.

"They're at a point in their lives where they need to care about themselves and the families they're starting."

He's a good man. Seeing this side of him makes me less cautious around the commitment-phobe in him. A warning bell should be going off, but it's not. Not when I'm enjoying the gorgeous weather with a guy like him. "Someday, I strive to be where your brothers are and not unemployed, dumped, and bunking with an old bachelor bull rider who didn't tell anyone he has a daughter."

His lips quirk. "I've heard that's not recommended either."

"Neither is his coffee, FYI. In case he ever offers you a cup."

"That bad?"

"Unless you like it as hot as molten lava and as strong and bitter as battery acid."

"You've only piqued my interest, Red. Is the cup also a dubious level of clean?"

My laugh is carried off on the breeze. He's grinning, with those sexy crinkles at the corners of his eyes. The fishing rods are slung over a shoulder, and the backdrop of the river and grasses only enhances his outdoorsy ruggedness. "This is where we're going to take your pictures."

Surprised, he looks around and nods. "Sounds like a plan, Red."

Haven

I load everything into the back of the pickup that I took out of it four hours ago.

"I can't believe we actually caught something." She sounds as stunned as she was when she first realized she had a fish on the other end of her line.

"*You* caught two fish. Didn't tell me you're a pro angler."

"I'm not, but then I never tried."

I almost ask her when we can go again, but that might scare her off. My stomach rumbles. She only put her pole down during our small snack break and picked up her camera instead. She must be hungry too. "Now we need to eat these. How about a fish fry?"

Her smile falls. "I told Papa I'd work at the bar."

"It won't take long. Those beef sticks aren't enough for dinner."

"You mean those beef sticks that were labeled with Hennessy Beef?"

"Only the best for you, Red."

She shoots me a mock scowl and takes her hat off. Some of her coppery strands have escaped the hold of her ponytail and flutter around her face. My reflection shines back at me from her sunglasses. I look more casual than I feel. If she joins me, it'd be at my place. She's been there before. It's not a big deal. Good fish fillets shouldn't be kept waiting, and she's the one who caught them. She should enjoy her work. So yeah, I'm using our trout as my bait.

She tucks some stray strands behind her ear. "I should get going. Clean up a little before work."

Damn. "All right. Let me know when we can take my pictures."

"Wednesday."

She planned it already? Is she looking forward to it? As much as I cringe when I think about saying *cheese* or some shit in front of her, I like having a set date to see her again. "See you then, Red."

I might've added a suggestive purr, but I can't help it. I want her to like me, and it's not like I've had girls for friends before. I've been friendly with them, but this thing with Prescott is different. Maybe it helps that she's basically passing through.

Her lips part before she shakes her head and starts for her driver's door. "See you then, Hennessy."

The way my last name rolls off those ripe lips is going to stick with me when it's not convenient.

After she drives away, I get in my pickup and take off home. What am I going to do with the fish? Hunger grumbles in my stomach again. They're both okay-sized trout, about what I'd expect this time of year. If I fry them up, I'm just going to think about her, and I've been doing too much of that lately for a guy who isn't interested in long-term relationships.

At my house, I unload all of the fishing gear in my garage and let Meadow out to use the bathroom. She runs around my feet, delighted I'm home.

"Hey, girl." I wait until she's done on the lawn before I let her into the house.

My gaze tracks across my clean house. I replaced the flooring shortly after I moved in and installed new windows. The doors have been replaced too, and the walls hold a new coat of paint. It's an old place, and it could use more remodeling, but it's clean and tidy. For all the guests who aren't going to see it. Especially one tall, curvy redhead.

Meadow's paws tap across the floor, and loud, sloppy sounds of her drinking water fill the air. I set the backpack and cooler on the counter.

My doorbell rings.

Did I miss a note from my brothers about stopping over? Even then, they just knock before opening the door and shouting for me. They know I never have anyone over. I check my phone on the way to the door. Nothing.

I open it to Prescott twisting her hands together. She's taken her sunglasses off, and her blue eyes dart around.

"I mean, I have to eat dinner anyway," she says with no other preamble.

A wide grin overtakes my face. She changed her mind and ended up on my doorstep. "I'll make it quick."

It's the only thing I'd do quickly with her.

Meadow runs to her, droplets dripping from her chin.

"Look at you," Prescott coos, uncaring about the water splatter and squats down. "Such a pretty girl."

"Go ahead and spoil her while I get some fish fried up."

I work in the kitchen, dragging dishes and batter ingredients out. When she's done petting Meadow, she ducks into the bathroom right off the hallway and returns. She creeps to the table, looking all over like she's trying to be subtle about gawking.

"I'm using my dad's recipe." I've never cooked it for anyone before, but it's the only one I've ever made.

"Is it a secret?"

"Only in that nothing's measured."

"Ah, the ol' go-with-your-heart measuring spoons. My mom liked to use those."

"What's your secret family recipe?" I dredge the fillets and put them into the hot oil. Sizzling fills the air.

"Mom made a killer lasagna. And short ribs. Then there's her birthday cake recipe."

"Vanilla or chocolate?"

"Marble. Homemade marble cake is nothing like store-bought. Not with Mom's recipe. What's your favorite flavor?"

"Don't really do birthday cakes."

"What?" She stands and charges to the opposite side of the counter where it wings out from the wall. She has to duck to see me from under the cabinets mounted overhead. "How do you not do birthday cakes?"

"Our birthdays were always low-key." Her attention prickles over me, and the back of my neck heats. Time to get off this topic. It's one I've never explored, and I don't want to. "Care for a drink? I've got whiskey, of course. Vodka and gin. A beer?"

"The distiller drinks beer?"

"If it's fermented, I'll drink it. But I won't pay five bucks for a bottle of kombucha."

"Especially since a distiller can make his own." She waves off the topic. "Back to the cake. Your birthday isn't a big deal? When is it?"

Too close. "In a few weeks. It's on a Saturday this year." I made sure I'm working that day. It's too close to the wedding for Durban and Campbell to get distracted. "You could say the wedding is a birthday gift."

Her expression turns dismayed, and she leans farther over the counter. "They're getting married on your birthday?"

"No, the week after." I'm not sure what's upsetting her. There'll be guests and cake. For the wedding, but it's not like I'll be sitting home alone. "It's just my birthday."

Her jaw drops, and a squeak leaves her. "Just your birthday? Are you going to tell me next that it's *only* Christmas?"

I give my head a shake and turn the fillets over. "Holidays are a big deal for you, aren't they?"

"Yes." She sticks her index finger in the air. "First, Mom would always rouse out of her doldrums to put on a big shindig. Special cake. Wrapped presents. Good food." She rolls her eyes and moans. My gut clenches. "The best food. She cooked so much, and it was usually just the two of us."

What food? If I make it, can I get that moan again? "Good food. What else?"

She sticks up a second finger. "Holidays were some of

the only days I got off from work. When I did photography, holiday shoots were *before* the holidays, so I usually never had to work. And I never scheduled sessions on my birthday. Those were to be spent with my mom."

"She sounds pretty special."

"She was. Fuck cancer." She adds a third finger. "And then when I got into influencing, I kept it up. No matter how much I chased views and content and algorithms, I kept the no-holidays rule, including my birthday. Mom said she was proud of me."

"Good."

"Thanks." Fleeting sadness passes over her face before her earlier holiday fervor returns. "So if I'm still here—and judging by my tips, I will be—you're getting a marbled cake for your birthday. A birthday cake for a fish fry. No!"

I almost startle at her shout. "No?"

"What's your favorite meal?"

I fight with my brain to keep my thoughts off her body and on her question. She's flush with excitement, and while the fried fish smells divine, my hunger is less food-related.

Her. She could very well be my favorite meal, and I don't know it. "Anything beef."

"You can get that all the time, Hennessy beef. What don't you usually make for yourself?"

"Ribs."

"Ribs and birthday cake." She crosses her arms. *Don't look at her tits. Don't look, goddammit.* "Who would you want at your party?"

My gut clenches, wiping away the urge to dive headfirst into her generous cleavage. "No one." Everyone showing up, just for me? Making a big deal out of what's usually a normal day, other than the dozen cupcakes I pick up from Dee's Sweets? I shudder. "No. No party."

"Okay," she says lightly, like she's coaxing me out of a ditch. "It's fine. Food only."

"And you."

Her lips curve up. "Well, I have to cook."

"And you have to eat with me."

"I'm not going to fight you when it comes to ribs and cake."

"Good. I don't want the drama." Which used to come with birthdays. Some sort of conflict or nothing, no in between. One more set day with Prescott. What about the time from the photo shoot to my birthday? Three weeks I can fill with Prescott. I think back to our conversation. "We still need an old movie."

"Then I would have to think of something else."

I watch the breaded fish cook. I'm not giving up. Something she said earlier comes back. "I haven't had lasagna in years."

"How many years?"

"Does the box stuff from the store count?"

She makes a gagging motion. "No. Ew. Okay. I'll get the ingredients, and I can cook for you."

"At Silas's place?"

Color leeches from her face. "I feel like Papa would have words."

I pull the fillets out and onto a rack to drain the oil. Then I move the pan and shut the burner off. The whole time, I'm suppressing a grin. The only place she can make that lasagna is right here, in this kitchen. For me.

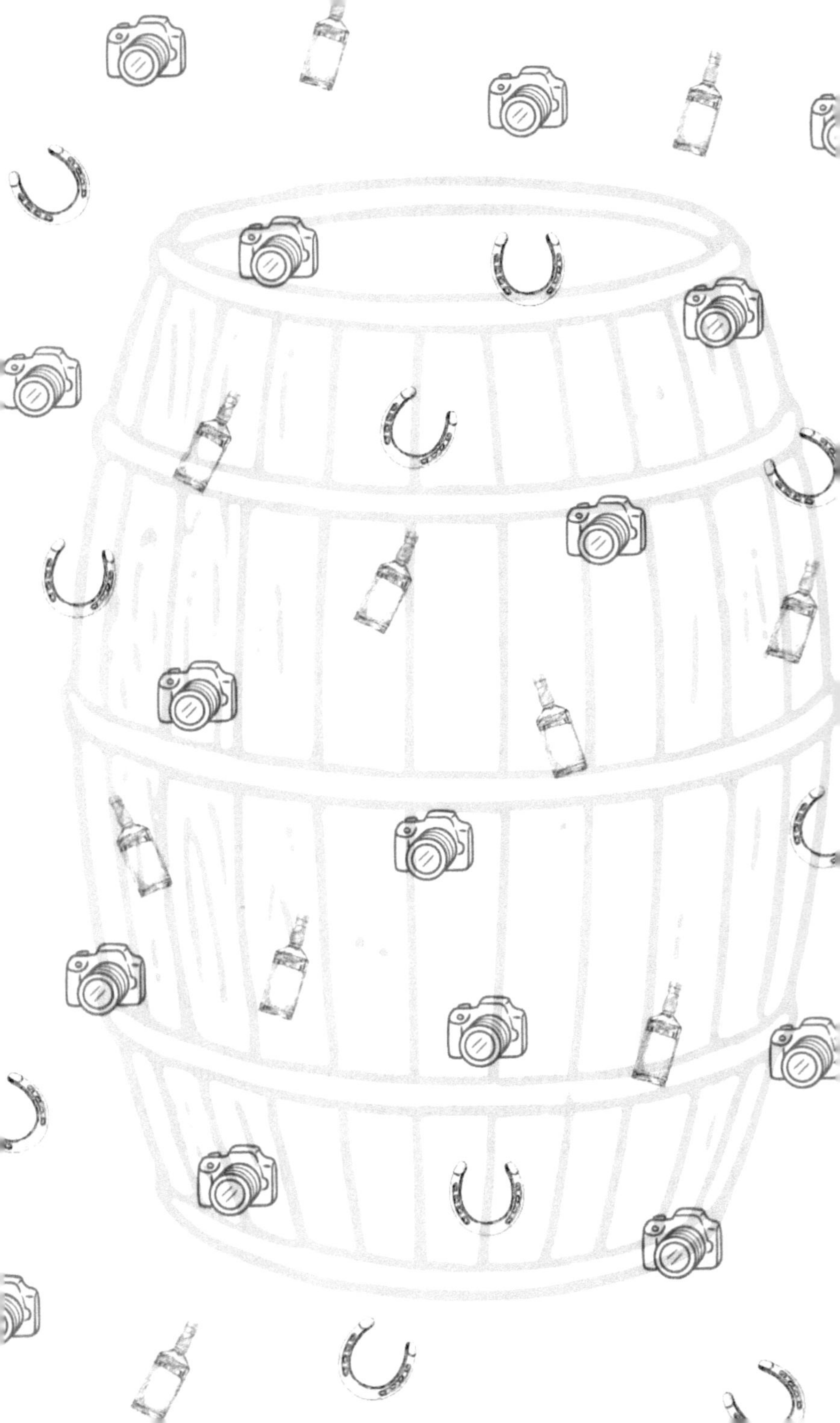

CHAPTER NINE

Prescott

"What drink would you have paired with this dish?" I cross my feet at the ankles and lean back in my chair. I really need to go. I'm already risking an interrogation from Papa. I've spent the whole day with Haven, and I'm still with him. It's just so comfortable. The conversation is flowing. And Haven cooking in the kitchen in his tight shirt with his wide shoulders is a treat I don't ever get. "Something from Foster House?"

"Whiskey. All the way." He stuffs the last bite of his coleslaw in his mouth. The man didn't just serve me fried fish. He had cubed melon and fresh coleslaw already in his fridge, and he took a box of cookies out of the freezer.

The guys I've dated before never had their shit together this well. "Butter Barrel or Haven's Rye?"

"Either. The food is mild enough. Our Golden Nugget would be good too. You haven't tried that yet."

He gets up and goes to a wooden stand in the corner.

It's like an armoire but for spirits. On one side, he selects a bottle of amber liquid. From the other side, he gathers two glasses in one hand, the same as the ones he had me drink from at the tasting room, and brings them to the table.

"You're prepared," I say, shifting my chair to face him more.

"I didn't have to be a Boy Scout to learn some skills." He moves his chair so we're facing each other and pours a small amount into each glass. "I know you have to work, but you have to taste Golden Nugget before you go."

He doesn't drink his. He watches me as I raise the glass. Awareness dances over my skin. Maybe it's because his attention is on me, but I take my time. I swirl the glass slowly. Sensually. His pupils dilate.

There should be nothing sexy about this moment. I'm in moisture-wicking material, the smell of the river and neoprene waders clinging to me. My hair must be a frizzed halo around my head, and my skin feels both sticky and oily from the sunscreen. Yet the way he's looking at me, it's like I'm in a slinky dress that flatters the flare of my hips and the pooch of my belly that no shapewear can hide.

I put the glass to my lips, and he leans forward. His gaze flicks from my mouth to my eyes and back down. The thin ring of his brown irises is midnight against the black pupil.

Tipping the glass ever so slightly, the whiskey hits my lips and then my tongue. My heart beats slow and steady, hard thump after thump fortifying my nerves. Why am I doing this? Why am I at his house? I should be at work.

"How is it?" His rough voice distracts me enough that I forget to shut off my nose. Whiskey sears the back of my throat and swoops up into my sinuses. I start coughing.

"Shit. Sorry." He jumps up and retrieves a glass of water.

I gather myself together enough to take the water. "It's not your fault." It is, but not in the way he thinks.

"Yes, it is. Golden Nugget is one of our strongest whiskeys, and it's a rye. Very peppery."

I'll say it is. I nod and polish off my water. "Whiskey just isn't my thing."

He scoots his chair closer. "Some of it just needs to be softened. Add a little water to it."

I eye him dubiously, but he reaches next to me, mere inches away, and takes my mostly empty glass of water. He shakes two drops into the glass of whiskey.

"Try it now." The stern but encouraging way he says it is apparently a new kink of mine. *Kneel and take it into your mouth.* I'd do it without thinking.

I have to be logical. It's just whiskey. "That little amount of water is going to make that much difference?"

"For some palates, it makes all the difference. Drink."

I go through the same motions, but only because he's on the edge of his seat, our knees touching. He needs me to put my lips on this glass. So I do.

This time, I don't burn my vocal cords or singe my sinuses. I roll the whiskey on my tongue.

No way. The peppery sting isn't as strong, and the flavors sink into my taste buds instead of assaulting them. "Oh, wow. It's better. Just a little water does that? What else?"

His gaze stays on mine, the brown swirling with his thoughts. My pulse kicks up a few notches. Why do I feel like I never want to move from this spot ever?

Then he picks up his untouched whiskey and takes a drink. But he doesn't swallow. Instead, he leans even closer and cups my chin. Despite my confusion, I sway toward him, closing the distance. He places his lips on mine, tickling the sensitive skin around my mouth, and scoots to the edge of his chair, coaxing me to do the same. Our legs are intertwined, and damn, my ass is barely on the seat. But his knee is right there. Close enough to grind on.

As if his voice is in my head, I part my lips. He opens his and a trickle of whiskey slips into my mouth.

I moan. The flavor is warmer, richer. Spicy.

I guess I am a whiskey girl.

More smooth liquid fills my mouth, and I drink him in. He sweeps his tongue in, and I grip his shirt, meeting him stroke for stroke. It's like I've been parched for months, and he's here with all the life-saving water I need in the form of whiskey.

My fingers are curled so tight in the material of his shirt that his heart hammers against them. I'm not the only one affected by this kiss.

Oh god. A kiss.

I'm kissing Haven, and I don't want to stop.

I rip away with a gasp, and he lurches forward. I've still got a hold on his shirt. My fingers are stiff when I let go. "Sorry."

"Why?" He hasn't backed away. His lips are glistening. Mine must be the same. Swollen and puffy. Demanding more.

I rise, pushing away the chair and dancing out from between it and him. Meadow raises her head from a bed that looks new.

He stands behind me. "Prescott."

"I've got to get to work." I continue through the kitchen. What was I thinking? Now I know how well he kisses. That wasn't just any lightning-fast make-out session either. He gave me a special tasting. He showed me what whiskey tastes like with him in it.

How many others have gotten that?

Ugh. This is why I don't mess around with guys like him. Attractive. Charming. Successful. Someone like me will never be enough.

"Red."

I push through the front door, but it doesn't slam shut behind me.

"Prescott, please."

It's the *please*. I stop and turn. Irritation rises like sandpaper across my skin.

Prescott, please. It was just a kiss.

Prescott, please. It didn't mean anything.

Prescott, please. Did you really think I would be happy with only you?

"I don't want a relationship," I say firmly, but his fraught gaze digs into my chest. "You really do seem like a decent guy, but I'm really not in a place to trust anyone. And I'm not in the mindset where I can kiss and have it mean nothing."

The stress in his features eases, but the concern remains. "You're telling me that it's not me, it's you?"

"Yes."

"It's not you, Prescott. It's everyone who let you down."

"Do you mean my dad? Or every cheating ex in my dating history? Because there's been more than one."

Anger flares in his eyes. "Fuck those guys." His expression flickers. "Well, not Silas, but you know what I mean."

"Usually, they fucked someone else. There's always someone better."

"Not all men are like them."

"So you're telling me that you're ready to get serious?" The way he draws back tells me everything. "I'm done being good enough for a good time, but not a long time." I continue to my car. "The next guy I get serious with is going to be endgame. There's going to be monogamy and vows. Commitment. Real commitment and not smoke and mirrors and endless hours, days, weeks to himself. No more excuses for *years* for why he can't settle."

Haven works his jaw back and forth. He stares into the distance.

Yep. That's what I thought. "Thanks for the fishing experience. I'll still honor the senior pictures. And the lasagna." Crap, there's more. "The old movie. And the birthday cake. But that's all. Experiences. Without kisses."

His brows draw together. "Experiences without kisses?" A muscle in the corner of his jaw flexes, but he nods. "See you."

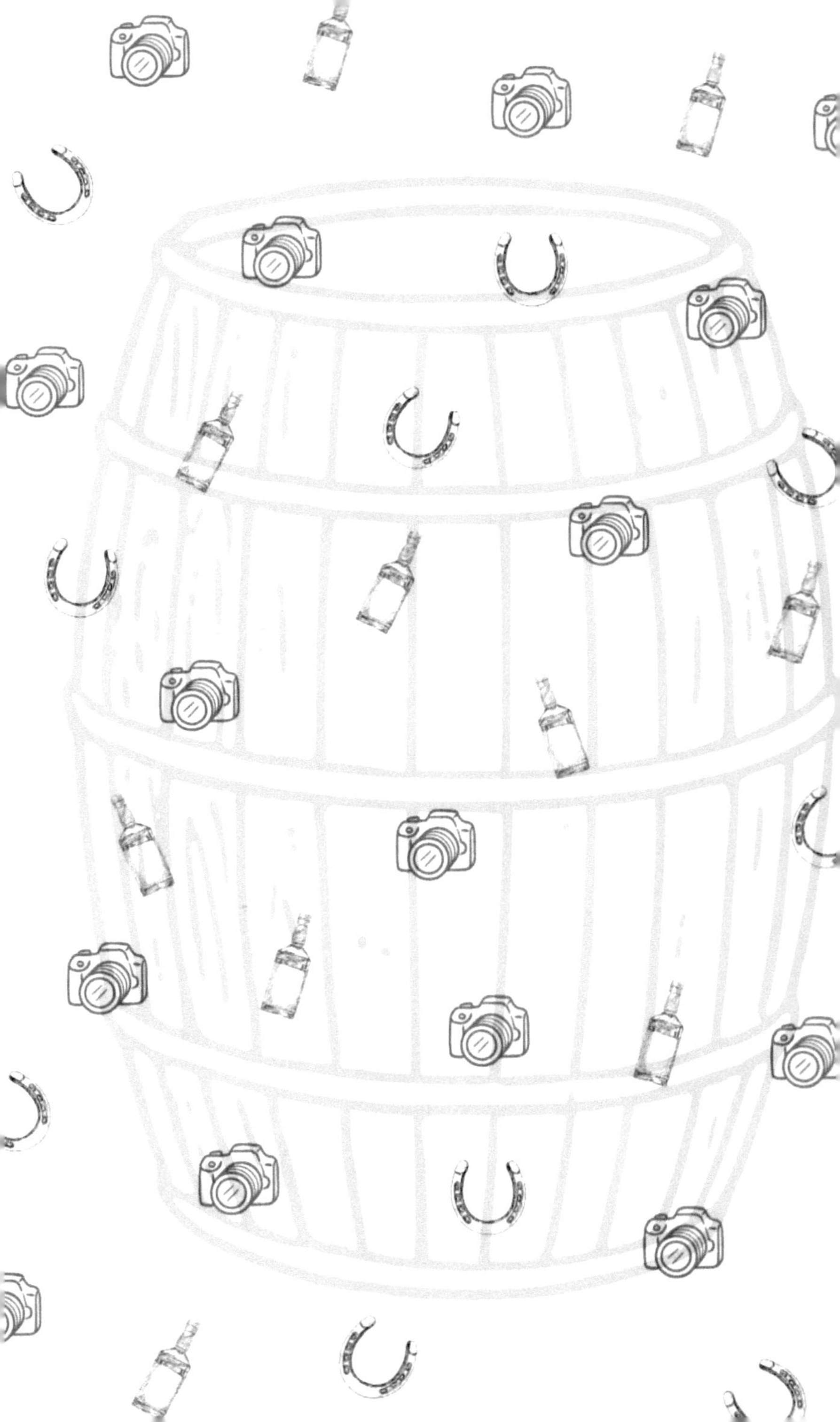

CHAPTER TEN

Haven

"You're doing what?" Jamison asks. She and Campbell cornered me by the pallets before I could duck out the back door. Prescott's car parked next to mine last Sunday didn't go unnoticed. I glance at the clock on the wall for the tenth time.

It's Wednesday, and I didn't want to freak out Prescott, so I told her to meet me here. She's gone back to checking on the animals when I'm out doing chores or working here. She must drive by to see if my pickup's parked in the Foster House lot.

"Senior pictures," I answer Jamison and brace myself for the barrage of questions.

"Like senior discount pictures?" she asks.

"No, like the ones I never got done in high school." They're the reason I dressed in my bluest pair of jeans, put on a crisp white dress shirt, and dug my nice cowboy hat out of the closet. I kept that in my pickup while I finished up in the distillery. I'm getting enough questions as it is.

Campbell claps her hands together and jumps up and down. "That's so sweet."

"No," I say firmly. "It's not that. She wanted to pay me back for taking her out on Biscuits and Gravy and for going fishing."

Jamison's expression turns greedy, like she's in gossip overload and loving it. "What else?"

"Nothing." I try to skirt around them, but I picked the wrong two country girls to try that with. They grew up working cattle and catching horses, and they've got me flanked so well, they might as well have a lead rope in hand. I exhale. I'm trapped. "She wants a serious relationship, to not live in a small town, and to start her career not in Huckleberry Springs. And you know how I am about women."

Campbell frowns. "How are you?"

"Not serious." My chest gets heavy.

Jamison's glee turns into confusion. "Why not?" Understanding fills her eyes. "*Oh*. Haven..."

I'm sure Iverson's filled her in on life with our mom. I don't want to talk about it. "So we're just friends. I'm making sure Huckleberry Springs doesn't suck for her, and she's trying to reciprocate the best she can."

"It's still sweet," Campbell says softly. "She seems really cool. Durban said he told you that you could invite her to the wedding."

"She is cool." I ignore the wedding comment. "Hopefully, she's also a good photographer." It doesn't matter if half the photos have me blinking or my mouth hanging open. They're not real senior pictures anyway.

Jamison digs out her phone. "One of my favorite pictures from our wedding is the one of you three."

I know the image she's talking about. Me, Iverson, and Durban. Those were the first family pictures taken of us since before our dad died.

She flashes it. "Look how happy and proud Iverson is."

That day, he was the happiest man in the world. He got married, something none of us thought would ever happen. The old mine was being refurbished, and we were a part of that project. For the first time since before we lost our dad, each day wasn't about scraping together the necessities. The future was ours.

"Will we get to see the pictures?" Campbell asks.

Durban appears in the packaging room, scanning from left to right. When his gaze lands on us, he smirks. "Need a hand, Haven?"

"We aren't bothering him," Campbell argues.

I grasp the lifeline and use the girls' distraction to sidle between them. If I take too much longer, I'm going to be late. "I gotta get going."

"Durban has all the dates and times for you," Campbell calls. "For the week before the wedding. I left your birthday free in case you want to do anything."

"Nope."

Jamison pouts. "You never do."

Except for this year, but I'm keeping that to myself. They'll see it as more than just tit for tat. I toss her a thumbs-up. I'm almost to the door, and wedding plans aren't my priority right now.

"Let me know if you're going to have a plus-one," Campbell adds. It'd be better if Campbell were a bridezilla nitpicking her guest list. "A *friend* or someone you're bringing?"

My gut clenches. I've never had a plus-one, and I'm not starting now. Besides, what if she said no? "I don't think my *friend* would feel comfortable at a wedding full of people she doesn't know."

"We can change that." There's nothing but determination in her voice.

"Or...you can both stay out of it." I look at Durban, but he's grinning and enjoying my discomfort.

"Hookers and Booze is Monday," Campbell adds before I escape outside. "She should come."

If I'm at Hookers and Booze, Prescott might decide *not* to join.

I reach my pickup just as she pulls in. I wait by the tailgate while she parks.

When she gets out, she scrutinizes the sky. "I'm just getting a feel for the lighting."

I stay where I am. I'm not going to make today uncomfortable for her. No whiskey will be exchanged between us. But I do steal a moment to appreciate her generous curves in her loose pants. Her pink shirt hugs her breasts and slopes down her waist.

Looking good, Red, hovers on my tongue, but that might ruin the evening before it starts.

She drapes the strap of the camera bag over her body, still avoiding my gaze. "You still okay taking some shots by the river?"

I gesture to the opening of the hiking trail with a flourish. "Ladies first."

Her smile is as tight as the rest of her body. Her shoulders are nearly to her ears. "No, it's fine. You know the way better."

I drop my arm, and my hand hits my thigh. She's jumpy, and she's not looking at me. She doesn't trust me, and she's here out of obligation. I fucked everything up when I discovered how sweet she tastes. How do I make it right?

"Are you afraid of me, Red?"

She stills but continues to study the sun. "No."

"The tip of your nose turns red when you're lying."

She touches her fingers to her nose. "It does?"

I laugh despite the gut punch of her unintentional confession. "I promise I won't touch you. I don't mess around with women who don't want me."

The tip of my nose should be glowing. I put my mouth on her, and I knew she didn't want to start a thing with me. She's been actively avoiding me over half the time I've known her.

A small frown ripples across her face before it's replaced with professional aloofness. "Understood. It's just awkward, you know?"

No, I do not. "You don't hang around many guys after they kiss you?"

The frown is back, and I'm just happy to have cracked her shell. "It's usually the other way around," she mutters. Her fingers are white where she's clinging to the strap of her camera. "The hanging around comes first and then the kissing."

She doesn't do casual, and that's all I've done. How can I make this better? "When I was scared to go into the classroom on the first day of school, my dad told me that when someone makes me feel awkward to picture them naked."

Her lips part, and her eyes go wide. She makes a choking sound, and I realize how I came off.

"Shit. No. Um…" Now I have the image of her nude in my head, all full curves and heavy breasts. Heat pools in my groin. I'm going to sport an erection if I don't distract myself. "I know it was inappropriate, but he was a single dad, and I mean, at five, it wasn't like..." I blow out a breath. If I keep talking, I'll make less sense.

I march to the trail and nearly take myself out on the "No Trespassing" sign.

Her footfalls rush behind me, but I don't turn around. My gaze would devour her morsel by morsel.

Prescott

After an hour positioning Haven and enjoying my old career again, we return to our vehicles. I'm sticky and sweaty, but it's not from the temperature. After taking pictures of the evening sun worshipping Haven and his strong body, after his shy smile and his almost timid questions about where to put his hands and his feet, my core temperature is set to nuclear. The neediness making me restless shouldn't be getting worse.

I didn't touch him. As much as I wanted to move an arm and angle his body, I refused. Now I'm left with a longing inside me that won't be ignored.

I need a shower after this anyway. I'll make it frigid. Shock my system into forgetting a smiling Haven in golden light with glittering blue behind him.

"Thanks for the experience, Red." Haven's still subdued, like he doesn't know how to act. "I'm not sure I would've enjoyed this back then."

"Kids either hated it, but their parents made them, or they loved it." We're done. I can get in my car and call it a night. I can drive home and attempt to not dive into editing these photos while I'm all hot and bothered. Instead, I linger outside my car.

He scratches the back of his neck, holding his cowboy hat in his other hand. "How was it for you?"

"When I took your pictures? Or when I had my own senior photos taken?"

"Both."

"Tonight was nice. No pressure." My camera loved the subject, and that always makes a session more fun. I lean against my car. The distillery soars on the other side of the parking lot, a beautiful piece of art that's now a part of nature. I dig out my phone instead of putting my camera and lens back together. "I got frustrated during my senior shoot because I thought I knew what would look better with my body and coloring."

"Did you?"

I smirk and frame the building in my phone's camera. "No, they ended up being really nice. That's when I was hooked. How could holding that pose feel so wrong, but in the pictures be so right?"

Satisfied I got some good shots, I stuff my phone away, but my gaze lingers on the lines of the metal and rock that make up the outside and how seamlessly the glass fits into it all. It suits the men who run it—rugged and pleasing to the eye.

The other guys who own this place don't get my heart racing like Haven.

I'm still not ready to leave. "We should get some shots in the distillery."

"Really?"

"If you want the whole senior-photo-shoot experience,

yes. I usually went to sites that made good backdrops or were important to the kids."

He crosses his arms, and I lose the battle not to peek at the muscles bulging under that white material. Now I have it immortalized in digital form.

"How many places would you go and where were the most popular?"

"Most often, it was a studio that I rented." I flash a grin. "Gymnasiums for the sports photos. Otherwise there were not-so-secret public places most of us photographers used. A popular bridge, a certain stretch of railroad tracks, a grassy pasture, or a field of sunflowers."

"The farmer always plants sunflowers?"

"There were some sad teens when he didn't."

He laughs, his Adam's apple bobbing. That unrestrained grin is also captured on my camera. I cannot wait to edit these photos. Instead of doing only the ones I think are the best, I'm going to comb through each one.

"The distillery it is." He ponders the restored old mine. "I don't think it's a service we can offer for other senior photos though."

"It's a shame. I'm sure there's a dispensary that would let us in for some shots to go with the theme."

"Nothing like drugs and alcohol to commemorate high school. Speaking of which, I was ordered by Jamison and Campbell to inform you about the Hookers and Booze club."

"Excuse me?" I'm trying to get a handle on my life and that doesn't sound like a club I should be a part of. But I'm intrigued.

"Our bookkeeper, Edna. She put together a monthly crochet club with Campbell. You just show up to the tasting room, crochet something—or don't—and enjoy a drink or two. Elodie usually brings some goodies."

"The bakery owner?"

He nods.

"I've never crocheted before. Or knitted."

"Edna won't care, and neither will anyone else. The cost is answering questions about you and your life. They're nosy as fuck."

It actually sounds...nice. "Sure. I'll go."

We start walking across the lot, slow and meandering like neither of us is ready for the evening to be over.

"Why did you leave it?" he asks almost hesitantly. "Professional photography? I know you said you moved, but why didn't you pick it up again?"

I've never told anyone the real reason. I always blamed the hours, and that's true, but there were ways around it. He knows about Papa. He knows about Buford. My cheating ex. Might as well put the cherry on top, in case I ever hoped he'd be interested.

"It got depressing." Humiliation doesn't swamp me as expected. Instead, pressure falls off my chest. "Seeing other people have what I want. The family photos where the couple argued and the kids were pills were weirdly easier than the happy families. Same with the weddings. When I looked through the lens and saw nothing but two people who couldn't wait to spend the rest of their lives together?" I went home and cried. "It was hard, and I needed a break."

"That's understandable." He leads me around the side of the distillery to another entrance for employees only. We can bypass any onlookers from the tasting room and have some privacy. I want this evening with Haven to myself.

"You really think so?" If Buford the Boss Cat hadn't hit like he did, I would've had a gap in my résumé and a failed adventure, and I would've probably been single a lot earlier.

"Of course. I loved being a cowboy, but sometimes, you just look at everything and wonder how it's serving your future."

"My ex would've said the benefits and retirement are serving my future."

"As he was fucking other women?" He clicks his tongue. "Doesn't sound like a guy I'd listen to."

Is it that easy for him to listen to me and support me? He does that for everyone around him. No wonder this guy couldn't close the door on his mom for good when his brothers did. "Who should I listen to?"

The corner of his mouth lifts. "Whoever lifts you up the most. Now. Where do you want me?"

With me.

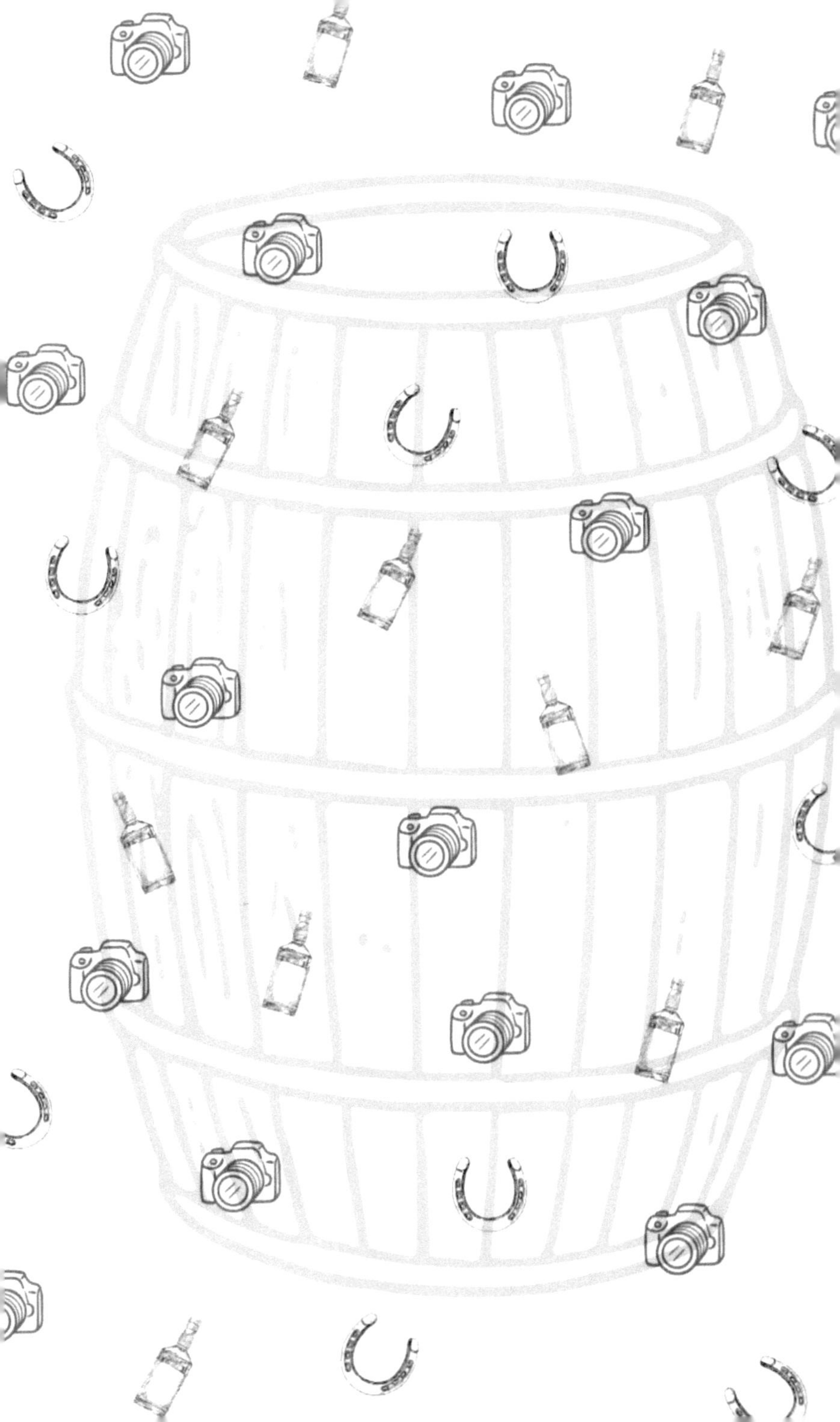

CHAPTER ELEVEN

Haven

It's not my day to work, but my mind is at the distillery. Hookers and Booze is going on now. Is Prescott meeting with the crochet club? Is she having fun? Do I have an excuse to show up at work that isn't obvious because I want to see a woman who's fun to be with?

"Meadow, come."

The puppy charges after me, her velvety black ears flopping. I give her a quick head scratch, and she follows me out the door. I hear the car before Prescott rolls down the driveway. She doesn't continue to the barn, but stops at the garage.

What's she doing here? "Sit."

The puppy does, and I give her a small treat. She's been a dream for a dog, and each day that goes by that Prescott doesn't notify me that a home has opened up for her, I'm relieved.

The kittens are worming their way into my heart too.

They get fed once a day, and yesterday, I saw one with a mouse. They would adapt to being inside, but they're making damn good barn cats. For someone.

Should I offer to keep them? They've settled in. I like having them around. Little buggers grew on me.

To be fair, I was wrapped around a furry toe as soon as I saw them. Beautiful woman rescuing them aside.

But if they went somewhere else, then Prescott wouldn't have a reason to stop by. Like now.

She gets out. Her sunglasses hide her gaze from me, but a pensive energy sizzles over her.

Something's bothering her. Is she worried about the kittens? "I wasn't sure if you'd get out here, so I gave the cats a little food."

"No, it's not that. I'd like to see them, but…" She scrunches up her face. "I'd like to go to crochet club, but I'm too nervous about just walking into a room full of people I don't know." It all comes out in a rush.

She's anxious, and she came to me? She might not trust me with her heart—for good reason—but she trusts me. I'm usually the guy people go to *after* they've tried my brothers.

"You need me to go with you?" I ask.

"You're busy, I know. I shouldn't be nervous. They're really nice people. Everyone here is so *nice*. I shouldn't bother you."

"It's ranching, Red. There's always something to do. Iverson says that if we don't purposely take time off, someday there'll be no time to take."

"The perk of being your own boss. Right?" She throws her hands up. "I've got all the time off in the world. You don't."

"Neither do you with all that bartending you're doing."

"It's not, like, a real job. I hang out with my dad, and he keeps asking when I'm going to get a real job." She bites her lower lip. "He pesters me like he's making up for lost time."

My lips twitch. She's adorably disgruntled. "He might be."

"He keeps bugging me about starting my own studio. I just told him I was thinking about it to get him off my back."

"Didn't work?"

"He's looking for open space in Billings and Bozeman."

He cares, and she's not used to it. Add in her nerves about the crochet club, and she turned to me. Does she realize that? "Let me get Meadow taken care of, and I'll be right out."

Once I have the puppy secured in my mudroom with promises to run the pastures after I get back, I sprint outside.

She's pacing by her car. "I should be able to go by myself."

"Relax, Red."

She stops and crosses her arms. "Does that ever work on girls? 'Relax.'"

"You'll have to tell me. You're the first."

She cocks her hip out, her dubious expression on me. A sexy siren standing right in front of me. I'd rather invite her inside, instead of sharing her with everyone.

Alarm bells go off, but I ignore them. She's been in my place before. It's not like she's moving in. She's not a rescue I get to decide if I'm going to keep or not. "Unless you count the horses and cattle I've said it to." I pretend to think for a moment. "And some chickens."

"Did they listen?"

"It's all in the tone." I give her a wink and enjoy the dusting of pink on her cheeks. "As for the crochet club, they'll be happy to see you." And to speculate about us, but I'll handle that.

"I bought yarn," she says as we get in.

I inhale the floral scent of her in the car. There are undertones of the coffee scent she's picked up since staying with her dad. "Whatcha making?"

"I have no clue. I just bought some skeins and a whole thing of crochet hooks of all sizes." She takes off down the road. "They're going to think I'm stupid."

"They're not."

"How do you know?"

"Because they've all taken me in. Durban's the smart one. Iverson's always been the boss. That whole crew lets me hang around. Trust me. They'll like you." A lot. Like I do.

"Right. I can see that." There's a thread of sarcasm in her voice. "Like, ugh. Here's Haven with his charm and the way he's always looking after people. I guess we'll let him stay."

I grin, but there's a weird twisting in my chest, right around my heart. "You're throwing around that *C* word again."

"I feel like that's not the only *C* word used around you." She chews on her lower lip as she grips the wheel. "Thank you. For coming with me."

Anytime, Red. "No trouble. This is my first time going as an attendee."

"Are guys not allowed?" She turns into the parking lot.

"No, there are guys, but since Campbell's usually there, Durban often covers it. Lane's working today though. I'll stop in to help because it's a good time." The laughter is a flame, and I'm a moth who loves Edna's crass jokes. Will Prescott get that blush when she hears them? Will I spend the whole time guessing how far down her body it goes?

"Let me get this straight—the crafting is pretty much an excuse to get together and eat and drink?"

"You're catching on."

She grins and parks. "Okay. We're here."

Well. If I thought I was offering her something special, I'm apparently not. "Want me to go in first? All eyes on me?"

"No, it's fine. I think I'm just not used to my presence not being justified. I've always worked events, not been invited."

The people in her life have been missing out. Prescott Keys has a big, sarcastic heart. When she points it toward a guy, he starts thinking about things he wrote off a long time ago. "Let's go learn how to crochet."

Prescott

I can't believe I was almost too timid to come to Hookers and Booze. The tasting room is over half full with the boisterous Edna and her equally riotous friends. I meet Elodie and her sister, Clementine, who works at Foster House Gold part-time. Jamison and Campbell are here, along with a couple more of Edna's friends who aren't from Huckleberry Springs. Thanks to Edna's crew, I've heard several dirty jokes that would make my dad blush.

My worry about feeling horribly out of place was unwarranted. I'm not even the only one learning to knit or crochet. Jamison is getting knitting lessons from the grandson of one of Edna's friends. Then there's Haven.

He has a big hand clamped around a size *H* crochet hook, and he's working on a dishcloth with one of the yarn skeins I bought. He swears the cranberry color will go with his dish towels. All I can remember from his kitchen is how hot he was cooking in it—and that kiss.

He holds out his cloth for inspection. "Whoever's is the most crooked owes the other a drink."

"It's going to be a close race." I gauge mine against his. "One of my sides looks like the switchbacks of a road going up a steep mountain."

"Both my edges look like that." He frowns and turns his cloth. "All of them, actually. I'm gonna owe you a drink."

Campbell turns our way but doesn't take her attention off the scarf she's making for Durban. It's a rich brown made from alpaca yarn. "You can settle up after we're done here."

Haven continues his row, his brows drawing together before relief crosses his face, and he starts his next single crochet. "It's whatever Prescott wants, but I might need you to stop by my house and let the dog out."

Campbell's face brightens. "Can I play with her too?"

"You're going to steal my dog," he says with fake accusation.

"You're keeping her?" she asks.

Haven's hands stall, and so do mine. His gaze meets mine, and an unspoken question passes between us. If Meadow's officially his, that's one less reason for me to be at his place. But she'd have a home, and a good one.

The electric awareness doesn't fade, and he gives me a

small nod. "She might be more of a birder than a herder, but it seems that she's mine."

My heartbeat stutters before a thrill surges. Can I be jealous of a puppy? He didn't want to take her in permanently, but less than three weeks later, she's his. "One down, three to go."

"You're not keeping the cats?" Campbell asks, oblivious to the second shot of tense awareness between me and Haven.

A band tightens around my chest. I want the kittens to have a good home, but I want to keep going out there and snuggling them. If they're not fosters, that'd be intruding.

Haven tears his gaze from mine and shrugs. "Word's out. I'm sure they'll get a good home."

I could sag with relief. "I'll have to touch base with the rescue again." I should've done it again before now.

The door from the distillery opens, and Cruz and Durban walk in. Each man's gaze lands on his respective woman, and it's like they've seen the sun after months of darkness. There's another wrench in my chest.

I want that.

The loving look from a bride to a groom. From a husband to a wife with their kids surrounding them. Partners who say so many things without saying a word, while they smile for the camera. I don't want to just be a witness to it.

Cruz veers toward where Elodie is crocheting with her feet outstretched. She's nice, but definitely more reserved than any of the other women here.

Durban goes straight to his fiancée. I crochet through their kisses, and Haven does the same thing.

"How many times do I gotta say," Lane calls from behind the bar with a grin, "no public make-out sessions."

The guys pull up chairs. Elodie shifts to put her feet up on Cruz's lap. Campbell and Durban are sitting so close, she's practically on top of him. Then there's me and Haven. Side by side, not touching.

A longing pulls at my chest. I've never been a part of a big group like this, and so far, I like it.

Edna's talking, her hands flying and punctuating her words in between packing up her stuff. She sees our part of the tasting room and waves. "Don't rush out on my account." She hitches a tote bag over her shoulder, spilling over with yarn and the block blanket she's making, as the rest of her group packs up.

"There's Iverson. Bye, everyone!" Jamison races to the door, but she stops to look back at me. "Thanks for coming, Prescott. Don't hold my lack of knitting skills against me."

Touched that she thought of me before she left, I smile. "Only if you don't hold a crooked dishcloth against me."

She dashes off, and Edna crosses to our table.

"It was so nice to meet you, Prescott." The corners of her eyes crinkle with her smile. "Will I see you next month?"

All eyes are on me, and my skin feels too tight.

"I don't know," I admit, and my cheeks flame. There's no blending into the background in this moment. "Everything's still up in the air."

"Don't be a stranger." She rubs my shoulder in a way my grandma used to do. "If you never crochet another stitch, come anyway. The club is Hookers and Booze, not just Hookers, though the booze ain't required either."

"I'll keep that in mind." Now I want to still be here in a month.

She scoots over to Durban and Campbell. "You two will be on your honeymoon. Gonna make some scarves while you're there?" She chortles at her own joke.

"Absolutely, Edna," Campbell says with all the seriousness in the world, and Edna laughs harder.

She gives their shoulders a grandmotherly pat. "If either of you comes back with a completed project, I'm going to be so disappointed in you. You're going to Tahiti, and it's your honeymoon. The three *B*s are all you need to be doing."

Durban and Campbell each give her a questioning look, and I'm as lost as them.

"Beach, booze, and banging." Edna sticks a finger up for each *B*.

Her friends erupt into laughter as they file out.

Edna waves both her hands in the air as she heads toward the door. "If I can't impart my wisdom on the younger folk, then what's the point of getting old?"

"So you can keep doing the three *B*s," Cruz replies.

Edna salutes and winks on the way out.

I keep crocheting, but a smile plays on my face.

Clem packs up next. "I'd better get going. I've got to do some work for the puppet show tomorrow, and I have an interview tonight."

"Clem's a writer," Haven says quietly to me. "And she works at the library in town."

In addition to being a tour guide at the distillery? I don't really have one job, and she's got three. "Oh, wow. That's a lot."

She shrugs. "I'm single." A mischievous smile spreads over her face. "Plus, I never get to see my sister anymore. She's seeing some guy, and he takes all her time."

Elodie rolls her eyes. "I see you more than ever."

Clem grins. "I know—and it's with that dreamy smile."

Cruz raises his hand in the air like he's in class. "Hope that's my fault."

Elodie nudges him, and the look they exchange should make steam rise between them. It's putting a green ribbon around my heart.

Cruz pats his fiancée's leg. "Should we get going? You've got those buns to knead."

"Aw, hell," Lane says from behind the bar. "I never know if he's talking about dough anymore."

Cruz's eyes twinkle as he stands. "It's rarely about the dough."

He and Elodie pack up and leave. Campbell and Durban are right behind her.

Haven jumps up to help Lane clean off the tables and move them back into place. I tidy the baked goods that Elodie brought. The bar is lined with small boxes of cupcakes, cookies, and slices of sweet bread. I consolidate the treats into one container and try not to steal another cookie.

Haven appears next to me. "Go ahead and take that home."

"I couldn't."

"Jamison snuck a tin home for Iverson."

"But he owns the place."

"So do I, and I want you to take some home." He leans in, and I instinctively sway closer to him. "We also get a lot of samples here. Elodie refuses to sell any wares made with a Foster House spirit unless we try it and bless it."

Well, when he puts it that way... I fold the lid over the leftover sweets. "Fine, you win."

"I also owe you a drink."

Lane drops a cloth in front of him. "Mind watching

this place for me for a bit? I've gotta check on Hutch, and then I'll be back."

"That's his neighbor," Haven explains for me. "Go ahead." He takes the cloth and wipes down the island. "Have a seat. Or do you have to get to Bootleg?"

"I've got some time." Unlike the tasting room, Bootleg is open seven days a week.

He steps behind the counter. "I feel like this is cheating. I can't really buy you a drink when it's my company's product."

"But we get the place to ourselves." I like the idea of that more and more, and from his small smile, he does too.

Why do I keep setting a boundary and then dancing on it? I'm not a good two-stepper.

"What would you like or do you want me to surprise you?" he asks.

Easy answer. "Surprise me."

A lock of dark hair falls over his forehead as he selects a bottle of huckleberry vodka. When he drops to a squat, I almost bodysurf over the counter to see where he went. But he soon rises with a small round glass in his hand.

"That looks like a fishbowl."

"I don't know if there's a fish small enough for this."

The container is too small for a dish but a little large for a drink. "The fish doesn't have to drive home, but I do."

"Don't worry. I'll add more Sprite and pink lemonade. It'll be more like a punch."

He stays true to his word. I'm served a gorgeous pink drink with a brown sugar rim. It's not even a boozy punch, and the huckleberry is faint but adds a dash of sweetness to an already sugary drink. I like it, and it's taking everything in me not to lick the rim in front of him.

Just a taste.

I'm using the little stir straw to sip from, but I try to discreetly drag my tongue along a small portion of the rim. Haven's gaze drops to my mouth, and his eyes go dark.

The need that courses through me steals my strength. I put the glass down before I drop it. "Brown sugar? That should make it too sweet."

He peels his gaze off my mouth. "We add a pinch of salt to our brown sugar to cut through it." His voice is gruff. Just from me licking a rim?

Yet there's a quiver running under my skin, from head to toe. "Who came up with it?"

"Me."

"You're a mixologist?"

"No, I just put a Foster House spin on cocktails. I don't come up with any of it myself."

"We all put our own spin on art." I take a drink from the glass so I can get more brown sugar. "Mmm."

"Red, you sure know how to torture a man." Before I can ask what he means, he draws his brows together. "What I do isn't art. It's just mixing drinks."

"It's not just anything. You really know what you're doing. All of you guys do." I lift my drink in a salute. "Especially you."

A light pink dusts his cheeks, and he looks down.

Oh my god, he's blushing. It's adorable, and it's sexy, and worse, it makes him attainable. "I didn't mean to embarrass you."

"You didn't," he says quickly. "I'm just not usually complimented for doing my job."

"I'm sure the girls who come in gush about you all the time."

The corner of his mouth lifts. "You mean Edna and her crew? Actually, they do."

I laugh. "I can imagine they get rowdy." That's not what I meant, and it's not like I want to think about all the other options he has. I'm not supposed to be interested.

Which means I need to leave.

I push my half-full glass away. "This really is yummy, but I should get going. Papa's waiting for me."

Surprise flits across his face. "Okay. Yeah. Thanks for coming."

"Thank *you* for coming." I snap my fingers. "Wait—I gave you a ride."

"Lane's coming back. He'll take me home."

"No, I can wait." Except the longer I stay, the larger my interest in all things Haven will grow.

"It's fine. Gotta stay on your dad's good side."

"If you insist." I gather my crochet bag. I'm never going to touch it again, or I'll think about his big hands and the way he concentrates on his work. Lucky yarn. He puts his all into his work. So why not a relationship?

Seems a shame that someone like him should isolate himself the way he does. My situation is by circumstance. His is by choice.

I'm in territory that's none of my business, but there are some things about him that *are* my business. "I've been going through your pictures, and I'll get them to you in a couple of weeks."

I can only do short batches of editing, or I start forming fantasies in my head starring the face staring back at me on the screen. The thoughts get faster and stronger. Why can't I see if Haven's really interested? Do I care if he isn't, as long as I get to see what he's offering? What's wrong with a little fun?

Then his soul-searching gaze into the camera becomes too much. The longing increases, and last night, I almost started crying.

I just miss Mom and Buford. That's all.

I'm almost to the door, outrunning the cacophony of feelings he creates. I need to go home, take a cool shower, remember why I'm single and jobless, and go work for Papa.

"Just let me know when," he calls.

I stop with my hand on the cool door handle. "What?"

He smiles, and his expression is so damn hopeful it burrows right into my chest and takes up residence next to my heart. "When you're making that lasagna dinner."

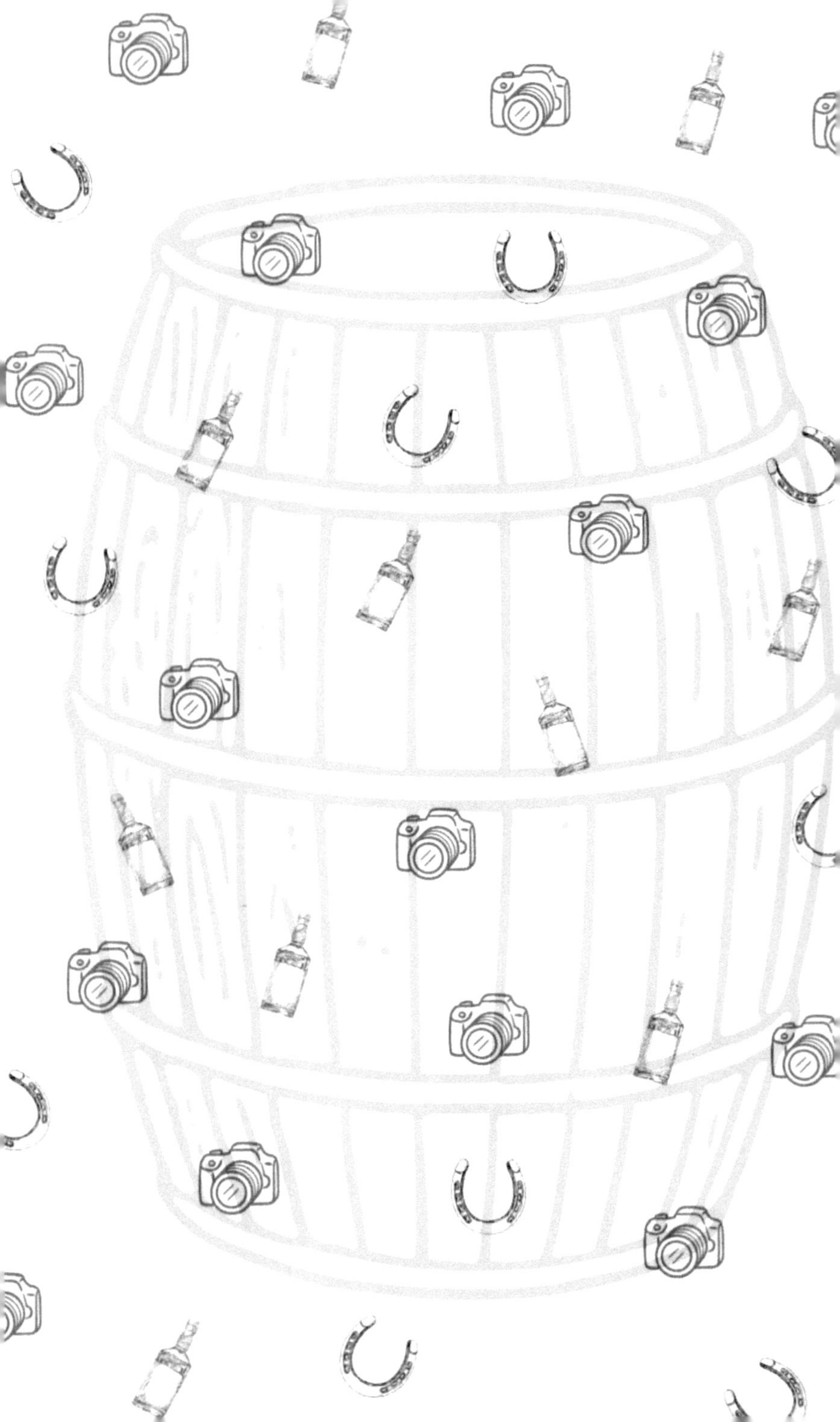

CHAPTER TWELVE

Prescott

Monday nights are surprisingly busy at Bootleg. The shift was long, and Papa spent most of his time talking to an old rodeo friend rather than helping me serve drinks and clean tables.

I smother a yawn and duck into the supply room. The scent of lemon-tinged mustiness fills the air. I flip the water on to fill the mop bucket. While it's filling, I stretch my back.

How has Papa kept this place going? There's so much to do, and he just roams the room, talking more than he's filling drinks. Tonight, I even heard him telling a story about when I was younger, when he led me around on one of his buddy's horses. I asked him why it wasn't bucking, and he laughed for an hour.

My lips curve up. That was a good day, and I liked hearing him recount it.

His hitching footsteps reach me. "Go home, Pressie. Get some rest."

"The floors are filthy." It rained earlier, and we got a lot of regulars tonight. Customers who were outside all day working and came in with gritty shoes. Many used the boot station outside the door, but it only gets the big chunks.

"They'll still be filthy in the morning. Let's go home."

I rub the back of my neck. I have all this restless energy coursing through me from the drink with Haven after the crochet club. "It's okay. I feel like doing it now."

He shakes his head like he normally does when he doesn't understand my reasoning. "You work too hard. Gotta make room for a little fun."

There's one guy I'd like to have fun with, but that's all he wants. I'm not in a place for a relationship anyway.

So why can't I have fun with him? Why can't I keep my hopes all locked up and just enjoy— No, he's not interested.

But *he* kissed *me*.

"Maybe I do." I go to the seating area and start sweeping. What am I going to do about it? The only fun I've had lately has all involved Haven.

He pushes the mop bucket to the side and slides a butt cheek on a stool. "You were at Foster House all day?"

"Crochet club."

"Haven there?"

"All of his brothers were." Not until the end, but I'll keep that to myself. Papa's fishing, and he might be afraid that Haven's going to put a ring on it and keep me in city limits, but he doesn't know Haven.

"How's studio hunting going?"

About as well as me finding a home for the kittens.

Hard to make progress when I'm not reaching out to anyone. To be fair, I work late, and then I sleep late. Now I have Haven's pictures to edit. Papa won't buy those excuses. "I'm saving as much as I can, but I don't want to find the perfect place only to not be able to afford it."

"What if I helped you?"

I keep sweeping, curving the broom around table legs. Papa already tipped chairs onto the tables. "How do you mean?"

"I'll put the money down for it."

That makes me stop. "You don't have the savings." Rodeo was Papa's main career, and the pay wasn't exactly steady. Then there's Bootleg.

"I can find some."

"Did you inherit money I don't know about?"

He chuffs. "Pressie, the Fosters, Hennessys, and Hawthornes aren't the only ones with means in Huckleberry Springs."

I arch a brow.

He smooths his fingers over his mustache. "I'm not well off like them, but I can get some quick cash."

Do I want to know how? Probably not. "I'll figure it out."

"You don't have to do it alone."

It's how I've been doing it since Mom died. I temper my attitude this time. Papa's offering, and it's not something he's done much of before. "I'll start looking just so I know what to expect for size and expense."

He rubs his hands together, and the scraping sounds from all his old callouses fill the air. "I've been doing some looking."

He's more invested in my future than I am. I've been spending my extra time with barn cats and Haven. The guilt isn't building like it should, but there's a spark of dread. What if Papa finds the perfect space? What if it's time for me to move on? I'm not ready. "Find anything?"

He makes a pleased sound, mistaking the tremor in my voice for excitement. "There are some options. It won't hurt to go look at them."

"Where exactly? Bozeman or Billings?" Are those big enough towns for me? In this state, they're cities, but I came here from Chicago. I've lived in Phoenix and Tucson. What's my small-town limit?

"Both. Either. I can check in other places too."

Now that dread's building in my gut. Hopefully, the reflux won't keep me awake. I'll sleep too late to call the rescue again. "Sure. That'd be a good idea, I guess."

He grunts. "Casper's a little over four hours away. There's Rapid City. Even Sioux Falls."

I choke on a swallow and start coughing. "Sioux Falls," I wheeze. "That's quite a drive." But it's the biggest city he named.

"Yeah," he says gruffly, and I peek at him before I return to sweeping. Is he going to miss me? "I heard something today," he says with a gravity I haven't heard very often. When he was around, he was the fun parent.

"Oh?" I leave my tidy little pile of dirt and pretzel bits close to him, then push the mop bucket toward the far corner I started sweeping in.

"You went fishing last weekend. With Haven Hennessy."

I spin around. "How'd you know?" Don't I sound guilty.

"Small town."

"I was in the middle of nowhere."

He gives me a knowing look. "The parking lot isn't."

The distillery. Someone must've been doing a tour or been in the tasting room when I walked off with Haven. "Is fishing a bad thing? I caught two trout."

"That's my girl." A flash of pride crosses his face. That damn little girl inside me soaks it up.

"Thanks." As long as I don't think about that kiss or Haven's tongue in my mouth, I won't turn red. Papa won't know what cooking those two fish led to. "He's a friend. That's all."

He grunts. Does he believe me?

I continue pushing the mop around. It's true. I consider Haven a friend. Honestly, he's the closest one I have. He's the only one I have who's more than an acquaintance.

Did Papa know Haven's parents? Curiosity wells inside me, and I have to stop mopping. "Were you gone while he was growing up?"

Papa scratches his cheek while he thinks. "I came back enough. His dad was a good guy. Had the patience of a saint with that woman as a wife."

"What does that mean?" I rest my arms on the top of the mop, thirsty for every scrap of information I can get on Haven.

"She was a piece of work. Left them boys." He shakes his head as if he didn't basically do the same thing with me. "Not well liked in town."

She still isn't, from what Haven said. "She's never returned?"

He puffs his lips out. "Would've been the best thing that happened to them boys if she never had. Losing their dad was the worst. Having to go live with her was a close second."

"That bad?"

"I don't like to get into other people's business." He ignores my pointed look. Yes, in fact, he does. He most likely opened Bootleg to keep talking about rodeo when he could no longer do it, and to be at the hub of gossip. "But if those boys have been able to get away and never talk to her again, it's for the best. She's bad news. Always has been, always will be."

My heart twists. I don't need a psychology degree to assume that Haven's commitment issues are rooted in his history with his mom. First, she left, then he lost his dad. And who knows what games she's playing now. Is Haven protecting himself or other people by isolating himself?

It's not my concern! But I do care about him. As a friend, of course.

Papa crosses to the broom. "I'll sweep this pile up, and then we're going home. My back hurts."

I look at the half of the floor that still needs to be cleaned. Thoughts of a young Haven dance in my head, mixing with my memories of him from the last few weeks. He's taken me horseback riding and fishing, and while it wasn't part of our experience swaps, he dropped everything to go to the crochet club with me.

Who's gone out of their way for him? The photos don't seem like much, and the birthday dinner is over two weeks away. What else was I going to do for him? I have to make sure I don't let him down. I rack my brain. Right! I dig my phone out.

Me: Lasagna. Lunch on Friday?

I hit send. He should get it in the morning, but at least he'll know I plan to follow through on my word.

I'm about to tuck my phone away before Papa returns, but it vibrates.

Haven: Noon. My place. Let yourself in when you need to.

Haven

My phone's going wild while I chat with Durban in his office. As much as I'd like to think it's Prescott in my house telling me to come home, fill my belly, and then sate myself with her, it's not. The only person who pings my phone a million times before giving up and sending me an angry text is Mom.

I jut my thumb over my shoulder at the door. "I've gotta finish some orders and then head home for lunch."

"I was going to meet Campbell at the café. You can join us."

"Thanks, but I've got something at the house."

Something sweet and delicious who licks sugar off the rim of her glass in a way that brings me to my knees. I duck out and rush up the stairs to the next level and into my office.

Just lunch. Just a friend.

Shutting the door, I take my phone out. Did Durban hear it vibrating? He would've made a comment if he had. I punch Mom's notification, and it rings.

"I thought you were ignoring me," she says, and the image of her fake pout enters my brain.

"I do have a job, Mom."

"What if it was an emergency? You're all I've got. Your brothers..." There's a loud inhale, like she's holding in a sob. Is it a real reaction? "I extend the olive branch, and they slap it away."

"Is something wrong?" I ask to bypass the subject of my brothers.

"Just checking in. You were being cagey the last time we talked."

I had been trying to get off the phone because Prescott had just arrived to go fishing. "There's nothing. I had to work."

"I thought you said you were off that day."

I wince. Damn. "I've got the ranch." Look at that. Mom's made me a good liar.

She sniffs. "Sure. Listen, my building manager's giving me a hard time about a rent increase."

My stomach falls like a brick. She's not calling to check on me or my brothers. She needs money. "That sucks."

"It does." She lets out a dramatic sigh, and I steel myself for the ask. "Can I borrow the difference? I'm supposed to get a raise at work, and then I can take care of the increase on the apartment that asshole refuses to maintain."

I pinch the bridge of my nose. "How much?"

"Two hundred."

That's not the most she's asked for, but the number doesn't make sense. "They raised your rent that much a month?"

"Well, you know, they worked out a little payment system for me. I got a little behind."

What about the money I sent her last month? I shake my head. I learned a long time ago not to ask what she did with it all. She doesn't drink, gamble, or do drugs. The rest isn't my business. "All right. I can send you some."

"When's Durban getting hitched?"

I rub between my eyes again. "You'll have to ask him."

"So they are getting married," she says in a gotcha tone.

"No, Mom," I say patiently. "I've told you before that anything you want to know about him or Iverson has to come from them."

"And after all I did for them."

They would argue differently. "Hey, I've gotta go. I'm meeting someone for lunch."

"You're going to send that cash first?"

No questions about my life? "Sure. Give me a few minutes."

"You know, I'm going to be in Billings for some training next week. You should meet me there. Buy me some lunch." She makes it sound like she's joking, but I will buy her lunch, and she'll take the receipt to get reimbursed. Still, I can't resist.

"Tell me when and what time."

"Yep." She disconnects.

I stare at my screen. It's an image from right out my front door. Sweeping pastures, my red barn, and foothills in the background. Then I notice the time.

Shit. I grab my hat and charge down the stairs and out the door. Within five minutes, I'm turning down my driveway. Her car's by my garage, and the knots from my mom's call loosen.

What would this be like every day?

Honey, I'm home. You probably don't want to ask about my day. Here's some money.

I toss my hat on the front seat and push a hand through my hair. This is just a simple lunch. A homemade meal. Part of our swap.

I enter my place to a savory, garlicky smell that's never emanated from my kitchen before and instantly feel lighter. Meadow lopes up to me, and I stoop to scratch her head. Then I go in search of Prescott. When I turn out of the living room, I stop, my mouth dry.

Prescott's bent over the oven, ass in the air, all round and full. "Look at you, you gorgeous, cheesy wench." She does a little wiggle that sends lust straight to my groin.

Her jeans shorts ride up in the back, and I'm never going to get the image of her thighs out of my head.

She sets the pan on a hot pad, drops the oven mitts by a tray of breadsticks, and dusts her hands. Her hair is piled in a floppy bun on top of her head. She turns, sees me, and adopts a big smile. "Just in time."

"I had a call. Sorry."

"No worries. You were working."

"It was my mom."

Her pink lips form a perfect *O*. "Bad?"

The call was average. "She's trying to get out of me what's going on with Durban and Campbell." But not with me.

"You held strong?"

"She's the one who taught me how to skirt around the truth."

"Which is why you don't want to feel like you ever have to lie otherwise." She spins around to inspect her work. "You know, like not leading anyone on. You're upfront."

"That's not..." Hell, is it? Prescott has daddy issues, and I have mommy issues. It's not like we don't know that. But I don't like hearing it out loud. I'm my own guy. "Smells delicious," I say instead. "Looks just as good."

She does that wiggle again, and I almost groan. "I hope you think it tastes even better. I use more cheese than the original recipe calls for, but I'm a hussy for melted cheese."

What else is she a hussy for? Can I find out? "Let me wash up, and I'll help— Oh. You already set the table."

She's been in my home, finding what she needs. Something about that sticks with me, sinking in like a soothing heat. When I return, the lasagna and breadsticks are on the table. She set our same spots that we ate in last time. Our chairs are farther apart than last time. No more kissing. Got it.

"Go ahead and sit. I'll dish up." She cuts through the steaming lasagna, and I snatch a breadstick.

Warm and fluffy, the flavor is perfect. I should've waited, but I can't regret it. "Where'd you get these?"

"Made them."

"No shit?"

"It's easy. I can show you." She puts a square heap of food on my plate.

"I don't bake, Red." My stomach growls, and I drag the breadstick through the red sauce and chomp off another bite. Fuck me. Eating her cooking is going to be as dangerous as putting my mouth on her. There's nothing I won't do to get a sample. "'S good."

I take my fork and dig in. Goddamn. This is a party on my taste buds. I like quality, homemade food after all the canned food I grew up on, but when I cook at home, it's a lot of meat. I don't bother even cooking many veggies unless I can throw them in with the beef, pork, or whatever protein I'm making.

I chow through my first piece and soon dig out a second, adding another breadstick. The self-satisfied smile on her face is enough to tempt me to eat the whole tray.

She finishes before me and wipes her mouth. "Oh my gosh, that was good, if I do say so myself. Mind if I snuggle the kittens for a while before I head back to town?

I washed everything while the lasagna was cooking, so you can just toss your plate into the dishwasher."

She's leaving? Already?

Disappointment fills the rest of my stomach, and I can't add another bite. It's not all about me. She's spent hours here, and she probably worked last night. She probably works tonight too. "I feel like I need to tip you for this."

"Kitten cuddles are enough. I can bring Meadow outside with me." She puts her silverware on her plate with her napkin and pushes her chair back.

She's not here to entertain me, but I like talking to her, and I've already missed the rest of her time here. "What if I choke on a breadstick?"

My gut's going to burst, and I'll need a nap, but I grab another breadstick and take a bite.

It works. She doesn't rise. "You need me around for the Heimlich?"

"Maybe mouth-to-mouth," I say around my mouthful.

Her laughter tinkles through the room. She selects another breadstick. "What if I swallow wrong?"

I catch the groan before it leaves me. To make things worse, I'm enraptured as she slips the breadstick between her lips and bites through it.

"I'm good at mouth-to-mouth," I say gutturally.

She cocks a red brow. "The Heimlich would be what I'd need."

I recline in my chair, food forgotten. "I just so happen to be good at wrapping my arms around a woman and thrusting."

Her throat works, and she tries to swallow, then sputters and coughs. The breadstick drops to the floor.

Shit. I get up, and she holds a hand up, using the other

one to press against her lips. When she's breathing normally, she shakes her head. "Hennessy, you're going to get me in trouble with that mouth."

"It'd be my pleasure—and yours."

Her gaze turns alarmed before she starts giggling. "I don't know whether to be scared or hope I choke for real."

"No dying on my watch, Red. I like your company."

"That's a shame. I only put up with you."

I smile and recline again, secure that she won't need life-saving measures. "I'm a hard guy to be around."

"Must be those muscles. They get hard to look at."

"I understand." I can't stop my gaze before it dips down to the barest hint of cleavage teasing me from her collar. "I happen to like some soft padding."

She barks out a laugh, and I flinch. I wasn't joking.

"Anyway," she drawls. "I really should get going. Papa wants to talk about touring studio spaces in Billings next week."

"You made your decision?"

"No." She gives me a wry smile. "Papa's offered to help cover expenses until I'm set up, and it's hard to tell him no when he wants to help."

She's getting the support she didn't get growing up. We go quiet, but the urge to talk about my phone call with my mom rises. I can't go to my brothers. They'll just tell me that I should quit answering, and they don't understand that I can't.

"Speaking of Billings." The delicious lunch I just ate turns to a lead ball in my gut. She's going to tell me to quit answering too. "My mom's going there for some training, and she wants me to meet up with her."

Prescott studies my face. "Are you looking forward to it?"

"No." My answer leaves my lips before I think about her question. "Maybe?"

She nods but doesn't respond. If she's waiting for me to talk, it's not necessary. I don't have anything to say about Mom, the phone call, or Billings. But I'm glad I told Prescott. A weight is gone that was there before.

"Want to make another swap?" she asks softly.

Anything. "Name it."

"I'll tell you about my visit to Billings, and you tell me about yours."

Another give and take. More importantly, the acid in my stomach calms at the thought. "It's a deal, Red."

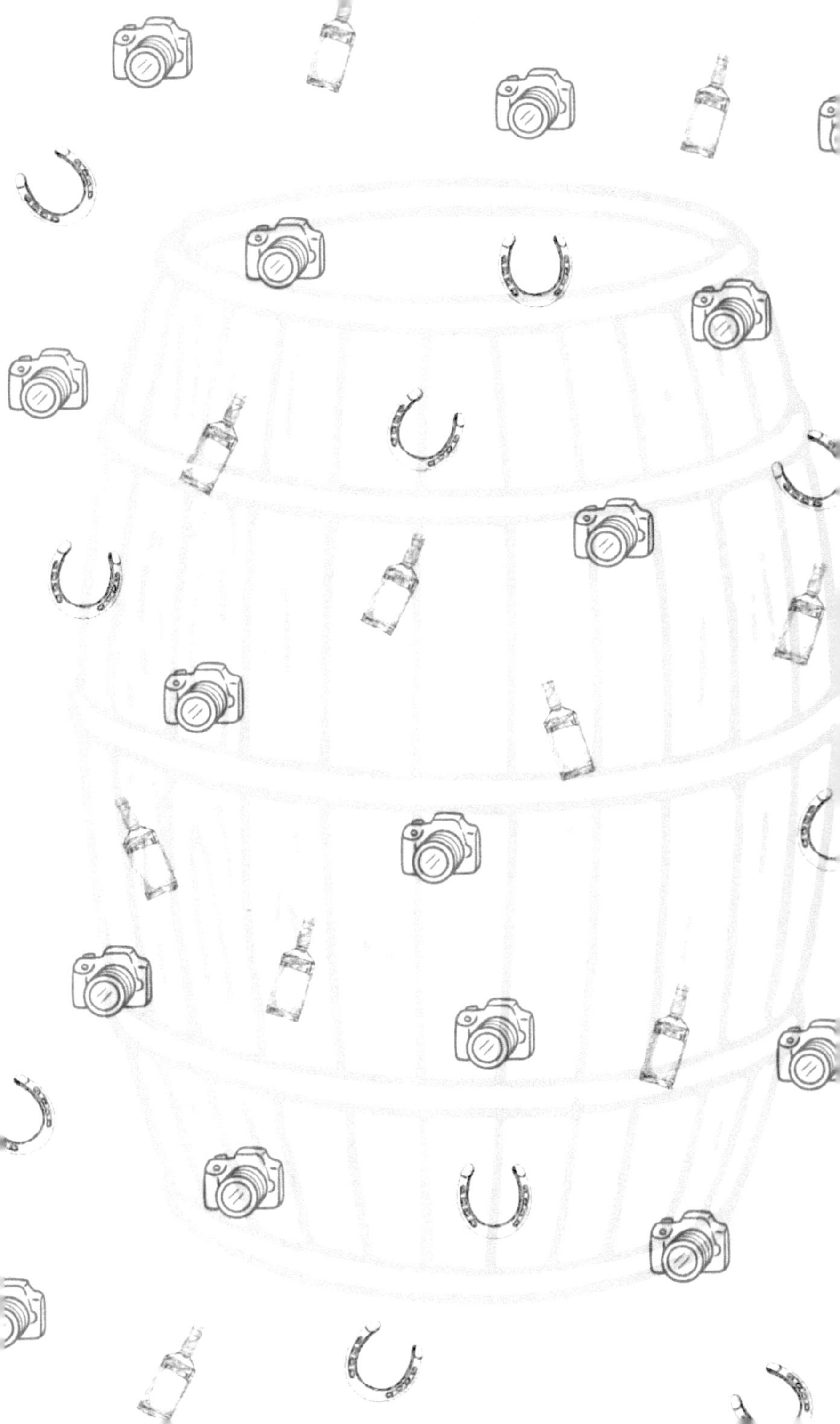

CHAPTER THIRTEEN

Haven

Lane enters my office Sunday afternoon and plops into the chair across from me. He's just come in from haying, and he's dressed like it. Cruz is in his office, and they usually take turns with their ranch duties like my brothers and I do with ours.

"How was the weekend?" he asks.

"More of the same." Work's been fine. Outside of Foster House, my weekends only change with the season—and if Prescott's around.

She's probably been working at Bootleg, but I haven't gone there. The only reason would be to see her, and that crosses a line. What would I do, sit at the bar and fight off every prick who hits on her? She's not interested, but tell my jealousy that. And if I wasn't pissing my territory around her, I'd be sitting and staring at her. Doesn't sound much better.

Lane picks a piece of grass off his pants and drops it

into my wastebasket. "Mae's coming out with Myles. Maybe next week."

I sit up. Our former foster mother comes to Huckleberry Springs a couple of times a year, and I look forward to it more each visit. Every time, she's just as calm as I remember, and it might be selfish, but she asks about my life, and she listens. "Yeah?"

"I'm not sure who else is joining them, but I invited them out. Everyone's welcome."

"I'll be there."

Lane's place is nice. He and Cruz live next to each other, a few miles in the other direction from the distillery.

He kicks an ankle over his knee and crosses his hands over his gut. "Bringing anyone?"

A pang of something hits between my ribs when I say, "No. Why?"

He rolls a shoulder. "Just heard that you and Prescott have been a thing."

"From who?"

"I stopped at Bootleg last night, and before Cruz showed up, I talked to Silas." He smirks. "Said he was glad it was me and not 'that single Hennessy that's been sniffing around.'"

I gawk at Lane. He's just the messenger, but damn. Sniffing around?

She smells nice, like the wildflowers in the ditch I found her in, but it's not like I'm secretly sniffing her hair. I'd have to get close to her, and I've been a damn good boy when it comes to that. "We're friends."

"Then invite her out."

Invite her by telling her I want her at a gathering of the

closest people in my life, but it doesn't mean anything? "I'm sure she'll be working."

He snorts. "Yeah, she will. When she's there, Silas thinks it's social hour. That girl is busting her ass while he's chatting up a storm, though she doesn't really seem to mind."

She's soaking up the time with him, but that's her business, not Lane's.

He slaps the arms of the chair and gets up. "Either way, come on over. Mae will be happy to see you."

"She's happy to see everyone." I state it as a fact. One I admire.

He adopts a fond smile. "She's amazing." He starts for the door.

I sit forward. "You going to Bootleg again tonight?"

He grips the back of his neck and blows out a breath. "No. Hutch is on a bender, and I should stick around home to make sure he doesn't fall asleep smoking and burn all our places down."

"He's getting worse?" Lane's neighbor is a known alcoholic, the sad type who misses his late wife and the kids he drove away. He's also a smoker and has had a lot of close calls with fire in and around his house.

"He was ranting last week about how his kids won't return his calls, and then he's just been tanked since. I found him weaving through the pasture this morning, trying to catch his horse."

"Shit."

"Yeah," he says grimly. "It's bad. I'm gonna do some work and then check on him. Cruz says he'll look in on him in the morning before he goes to the bakery to help Elodie."

"Let me know if you need help. I can always make some excuse to swing by his house."

"Appreciate it, man." He throws me a wave when he leaves.

He won't ask. Lane is good at delegating at work, but he and Cruz are almost like twins despite their three-year difference.

I finished all my cleaning this morning, and my paperwork is done. Iverson's working the tasting room, and normally I'd go home. There's always something to fix, but restless energy teases my muscles. I'll go home and play with Meadow for a while, but I don't want to stay there.

My phone buzzes on my desk.

Red: Do you have a few minutes today to stop by Bootleg?

I snatch it up so fast I fumble it.

Me: Yes. Just got done with work.

Red: I have your images. I can send you the link, but I want to explain how I did the edits.

I don't care. I just want to see her. I'm about to text back when another one comes through.

Mom: Three on Saturday. Late lunch? I'll text you the place later.

I stare at it for a moment before I reply to Prescott instead.

Me: I'll stop at home first and then be right there.

I send Mom a quick yes and leave work. At home, I let Meadow out of the mudroom, and she follows me as I check on the kittens, give the horses their evening meal, and feed and water the chickens. Once I'm done caring for my animals, I dart into the house to clean up. I don't change clothes. That'll look like I'm trying too hard. I shove a ball cap on my head, say goodbye to Meadow, and hop back into the pickup.

Bootleg doesn't have many cars around it yet, but it's a Sunday night. Those are usually quiet, and sometimes that's why I come. I can unwind somewhere that isn't my own place of employment, and I don't have to think about chatting up a woman. Now I want it to stay slow so I can talk to my girl.

After I park, I trot to the door. Inside, there're only a few people sitting around a couple tables. Rafting guides, probably, around one. At the other is a guy that owns some rentals in the area and a woman—not the wife he's divorcing.

Prescott's leaning against the counter, scrolling through her phone. Her coppery hair is in a thick braid again. I have yet to see it unbound in all its wavy glory. The braid gives me enough naughty ideas, along with the image of her bending over in my kitchen. The two fantasies clash together in a glorious display of sparks.

She looks up and smiles. My whole world slows. Damn, she's beautiful. Those eyes that see right into me should make me feel exposed. Instead, I feel seen.

"Working hard or hardly working?" I joke and take a stool across from her.

She rolls her eyes at my lame humor. "You sound like Papa."

"Where is he?"

"Another one of his rodeo friends is in town, and they went out for Mexican." She pulls out her phone. "I'm going to send you a link to the photo gallery I uploaded."

"All right." I pull out my phone too, and when the link comes through, I click on it. An image of my smiling face at the river appears on the screen. "Damn."

She skirts around the bar and sits next to me. "You like it?"

I don't look like myself, but I do. I'm smiling as if I like what I see, and since she's holding the camera, that's exactly what's going on. There's also a shyness. I don't want to make an idiot of myself, but from the crisp colors and the slight fade to the background, she would've made me look good no matter what.

"I'm too damn old to pose like some eighteen-year-old, but you make it look natural."

Satisfaction fills her face. "It's not hard with you."

"There's no better photo of me on this earth."

"Trust me, there are." She reaches over me to scroll, and I let her get as close as she wants. When her chest grazes my arm, my vision goes blurry. "I love the outdoor ones, but the distillery ones blow those out of the water." Her voice is in my ear. Pressure builds behind my zipper. I could come from a tit swipe. That's how bad off I am. "You'll notice some are more polished, maybe a little shinier. Those are the ones I've edited, but I didn't Photoshop you or anything. You don't need it."

"Are you telling me that I'm handsome?"

"You know you are." She pokes my screen to bring up the next image, and there's that brush of her shirt again. My gut clenches. "There are over a hundred and fifty." She thinks for a moment. "Or was it a hundred seventy? I got a little carried away in Foster House."

"A hundred and seventy? Of just me? That's more pictures than have been taken of me my whole life."

She laughs and then peers at me, her smile dying. "Are you serious?"

I nod.

"Haven, I used to take that many pictures in a week when I was posting regularly."

"I'd take that many of you too." Before I creep her out, I scroll through her work. Image after image of me, and not a bad one in the bunch. "Didn't you catch me blinking or with my mouth open?"

"Yes, and each one made me feel better." She points at my phone. "You could be a model."

"Yeah, right."

"That grin can sell anything. Probably panties to replace the ones that smoldering look destroys."

It's my turn to stare at her, stunned. "And yours? Are they safe around me, Red?"

A flush blazes into her cheeks. "You'll never know."

Never say never. I tip my head toward her so none of the customers can hear. "You think I call you Red because of your hair, but, honey, that's the color of the underwear you were wearing the day the wind blew your skirt up."

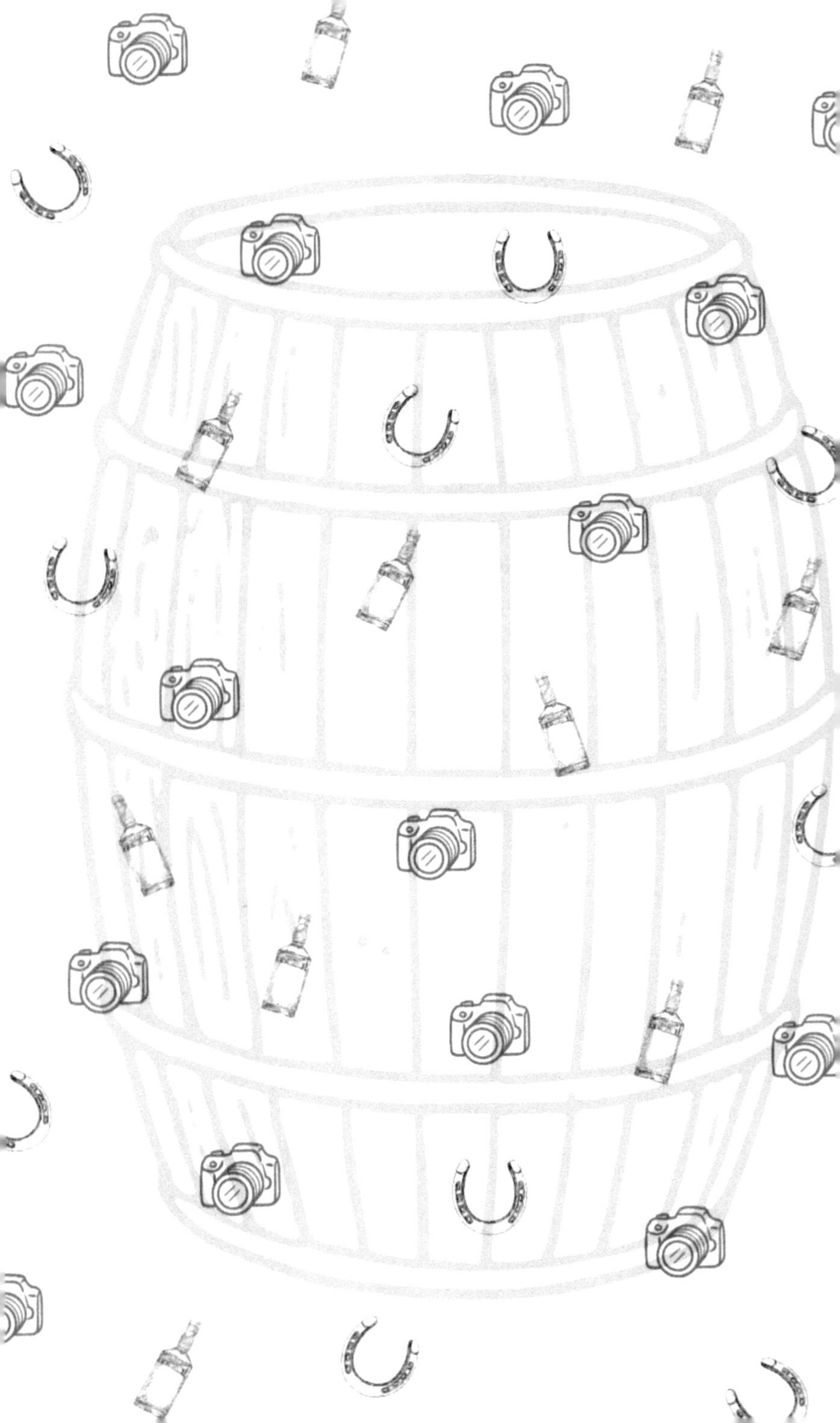

CHAPTER FOURTEEN

Prescott

The leasing agent strides through the empty room sandwiched between a game shop and a day care in a strip mall in Billings. "The keypad can easily be reprogrammed, and you can even give each client their own code."

I'm staring out the window. A small piece of paper dances across the street, blown by the wind. He saw my underwear. If he saw my underwear, he pretty much got the whole full moon. And he calls me Red.

I accused him of going for the low-hanging fruit of nicknames because I'm a redhead. He was being cheeky.

Well, *I* was cheeky first.

My reflection in the glass smirks back at me. My eyes shine. Do I like that he calls me Red after my underwear?

God, I'm afraid of the answer.

Now's not the time to be thinking about any of this. How's his meeting with his mom going? He was supposed to have lunch with her an hour before my viewing. Is he still in town?

"Pressie?" Dad asks roughly. "You here on earth with us?"

Startled, I spin around. "Yes, sorry. I was thinking about..." How Haven's first impression of me was practically obscene, yet he wasn't overwhelmed with lust. But he still kissed me.

"What do you think?" the agent asks with a smile.

I think I sold all my shit and would have to purchase new backgrounds and props. Mine were out of style anyway. What is even in?

Shouldn't I be more prepared if I'm thinking of opening a studio? I can rent it out, but there's already a space that does that. My questions are signs that I still don't know what I want to be when I grow up. "I'll have to think about it."

"Pressie." Papa's impulsiveness is palpable. Does he want me out of the house?

"I need to consider everything." Like whether I'd like to be a photographer again. I can't take pictures of Haven all my life. Is it an option?

"What's there to consider?" He holds his arms out, heedless of the agent listening to every word. "It's not far from Huckleberry Springs. You can commute, or hell, live in the back room."

My cheeks flush. The agent is dressed in a maroon skirt and cream shirt, a summery yet business-casual ensemble. I'm in the same skirt that flew up on me when Haven drove by. I'm even wearing the same underwear.

"Go ahead and take the time you need," she says. "There's *a lot* of interest. No pressure, of course, but I just wanted to let you know."

"Thanks." I summon the professional smile I used on prospective clients back in the day. I didn't need it when I worked with Buford. "I'll keep that in mind."

I start for the exit. I don't have to make the decision now. I should have a business plan before I do. An idea of the clients I'm willing to take. Studio only? Events? Ugh. Weddings.

"I don't get to the city much," Papa says to the agent behind me. "I used to travel a lot when I rode bulls."

"Really?" she says, politely interested.

Papa always finds a way to talk rodeo, and he's found a brand-new subject. The poor woman might regret this whole showing and never take a call from me or Papa again.

While he's regaling her with his wins, I take out my phone and send Haven a text.

Me: How's it going?

The reply is quick.

Haven: It's not. She didn't show.

My heart falls like a rock. Oh no.

Me: I'm so sorry.

Haven: Maybe she's late.

I look at the time. Really late.

Me: Are you still at the restaurant?

His mom recommended a brewery not far from the zoo. It's a place I'd love to go to, but Papa likes cheap beer, hard liquor, and plain food. When I looked at the place online, it was the kind to repel him.

Haven: Yep.

That poor guy. She puts him through so much, and he keeps taking it. He's doing it all alone. It's not right.

"Papa," I interrupt him while he's mid-story about the

ride in Prescott, Arizona, that earned me my name. "Can you give me a ride somewhere?"

Haven

I gave up and ordered after an hour of waiting. My steak and pasta plate were whisked away fifteen minutes ago. My mom still hasn't arrived. To justify how long I've taken up a seat on what seems to be a busy day, I ordered a couple appetizers and their IPA. It'll take me a while to chew through that drink.

I pick up my phone. Maybe my mom's training went long. Again.

Me: Hey, I'm leaving soon. You coming?

I set the damn thing face down. She isn't going to reply. I don't know when I'll hear from her, but she'll have some excuse about today.

Squinting out the window, I frown. A familiar pickup leaves the parking lot.

"Hi."

I whip my head around at the heavenly sound. Prescott has on the same outfit I first saw her in. Too bad there's no wind in the brewery. "Hey. What are you doing here?" I point to the window. "Was that Silas leaving?"

She nibbles on her lower lip. "I took a chance that you'd still be here, and that I could ride back to Huckleberry Springs with you."

My mood rises out of the gutter. "Yeah, of course. Have you eaten?"

The young server who's been slowly losing her patience

with me arrives with my beer, a basket of mozzarella sticks, and a tray of wings.

"Your guest arrived?" she asks lightly while giving Prescott a hard look.

"No, but someone found me. Order whatever you want, Prescott, or help yourself. Or both. It's on me." I slide the menu across the table.

She sits in the booth across from me. "I'll try what he's having."

"It's an IPA," I warn her.

She grimaces. "In that case, I'll have your most popular beer, which I assume is not the IPA."

"It's not." The girl grins, already enamored with Prescott. I know the feeling. "I'll be right back."

I position the apps between us. "I'm not too hungry. I already ate." My stomach acid flares just admitting that.

Sympathy fills her eyes, but she grabs a mozzarella stick. "I'm sorry. But I really am a sucker for melted cheese of any sort."

"What about wings?"

"As long as there's ranch." Her eyes light up when she spots the container of ranch along with the blue cheese dip. "Perfect." She scoops up marinara with her appetizer and bites off the end.

Her eyelids flutter, like it's the most delicious food she's ever eaten. And just like that, I'm grateful that I waited so long for my mom.

Sitting alone for over two hours, thinking about whether I should leave or not, when I know I should, has mentally taxed me. I'm tired. I'm stressed. But I can't call Iverson or Durban. I can't tell them that Mom most likely stood me up. They'd ask what else I expected.

So I sat here. Both wishing for Mom to show up and

hoping that she would keep her brand of whirlwind away from me.

It's funny, I usually avoid whirlwinds, and yet when Prescott's particular unpredictability twists me up, it's not the same. Prescott seems like she'd be chaos, but she's steady, even when she doesn't know what she wants. Because she knows what she *deserves*. A guy could learn a thing or two from that.

Prescott grabs another cheese stick. The server drops off her beer, and Prescott smiles around her food. She finishes chewing and takes a big gulp of her beer.

Her gaze finds mine, and she raises her brows. I'm watching her. Staring.

"Sorry, but bar food is my weakness. I've told Papa that he should serve it when I know damn well he wouldn't follow code on anything."

"Don't be sorry. I ordered them out of guilt. How's the beer?"

She turns the handle toward me. "Better than yours, I bet. Try it."

"People love to hate on IPAs."

"I don't like to gnaw through my beer."

"I'm going to have to get you to like IPAs now too?"

"You're doing it with whiskey. Want the last mozzarella stick?"

Not if I get to hear her moan again. "All yours. How was the studio?"

She slows her chewing and dabs a napkin at her mouth. Sucking in a big breath, she sets her food down.

"It was great. Ideal." Her wooden tone says otherwise. "Spacious, good lighting. Nice bathrooms for changing rooms and ample storage. If I said the word, Papa would sign the lease."

"But?"

Her pretty pink lips shine from the grease of the food. She'd taste sweet and savory right now. "But I don't know if it's what I want to do." Her expression turns sheepish. "Is it bad to admit that I kind of enjoy bartending?"

Nothing she enjoys should be shameful. "Is it getting hit on? Didn't happen enough at weddings?"

"Funnily enough, it did happen more than I would've thought. But with men old enough to be my dad—or grandpa."

"Oof, and here I am with only six years on you."

She laughs. "You think your pickup game is good enough to rival theirs?"

"Did they try the 'are you from Tennessee' line?"

"I believe it was more like, 'I'm in room three fourteen. Bring your camera.'"

"You didn't jump on that?" I make sure to sound scandalized, and she rolls her eyes. "One time, one of Edna's friends told me she'd pay me two hundred dollars to mow her lawn naked." When Prescott's jaw drops, I chuckle. "She lives on eight hundred acres."

"That's so inappropriate."

"Edna never invited her back for that reason. She might tell dirty jokes, but she has her limits." I fold my hands, enjoying today more than I thought I would. "You like bartending?"

"I like tending bar at Bootleg." She frowns and stares out the window. "It's not a quiet house. Papa's an odd mix of laid back and uptight, and he must've been a hottie back in the day, or he would've driven Mom crazy."

"He drove her wild instead."

"Eew, Hennessy. Why'd you go there?" Our laughter draws attention, and that's a first for me. She rolls her lips in. "I thought I'd be upset at him the whole time, but I don't know. With Mom gone, it just seems too hard to be mad at him. He is who he is, and I'm tired."

"You've been through a lot."

"I guess." She shrugs. "Eh. Could've been worse. To cap off losing my mom, my cat, my career, and my boyfriend, my skirt could've blown up in front of a complete stranger on my first day in town."

That might've been the cherry on top of an awful few years for her, but the memory of seeing her ass still brightens my day.

Prescott

I chowed down all of the food Haven ordered, and then had another beer while he nursed his IPA. We stayed at the brewery for another two hours after I arrived. I didn't see how much he tipped the server, but she almost bum-rushed him at the door to thank him.

We're not quite to his pickup, and I'm enjoying the warm summer air.

He slows the closer we get. "Time to head back?"

"We could. Or..." I look around. We're on the edge of town, and leaving would put an end to a really pleasant afternoon. Can we make it a nice evening? "We could see what they have for distilleries."

He stops at the hood of his pickup. "Red, you wound me. Don't you think I've been to them and tried everything they have?"

A stroke of jealousy paints my insides. Why? I've never

wanted to go to a distillery before. "Haven, it's official. You're cooler than me."

"Nah."

"How could you not be? You're a cowboy, for one." It has to be the beer that keeps me talking even though I drank them over a span of hours with food. "And two, you make whiskey."

"And vodka and gin."

"Cool vodka and gin. Hennessy, this is the most fun date I've ever had, and it's not even a date."

His smile freezes for a second before he laughs. "You know what? I'll take it." He jogs around to the passenger side of his pickup. "In that case, we should keep this nondate going. How about we get some samples and go to a park?"

"Isn't that illegal or something?"

"Just a tasting. Mostly for you because I have to drive."

"I haven't drunk in a park since I was a teen."

"Prescott Keys, are you telling me you were a wild child?"

A grin spreads across my lips. "It was actually my mom." I get into his pickup, and I'm surrounded by his sandalwood scent. "She thought if she made it less forbidden, I wouldn't be as interested."

"Did it work?" he asks in a low voice. He props his hands on the top of the pickup, and the frame surrounds his strong body. My heart stutters.

"Actually, yes, but I was eighteen and didn't have a lot of friends." Maybe I shouldn't drink more. I'm telling him that I only get hit on by grandpas and was a reluctant loner. "I could use another memory of park drinking."

"Park tasting," he says seriously. "I won't let you get tanked."

"I trust you with my alcohol, Haven Hennessy." I like hearing him say my whole name, and I like saying his.

He pushes away. "Let's go get some samples."

I'm more excited than I've ever been to do something with a guy. This isn't a date. That's why it's better. I'm just hanging out with a cool guy.

He climbs in. "Too bad you missed the street fair they had in town right before you came. Huckleberry Springs had one too, but they're only going to hold it every other year."

"I love street fairs. The energy. The people. The booths. They inspire me."

He gives me a lopsided smile when he pulls out of the parking lot. "I worked them both with Cruz last year. Elodie had a booth at each one."

"I haven't been to the bakery yet. I keep meaning to go."

"How 'bout lunch on Monday? She's added soup and sandwiches now."

"I do owe you a meal." I should be talking myself out of meeting up with him again, but he covered the restaurant.

"And a movie."

"Can we watch a movie at the park?"

His brow furrows as he pulls into another parking lot. A distillery looms in front of us. It has character, but nothing like an old gold mine that's been in the owner's family for decades.

He works his lower lip between his finger and thumb. The light scrape of his whiskers scratching against his skin fills the cab. What would those feel like on my skin?

He's taking too long to answer. I'm going all in on

tonight, and he's pulling back. Was I coming on a little strong? I'm just really enjoying myself.

I tear my gaze away. "You probably can't get a signal."

"With all the industry in Billings, there's no shortage of signal. I'm just trying to think of what movie would be good."

"What'd your dad like?"

The corner of his mouth lifts. "Everything, but he loved shoot-'em-ups, especially if they were cop dramas."

"Then pick one of those."

A full smile takes over. "All right, then. We'll go to the park that overlooks town. I have a blanket and a strong signal. We can lie in the back."

"It's a nondate." I say it for myself more than to make it clear to him. I'm the one who thrust myself onto him.

Something I'd like to do in so many ways.

Watching a movie with him in the bed of his pickup is like climbing into the coals and hoping I don't get burned. Yet I'm wedging my way in.

He dips his head, heat simmering in his eyes.

"A nondate." His jaw goes tight. Like he doesn't like the *non*? It's just my wishful thinking. "Tasting first. Then we'll go watch a movie and drink lots of water. And if things go well, the wind will blow your skirt up again."

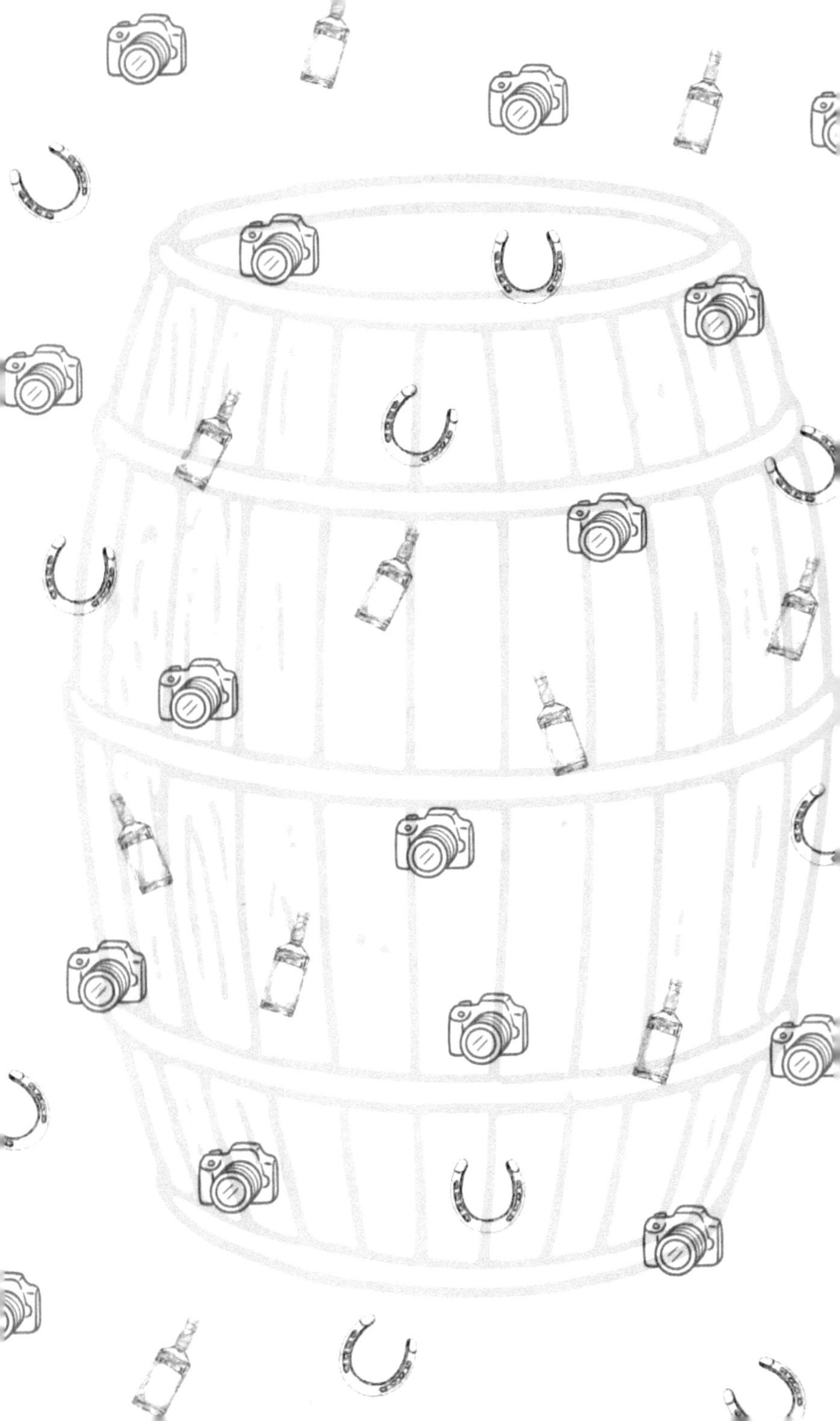

CHAPTER FIFTEEN

Haven

My blanket does not make the bed of the pickup comfortable. I'm parked to the side of the lot, but it's a gorgeous Saturday night, and several people have walked by. We get curious glances, but we're fully clothed and not curled in each other's laps.

Unfortunately.

Sitting next to her with our lemonade and a bag of Nerds Clusters that are more addictive than any alcohol I've drunk has been a torturous test of my restraint. I've wanted to put my arm around her. Bad idea. Her claim that tonight is a nondate runs through my head. Of course, we're not dating.

But do we have to be dating for me to lean over and kiss those red lips?

So far, I've survived a movie in the bed of my truck and a brutal tasting. We weren't in Foster House. I wasn't working, but I walked her through sipping small amounts of different whiskeys. I'm still floating on the high of hearing her say she likes my rye better than the one she had tonight.

The credits roll for *The Untouchables*, and I shut the screen off.

"You watched that as a kid?" She looks at me with incredulous concern. "It was really good, but also— violent."

"Way too young, but I think I closed my eyes a lot. Dad loved it, and he'd always make lemonade for movie nights."

"Thanks for sharing it with me." Her hand is tantalizingly close to mine. I could inch my fingers over and entwine them with hers.

Holding hands? Who am I?

This whole night is something new. Dinner. Drinks. But in a way that's not the norm. Then a show where the backdrop of the screen is her bare legs stretched out next to mine. Her sandals by my boots.

She starts picking up the bottles and the empty candy bag. "It's the world's smallest drive-in, but we made it work."

I hop over the side of the pickup and drop the tailgate so she can crawl out more easily. I take the garbage from her and toss it in the trash can a few feet from where I'm parked. By the time I turn around, her feet are hitting the ground. She straightens out her clothing. When she looks up and catches my eyes, the faintest blush stains her cheeks. Is she remembering that I saw that skirt flying over her ass?

I recall every detail. Especially the red, lacy underwear.

I open the passenger door for her again. When she

swings in, I follow her with my hand hovering over her lower back. I don't touch her. Did she notice?

She's yawning when I hop in behind the wheel.

"Sorry." She covers her mouth. "I didn't sleep well last night."

"Too used to staying up late working at Bootleg?" I take off in the direction of Huckleberry Springs. Tonight's not even going to end in an orgasm, but I wish we could do this again. And again and again.

Pressure grows behind my zipper, and I shift in my seat. It might end with a solo session in the shower. Fuck, there's only so much a guy can take. Her skirt is riding up her lush thighs, and her skin glowing under the streetlights is my tipping point.

"I was nervous for the showing." She curls her arm along the edge of the window and rests her head on it. "Embarrassed that I had to go with my dad."

"It's smart to go to a showing with someone else. You never know who's there."

"But it wasn't for safety. He was going to sign with me and put down the deposit. I just want to have my shit together, and today didn't feel like I was making progress." She lets out a delicate snort. "Not to mention it's the only thing we've done together in years outside of Bootleg."

"No kidding?"

"Yeah." She yawns and snuggles against the door even more. My side aches, like there's an emptiness that she could fill. She could cuddle against me instead. But I don't have a bench seat, and that's not what tonight is about. "And in a weird twist, I'm the one who left him to hang out with a friend."

"Serves him right. I've been meaning to ask. How'd you get him to leave you with me anyway?"

"I told him that a friend from Colorado was in town. He doesn't know anyone I hang out with, so he didn't question it."

I chuckle. "Lying to your dad."

"Getting that teenage experience now that I didn't get back then." She falls quiet. By the time I turn off the interstate, her breathing is even.

Goddamn, I'm smiling the whole way back, driving in the dark with a pretty girl asleep in my passenger seat.

She's not mine.

But there's something between us, something I'd like to explore more. Except she's a girl who wants it all, and I can't give her that.

I pull into the driveway of Silas's small white house and kill my headlights. It's dark, and neighbors are nosy enough. Silas must be at the bar.

Prescott inhales deeply and sits up, unbuckling her seat belt. "I can't believe I slept all that way."

"It wasn't far." I free my seat belt and lean my elbow on the console. "You didn't snore very loud."

She twists toward me, eyes wide and horrified. "Did I really snore?"

Her eyes are luminous in the dash lights. "No, Red," I say softly, "you didn't snore."

Her gaze dips to my mouth. "You like to mess with me."

"You have no idea." My face is only inches away from hers.

"I should go." Her words are barely a whisper.

We hold our positions for a few seconds, then she rips herself away.

"Good night, Haven. Thanks for the ride." She slips out the door.

"'Night," I say after the door shuts.

She scurries around the hood to the front door. A sense that I missed something develops in the center of my chest. She digs in her purse for a key as she takes the few stairs to the door. Soon she'll be gone from my sight. The emptiness inside me grows vast.

Dammit. I get out and swing the door shut. My long strides eat up the pavement toward her.

She looks up just as I jump to the top step. "Is everything—"

I grip the sides of her face and plant my mouth on hers. Her lips are warm and soft. She grips my shirt and a little whimper leaves her.

I push her into the nook beside the door and deepen the kiss. I lick into her mouth, and she meets my tongue stroke for stroke. She's so damn sweet, I could drink her in all night. But we're outside.

I crowd her farther into the little corner and block out everything behind us, and I do it while devouring her. A needy moan escapes her. I grind against her, hounded by a need of my own. She's air, and I'm suffocating. She's sustenance, and I'm starving. She's understanding, and I'm so damn confused. But not about this. Not now, and not with her.

Her curves press against me. Round tits and lush hips. I grab on to them, yanking her even closer, though it's not possible.

I release her mouth, and she gulps in air while I lave kisses to her ear.

"Haven?" It's a question and a demand.

I slide a hand up her torso. She shivers under my touch, like it's been forever, or it's overwhelming, and both appeal to me. Her nipple pokes against the fabric of her top, and I circle it with my palm. I'm rewarded with a whimper.

"Do you need more, Red?"

"Yes," she whispers.

I use my other hand to grab her ass just as I wedge a knee between her legs. "Are you wet for me?"

She groans in answer and starts rocking her hips against me. Her skirt gets caught between us, hindering her movement.

I let go of her ass and scrunch up the hem of her skirt, tugging it free from the lock our bodies have on it. My fingers graze the velvety soft skin of her thighs.

"You're so fucking soft." I flatten my hand on her leg, and a shiver runs through her. I hitch her leg up to my hip and pin it between me and the wall. It's like this nook was made for us. "Are you soft everywhere?"

"I...I don't know..." The night swallows her words. Whatever we say is just between us. "Yes."

"Do you touch yourself?" I brush my palm up her leg to her hip. If there's a way to feel all of her at once, I want to know it. But I don't want to leave this position. No interruptions.

"Yes." She frees her fists from my shirt and braces herself on my shoulders. Heat seeps through the denim of my jeans. A siren's call that makes the zipper of my pants dig into my dick.

"What do you think about when you do?" My fingertips touch her underwear. Delicate, uneven fabric slides under my touch.

"Lately?" she says breathlessly. "You."

Lust hits me so hard my gut clenches. She thinks about me when she touches that wet pussy of hers? There's nothing I could hear that sounds so good. "Goddamn, Red. Do you call out my name?"

A sliver of stiffness lines her body. "It's not private enough."

Good point, and I don't want to dance any closer to the topic of her dad. He'd be a helluva interruption.

"Do you know what I think about when I jack off?" I whisper against the shell of her ear.

She turns her face into me. "No."

"How bad do you want to know?" My breath tickles her hair.

"God, Haven."

I smile. "That's not enough. Do you want to know bad enough to tell me if this underwear is the same red pair you wore on the day we met?"

"It is."

"Fuck, Prescott." Need pounds through me. From my temples to my erection, I'm a live wire. My muscles are taut. I could drag my zipper down and plunge into her until I release, and the misery would be over. But I wouldn't know.

How does her wet cunt feel?

How needy is her clit?

How can I get that underwear off her so I can strangle my cock with it?

I've got a handful of her breast. Her shirt material is in the way, and then there's her bra, but later. I have now, and my other hand is right beside heaven.

I rim my fingers underneath the fabric of her panties. Someday, I'll see those again too—up close, and I'll take them off her.

Scalding heat meets me, and fuck yes, she's soaked.

The fabric, her skin. "This is for me?" I need to hear her say it.

"Yes."

Staying underneath her underwear, I slide a finger through her pussy lips. "Fuck, I knew you'd be dripping." I kiss along her jaw. Her chest is heaving against me, and my breath is sawing in and out of me. "I bet you taste so fucking sweet."

I hit her clit and she moans. If my fingers were in her, she'd be clenched around me. I'll enjoy the quiver moving through her for a bit longer before I find out.

I circle her tight bud and get another moan out of her. My patience is a razor wire. I change the angle of my hand and thrum her clit with my thumb and thrust two fingers inside her.

"Oh god, Haven."

Her body grips me. If my dick was in her instead, I wouldn't be able to move. I'd be locked in place and fucking loving it. "Ride it, Red. Now."

She doesn't argue. For once, we're not dancing around attraction. This connection we have should be explored. I'm too drawn to her, and if she's only here for a little while, why not live it up?

I push in and out of her. She rolls those full hips of hers, and my thigh between her legs props us both up. Energy builds within her. I can feel it vibrating through the walls of her pussy.

I brush my mouth against hers. "You're ready to come, Red. Let yourself go." Then I crush her lips with a punishing kiss that matches the frenzy I'm stroking her clit with.

She goes taut, and her mouth falls open. Her cry gets strangled in her throat, and I catch the rest. Heat floods my hand, and her nipple against my other palm is hard enough to carve wood.

She drenches my hand, and her breathing is ragged. She's sucking and nibbling at my lips. Delicate tremors run through her.

I ease back, but I don't withdraw my fingers quickly. I tip my forehead onto hers. She fits against me perfectly. I'm not towering over her, and I don't feel like I'm going to crush her. "That was even better than I thought it'd be."

"I can't believe we did that."

"Believe it. That orgasm was mine."

She licks her lips, and my dick bangs against the clasp of my pants. Exquisite pain courses through my veins. As much as I want relief, any more will be too much. We haven't skirted around each other for weeks just to dive into bed. Not on the stoop of her dad's house.

"What about you?" Her gaze darts around, scanning the street behind me. "You didn't..."

"Come in my pants? It was fucking close. There is something I want." I tug her panties down. "Step out of these. They're mine too."

She does as I ask. "You want my underwear?"

"Yes." I fist them in my hand and caress my knuckles down her cheek. "Because when I go home tonight, I'm going to think about those needy moans, and I'm going to remember how hot and fucking tight you were, and I'm going to come. These are going to catch my whole load. Then I'll wash and return them. You won't know when, but I'll give them back, and you'll know I jacked off in them and thought of you the whole time."

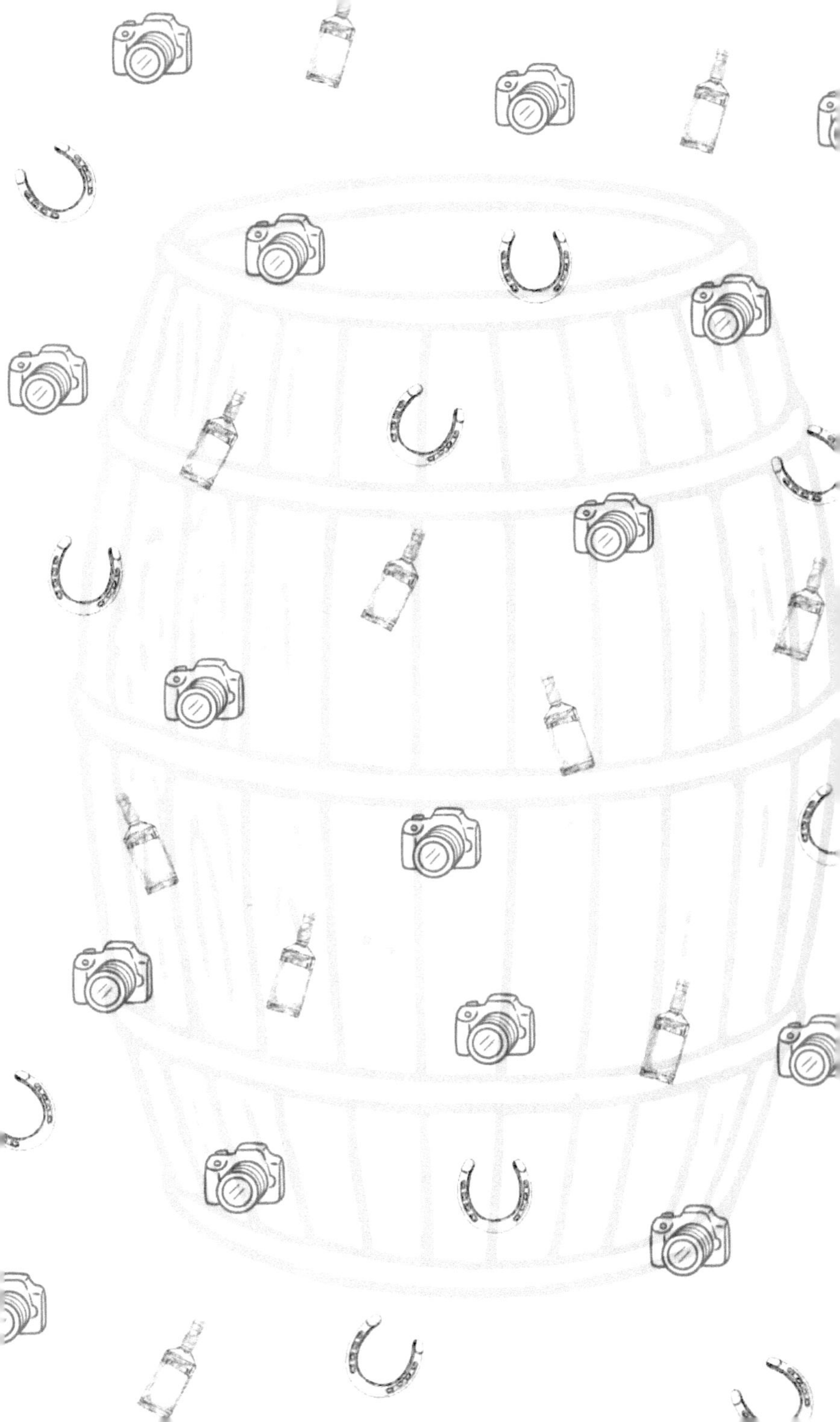

CHAPTER SIXTEEN

Prescott

Will he remember?

I pace the few feet of space I have in front of the futon. It's Monday, and Haven offered to meet me at the bakery for lunch. But that was before he drove me home. That was before he gave me the most explosive orgasm of my life. That was before he dragged my underwear off. Before he told me all the naughty things he was going to do with them.

I'm mortified, and I don't know if he really did it. But I *can't wait* until he returns them. Because then that means he did. Right?

Ugh. What do I do? If I go to the bakery and he's not there, then what?

Did he get home, look at my panties, and wonder what the hell he saw in me?

How was Saturday the most romantic date of my life, and it wasn't even a date?

There's a knock on my door.

I open it to Papa. "Hey. I was just leaving."

He frowns at the beige summer dress I have on. "Michelle called."

"Who?" Am I too dressed up? Trying too hard?

He narrows his eyes. "The agent from Saturday."

Oh. Did I ever catch her name, or was my head in the Haven cloud it's been lost in for weeks? "Is the studio gone?"

"Yes. You missed your chance."

"It was a good place, but I'm not sure studio work is for me." I have all the pictures of the cats and Meadow. Although the puppy is Haven's now, so I can't post her. Should I try influencing again? What would be my goal? It's not like I can adopt the kittens and make them stars.

"You should start getting clients. I saw Jack heading out of town with Ellie."

"Who?" Usually Papa's throwing around friends from his rodeo years, but none of those names are familiar.

He points to a wall of the house. "Kid next door. Ellie takes their pictures."

"Oh." A hope I didn't know I had sinks. There's already a photographer people turn to. Huckleberry Springs isn't big enough for another.

Is it?

I wasn't planning on it, but a few jobs would help.

"I'll think about it." I can give Papa that. "What time do you need me in tonight?"

He shrugs. I really should be used to the lackadaisical way he runs Bootleg.

"Okay," I say. "I'll be there when I'm done. I've heard so much about the bakery, I'm going there today."

Interest lights his face. "If she's got cruffins, can you bring a couple home?"

After I look up what a cruffin is. "Sure." I step around him and start down the hallway.

"Want me to book a showing in Bozeman? It'll be overpriced," he grumbles.

"Maybe I should look in Wyoming." I don't want to look in Wyoming, but Papa's going to start to think I'm a deadbeat.

He grunts. "Gettin' a little far away."

I stop before the door and turn. "Do you want me close?" My face warms. On the other side of this wall, I was grinding against Haven and coming in his arms.

His expression morphs into astonishment. "Of course. Why wouldn't I?"

"You never wanted me around when I was a kid."

He draws back. "Pressie, I was working." He sucks in a breath, like he knows that excuse no longer works, and lets it out in a quick exhale. "I couldn't give your mom what she wanted."

If I had a nickel for every guy who knew his limits when it came to relationships, and it was me...

"Wyoming is closer than Chicago," he says.

"Just as windy." Regardless of whether Haven remembers or not, I'll cheer myself up with some sweets. "See ya later."

I pull up to the bakery right at noon, and the line from the register is to the door. I creep inside. A bell dings, but the chatter doesn't die down. People look me over. Some faces are familiar from Bootleg.

"Hey, bartender girl." The guy who hit on me the first week I was here is in line in front of me. "I never did get your name."

My ex's face overwrites the stranger's face. He becomes Not Milo. His voice even has the same nasal quality. "But you haven't needed it, have you?"

His smile widens. "I could've used it now." He snaps his fingers. "Wait. Someone called you Red."

He knows very well it was a man. "But do you know why?"

Frowning, he glances at my hair like it should be obvious. I just shake my head.

The door dings open, and I shuffle forward to make room for the new arrival.

A wall of heat surrounds me, and my nostrils fill with the scent of sandalwood. Warm fingers touch my hip right behind my arm, where few people, if any, can see. "Hey, Red."

Not Milo's gaze touches on Haven, and a rueful smile fills his face. "You're a Hennessy, right?"

"Haven." The touch is gone from my back, and he holds a hand out.

"Kade, I should go to Foster House more." Kade drops his grip from Haven's. "Lots of women like to go there."

"There's only one I keep trying to get through the doors," Haven says easily.

I twist to see his expression better. Me?

Not Milo turns back around, and we shuffle forward even more.

"I wasn't sure you remembered about today," I say quietly.

"Red, I wasn't about to forget a nondate with you."

"Another nondate? Is this a regular thing?" Say yes.

He shrugs. "It has to be. I hear you don't date guys who go to bars or own them."

"I don't."

"And you don't date men who wear cowboy boots." He's only speaking loud enough for me to hear.

I smirk, still facing forward, but my body's cocked sideways. "That's a hard one. Some guys can really pull the look off."

"For some guys, it's more than a look."

Don't I know it. "And it makes him sexier."

His deep chuckles rumble right into my veins, like a mainline of the most potent drug. The line shuffles forward, and so do I, breaking the link between me and Haven.

A young girl, probably in high school, is working the register, and a woman a little older is rushing behind the counter, fulfilling orders. I want one of everything in the case, but I order a soup in a bread bowl. Haven gets the same thing. There were no cruffins.

After I pay, I slide into a booth, and he sits across from me. "Now I'm going to have to pay rent. I'm cruffin-less."

"You can always put in an order if Silas gets that grumpy."

People are glancing at us. A few are outright staring. What are they thinking? Is it me? Haven? Does he come to the bakery with lots of girls?

Does he make them come on the front steps?

Heat infuses my face, and I trace the wood grain of the tabletop. The surface is cool. Maybe it'll reach my cheeks.

Haven folds his hands. His legs are stretched out, and he's crossed his boots. My bare legs brush against his jeans. "Silas getting down on you?"

I don't reposition myself. "No, actually. He complained that Wyoming was too far away."

A frown plays along his lips. "Wyoming? What's there?"

"Maybe a place to rent. A larger population that can handle more photographers."

Awareness fills his face, but his mouth stays in a flat line.

The front door dings open. Clementine Palmer enters and waves at practically everyone in the bakery.

When she sees me, her face brightens. "Prescott. What timing!"

"Oh?" Did I do something wrong? I haven't seen her since the crochet club.

She stops at the end of the booth, a smile on her face. "I hear you're a legit photographer."

Surprise flits through me. I haven't been sure about returning to my former career, but it's got its claws in me, trying to drag me back behind the lens. I'm not upset about it.

My skills were always in demand. I loved Buford. He was an amazing cat, but it was *my* photography and videography skills that captured his stubborn, impertinent personality. It's just that people don't usually care to go deeper. "I am, but I'm a little rusty."

"Don't believe her," Haven says in a tone that no one would argue with.

"You were an easy subject."

"I saw what you did," Clem says excitedly. "Those distillery images? Stunning."

He showed them off? He should've. If I had a studio, I'd put some of his shots front and center. But I can't take all the credit. "With the backdrop and the model, I wouldn't have needed more than a phone camera."

She snorts and puts a hand up. "Trust me, I've seen the pictures tourists take, and while they're amazing, they don't match the shine and polish of yours. The detail? I felt like I could walk right into the screen. Anyway, I wanted to talk to you about maybe doing some pictures for me at the library."

"Headshots?"

Elodie comes out of the back and circles around the counter, heading for Clem. "Hey. You're early."

"Good thing," Clem says, "or I wouldn't've been able to interrupt their lunch."

"There you go. Harassing my customers again." She bends down by me. "I have some cruffins in the back. I'll send some with you."

Surprised, I jerk my head around, almost whacking her in the nose. "Oh, no, I couldn't."

"They're ones that aren't pretty enough to sell, but I feel like Silas won't mind."

No. He will not at all, but doesn't she need to get paid? "He would understand, and I can still pay you for them."

She waves a hand. "It's my welcome-to-town gift."

"It's how she lures you here for more goodies," Clem adds.

Elodie shrugs. "A few freebies to create a regular customer never hurt anyone."

"Thank you." I'll come here every day before work to pay her back.

When Elodie disappears into the back, Clem puts her fingertips on the table. "Can I buy you a sandwich tomorrow and tell you all about my idea, and you can think I'm crazy?"

"Do you and your sister have a compulsive need to feed people?" I joke.

Clem snickers. "It's easier to get them to do our bidding, and I need to persuade you to take some pictures for me."

"It might be surprisingly easy. I've been asked to take a lot of questionable photos."

Haven grunts like he's incensed about the inappropriate offers I'd get at weddings. At least I'll tell myself that's why. Only Mom was ever concerned about the situations I found myself in before.

"I'll give you a hint. I really like what you did with Buford."

"You saw that?" My excitement rises. The melancholy is still there. I miss my cat, but finding a fan in the wild immortalizes him.

"Prescott, I'm a single woman in my thirties. If you think there's a cat account I don't know about, please tell me. Those are my comfort watches before bed." She puts a hand on my shoulder. "I really am sorry. Your tribute to him made me sob for an hour."

I pat her hand. "Thank you. That didn't get many views, so I appreciate you telling me."

Buford's not living on only in my memories. Social media is a powerful medium. The loss shifts. I should've kept going and wielded that influence for...something.

Instead, I drained my savings and had to move.

"Tomorrow?" Clem asks. "I'm free anytime, and I know it's an ambitious ask. I thought I'd try before school started."

"Tomorrow."

Clem's grin is wide. "It's a date."

When she leaves, Haven sits forward. "So you'll date her and not me?"

Haven

. . .

Prescott's cheeks turn beet red. I'm joking. Mostly. I'm not looking for a date. I want more of that sweetness I got on the porch.

"It's not—it's just—" She works her jaw like she's straightening her tongue out. "It's business."

The woman from behind the counter swoops by with our drinks and bread bowls, and she drops a to-go container with the cruffins.

Prescott peeks inside at the goods and pins me with an accusing gaze. "You're behind this, aren't you?"

"Don't know what you're talking about." I pick up the top of the bowl and rip a chunk off. "Whatever it is that Clem wants, I think you should do it."

There's a lot Prescott should do. Starting with me.

My time with her red panties and those steamy front-step memories have changed me. I'm not the same man I was before she came in my arms. I'm starving. I can't concentrate. I got fuck all done this morning. All my fingers and toes are crossed that I didn't fuck up the amount of grain I dumped into the mash tun, or Durban's going to have my ass.

She mimics me and dips a piece of bread into her beer cheese soup. "Do you know what she wants?"

"Nope, but it's probably for the library. She does the kids' part of it."

"Maybe the library is having a festival day, and they want someone to capture it." Anyone could do that with a phone. "But she mentioned Buford."

"Buford's worth mentioning." The cat is safe territory. I won't be captivated by the way her red lips close around the soaked bread. Or how her pupils widen, just slightly, as she gets her first taste of the soup. It's fucking amazing, but now each time I eat it, her pleased expression will be in my head.

"You've seen him?"

Busted. "I might've snooped a little."

"Oh." She gets quiet and tears off another chunk of bread. "What'd you think?"

I thought it was a humorous but touching account. She showed off a fancy, mellow cat and talked for him in a way that anyone could relate to. I was enraptured by her voice and drawn into the vibrant imagery. "I liked it. I watched for an hour."

Then she flashed to some prick and I almost smashed my phone into the desk. The jackass ex who'd fucked around on her.

Her eyes widen. "Really?"

If she needs me to make a sap of myself, I will. "You know how sometimes you can skip posts over and over again, but there's no way to pinpoint why. Was it the lighting? The hesitation of the speaker? No animals?" The corner of her mouth tilts up. "You nailed all of it. Each time that cat appeared on the screen, I wanted to stay." Only it wasn't for the kitty, though Buford was a cute bugger. *She* was in those posts. She left a part of herself in each one, and I wanted to collect them all.

"I wish I could've had the same effect," she mutters and dunks another chunk of bread.

"You would've, but you were mourning."

She lifts a shoulder noncommittally. "I guess. I didn't have a purpose though, and I wasn't enough of a draw to get beyond that."

She is an attraction. I walked in on an asshole hitting on her. She wasn't interested, nor does she seem to read into her worth about the guys who come on to her. Superficial isn't what wins Prescott Keys over.

"I didn't know if you'd show up today," she says after we take a few more bites.

"If I didn't, would you have kept talking to Slick?" Okay, maybe that bothered me more than I thought. It's one thing to walk into the bar and some guy is always on her heels, but the bakery too? Sure, it was one of the same men, but what if some Slick makes it through her defenses? What if he gets her alone on the front step of her dad's house?

"Slick?" Her red lips twist up. "The guy in line?" She shakes her head. Her hair's in another loose bun. A different one than I've seen yet, and I'm apparently keeping track. "No. I know his type. Maybe he'd make a good friend. Or a fishing buddy."

A crumb goes down the wrong tube, and I start coughing. I guzzle my Sprite. A good fucking friend? Why the hell would she think about fishing with someone other than me?

What, have I staked my claim?

"You okay?" She ducks her head to get a better look at me. "I'm kidding. He probably doesn't pack Hennessy beef sticks."

"I'm fine," I wheeze. When I fully recover, I chug half my drink.

She gives me a once-over before diving into the remains of her soup bowl. "All I'm saying is that, no, I wouldn't have done more than chat. He reminds me too much of Milo."

"The Slick in Buford's posts?"

"That's the one." She giggles. "'Slick.' Is that from your dad's shows?"

Touched she'd remember, I grin. "Probably. If it was from my mom, it'd be something like 'goddamn cocksucking motherfucker.'"

She coughs and puts her fingers on her lips. I spoke low enough that I didn't shatter anyone's impression of me. "Slick is much better."

As if I summoned her, my phone screen lights up. A text from my mom.

I flip it over. Prescott watches the move but doesn't say anything.

My phone buzzes again. And again. Sighing, I check the messages.

Mom: I had to work Saturday night.
Mom: Have you seen the price of eggs?
Mom: Call me.

My stomach cramps around my lunch. I put the phone face down on the tabletop again and push my bread bowl to the side. The bottom is my favorite part too.

Prescott rips a soup-soaked strip from hers. She doesn't pry.

"It's my mom." There goes a pleasant meal. "She needs money," I say woodenly.

Surprise and concern fill her eyes. "Does she ask for financial help a lot?"

My laugh comes out empty. She makes it sound so formal. "She goes through seasons. It's not a lot, and I mean, it was hard on her, raising all of us on one income. Everything my dad left behind stayed in a trust, and Iverson was in charge of that once he turned eighteen. By then, he knew better than to hand it over."

"The trust had the mine and the land?"

I nod. "And that's it. No money. We hunted a lot of our

food." Hoping to lighten the mood, I grin. "I didn't contribute a whole lot other than being told to be quiet."

She smiles, and just when I think she's going to ask something that'll veer us into the depressing and serious, she tips her head. Her bun flops with the move. "You probably couldn't contribute a whole lot fishing either."

I bark out a laugh, and it draws attention, but I don't care. "Holding all the time I took teaching you over my head? Low blow."

"I mean, we could try again."

Now I'm serious. "You mean that?"

She thinks for a moment. "Will it cheer you up?"

"Yes." Without a doubt.

"Then let me know when you're free again. Isn't that what fishing buddies are for?" she asks lightly.

Fishing buddies?

I know how she moans when she's turned on. I know how wet she gets when she comes. And I've got her panties in my house. "Just an FYI, Red. This fishing buddy is wondering what color underwear you're wearing today."

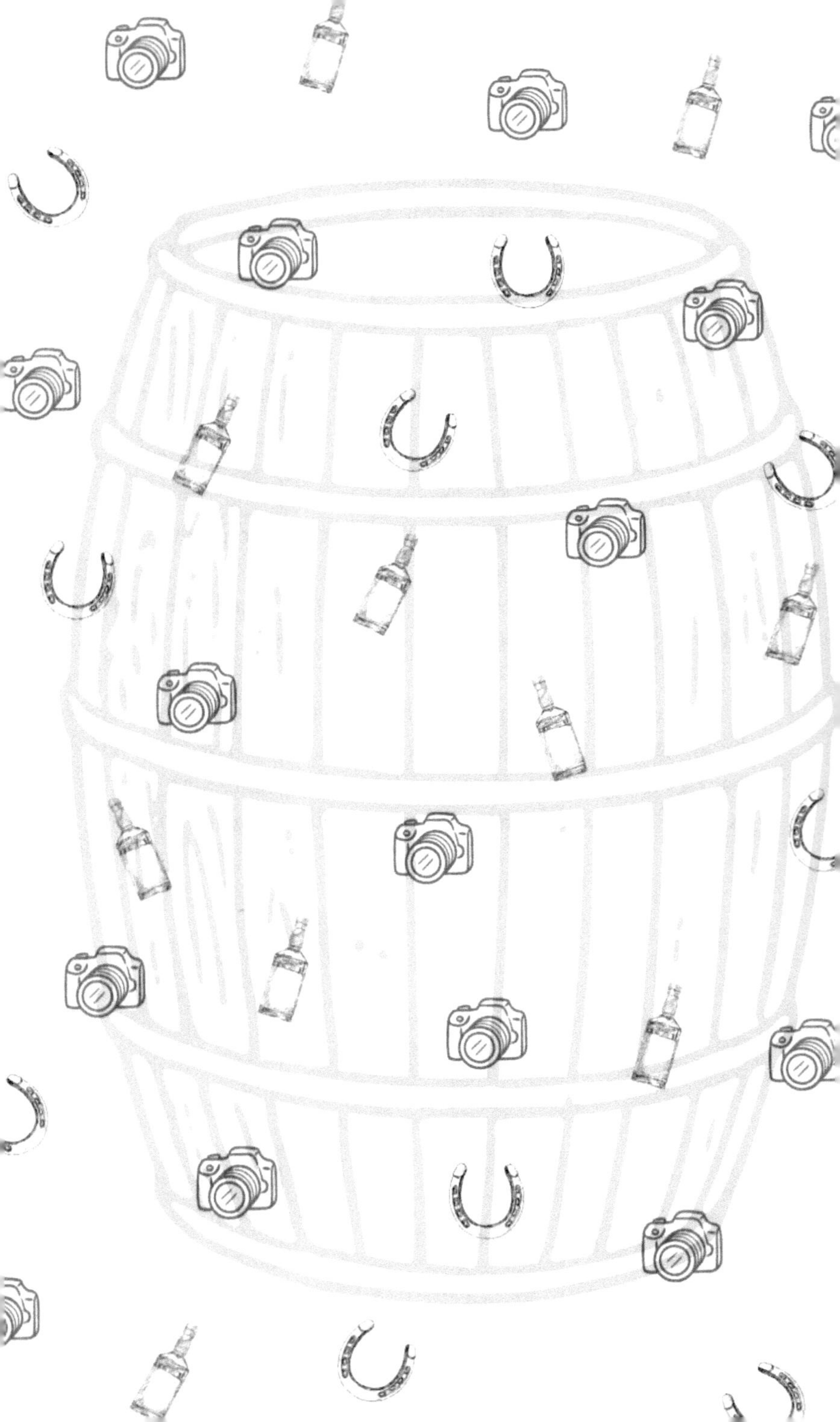

CHAPTER SEVENTEEN

Prescott

I pull up to Haven's barn and park. Why did I volunteer to go fishing again? We didn't set a date, but he mentioned having Friday off. That's perfect. I specifically told Papa that I'd work Friday night. I might've done it after we made plans to fish again, but Haven doesn't need to know that.

Nor does he need to know I'm wearing a pale-blue pair of panties that's a lacy match to the red ones he took.

Will I get those back? Do I want to? Every time I put them on, I'm going to feel his fingers thrusting inside me.

I get out and look around. He's usually at the distillery at this time of day, and I passed a tractor sitting empty in a ditch. Haying.

I gambled that he's busy with either one. I also purposely came out to play with the kittens less than two hours before I'm supposed to meet Clem and talk about the project she wants to hire me for.

Armed with the treats I bought before I left town, I call for the kittens. They're friendly, but they're getting older and are exploring farther. I still need to call the rescue again and see if they have any leads on homes.

How long have I put that off?

Thinking back, I grimace. Way to go, Prescott. Taking advantage of a hot distilling rancher and his soft spot for cute animals. And a really hard spot for a lost woman living with her papa.

If the rescue asks for photos, I have the ones I took when we first found them, but they've changed so much. Round little bellies stretched out with their bodies, they don't look like fuzzy tumbleweeds ready to blow away anymore.

Thistle runs from the back of the barn once I call him. I shake a treat out of the bag to the ground, but the other two don't show yet.

Digging my camera out, I squat. "Smile and say dead mouse." I take a picture of Thistle curled over his fish goodie. Once he eats, he darts off, and I get a video of it. I'll have to tell the rescue that they're better as barn cats. They like their freedom and all the hunting they're doing.

Well. I might as well leave the treats here. I duck into the tack room and stick the bag on a shelf next to the cans that Haven has stockpiled.

I should message the rescue while I'm here. I should do something. Digging out my phone, I stare at my lock screen. Buford's soulful eyes stare back at me.

Boots crunch on the ground behind me. I spin around.

Haven's in the doorway. His shirt is stretched obscenely over his shoulders and plastered to his chest just like I want to be. "Did you find them all?"

"Just Thistle."

He takes his cowboy hat off and pushes a hand through his hair and then sets the hat back on his head. "They're around somewhere. Nice little hunters, especially Tan."

"I was going to ask the rescue for an update and send them some images." I lift my phone like I need to show him proof. "I can tell them that they're good barn cats."

He runs his gaze lazily down my body. My nipples stiffen, at attention, and the slight rasp of the bra that matches my underwear is acute. His gaze continues down the jean shorts I almost didn't wear because they are *short*, but it's hot today, and I had the good sense not to wear another dress or skirt around him.

I regret that at the moment.

He drags his heated gaze back up, and it's like each article of clothing flies off me, leaving me bare. Can he tell how much I want him? Is my shirt hiding the peaks my bra can barely contain? If he thought I was wet Saturday, it's nothing like I am after seeing that hot look of his in broad daylight.

"How upset would you be," he drawls, "if I told you that the only reason I haven't admitted I'm keeping all the kittens is because there'd be no reason for you to keep dropping by?"

I should be irritated. Furious. Scandalized. And I should storm away from the barn and him, and never look back. But I remain rooted to my spot. "I'd be relieved our little wildflowers have a good home."

He drifts closer, the heels of his boots scraping on the barn floor. "You wouldn't be mad?"

"The rescue would be happy." I would be disappointed to have no excuse to return. Perhaps that's too light a description. Devastated. Yeah. That fits better.

He's standing in front of me now, so close the brim of

his hat shades my face. "How do I solve the problem of getting you back out here?"

"There's the fishing." I lick my suddenly parched lips, and his gaze snags on the tip of my tongue. "And your birthday is coming up soon."

"It's still two weeks away." He rests his hands on my hips.

I brush my fingers over the warm fabric of his shirt and trace his shoulders down to his hard biceps. "I have no business being at your place."

"Because you don't want to waste your time on a guy like me."

But I do almost escapes me. My sense of self-preservation might be fragile, but it remains intact. "You don't want a relationship."

"Yet I sure liked hearing you moan my name." His grip on me tightens. If he yanks me to him, I'll be pressed against the big ridge behind the fly of his jeans.

I also liked moaning his name. He blocked me from view and then dominated my senses. He turned me inside out and only took my underwear off. I dreamed about the way he slipped them off and told me exactly what he had planned for them.

The pair I'm wearing today is just for him.

The truth is, I wouldn't be out here if it wasn't for the cats, and I dreaded that the rescue would find homes for them. I don't need to talk to a professional to figure out why I haven't called. I'd have to ask them what it means that Haven hasn't kept me on task. He likes the kittens. Does he like me?

So do I wait to go fishing to see him again? Anticipate his birthday dinner? Do I keep my fingers crossed and make my own wish when he blows out his candles?

It's Tuesday. If we fish on Friday, that's days away. Need is pounding through me now. I'm approaching desperation, and I don't make good decisions in that mental place. It's how I ended up here, not that I'm in a place to complain.

How much sooner can I see him? "What if I came back to get my underwear?"

"I only have one pair." His voice is gruff, and his pupils are wide.

How about now? How about he takes my panties off again? No, dammit. "I need the pair I'm wearing for my meeting later."

"You sure about that?" He crowds closer, and his sandalwood scent wraps around me.

Small, blistering tendrils curl through my bloodstream. A persistent throb grows between my thighs. I've been half aroused since he saw me into the house like a gentleman after being filthy just seconds before.

"I'm sure," I breathe. "But you can find out the color." Did I seriously just offer that? "If you want."

His nostrils flare. "Fuck yes."

Desire cascades through me from head to toe. "I have a meeting in an hour."

A sexy smile curves his lips. "Well then. I'll make sure I'm quick."

His grip eases on my waist only so he can tunnel his fingers between my skin and my waistband. Carefully, he eases the material over my hips. Stopping there, he straightens.

"Are you sure about this?" he murmurs, his lips inches away from mine.

I'm not sure about anything. I haven't been for a long time. The one thing I know for certain is that the sensations he can give me are unrivaled. Maybe that's what I'm clinging to. No surprises. Just pleasure. "I'm sure that you can't guess what color I'm wearing."

Does my sassy tone cover my insecurity?

Can I do this? Can I keep my heart out of whatever it is we're going to do? Playing it safe has only left me alone and heartbroken. So, yes. I'm going to take what I can get. I'm not everything a guy would want, but I'm gambling that I'll be out of town before Haven finds his next fling.

The thought dulls the edge of my raging hormones.

"Blue," he says roughly. "Light and crisp, just like the color of your eyes."

I blink at him. He's standing. How did he guess correctly? "How in the world did you know that?"

Mischief enters his smile. "I peeked when I was pulling down your shorts."

Laughter erupts from me, and I lightly swat at his shoulders. "You had me thinking your sweet words were real."

His expression sobers. "They are one hundred percent real. I just didn't have to guess."

Instead of responding, I slip my hand behind his neck and pull him down for a kiss. He's right. He's been truthful with me so far, yet I expect him to lie like the rest. He's a man of his word, and I need to quit lumping him in with everyone else. He's...special.

He smashes his mouth against mine and sweeps his tongue inside. He tastes like toothpaste and sunshine. I wrap both my arms around him and meet his tongue stroke for stroke.

When he breaks away, his breathing is raspy. "I don't have much time, and I wanna make this good for you."

"I'm wearing a matching bra too."

A ragged groan leaves him. He lifts my shirt over my head and takes in the sight. My nipples tighten to the point of pain, and my breathing becomes shallow.

"Fuck me," he whispers and tosses my shirt onto the closest shelf. "You're the sexiest damn thing I've ever seen. I'm not gonna be able to use that saddle you're leaning on without thinking about your creamy tits under that blue lace."

His words wiggle their way inside my chest and warm me from the inside out as if I'm not already sweltering for him.

I pat the saddle behind me. "Is this yours?" I know it is thanks to the trail ride he took me on weeks ago.

He nudges me backward, and my ass hits leather. "Hang on, Red. I'm going to give you a little ride."

I grip the edges of the saddle, and instead of getting closer, he steps back. Appreciation and desire darken his eyes. The raw need scribbled across his face burrows inside me. Light streams through the window of the tack room. There's nowhere for me to hide, but I can't be self-conscious when he's looking at me like that.

He puts his warm hands on my hips again, only this time, there's no fabric between our skin. Slowly, he lowers to a squat and sets a knee on the floor. Hooking his fingers around the underwear, he doesn't drag them down. Instead, he traces the hem, skimming around my thighs until he hits the juncture.

"Spread your legs, Prescott, and let me in."

My stomach clenches, but I do what he says. I won't disobey and risk losing the heat simmering in his eyes. He pulls the damp fabric to the side, framing my pussy with his hands. All I can see is my chest heaving up and down, the swell of my belly, and then his hungry gaze.

"There it is. So fucking wet and sweet." He swoops in and licks right to my clit.

"Haven!" I don't have to be quiet, but the pleasure coursing through me is building with so much energy, I might bring the neighbors running from miles away.

He strokes perfect circles with his tongue, sucking at intervals that rob all the strength from my legs. As if sensing my growing weakness, he wedges his shoulders between my thighs. A foot lifts off the ground, but he's supporting me.

I thrust my hips into him. Desire's building inside me like a thundercloud. The lightning's going to stop my heart, but I can't slow this down. The teaser on the front porch left me with an obsession for finding out how much more he has to give.

As I'm rocking, the saddle stand is creaking. The leather of the saddle is rough but soft against my butt, and it's like having him brushing his hands all over my backside. It only heightens the sensation of what he's doing to me.

The storm inside me starts to swirl. "Haven." Am I begging him? Warning him of an explosion? Stating a fact?

He replaces his tongue with his thumb and pushes two fingers inside me. "Look at you."

A ragged gasp leaves me at the fullness. I miss his mouth, but he's inside me and still making those thought-stealing circles. I tip my head back and roll my hips into his touch.

"Am I going to see you with your hair down one day?" he asks roughly. "Buck fucking naked and open for me?"

Will it keep him doing this? "Yes."

A satisfied grunt leaves him, and his tongue is back on me. He thrusts his fingers in and out of me.

I implode without warning. Energy bursts outward, and I stiffen, yanking at the saddle. Then I shake from head to toe as I weather the onslaught. "Oh god—yes!"

He doesn't let up until I release my purchase, and our whole situation starts to topple. His strong arms wrap around my legs. The saddle stand rocks back into place until it finally comes to a stop, still upright.

"You good?" he asks, but he doesn't let go of me.

"Yes." So good. I'm panting, and the aftershocks are still rolling through me, but I don't want to move.

He's on a knee in front of me. My traitorous mind paints a whole new picture. We're outside, with the rolling green hills and the backdrop of the mountains behind him. He's still on a knee, only the look in his eye has more yearning. It's filled with desire of a different sort. And in his hand is a little velvet box.

No. That's not happening, and that's what's dangerous with messing around. I'm going to catch feelings. I can deal with those. I *will* deal with those, and these foolish little dreams that pop into my head.

Inside my heart, a cord is pulled tight. I need to leave. I take hold of the saddle again and lift my leg down. "So. I have that meeting to get to."

If he senses my inner conflict, he doesn't let me scurry away. He rests his forehead on my abdomen. "I'm gonna need a minute after that spectacular show," he murmurs.

Pride blooms inside me, but I did nothing to earn it. I'm trying to run out on him, and he's only been generous. "I should, uh, get cleaned up before I go to the bakery."

I smell like sex and faintly of horse sweat.

He skims his hands up and down the backs of my thighs. The picture we make is still sexy, but my heart warms regardless. This is dangerously close to cuddling after sex.

The back of my throat gets thick. This. *This* looks too much like what I want. Still, I push my hands into his hair.

"I've gotta get you cleaned up."

Panic wells to the top. However that would happen sounds even more intimate. "No, it's fine."

He sits back on a heel and smirks. "If you insist on being in a hurry..." He reaches behind him and yanks his shirt over his head.

"Oh, don't..." Once his abs come into view, I have no self-respect. *Take that damn shirt all the way off.* "Nice."

His sexy smirk tempts me to stay as naked as possible around this man. His stomach is crinkled by his position, but it doesn't diminish the effect. His pecs ripple as he sticks his hand inside his shirt. I jump when he starts to wipe me down.

Embarrassment flames in my cheeks. "Did I make a mess?"

"*We* made a mess." His grin widens. "In the best way."

"But you didn't..." I'm the queen of unfinished sentences. Twice now, he's gotten me off with no release for himself. "We're two and oh."

"It ain't like that. I got plenty of pleasure." He straightens, letting out a little groan. Giving his head a little shake, he chuckles. "But maybe next time I don't kneel on a hard floor. I'm feeling every one of my nearly forty years."

"Oh, crap. My age limit is thirty-five."

He picks my shorts up off the other saddle he draped them on. "Not for you, Red. An older guy is like aged whiskey. Bolder, richer, and strong enough to shoot down in one swallow."

I park in front of the old brick library. It's a good size for a town the size of Huckleberry Springs. Yesterday, I had my meeting with Clem, and she invited me out today to make a plan.

The place closed a half hour ago, and Clem thought it'd be easier if I could do a walk-through. The library director wants custom headshots for each employee, and then the library is sponsoring a photo shoot for the local rescue and the animals that are in the jail's pound. There weren't many, but they hoped that fun photos would find the critters homes faster than a picture in a cage.

Now I don't feel so irresponsible for not calling the rescue. Like the rest, they are bursting at the seams.

The pay they offered would help me with a down payment on my own place. Whenever I move...or find a job.

Clem opens the library door and waves. "Come on in."

I go inside and inhale the smell of books. Clem clasps her hands and lets me take in the small space. Her hair's done in two rows of neat French braids, and she's wearing bold red shorts with a white shirt and navy boat shoes. She looks like she's about to leave for a second job working on a yacht, but it suits her.

She gives me a whirlwind tour of the fiction and nonfiction sections, the small sitting area with a few tables and chairs, along with just as many computers, then the new wing that houses the meeting room and the children's section. The large windows make my decision easy.

"I think the light is better in here." The large picture windows and the skylight give it life. "I don't have much of my old equipment, but I can do the shoot in the afternoon. That'll be the best."

"How about the animals? Will you be able to photograph them?" She rises to her tiptoes like she's on the brink of begging. I didn't want to commit until I knew I could earn the paycheck.

"I can do that in my sleep."

"Aren't animals harder?"

I tip my head from side to side. I'm boasting just a little. Buford was an older rescue, and he didn't have the energy of the kittens or Meadow. My camera phone shots of them turned out just fine. "Depends who we're talking about. My first job included going to day cares and preschools."

Clem grimaces. "Like hitting a moving target?"

"Wiggling, crying, distracted—take your pick. Animals can be a challenge, but I miss it."

"He was such a sweetie. It was clear how much you cared for him." She folds her arms, uncertainty playing across her face. "Do you mind me asking—"

"Why I didn't start over with a new cat?" I smile to let her know her question doesn't diminish how much my cat meant to me. "I thought about it a lot, but, uh, it was clear that I needed an animal to continue posting."

"That can't be true." She inspects my face and sighs. "Sorry. I know online stuff is like a popularity contest."

How'd she understand so quickly? "Do you do some influencing?"

"No, but I have to post stuff for my other job."

"Foster House?"

She shakes her head. "My books." She glances around like she's going to get busted. Just what does she write?

"But I always feel like I'm on the outside looking in, you know?"

I know all too well. "It's like a glass house, and everyone's having a party. You were invited, but no one will let you inside."

Relief fills her eyes. "No kidding."

"You could add a cat to your books," I joke. Shit. Did I just insult her work?

She laughs. "I always forget to add pets to my books." Snapping her fingers, she looks around. "Where's my phone? I told Ellie I'd ask if she could get your number."

That name is familiar. Her name in my dad's voice runs through my head, reminding me. "She does senior photos?"

"Yes, she does everyone's photos in Huckleberry Springs. She was telling me how overwhelmed she is, and I mentioned that maybe you were hanging a shingle."

"Oh, I haven't thought about it." I have thought about it. A lot. "Probably not in Huckleberry Springs."

Interest infuses her eyes, but she doesn't reply. Is she waiting for me to elaborate?

I've only talked to Clem a few times, but it's not like I have a pool of friends to chat with. Haven would listen, but I've been keeping my distance from him. Except the times I let him get up close and personal.

"I'm not sure how well I can build a client base." There. That didn't sound like I hold a grudge based on population size.

"That's too bad. We could use someone with your skills in the area."

"It's too much of what I grew up with." I lift my hands like *whaddya do?*

"Oh, god. I'm sorry. You must think I'm being pushy."

"No, I understand, and it's a valid assumption." Maybe I should be considering what Huckleberry Springs holds for me. If Ellie can't field all the requests she gets, and if I could get a steady client base, then I could supplement with bartending for Papa.

I could be around Haven more.

But he will not factor into this decision. He can't. I don't want to be bartending one night and hear all about the hot guy some tourists have hooked up with. I don't want to scroll through feeds again and see my boyfriend's favorite watch on some other girl's nightstand in the same town he has a business meeting in.

I hate to leave this conversation on an awkward note. Clem's been so nice, and I would love to have her as a friend if I had long-term plans in the same zip code. "What kind of work is Ellie looking at sending my way?"

"She's doing Campbell and Durban's wedding, and she says since Hawthorne Ranch is hosting more weddings, she's gotten a lot of queries, but she can't accept many."

"Because they take longer, and they suck up every single weekend in the summer."

She nods. "You feel the same?"

"Yes. But weddings aren't just a glass house. They're the biggest, happiest glass *castle*. I'm on the outside looking in."

"Always a bridesmaid and never a bride?" Her smile is full of understanding. "I think I'm starting to feel like that too. Elodie and Cruz are getting married in October. There's Campbell's in a few weeks. I've been to Vegas twice as a bridesmaid in the last five years and to Cancun once. Three more right here in Huckleberry Springs in the last decade, and my librarian bestie in Salt Lake City called to share the good news that she got engaged just last week."

"I was only ever invited as the help, not to participate. Adding to that, I was with a guy who strung me along for years, and I stayed with him, hoping and waiting."

She winces. "I saw the fallout." She puts her fingers over her lips. "God, I'm sorry. I shouldn't have told you that."

Yeah, that part sucked. People I know saw everyone tagging me and sharing the infamous posts with my ex. It's online for eternity. "It's nice not to have to explain it all." I check the time. "I hate to cut out. I told Papa that I'd be there by seven."

Clem folds her arms like she's hugging herself. "You mind if I show up there? I'm a little stuck in my book, and I could use a night with no work. But if it's weird, and you're busy—"

"No, not at all." I'm almost giddy. Did I make a friend? "Papa sits and talks to customers all the time. Besides, it's Wednesday. A pretty slow night the later it gets." I tip my head toward where our cars are the only ones in the small lot. "Let's go."

Two hours later, Clem's sitting at the end of the bar, and there are only two other groups in the building. The pool tables are empty, and no one's playing darts. The jukebox is quiet, and Papa's parked with one of the groups.

I check the message on my phone that just came in.

Haven: Still on for Friday?

I stuff my phone in my pocket.

"Is it Haven?" Clem asks in a singsong voice, stirring the ice in the drink she's been nursing for an hour.

"No? Why?"

She taps her lips with her finger. "Every time you look at your phone, you smile."

"Not every time." He's only messaged twice. Damn, she's right. "He wants to take me fishing again."

But does he want to strip me down in the tack room again? A wave of heat rolls over my skin.

Twice now I've fallen under his spell. I want to tumble again and again. But I also want to keep my heart intact.

She abandons the little straw. "Do you want to go?"

"I caught two fish last time."

"Nice." She holds her fist out. I laugh and fist-bump her. "So why are you undecided? Sorry if I'm being nosy again. I ask a lot of questions, and sometimes, it's not appreciated."

"I'm usually an open book." Except when it comes to what Haven and I have done. "It was my first time fly-fishing." And then he kissed me. "But I mean, it's fishing."

"So you two aren't a thing? I don't want to make innuendos if you're like, 'ew, no.'"

"Would anyone 'ew, no' Haven?"

She giggles. "Honestly, I would. I know the Hennessys and the Fosters are *very* good-looking, but they're not my type."

"What is your type?" I'm truly curious, but maybe she'll also forget about following up on my reason for avoiding Haven.

"Tall, dark, and brooding. Shaved head. A whole *Fast & Furious* vibe."

"Paul Walker or Vin Diesel?"

Her eyes grow dreamy. "Vin all the way. He'd have major resting dick face, but he'd be all soft and gooey when it counts. And he'd be able to crack a girl's back so many ways, in so many positions, until she couldn't walk, but make her breakfast in bed and give her foot massages."

"I don't know," I say drily, "that seems too general."

She snickers and takes a drink of her watered-down amaretto sour. "What about you? Is your type a tall, thoughtful country boy who loves his brothers and seems enamored with a tall, gorgeous photographer?"

"No." My cheeks are hotter than the July sun, both at her compliments and the thought of Haven being enamored with me. "Don't get me wrong, he's a catch. But no one can catch him, and I'm done with the chase."

"What if he's trying to catch you?"

"If anything, it's to release, and I don't want to be hooked. I want to move somewhere there are more options."

"Don't you see? You're not hooked when you're released. If you like hanging out with him, why not do it while you're here?"

I've thought of that. "What if he can walk away, but I can't?"

"Oh." Her shoulders slump. "That is the risk, and I get your reluctance with Haven. I've known him for years, and he's been single the whole time. All I'm saying is, you can relax and have fun for a while, without your clothes on. Just don't picture Haven as your future husband."

A pit opens in my stomach, and I drop through. Too late.

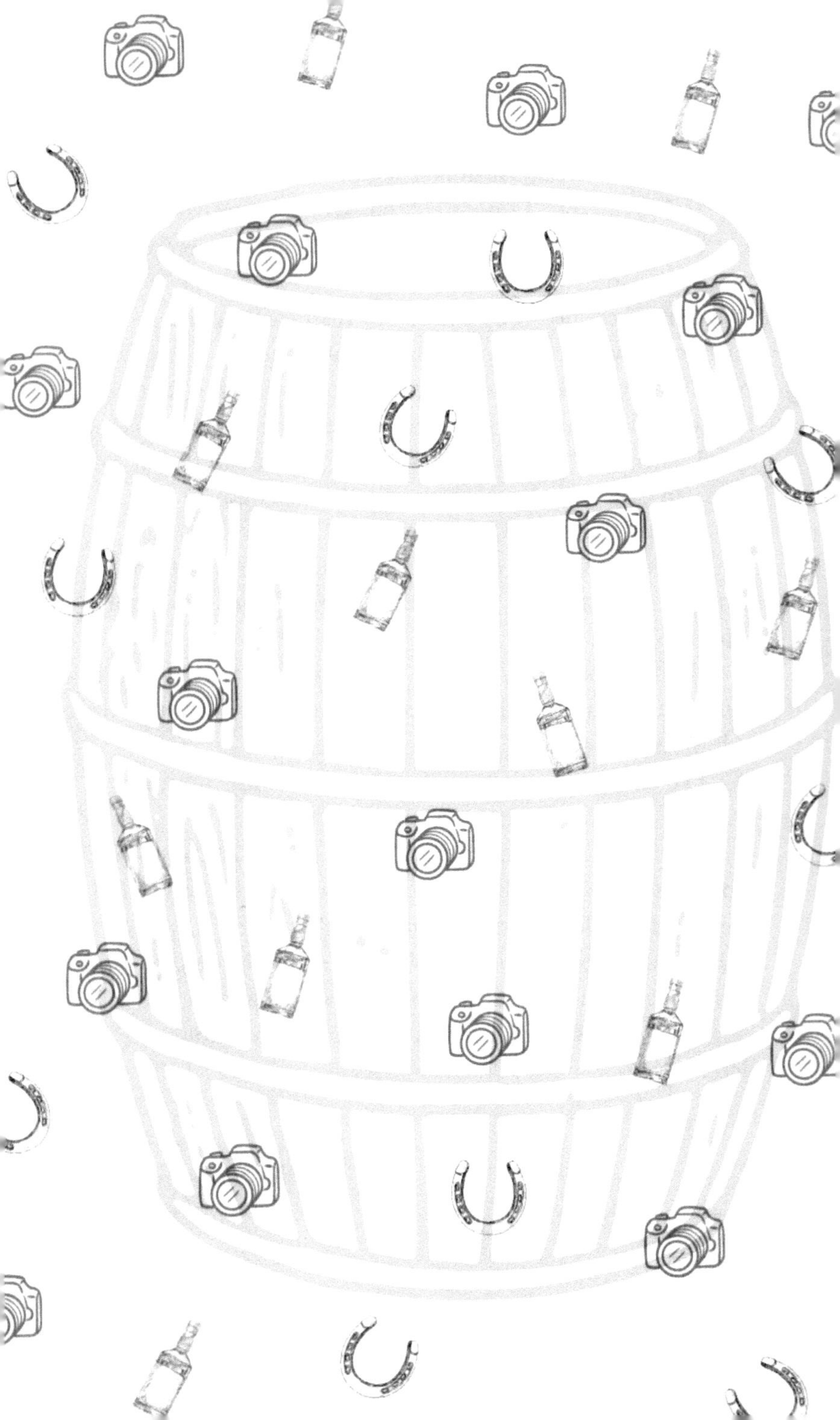

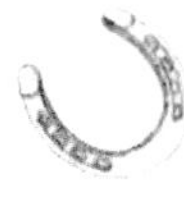

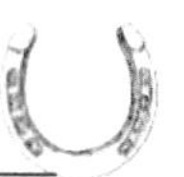

CHAPTER EIGHTEEN

Haven

She's not coming.

I wander behind my pickup. I'm parked at the distillery, and my brothers are probably inside, wondering what the hell I'm doing.

They've probably guessed. I'm in the spot we normally park in when we go fishing.

Is she coming?

I've texted her. I've debated stopping in at Bootleg. I've even driven by Silas's place. She never said if she was going fishing with me or not.

I went too far in the barn. I can't keep my damn hands off her, and she keeps letting me put my mouth on her.

It's a half hour past when I told her I'd be ready. If she wanted to go, she'd be here, or she would've let me know.

Message received loud and clear.

I don't feel like fishing anymore.

Swallowing past the burn in my esophagus, I head to

the distillery. I took the day off to fish, but that was unnecessary.

Clem's busy with customers at the merch counter. I keep going, dipping my head down. Lane's at a mash tank. He does a double take, and I toss him a wave.

"Change of plans," I say, trying to sound unbothered. "I'm going to pull the whiskey for Durban's wedding favors." I planned on doing it all tomorrow, but yay me. I have extra time.

"Mind double-checking everything we're bottling next week?"

"Sure thing." I walk right through into the packaging area and out the back door. I could have gone through the parking lot, but the excuse didn't come to me until I saw Lane was in there. He's working the tasting room tonight. Everyone but him and Clem is gone for the day.

I push into the rickhouse. I don't have to go hunting. The five-gallon white oak barrel is by the station where we sample a barrel before bringing it into the distillery. We have the same station set up inside the packaging area too.

After carrying the barrel to the table, I pause for a moment and puff out a breath. Do I try again with Prescott? She has no reason to step foot on my property. I told her I'm keeping the cats.

No. I won't try again.

The door pushes open with a squeak. Light filters through the dust hanging in the air.

I straighten. "Forget a barrel for tomorrow?"

"No?"

I spin at *her* voice. Prescott steps through the opening, her timid gaze finding mine.

"Red. Hey." I scratch the back of my neck. Why's she here? Did she arrive late, and I wasn't there?

"Haven, hi. Clem said I'd find you out here." She lets the door swing shut. She's wearing a loose cream dress with spaghetti straps and some sort of faint design. The flat sandals she has on aren't fishing shoes. "I'm...sorry."

"For what?" I'm the one always trying to paw her.

"For standing you up. Ignoring your texts. Getting weird after every time you touch me."

"I haven't noticed."

She does a double take before a quiet laugh leaves her. "I know. I can be subtle." She lifts her hands and lets them fall. "What are we doing? I mean, really."

She's talking about us, of course. Messing around with no strings attached isn't part of her routine, but it's my only one. She probably wants me to reassure her that we won't fall madly in love and won't be able to live apart. Words only go so far. How can I show her?

"We're standing in the rickhouse right now." When she scowls, I give her an encouraging smile. "We're not planning our future, we're not figuring out how to sneak out of each other's beds." I don't do that. I'm straightforward, but her ex was a liar. "We're talking. Just us. In the moment. Not worried about what tomorrow is."

"I've done nothing but worry about tomorrow. And wonder."

About whether she'll have work or get back on her feet financially? About me? She's opening up, so I continue with being in the moment. "Since I don't have a fishing partner, I'm working on Campbell and Durban's wedding favors."

That gets her to take a step forward. "Yeah? They're something from Foster House?"

I slap the small barrel. "They'll be little single-serve bottles of whiskey. I double-barreled a small amount of a batch we packaged a few months ago, one that we intend to do holiday infusions with."

She comes closer. "Like what?"

Now we're making headway. Getting back to being friends. The rest...maybe it'll come. "Apple and cinnamon."

"Yum. What flavor are you doing for the favors?"

"Vanilla and orange." I pick up the small copper whiskey thief. "I came out here to test it and see if it's ready."

"How do you do that?"

Smiling, I set out two tasting glasses. I remove the bung and extract a sample from the round hole. Then I splash some whiskey into each glass and hand her one.

She swirls the glass while I replace the bung. "Smells... woody?"

"It's stronger since I aged it again in a smaller barrel. I think it'll dampen the citrus but pair well with the vanilla. It'll be strong, but with only one serving, it should be the perfect strength." I lightly touch my glass to hers. "To the here and now."

"To the here and now," she says almost shyly and sniffs the whiskey. Her gaze gets a faraway look. "Whiskey, naturally. Also wood." She sniffs again. "Cherry?"

I swirl and smell. "Definitely cherry, which is why I think it'll also fit with vanilla and citrus."

"You put a lot of thought into this."

"I'm bottling a fifth for him and Campbell to celebrate on their one-year anniversary. I want to make sure it's good. He's usually the flavor guy, but he trusted me with this."

"It's clearly something you're good at."

Heat flushes through me, and my chest puffs up a little. It's not even a compliment. She stated it like a fact.

She takes a small sip and rolls it around, using all the skill I showed her. "I can't say I love it, but I can taste all the notes."

"That's my girl." We might go our separate ways, but she'll always remember me when she drinks or serves whiskey.

She blushes and inspects her drink. "So what barrels did I forget? When I entered, you asked if I forgot them."

"I thought you were Lane. He wanted me to find what we're bottling tomorrow and pull them."

She spins on a heel to take in the whole space. "It's quiet and peaceful." Inhaling, her eyelids drift shut. "It smells like dust with a hint of bread, wood, and also whiskey. How do you move the barrels?"

"The big warehouse in Denver has barrel elevators, tracks, and forklifts. We have a portable lift and a forklift to haul it to the main building." I gesture to the track that runs down the middle of the rickhouse. "We use that if we have several to move, but we usually work with single barrels and small batches because we're a novelty facility. Our goal is to play and let the public have fun with what we make."

"It's perfect. I'm itching to take pictures. There's so much I could do with lighting in here."

That gives me an idea, but it might just be an excuse to see her again. "What if I talked to the guys, and we hired you to do some shoots for this place?"

She opens her mouth and closes it again.

"We haven't updated our look online since we opened." Should I drop it? I don't even know if the guys would agree. The ones she took of me by the tanks were impressive, and it's not because I was the focus. "I'm not throwing work your way because I think you need it. The stuff you took with me, you really brought out the life in the place, and that's hard to do when nothing's moving."

"That'd be two freelance jobs I've gotten since I moved in with Papa, and I'm not counting your faux senior photo shoot."

"You took the library gig?"

"It's headshots and get this—animals for the rescue I was calling." She quirks her shoulders. "The one I called once."

"Because you knew those rescues found a sucker with me."

"I think I was the sucker." She flashes a tentative smile. "Apparently, Ellie checked with Clem to see if I was open to throwing my name out there for events. Mostly weddings."

"You said no to the 'I do.'"

Her laugh is a puff of air. "I never got a chance to say yes to my own, so I'm saying no to everyone else's."

"Never got a chance?" I scoff. "You're young yet."

"I'm factoring in getting strung along for another five years."

Damn. She sounds like she's joking, but there's a gravity in her eyes that's permanent.

She lifts her chin and gestures with the glass. "I'm really looking forward to working with the rescue though. It's nice to be behind the camera again. Taking pictures for the rescue gives it a little more oomph. I'm working for a cause instead of hustling for the bottom line."

Plus, if she's booking work in the area, that might mean she's going to stay longer.

I can't start thinking about a future with her. Here and now. "Do I get a sneak peek at the rescue images?"

"You'd be interested in that?"

"Cute animals?" I might end up with another dog and more cats. "Always, but mostly if it's you showing them to me." The fewer clothes she has on while doing it, the better.

Emotions ripple through her expression so fast I can't keep up. She sets her glass down. "How are you such a good guy and so off-limits?"

"I hear it's the boots."

"It is. They make a girl make bad decisions." She chuckles and shakes her head. Her hair is in a clip, and the ends swing around it.

"They can be some of the most earth-shattering ones though." I brush a loose copper curl behind her ear. "Take that clip out, Red. I haven't seen how long your hair is yet."

Her expression freezes. "Haven."

"If you don't want to do anything, we won't. If you want to seize the moment, fuck, I'm here with you."

Her eyes shine, and neither of us moves.

"What about Lane?" she whispers, holding my gaze. "And Clem."

"The merch store is closed, so Clem's probably gone home. The tasting room is open. Lane's working that." And if he saw her walk out here at all, he'll leave us alone.

"Is there..." She looks furtively around. "Is there anyone else here?"

"Everyone who might have business in the rickhouse is done for the day." I trail my fingers along her jaw. I drag my thumb down her chin and trace the column of her throat to her collarbone. The dress she's wearing only hints at her cleavage. A fucking tease.

Timidly, she reaches back and removes the claw clip. I shove my hands through her hair, spreading it around her shoulders. Curls spring to life and the silky strands caress my skin.

Letting her hair down is somehow more intimate than when I stripped her down in the barn. "You're a damn angel, and you make me want to sin so bad."

"Haven?" Her voice resonates with questions and so much more.

"Tell me what you need." I push through her brilliant strands to trace her collarbone.

"I need…" She squeezes her eyes shut. "I need to feel like I'm enough for now."

Her statement tears through me. The vulnerability. The assumption that it would only be temporary, pretend, because she'll never measure up.

"Will you let me show you that you are?" I back her to the table and move our glasses to the side. Her ass hits the edge just perfectly. "Will you let me show you that you're always enough? That if you ever feel like you're not, it's because the other person isn't worthy of you?"

A breath puffs out of her lips. "Wow." She pokes me lightly in the shoulder. "Are you real?"

"I very much want you to find out that I am."

She glances furtively around. "Is it okay? In here?"

"We can do a lot fully dressed, Red." We can do it all. I drag my wallet out of my pocket and find the emergency condom I keep on me. I haven't needed one for months, but I refreshed it after I kissed her. I think about the future too.

I set it next to her and cup the back of her neck. I don't smash my mouth onto her. True, we're in a place for a quick fuck. The possibility that someone could walk in isn't zero. But I want to make sure she comes so fucking hard she can barely walk. I'll take care of her.

I brush my lips over hers once, twice. Then I press my mouth against hers and run my hands down her arms. Tipping her chin up to give me better access, I delve inside. She's warm and sweet, and all the notes she named on my whiskey are still on her tongue. She's my very own tasting. I just have to make sure that when we're done, I don't walk away wanting the whole bottle.

Dragging her straps down, I kiss down the same path I took with my fingers. Her pulse hammers against my breath and matches the pounding in my dick. I stop at the base of her throat.

"Are you nervous?" I lick a short path on her skin. The slight saltiness is like tasting the richest whiskey.

"Yes. And no."

Goddamn, she's unraveling me while stringing me into the tightest damn knot. My erection begs to be released. Soon.

I kiss back up her neck and line her jaw. I press against the shell of her ear. "Open your legs for me." When she widens them, I don't do anything more than fist my hands in the material of her skirt. "Did you wear this hoping I'd fuck you today?"

"No. I was determined to resist the fishing trip." She draws in a shuddering inhale. "But also...yes."

Triumph slams through my veins. I claim her mouth again, and our tongues dance together. Tugging her skirt up, my knuckles brush her thighs and a groan leaves me.

Are we really going to do this?

I've wanted to for so long, but here? Now?

She answers my unspoken question by yanking and tugging at the button and zipper of my fly. She succeeds in opening it, and when her fingers graze my cock, I jolt like

I got slapped by a downed power line. Then she curls her warm hand around my erection and strokes it.

I have to break our kiss and suck in a breath. "Fuck."

"I want to look at you."

We're both still standing. I don't release her skirt, but I let her study as much of me as she wants. She rubs her thumb over the glistening tip, then circles around the blunt head. My abs clench so hard I'm going to be stiff tomorrow.

"I knew you'd have a nice dick." She slides her hand up and down again. My stomach clenches, and air saws in and out of me. "It's so strong. Just like you."

"You're gonna make me blush."

She shoots me the sexiest smirk before grabbing the condom. Without letting me go, she uses her teeth to open it and shakes the wrapper off. Shoving the flaps of my pants and my underwear farther out of the way, she rolls it on, taking her damn time.

"If you take any longer, I'll come from that alone."

"You make a girl feel good, Hennessy."

Good isn't enough. She needs to feel how hard she makes me. How close to the brink she pushes me. How much I can't quit thinking about that ass, those tits, or the smile that brightens a sunny day. This might not be the ideal place, but it's the perfect moment. Because we're both here. And we both need it.

I yank up her skirt. As soon as I see her underwear, a grunt escapes. "We're going to keep these in place. No one's going to come in, but if it happens, you'll be fully clothed."

"But your hard-on will be on display."

"And it'll be irritated as hell at the interruption." I hitch her onto the table, and she automatically wraps her legs around my waist. The height is so damn perfect, it's like this time and place is exactly when we were supposed to finally give in. The way we line up? Can it be any more fitting?

She grips my shoulders, and I hold her gaze as I lick my thumb. Her pupils widen as I find her hot little clit. "Red, baby. You're soaked."

"Haven." She whimpers and wiggles against me.

My cock is getting throttled between us, but she's wet and ready. I scoot her skirt farther up. "Hold this," I say gruffly. "And watch me fuck you."

Her hands tremble when her fingers curl around the material. I press her panties—a cream pair this time that blends perfectly with the color of her dress—to the side.

My grip has a tremor when I fist my cock and place myself. Slowly, I rock my hips forward. The tip disappears inside, and I hiss. Heat sears my skin, and I use every ounce of restraint to keep from driving in.

She moans as I feed myself inside her. My muscles quiver, but I hold as still as possible, only my hips moving.

"Watch yourself take all of me." My words are guttural. Most of my brain has shut off, but the pleasure centers are lit like a big city on a dark night.

She rocks ever so slightly, and I snap, pushing in the rest of the way.

Her, "God, Haven," gets mixed with my groan.

I grip her legs, helping hold them up and hinge my hips back before plunging once again inside. "Fuck, Red." I do it again. "Just fuck."

We watch as I thrust in and out of her. Pleasure swells and builds, and I have tunnel vision. Only her and her sweet pussy fill my sight. The way her eyes gleam, dazed and stunned, pushes me closer to an edge that I might not recover from. Her cheeks are flushed, and if I had her naked with her hair spread around her, I'd know how far the blush spread over her lush body.

My whole body is tense. I'm fighting off a climax until I can't anymore. "Touch yourself like you do when you're thinking of me."

She puts her index and middle finger on her clit and circles, going faster than I would, but my rhythm's also increasing. I grab one of the tasting glasses, shoot the whiskey back, and manage to set it down without breaking it. Then I claim her mouth.

She opens for me. Whiskey flows between us, back and forth, heating us as much as we're warming it. A drop escapes, and another. The sound of our sloppy kiss fills the room, matching the beat of our flesh slamming together.

Her legs clamp around me, tighter than a vise. She rips her mouth from mine and tips her head back. Her body fists me hard. "Haven!"

My orgasm rams into me so fast and hard. I hang on to her legs, but this time it's to keep me standing. I explode inside her, and goddamn, nothing has ever felt better.

We buck against each other until our movements slow. Until we're still and holding on to each other. This would be considered a quickie, but it rocked my entire existence. Something's changed, and I can't put a finger on it. I don't want to. Live in the moment.

She has her arms wrapped loosely around my neck, and she's fiddling with the ends of my hair.

"Red?"

"Yeah?" She sounds drowsy.

"I know I said that we should just enjoy the here and now, but I've gotta know when we can do this again."

Prescott

"Fuck. Ride me," Haven grips my hips.

We're sprawled on a blanket on the ground. His jeans are shoved to his knees, and I've pushed his shirt up as far as it'll go without taking it off. My pants are on the blanket he packed for our riding session, and my tank top is twisted to show my sports bra. Biscuits and Gravy are tied off on a fence post and grazing, while Haven and I are partially concealed by a small copse of trees that found purchase in the valley we're in.

I'm astride him, and he's inside me. The sun beats down on us as if we aren't working up a sweat on our own. Pleasure presses outward inside of me, seeking an escape. His mouth is at my neck, the nibble of his teeth sending electric bolts up and down my spine. But there's one thing that's keeping me from exploding. A pain that doesn't usually go along with sex. Definitely not the sex I've had.

"Haven?"

"Yeah?" he grunts.

"There's a rock digging into my knee."

He immediately hugs me to him, and in one roll, I'm on my back, knees in the air, bracketing his body. He doesn't bother shoving his belongings out of the way. It's like he has a single-minded focus on making me peak. I wiggle to the side, but he clamps his hands back on my hips.

"Your hat!" My head is almost crushing his cowboy hat, but he plunges in, filling me more completely than ever.

"Don't worry about it." He punctuates each word with

a thrust, and it pushes me right to the edge. I'm teetering. "Concentrate on me." Thrust. "On this." Thrust.

I dig my heels into his ass. He dips his head and nibbles along my neck. Shivers rack my body, and that's all I need. I fly over my peak into oblivion, soaring and floating in a way that's only happened with him.

"Haven!" My voice carries through the valley.

"Fuck, yes." He braces himself on his hands, like he's watching me, and it makes the orgasm hit stronger and continue longer.

One of the horses whinnies, but I'm focused on him bucking inside me, his hot release filling me. When he collapses, I catch him, wrapping my arms around his shoulders and hooking my ankles around his waist.

He can throw me around like I'm no more than a bag of potatoes, and damn, it makes me feel dainty. That's not a normal sensation for me. I wouldn't trade my height for anything. I like reaching the top of the cabinets, grabbing canned goods for random strangers in the grocery store, and sitting farther away from the steering wheel. Yet I didn't realize the trade-off was feeling bulky with men—but not Haven.

"What's going on in that beautiful head of yours?" he murmurs into my neck.

I pet his silky hair. Does he have a special product, or is everything about him the highest quality? "You mean other than how our fishing trip and horseback ride turned into a sex fest?"

He chuckles, his breath gusting across my skin and sending shivers rolling over me. "Unlike yesterday, we actually went horseback riding."

I could keep my earlier thoughts to myself, but it doesn't seem right around him. I've been able to talk to

Haven about stuff that would normally embarrass me. Not that my height or size does. It's just another thing that's different with him than anyone else. "I was thinking about how you make me feel petite."

He lifts his head. "You never been thrown around, Red?"

"Uh, no." I laugh. "Not picked up, or thrown, or carried."

"I'd carry you back, but Biscuits gets a little distracted without a rider."

"They're a good match. Gravy gets distracted *with* a rider."

He grins and props himself on an elbow. A cabbage moth flutters by, and the sound of insects buzzing grows louder now that we're quieter. "This worked out better than I thought."

"You make it sound like you've never taken a girl out on horseback just to get laid."

He arches a brow. "I haven't. Have you?"

"Before you took me out, I hadn't ridden since I was a kid." I gently push him away. He withdraws, and I roll to find my pants. "I could've told you it'd work. I suspect Papa did it a lot back in the day."

"I don't care to imagine that, nor can I promise that Biscuits and Gravy haven't stood by while someone else had sex around them. They were both older when I got them."

"The stories they could tell."

I squirm into my pants without rolling all over the blanket, while he dresses and takes care of the condom with an empty baggie from the snacks he packed.

I'm about to get up when he plops down next to me. "We got time. Unless you need to rush off."

"I do have a busy life." I sit with my legs crossed.

He smirks and stretches out on his stomach next to me. "I'm sucking up all your precious time."

I treasure each minute with him. "Well, I have this guy's birthday to plan. It's coming up soon."

He rests his head on his arms. "He probably doesn't deserve it."

I scowl at him, but his eyes are closed, and there's a contented smile on his face. "I think he does, and he should know it."

He cracks an eye open. "It's just a birthday."

I pluck a piece of grass from next to the blanket. The strand is crunched from us moving around, and I run it through my fingers. "My mom used to make them a big deal, and when I asked her why, she said it's because *I'm* a big deal."

"She's right."

"She would say that about you too."

His lips form a troubled line. "Why?"

"Because she was like that. Wanted people to feel special because no one made her feel that way."

He's quiet for a moment. "What would she have done for my birthday?"

"What age are we talking?"

He flips to his back and folds his hands behind his head and crosses his feet. He's a plank of sexy cowboy, and if we were in a private space instead of the wide-open pasture, we'd both probably be naked. "Does age matter?"

I scoff. "Oh, it matters. I got bouncy house parties and pool parties and arcade-slash-bowling parties when I was in elementary school. Then it turned into slumber parties with movies and spa nights. When I was a teen, she would call me out of school if my birthday was on a weekday.

We'd get our nails done, go to lunch, and she'd take me shopping."

"Damn. What if it was a weekend?"

"That's when she could really go big. One year, she took me to Disneyland."

"For a birthday present?"

"My present that year was my first digital camera." I let out a wistful sigh. "She took me to Disneyland so I could practice. Where else would I find people and characters and castles and fireworks? I took so many pictures."

"She sounds like an amazing person."

"She was." I run the grass stem through my fingers. "I wish she had found her person. Someone who would've spent their life loving her and making her feel as special as she made everyone else feel. I tried, but it was important to her that I live my own life."

I lie back and align my legs with his. The edges of the blanket rustle in the breeze. This is the closest to cuddling we're going to get.

After a few minutes, he props himself on an elbow and faces me. He trails a finger from the middle of my sternum to my belly button and flattens his hand. A furrow creases his forehead, but he doesn't speak right away. "Are you working Wednesday night?"

"Probably. Why? Got something in your tack room to inspect?"

"Yes, and it's best to look at it without clothes." He flashes me a grin. "No, Myles is coming out, and he's bringing Mae."

"Mae Bailey?" His foster mom?

"Yeah. Usually, when she comes, one of us will host a meal, and it's my turn. I'll open up the garage, and we'll all gather. Do you... Do you wanna come?"

I want to shout *absolutely*!, but I also want to forget he asked. "Is it a party?"

"Sort of. We just all get together."

"Who's we?"

"Me. Iverson and his family. Durban and Campbell. Lane and Cruz. Elodie will probably be there. Clem and Edna sometimes come too. Anyone associated with Foster House."

A burn sets in the back of my throat. I'm not a part of that group. "I don't know. I'd feel like a third wheel. I don't really have much to do with the distillery." Other than hooking up with one of its owners.

"If you take pictures for us, you'll be part of the crew."

"You haven't gotten approval yet." I didn't truly expect him to ask.

"I will." His answer rings with confidence.

"Before Wednesday?"

"If you need it before then."

I could show up and be one of the Foster House gang. I've talked to Jamison and Campbell a little. Clem slightly more. But I don't know any of them, and one crochet club doesn't seem like enough not to make everyone think there's something between me and Haven.

Is there? We're supposed to be living in the moment, not planning family functions together. Will everyone get the wrong idea about us?

Will I?

Have I already? Am I harboring a hope built out of a fantasy?

Come on, Prescott. Make one smart decision around this guy and tell him no.

"I told Papa that I'd help him do a deep clean." I'll tell him tonight, anyway.

His expression shutters. "Oh, yeah. No problem. Just thought if you could make it, I'd throw it out there. You gonna go to Hookers and Booze on Monday?"

A huge boulder lands on my chest. The urge to tell him, *no, it's fine, I'll be there, what can I bring?* rests heavy on my tongue. But we've crossed so many lines already. If I'm not careful, I'll fall off the edge.

Since I held strong for that, I'll dig out the crochet bag I haven't touched since the last Hookers and Booze. "Yes. I'm going."

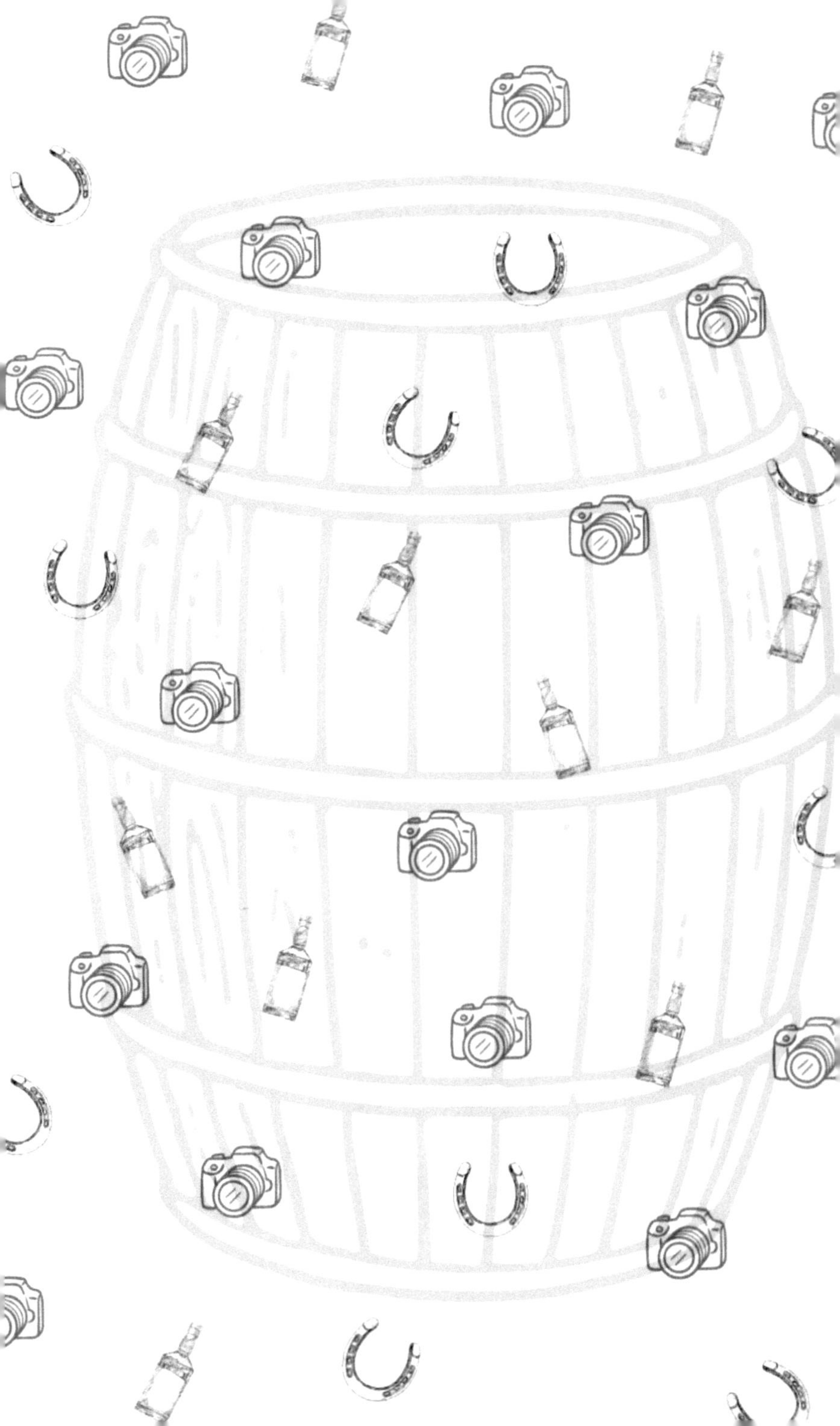

CHAPTER NINETEEN

Haven

"That's what I was thinking to update our image." I tap my fingers on the long table in our meeting room on the second floor of the distillery. Windows overlook the stills on one side.

Four pairs of eyes scrutinize me.

Iverson wiggles a pen between two fingers. "Have you shown all the guys the pictures your girlfriend took?"

Durban folds his hands in front of his stomach and rocks in the office chair. "They're really good."

"She's not my girlfriend." Sourness stains my tongue. If she were my girlfriend, she'd probably come to the gathering Wednesday night.

"What pictures?" Lane looks around. Cruz shrugs.

I dig out my phone and pull up the gallery. "I let Prescott pretend she was taking my senior photos since I never did it when I was actually a senior. She suggested using the distillery."

I flip to the first image. The one when I led her inside and gazed at the place like it was heaven. Is that how I usually look?

Lane takes my phone, and his dark brows draw together. He and Cruz lean toward each other and scroll through them. I swivel back and forth in my chair. The back of my neck heats like there's a spotlight shining right on me.

Cruz lets out a low whistle. "Those are really good."

Lane slides my phone back to me. "You don't look like you're pretending."

"Maybe because I really did graduate. They're just twenty-two years too late." I shut the screen off, or I'll slide through the gallery, letting memories of that day sweep over me. Not that I've done that a time or two, when I'm going to bed and wishing Prescott was with me.

"Too bad she didn't get here earlier," Durban says. "We could've hired her for our wedding."

"She doesn't do weddings." When he gives me a quizzical look, I just shrug. The story isn't his business.

Lane glances at each of us. "Seems none of us mind. I can't argue her work is better than the guy Myles sent down."

Cruz shakes his head. "No, that guy had some great shots, but Prescott captured the vibe." The essence. She gets right to the heart of her subjects.

"Agreed," Iverson says. "She managed to keep Haven from looking hideous."

I rub my eye with my middle finger, and Iverson smirks at me.

"Go ahead and set it up," Lane says. "Website photos and new brochure shots. Maybe she can get us some for socials. Wynter got a lot of videos, but maybe she won't mind new stuff. Get her pricing before we agree."

Be cool, or they'll think it's more serious than it is. "She'll be here for crochet club. I can ask her."

Durban threads his hands behind his head. "Is that why you wanted to work today?"

"It's my turn." Do I sound believable? None of them looks like they are buying it. I push out of my chair. "I'm going to open the tasting room. How many of you are heading down?"

Iverson sticks a finger in the air. Durban nods. Cruz grins, shameless.

Lane scrubs a hand down his face. "Unless I'm going to hit on Edna, which is not allowed as her supervisor—"

"Could be the thirty-year age difference," Cruz interrupts.

Lane gives him a flat stare, but humor dances in his eyes. "No. I'll be the only one not joining in. You hussies have fun."

I push out of my chair and race downstairs. Will Prescott really come? Will I get a chance to be alone with her?

The way she declined my invite for Wednesday gave me a steady stream of heartburn. What did she think? That I was getting too serious? Like I was trying to introduce her to my mother?

That won't be happening. Ever. Prescott doesn't need my mother's chaos in her life. No one close to me does.

My phone buzzes, and a dark cloud shadows me. The ominous feeling crests when I look at the text. It's like she has a sixth sense.

Mom: Fucking landlord is threatening eviction.

She needs money, of course.

Me: How much do you need?
Mom: Two hundred.
I pull up my bank app and send her the amount.
Me: Done.
Mom: Thank you. How are your brothers?
My stomach knots.
Me: You should ask them.
Mom: You should come down.
Shocked, I look around. Do I tell my brothers she invited me to Gillette?
Me: Something wrong?
Mom: Miss you. That's all.
The ends of the knot pull taut. Does she mean it? Or will I get down there and be left outside knocking on her door?
Does she remember that my birthday is coming up?
Me: Any specific day?
Mom: Why not for your birthday?
She remembered! I'm like a kid getting told we're going to Disneyland to use my new camera. Mom remembered my birthday.
Me: How about Sunday? I work on my birthday.
I glance around again. My brothers would tell me it's a bad idea. Going to Gillette is the minimum I can do, and the fact I'm surprised is a red flag. But I'm thrilled. There's only one person I want to tell about this conversation and she should be arriving soon.

Good thing I brought my sad dishcloth to work with me today. When I arrived, I stuffed it under the tasting room counter. Now that everyone's been served, it's giving me an excuse to sit with Prescott and Campbell.

My ass should be behind the bar, building some resistance to Prescott. I should back off a little instead of finding reasons to be around her, but each orgasm she gives me knocks my determination back. She's a single barrel, and now that I've tasted her, I can only think about having another sip.

"This is going to be my something blue." Campbell holds up a circular piece she's been working on. It's lacey and a light enough blue that it won't show through the material of her dress. "A garter."

"That's going in the TMI pile," I say, finishing off a row and turning. This dishcloth is going to be a rag in the barn. It's atrocious.

Prescott smiles. "I think it's wonderful to incorporate a part of your life into the wedding tradition. You need to make sure your photographer gets a picture of it."

Campbell stands and slaps the garter to the side of her cocked leg. "Like hold my dress up and show it off?" She tilts her head like she's picturing how it'll look. "Yeah, I like it."

"That," Prescott says while concentrating, "and you can have Durban on his knees, looking at you like he's ready to rip it off with his teeth."

Christ. All that flashes through my head is me, with a knee on the ground, gazing up at her. She'd have her hair piled on her head, those impressive tits spilling out of a slinky wedding dress, and her thigh playing peekaboo until I can barely get through the night without ripping her clothes off.

I clear my throat. Those dreams aren't for me. I'm not

the type who makes a woman want to stick around for the long haul, but the image is emblazoned into my brain.

Edna gasps from the next table over and covers her mouth. "Prescott, that's the most perfect idea for a pose. If only I were in my twenties again and trolling for a husband."

"Edna, I'm surprised," I cut in. My voice is gruff, but I wrestle it under control. "You don't need to be in your twenties to do that."

She winks and gives me an indulgent grin. "I've taught you well."

Campbell takes a seat again. "Your wedding photos are so gorgeous. Yes—I snooped. Couples must've been knocking down your door to book you."

I stiffen, but Prescott just shrugs. "I was doing okay. I would be recovering from one right now if I had stayed, and yeah, weddings would've been what I did the most. But when I moved, I decided not to go back."

"Instead, you get your gorgeous summer weekends to yourself." Campbell focuses on tying off her garter.

When Prescott slides a discreet look my way, I cock a brow. I had her to myself for some of a gorgeous summer weekend.

"I have the wedding favors all packaged," I tell Campbell.

She grins. "I love the label you made. It's perfect, thank you."

A couple on a horse riding off into the sunset has meaning for them. "You're welcome."

Campbell drops her hands to the tabletop, her project still clutched in her fingers. "Oh my god, Prescott, you must think I'm so rude. You are invited, of course. I would've gotten you an invitation sooner, but I was waiting to see—" She looks at me, and her gaze skitters to Prescott. "Um, I think I have an extra."

Shit. I didn't ask Prescott. A band cinches around my chest. A wedding is just so... It's not sex in the rickhouse or making out on the porch. It's a hardcore date, and we don't do that. *I* don't do that. Although with Prescott, it might be fun. But she hates weddings. So that's that.

"Oh, no." Prescott tucks her chin down and concentrates on her next double crochet. "It's fine. I don't want to intrude on your special day."

Campbell shakes her head. "Silas said he's going to close the bar that day since he wants to come."

"Papa said that?"

"To be fair, it was months ago," I say. I was at the bar that night, and it was before invites were sent out. Silas brought it up like he was excited. Not what we usually see out of the mellow bar owner.

"I'm sure he'll keep his word." Prescott's smile is tight. "Do you, uh, need an RSVP?"

"Nope." Campbell starts packing up her bag when Durban enters. "You come if you can. The more the merrier—I mean it. Durban and I really just want to celebrate with our friends and family. If it storms, if it snows, if every single cow gets out, we're going with the flow. No uptight bride and groom allowed."

Iverson and I will make sure of it. And if Iverson gets wrapped up with his wife and kids, I'll see that all the details are carried out. Since I won't have a date.

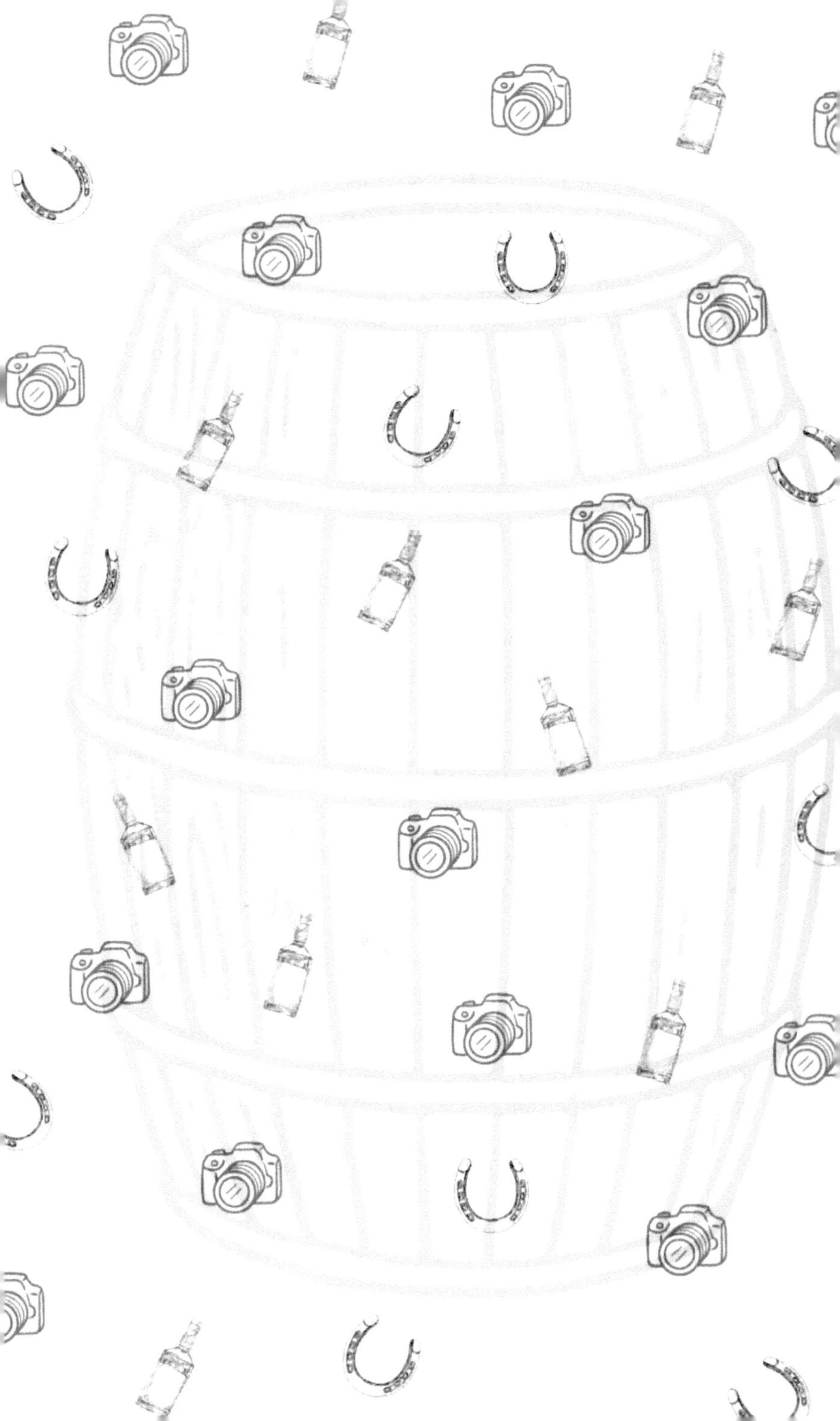

CHAPTER TWENTY

Prescott

I missed the Hennessy, Foster, and Bailey festivities last night, but I'm once again behind my camera. I get lost in my work, arranging the few employees of the Huckleberry Springs Public Library for their headshots. I'm taking it above and beyond the typical headshot. They're paying for the simple photo, but I want to hand them back a personalized, yet professional reflection of themselves. Everyone deserves to be seen.

Clem's sitting on the reading chair she uses when she reads to kids. Her legs are crossed, and the two buns in her hair have glittery gold strands twisted in them. She hitches her shoulders up, smiles, and looks up. It's a cute and quirky pose. The rapid clicks of my camera fill the room, then I look through the images.

"Perfect." I take the camera to her and let her see.

Her eyes flare. "Oh my god. I look fun and cute."

"Probably because you are." I flip through all the

images from today. I have several of each employee for them to choose from. "Are the animals ready?"

"Yes. Dr. Small is with Janelle from the rescue to wrangle and do some checkups and vaccinations."

"It's like a full-service spa day." Bring it on. I need the distraction.

The bar was dead last night, giving me ample time to wonder how the meal was going. Was Haven talking about me? Am I only a nameless friend? Was there no reason to bring me up at all?

What do I want the answers to be?

I follow Clem outside.

"We'll do the dogs first, if you don't mind," she says over her shoulder. "The foster families are bringing them by."

So many rescues for such a small town. "Point me toward a critter, and I'll shoot."

"Depending on who says that, it can have different meanings around here."

The sound of a dog barking comes from a car. "That one's excited." Time to put my reaction time to the test.

For the next two hours, I have the time of my life. Clem and I laugh until our bellies hurt. I have images of dogs jumping in the air for a treat or a ball, an older Great Pyrenees that was surrendered to the vet clinic curled up in the bed of a pickup, and puppies rolling around together like multicolored cotton balls. After them, I gather shots of cats stalking feathers, kittens batting at each other, and one adorable tortie curled up in the crook of Janelle's arm. In between everything, I gather videos and act like both a stalker and a paparazzo.

I'm packing up my camera when Dr. Small stops next to me.

"This is a good thing you're doing." She runs a hand down her long black braid and squints around. "It feels like a losing battle, finding every stray a home. Your efforts are really going to help."

"I'm happy to try. Janelle says the rescue has at least one online profile?"

"Between the two of us, we manage to post sort of regularly. It can get overwhelming."

Ideas swirl in my head. "I can't promise any reach, but I can start a couple of new accounts and tailor them as locally as possible. At least to the four-oh-six."

"Just Montana?" She nods, her expression thoughtful. "I'm sure we'd have volunteers to relocate rescues an hour or two away. Even to some parts of Wyoming. Yeah. We need all the help we can get. Our seams are bursting. You talked Haven into keeping all the others?"

I shake my head. "He came to that conclusion himself. They're good mousers."

She flips her braid over her shoulder. "He's a good guy, and he needed a dog. Told him all ranchers do, but he hated losing the last one. And his cats."

Because Haven has a gigantic heart.

Her phone goes off, and she grimaces. "Almost made it through the day without an emergency call, but at least I made it through all the animals. Nice to see you again, Prescott." She turns her back and answers her phone.

I don't have time to run home. I told Papa I'd be later than normal tonight. I didn't want to be rushed, but I hate to leave him hanging. Last Friday, when I tracked down Haven after standing him up, Papa got slammed. He slept all through the next morning until lunchtime.

I'll bring my camera with me.

By the time I get to Bootleg, I have a message.

Haven: Can you take distillery pictures on Friday? Myles can come back for them.

Let me check my busy schedule. Haven's birthday is the next day, but I can grab what I need before then and prepare it all on Saturday while Haven works.

Me: No problem.

As I enter the bar, Papa's serving a group of tourists. They probably came from the river. They're all dressed in loose, breathable clothing, and one girl didn't put a shirt over her swim top.

After stowing my camera under the bar counter, I get to work, taking orders and grabbing refills. The night goes by fast. At closing time, Papa shuffles everyone out the door and comes over.

"I can clean up," I tell him. "You go home."

Fatigue lines his face. How much longer can he work day after day in this place? Holding it all up on his aging shoulders?

"I'll sweep up first. Hate doing dishes."

"I know." Anyone who's frequented Bootleg before knows he hates washing dishes. "You feeling okay?"

"I'm feeling like I got bucked around on too many bulls when I was younger." He disappears down the hallway to grab the broom. When he returns, I'm at the sink, my hands in soapy water. If he'd let me look at the books, I could see if he could afford a small dishwasher.

He rests a hand on the broom. "You and that Hennessy boy still talking?"

We're doing more than talking every chance we get, which hasn't been a lot. "Sort of, yeah."

"He hasn't charmed you?"

In so many ways and in a few positions. Papa's worried

I'll lose my heart with my pants. He doesn't know Haven very well. "No."

"Good."

"Yeah. Good."

When I get to the last glass, he's finished a light sweep and closed all the blinds on the windows. He heads to the door, throwing me a wave. "No one's in the lot, and Deputy Palmer is on duty. You got this?"

"I'm too wired to sleep, so I'll probably mop."

"I'll lock this behind me. Check before you go out."

"Night, Papa." I'm parked right by the door, just in case. Papa's quit worrying about leaving me alone to lock up, but he still tosses out warnings like a worried dad. I don't hate it.

After he's gone, quiet sets in, and I sigh. Time to mop. At least I can look forward to editing cute images of animals after I wake in the morning. Just as I'm rounding the counter, there's a knock on the door. My heart lurches into my throat.

Who the hell would be here at this time of night? I creep toward the entrance.

"Who is it?" Can I sound any less intimidating?

"Haven."

I practically leap to the door and whip it open. I should've checked first, but I know what he sounds like.

He's bracing himself on the frame, no hat, his eyes dark in the dim glow of the outside light. "Hey. I couldn't sleep."

I step back to let him in and flip the lock behind him. "That wild of a party?"

"Must've been. Meadow loved it, and she's gonna sleep for twelve hours straight. I think it's safe to say she's been exposed to a lot of kids now."

It's good for her. And for Haven to have everyone at his house. "I was just going to mop and head out."

He runs a hand through his hair. "Yeah. Of course. You want to get home."

Wait—he's here. I have him to myself. There's no need to rush. There's nowhere else for us to go. Bootleg is the last business open. Not even the gas station is open twenty-four hours. An idea sparks. "I'm not in a big hurry. Papa groans a lot when he's getting settled. Want to see the photos I took today?"

A grin spreads across his handsome face. "Can I?"

"Of the animals. You'll have to wait for the library's headshots until they post them."

"There's only one headshot I want to see."

"I haven't had one for years." I grab my camera case from under the bar. He takes a stool, and I sit next to him. "The dogs are first."

He chuckles going through them. "There are a lot of blurs."

"Those buggers took all my skill to get some decent shots. I'm not a sports photographer." I rub my hands on my shorts. "I offered to start some online accounts for them. Try to hustle for them."

"Yeah? You're opening your influencer doors again?"

"No," I say quickly. "I'm just going to get them more visibility. I can hand over the logins when I move."

A muscle jumps in his jaw. "Right. I'm sure they'll appreciate any help." He continues to scroll through photos. "Which is your favorite?"

"The puppies, when they got tired and passed out in random spots."

"What about of all time?"

His. Hands down every single one I took of Haven.

"Um...probably Buford." He's a close second. "I have one when he's in a sunbeam and his eyes glow. It's like he had powers."

"That was your first post."

My brows lift. "You scrolled all the way through them?"

He focuses hard on the dog image we stopped on. "Sometimes I can't sleep. What's your favorite photo of you?"

"None." When he gives me a *seriously?* look, I shrug. "It's not that I don't like pictures of myself. I'm usually *behind* the camera."

He nudges the camera. "Show me how to use this."

"Why?" Surely, he can't be thinking about—

"You should have pictures of yourself. Show me."

I like the idea of Haven using my equipment way too much. "Okay, well, right now, it's just a plain camera." I poke at the screen and adjust the settings for the dim indoors of Bootleg. "Just press and hold that button. It'll autofocus on the subject."

"Like this?" He aims the lens at me.

I sway to the side. "Whoa. Whoa. That's going to be up my nose."

He chuckles and hops off the stool. "How would you pose yourself?"

I'm not self-conscious. I'm *not*. Yet I don't answer seriously. "Reclining on a settee with a sheet artfully draped over me like a Renaissance painting."

"We're a local bar. No settee." He snaps a picture. "No sheet."

I throw a hand up. "Hey!" I huff out a breath. He's set to do this. I might as well humor him. I can delete all the images later. "Fine. Stay there."

I twist to the side, put an elbow on the bar, and rest my chin in my hand. The rapid fire of clicks fills the air.

He lowers the camera. "Next pose."

I slip off the stool and go behind the counter. "Get me from the side, almost like an action shot."

"Do you have to change the speed or something?" He lines himself up at my right.

"Nope. I'll do short motions to add depth." I dig out the silver shaker Papa and I almost never use. I hold it to the side opposite Haven. "Get ready."

Once we're done with that pose, he lowers the camera and rakes his gaze down my body. "Now take your clothes off."

Haven

She's not going to do it. Standing in her dad's bar, wearing a pale-green shirt and jean shorts, she's going to tell me I'm being ridiculous. She's going to tell me how tired she is and ask to call it a night. Then she grips the hem of her shirt and drags it over her head. Her creamy tits jiggle in the same pale-blue bra she wore when we were in the tack room.

Blood rushes to my dick. I've been talking it down since I arrived, but this time I don't. Pressure grows behind my zipper, and I look into the screen of the camera. I snap some pictures.

Her gaze drifts from my hands to my face. "I can't believe I'm doing this," she murmurs, and shucks her pants off. She leaves her sandals piled with her pants.

"Underclothes too."

"Haven!"

"You're right. I need some pictures like this." She's an angelic beauty in the viewfinder. Her comment about the Renaissance painting is spot on. The curves, the demure expression, the pink tint to the apples of her cheeks. Where can I fit a settee in my house? "Grip the counter behind you."

She licks her lower lip, hesitant, but she does it. The pose pushes her breasts out, and she bends a knee. Instinctive. After I get some shots that only fuel the heat pounding through my veins, I'm not ready to quit. "Turn around. Get that ass in the air."

She sticks her hips out, and her ass rounds in a way that robs all the moisture from my mouth. So fucking perfect.

I take more pictures as she rolls through poses. When she reaches up to free her hair from its clip, I'm struck with dizziness. There's no damn blood left for my brain. It's all in my raging erection.

Only because I need to immortalize the fantasy she's bringing to life, I get several more shots before lust makes me stop. "Come here."

She pauses for a second, then picks her way toward me. The vulnerability in her eyes is a stark reminder of the power I have. I slide her bra straps down and reach behind her to unhook her bra. It falls loose, and her tits are free.

I caress down one soft globe before I pull out a stool and pat the surface. Then I take a few steps back. Like before, she has to think for a moment before complying.

"I can't believe I'm doing this," she says again before planting her sweet ass on the stool.

"Think of me as your personal boudoir photographer."

She chuckles, and *damn*, it does things to her boobs that could drive me to my knees. But she crosses one leg over the other, angles herself to the side, and looks coquettishly over her shoulder. "I'd need more equipment for that."

"My god, Red." I press the button like my life depends on it. "You're determined to make sure I'm never going to sleep again." Not with these memories to haunt me.

I close the distance between us and set her camera on the bar. Her hair's off her shoulders, and I spread out the brilliant strands and drape the tresses over her shoulders. They fall down her chest and I tunnel through them to palm her breasts.

Lust beats at my temples. "You're like my very own mermaid."

"I don't have a tail or scales."

"Trust me." I drag her underwear down. She lifts her hips so I can get them all the way down to her thighs. I push my knee between hers. "That's for the best, or I couldn't do this."

Sinking to the floor, I'm at eye level with her navel. She tries to suck in her stomach and starts to squirm. To keep her distracted, I tug her underwear all the way off.

She pulls her legs in, but I still her with my hands on her knees. "Don't hide from me." I brush up her satiny skin. "Since I first saw your creamy butt cheeks in the ditch, I've only wanted to see more."

"You say the sweetest nothings." A smile plays over her lips.

"With you, it's never nothing."

"Oh my god, that's going to get you laid." There's something in her tone, a playfulness, but also disregard.

"I'm not saying whatever I can just to get laid." I don't need help with that.

Her eyes go wide. "Oh, I know. It's just that you make me comfortable. I'm not usually this…brazen."

"I get it." Why did I get so defensive?

Because she means a lot. More than she should, and it's critical that she feels safe with me. I told her that I'm not looking for something long-term. I don't do complications, and this girl could tangle the hell out of my heart.

I'm not what she needs. Not like that. Like this, though? I know exactly what to do. "Oh, sweet Red. I think you've been like this a lot longer than you know."

"That makes one of us."

No one's made her feel desired like this. No one's made her willing to open up. They've only closed the door and moved on. We know where we stand, and as long as we're messing around, she can be wide open.

I push her knees apart. "Let me show you."

CHAPTER TWENTY-ONE

Haven

Mom: Can you come down before your birthday?

I look at the text for the third time, and dammit, I'm hiding in the rickhouse to do it. If I go before my birthday, then I won't be around when Prescott is taking pictures of Foster House Gold. If I go, I can't tell my brothers. They don't know how much I've been talking to her or helping her. If I go, I'll also have to be careful not to discuss what's going on in my brothers' lives.

What would I tell everyone?

Me: What time?

Mom: Come for dinner.

I could leave after lunch. I'd get there for a quick dinner, and then I'd return to Huckleberry Springs before too late. Not enough time to incriminate myself, but short enough that I wouldn't have to make excuses. I'll tell my brothers I went fishing, if they even notice. Both of them are too busy with their lives to notice.

I'm leaning against the table I fucked Prescott on for the first time. What about her? I could tell her, but after how it turned out last time, will she think I'm foolish to think Mom will even be home?

No, I want to keep this to myself. It might be a fool's errand, but she's my mom, and she remembered my birthday. Prescott doesn't need to worry.

We're not serious. I push off the table and rub at the ache in my chest. I can do what I want, and no one gets hurt.

Me: I'll be there. Need me to bring anything?
Mom: Grab whatever you like to eat.

I bark out a laugh. Nothing responds other than dust filtering through the light.

Bring my own fucking food for the birthday celebration she wants to throw me. Does she even know what my favorite food is? Shaking my head, I tuck my phone away and head back to the main building.

Lane's pacing behind the employee entrance in the back, punctuating the air with a hand. He has his phone to his ear. "Hutch!" He looks up at the sky like he's begging for patience. "Hutch! Goddammit."

He drops the arm holding his phone.

"Having trouble with your neighbor?" I ask.

"You can say that." He pinches the bridge of his nose. He might be dressed like me in jeans and boots, with his standard Foster House polo, but he's all business. "He keeps asking me what to do about his place when he dies."

"He sick or something?"

He snorts. "Probably. His liver can't be keeping him healthy."

My brothers and I weren't living in town when Hutch lost his kids after his wife died. My dad would've known if

Hutch was a drinker before that, but we lost all access to the historical gossip hotline when he died.

He sticks his phone in his pocket. "He managed to find a lawyer, and he's talking about making up some trust for his house and property."

"You make it sound like that's not a good idea."

Lane's lips thin. "He wants to, *fuck*— Never mind. He'll probably change his mind. He'd better."

"Trusts are pretty straightforward." The arrangement kept our mom out of our funds and away from the property. It's why we all have careers and homes now.

Lane stuffs a hand through his hair. "He's coming up with some crazy ideas."

"Like what? He's got kids. Don't they get along?"

"A boy and a girl, and I've heard they do, and he's desperate to get them back in Huckleberry Springs. He's even mentioned—" He blows out a breath. "It's just the beer talking. I'll jam some sense into him in the morning." He props his hands on his hips. "I'm going to be traveling to Denver a little more in the next few months. I'll be here for the wedding though."

Mentioning the upcoming nuptials gives me an idea. "Speaking of that, I'd like to take a little more time off next Friday. I can be here in the morning when Prescott's taking pictures. But then I'd like to get away. Before everything."

He grunts. "Right? It gets to be a lot, and Elodie and Cruz are next. Then it's just us."

The last two single guys of Foster House. "Unless you meet some girl and tie the knot before you know it."

The bemused look he shoots me isn't expected. "If Hutch has his way." Shaking his head, he rolls his shoulders. "Shouldn't be a problem. Taking your birthday off?"

"Just the evening. Prescott insisted on making me dinner."

"Nice. You two getting serious?"

"Nope."

Surprise lifts his brows. "It's like that?"

"She's not planting roots in town, and I'm not leaving."

He nods. "If you both know what you want, more power to ya."

I bob my head, relieved he doesn't grill me more than that. "Yep. We both know."

He shifts his gaze toward me. "Wherever she settles, I'm sure some guy will sweep her off her feet."

The fuck he will. He won't know that she doesn't want to like photography again because she's afraid of disappearing behind the camera once more. He won't know that she's loyal to her dad even though he's the man who hurt her the most. And worst of all, he might not realize that her birthdays are precious to her, and she hasn't had a good one since her mom died.

Lane slaps me on the shoulder. "Like I said, as long as you both know what you want."

Prescott

Me: Can I get some more footage of the cats before I go to work? I have an idea for the new account.

I stare at the phone, waiting, as if Haven's going to drop everything and jump on my text.

"Excuse me, please," an older man says.

I jump out of the way. "Sorry!"

He chuckles as he pushes his cart by. I'm in the middle of the Tractor Supply store. I have a handbasket full of cat treats, a puppy toy, and some kitty toys. The money from the library photo shoot is burning a hole in my pocket, and I should save it for whenever I actually move. But I continue shopping.

My phone buzzes, and I hug the boot aisle to read it without blocking anyone's way.

Haven: You know where the key is.

I smile. He doesn't have a key. The guy lets anyone come and go, but from what I can tell, I'm the only one doing so.

I finish up in the store, load my items into the car, and head for Haven's place. The drive is so damn familiar by now, it's second nature. It's...wishful thinking. I cannot catch feelings. I'm barely over my titillating embarrassment from going through the images he took of me in the bar. I even edited a few.

The man has an eye for...me.

I pull in a breath and slowly let it out. The impromptu boudoir session, what he did to me on the stool after...a cold shower isn't enough. Can I swim in the Stillwater? Is it icy? Glacial? That's the only thing that's going to cut through the haze of lust from that night. It's that daze that made me upload one of the edited images in my pale-blue underwear set to his gallery.

I don't have the guts to tell him.

When I reach his house, his pickup's gone. I figured he was at work, but the disappointment is still there. I got myself all bothered on the drive.

I park by the barn, grab the bag with my purchases and my camera, and head inside. "Here, kitty, kitty, kitty."

Daisy sprints from the back of the barn, her tail held high.

"Hey there, girl." I take out the treats and rip the top off. The sound attracts Thistle. Good.

I dig out my camera, set the bag on the floor, and squat. Aiming toward the anxiously waiting kittens, I hit record and toss out a few treats. The kittens dive for them and gobble them up. The shot is perfect with the visible treat bag.

For the next twenty minutes, I get video and stills of the cats eating and playing with the toys. I'm so engrossed in the work, laughing at their antics, and being delighted that I even got some of Tan, that I don't hear Haven pull up until he's standing in the doorway.

"Hey!" I was having a lot of fun, but seeing him adds a whole new level.

He crosses his arms and leans against the frame of the barn door. "I have to hear what this idea is."

"I'm not sure if I'll go through with it." I gather up the treats and toys. Thistle's twining around Haven's legs. I stuff the cat items into my tote. "So, there's this cat company based out of Chicago. They were one of the first to approach me, and they've really grown, but they stuck with me until the end. I just thought, I don't know. Maybe they could help the rescues, get them some exposure."

"That's an awesome idea."

"It probably won't amount to anything," I say quickly.

"Don't discount yourself—or how much people want to work with you."

"Yeah, I guess." I'm more emboldened than I was this morning. I was looking forward to playing with the cats and having an excuse to come out and do so. Add in Haven, and it's been a fantastic morning. "All they can do is say no, and that's fair. The animals I'll be posting are in Montana."

"But you bought their stuff, right here in town."

"I'll make sure to add that." I take the cat supplies to the tack room, and he follows me in.

The air grows thick and sultry, rippling over my skin. I'm hyperaware of his proximity, overly sensitive from my nipples down to the juncture of my thighs. Maybe it's what we've done in here before. Maybe it's seeing his long, hard body leaning against the doorframe. Maybe it's his unyielding support and confidence in me.

All of it. The whole package that is Haven is perfect. Except...crochet club flits through my mind, dumping a tidy little cup of water on my building desire.

I set my stuff on the shelf he's reserved for the cats and turn. He lifts his gaze from my ass.

There it is. The way he makes me feel...special. But then... "If you don't want me at the wedding, I won't go. I mean, I probably wasn't going to go anyway," I rush to tack on.

"Oh, that." He stuffs his hands in his pockets. "It's up to you. I'll be helping Durban and Iverson. I want to make sure Durban and Campbell don't have a thing to worry about."

Makes sense. Yet I'm let down in a way I can't explain. Did I want him to ask me out? A wedding date?

It would be a promotion from working a wedding, but that's kind of what Haven's doing.

"Campbell said I could ask you." He rocks on his heels. "But I know how you feel about weddings, and I didn't want you to feel ditched if you came with me."

"Oh." He doesn't want a plus-one. He doesn't want *me* as a plus-one. But he's looking out for me. The middle of my chest burns. I had a late breakfast. Is it heartburn?

"You should come. If you want."

The way he hesitates doesn't invite me in. "I'll see what I'm doing. Who knows, maybe I'll go viral by then." I summon a weak smile.

"You will." He closes the distance between us. "You're going to find all those cats and dogs a home."

The unwavering confidence in me. As a pet influencer. Not as his—I can't finish that. It's not what I'm looking for. "I could do other animals too."

The corner of his mouth tips up. "You're going to help every critter."

Sizzling heat returns, licking up and down my body. I'm so primed for him that it helps chase off the doubts from earlier. Those have no place in this moment. What did he say before? Here and now.

I nudge him backward until his butt hits the saddle stand he propped me against when he stripped me down. "It's your turn."

He sucks in a breath. "Red, you don't have to—"

I yank his zipper down, and he groans, long and loud. His erection's already raging when I free him from his underwear. His lips are parted, and his breathing's heavy. He looks from my hand around his dick up to my face. I hold his gaze as I sink to my knees and take him into my mouth.

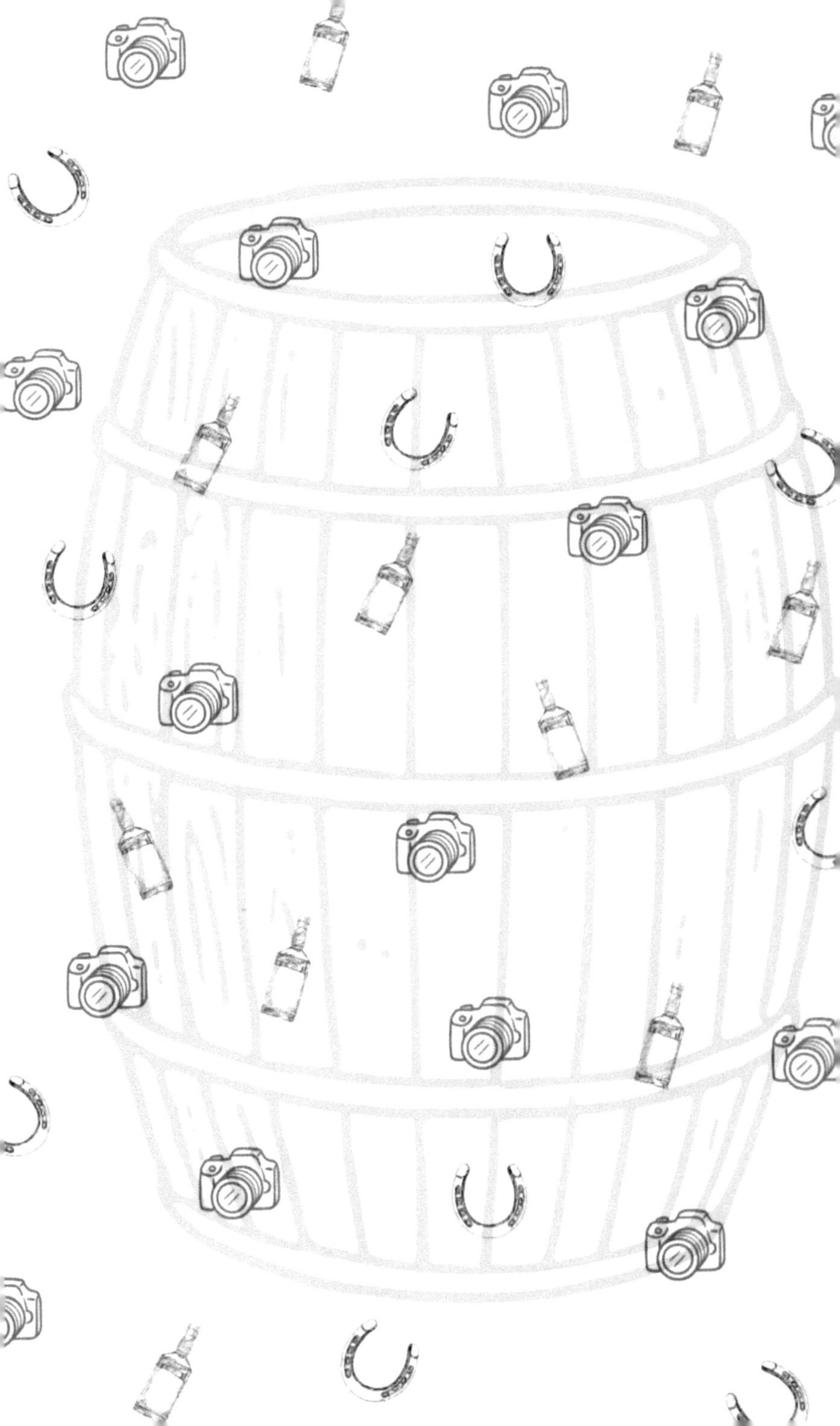

CHAPTER TWENTY-TWO

Prescott

Dad's sitting at a table with his hotter-than-the-surface-of-the-sun coffee when I emerge from my room. "You making something big tomorrow?" he asks.

"Yes, but not here." Last night, I bought all the groceries for Haven's birthday cake. I was tempted to order one from Elodie, but making a homemade cake fits the day better. Makes it more special. And ordering a birthday cake when we're not inviting anyone else would only make people question things.

It's making me question things.

That's not all that's running through my head. The messages I woke up to this morning are dominating my thoughts. I sent off the email to the cat supply company I collaborated with the most, and they already replied.

Prescott, we're so happy to hear that you're returning to the pet influencer world. While we're interested in partnering with you on your rescue and foster animal awareness endeavor, your query came at a fortuitous time. We're also interested in working with you on a more permanent basis in our PR department. If you'd like to discuss the opportunity further, please let us know when we can meet. We'll fly you out so you can tour our new Toe Beans facility.

New facility. Fly me out. Permanent.

Everything I wanted dropped into my lap like it was predestined. Because Haven gave me the confidence, I emailed some information with example posts and videos and it happened to be when they were looking for someone like me to be on their staff.

Just like that.

I drag in a lungful of air. I have to figure out what to tell them. My response will determine my future—my very near future—and where I might end up.

Papa cocks a brow and takes a slurping sip. "Whoever it is must have a birthday."

Here and now. I'll give myself the weekend. "Yes. I'm going to make dinner and a cake tomorrow. I got everything today because I'm working at Foster House all morning."

"You getting clients?"

"No, just some gig work."

He gives me a steady look and takes another drink of his acid-washed coffee. The cloud of steam doesn't hide his piercing gaze. "Haven Hennessy has a birthday tomorrow."

Do I pretend to be surprised? There's one thing Papa has always been with me, and that's honest. "He does. He also hasn't really celebrated it."

"You and him a thing?"

I'm not even a wedding date. *Get over it, Prescott.* "No."

"But you're something?"

"I don't know. I guess."

"You guess? How long you been in town?"

I met Haven as soon as I entered the city limits almost two months ago. I used to know by the third date how I stood—do we break it off or keep trying? I kept trying too much while the guy always gave up. But Haven and I aren't dating. We aren't...something. The back of my throat hurts. "We're just living in the moment."

He arches a brow again. "'Bout time. You always were worried about tomorrow."

"I wasn't worried, Papa. I just wanted someone to spend my tomorrows with."

"That ain't Haven."

I recoil like he's swatted me across the cheek. "Okay, well, I've gotta get to Foster House today, and I'd like to edit a bunch tonight." Especially if I'm going to be planning meetings with possible sponsors. "You okay for tonight and tomorrow?"

"I did just fine before you whirled into town," he grumbles, but there's no heat behind his words. He draws his brows together, and his mustache puffs out. "But when you leave town, I might have to find someone to work a few hours."

"Oh. What if I stay—"

"No, Pressie. You go out and live your life. When you're old and can't move so good anymore, like me, you find a place to hide and lick your wounds."

That sounds dismal. "Bootleg is that spot?"

"Sure is. For me. You leave here, and you live like I did. Go where the wind takes you."

I nod, but I almost shake my head instead. "Some people think it's being asked to stay that's really special."

He only grunts, and it's like an uppercut to my sternum. Hurt spreads between my ribs, but it's my fault. Did

I expect him to ask me to stay? It's always been temporary. Here and fucking now.

Yes. I knew the arrangement, and I still got my hopes up.

Just like I'm doing with Haven.

I grab my camera bag and head out. If I was working a wedding, I'd usually be in a dressy black top and black slacks or leggings to fade into the background. Today, I'm in black athletic shorts that won't show my crotch if I have to squat in front of anyone, and a loose white top that hopefully won't show pit stains if I start sweating.

The drive to the distillery helps diminish the lingering hurt that always rises when I talk with Papa. I'm too old for daddy issues. I have one tall, dark, and handsome issue that I'd rather focus on.

By the time I arrive at the distillery, the tension has drained from my shoulders. I have a prospective job. I'd have to move. Which is what I want. But I may also be able to work with them and keep doing my thing. Right here in Huckleberry Springs.

Could I be happy here?

When I enter, Haven's chatting with Clem at the cashier's desk. His gaze goes straight to me, and his eyes heat. He's dressed a little nicer than normal, wearing jeans and a black polo shirt that has a yellow Foster House logo.

"There she is," he says with a grin.

There is a scenario where I'm happy in a small town.

I'm here to work. I pat my camera bag. "I'm ready to work. Clem, do you get another headshot?"

She holds her hands up like she's blocking the paparazzi. "I'm not being immortalized. I'm in enough pictures from the tourists, and that's good enough for me."

Haven pushes away from the desk. "I'll let the others know, and you can boss us all around."

The next few hours go by in a whirlwind of laughter and the clicking of my camera. I'm going to have hundreds of images to go through, but none of it is going to be hard work. The rich copper and silver of the tanks and stills only highlight how ruggedly handsome all the owners are.

Haven looks at his watch. He's been doing that a lot today. Does he have a pressing appointment other than my photo shoot?

I'm thinking too hard, but Haven's at the center of most of my thoughts today. I aim and click at the guys chatting at the base of the stairs. The sun's high enough to keep from glaring through the windows, and the relaxed way they're standing will be perfect for their socials.

A tall man with starkly combed dark hair, a blue dress shirt, and black slacks wanders in. "Am I late?"

Cruz smirks. "Just in time to get in on the photo shoot and act like you've been working hard the whole time."

When he grins, the resemblance to Cruz and Lane is clear.

He crosses toward me and sticks his hand out. "Myles Foster. Thanks for helping Foster House update our look."

I give his hand a quick squeeze. "Thanks for taking a chance on me."

Myles's smile is more professionally aloof than his brothers'. "It was a no-brainer after Haven showed us those pictures you took of him. My wife said if we don't hire you, she'll do it herself."

My insides warm. Haven talked about me? Was it just in the capacity of Foster House?

When I glance at Haven, he's peeking at his watch. My

ego shrivels. What did I think he'd be doing? Gazing adoringly at me while I got showered with praise?

"I'm just here to get in the group shot," Myles says, wandering toward the rest of the guys. "Lane insisted."

Lane nods and starts for the stills where we'll do another group shot. "It's because I love having to answer where you are to everyone. People don't believe you're ever here. This is proof."

All the guys follow Lane. Haven falls back with me. I'm looking too hard into how he's acting. Thinking about tomorrow—and what I want to come after—is making me uptight.

Haven touches the small of my back and drains half the stress in my body. "Where do you want us, Red?"

We haven't been around a lot of people together. Do they know he calls me Red? My face gets hot. If they do, they don't know why.

I arrange all the owners, and it doesn't take much to get billboard-worthy images. "Okay. That's it."

I loosen the harness and let my camera arm go slack. It's been years since I worked this long. My shoulders are sore, and my cheeks ache from laughing. And with the way Haven's heading toward me, I feel like part of the crew.

"Was it like the old days?" he asks.

"More fun, actually. You guys don't fight like married couples."

"No, we do. We wrestle sometimes too."

"Then I'll have to tell you about the headlock a wife put her husband in."

He laughs, and we draw attention, but he doesn't seem to mind. "I can't wait to hear about it. You heading to Bootleg?"

I shake my head. "I told Papa that I needed to bond with my computer tonight and edit."

He nods, but I can't read his expression. "See you tomorrow, then?"

"If you're still up for it."

"I am. Let yourself in. The house will be open."

The smile tugging at me is almost triumphant. This isn't the first time I've gotten free access to his place, and I don't take it lightly. My mind might be seeing more than he's presenting, but what if? What if it means he's willing to let me into more than his home?

Haven

I hold the pepperoni pizza in one arm while I walk up to the door of the place my mom rents. The square brick building is an old house that was converted into apartments. Probably by the landlord who supposedly keeps raising Mom's rent.

I knock and wait.

Thirty seconds later, I knock again.

The warmth of the box seeps into my arm. My stomach cramps, but it's not from hunger. More from the stress I've carried all day. I couldn't enjoy the session with Prescott as much as I wanted. She was in her element. The only thing missing was some kittens or a puppy or two. She couldn't talk to us in the same cooing voice she does with our little wildflowers.

Ours.

I shake my head and knock louder. I'm getting ahead of myself.

Or am I right on track? What if—

The door whips open, and Mom blinks at me. Her dark hair is mussed on one side, and she's in tan sweats. She blinks at me with eyes that are a lot like Iverson's. I guess it's more accurate to say Iverson's are like hers, but it's hard to think that my brothers got much from my mom other than bitterness.

"Haven." Her voice is scratchy. "You're early."

Five minutes. "Sorry."

She grunts and steps to the side. "What kind of pizza did you get?"

The acid in my stomach intensifies. Happy birthday to me too. I step inside, and I'm surrounded by a cloying flower smell. The kind that sticks in your nose and seeps into the fibers of your clothing. Nothing like the light, pleasing scent of Prescott. "Pepperoni."

"You know that gives me heartburn."

"Sorry," I say again. "I didn't remember. You just told me to pick up something I like."

"Thought you'd have better taste than that." She grunts and goes up the stairs to the table. Has she gotten thinner since the last time I saw her? Each visit I have with her, she's a slow disappearing act. She chuckles. "But then, you make whiskey for a living."

"Good whiskey, vodka, and gin." An open bottle of red wine is in the middle of the table. Only one glass is by the spot she normally sits. I set the pizza on the table and find my own glass and get us a couple of plates and napkins.

When I return, she's already got a slice in her hand with her leg cocked so her foot is on the chair. I take the spot across from her.

"How was work?" I ask to have something to say, and pour us each some wine. The mystery of how long it's been open and sitting out will have to remain unsolved. Sometimes it's better that way.

"It's work. What are Iverson and Durban up to?"

"Same as us. Work." I stuff some pizza into my mouth.

She tips her head to study me before she takes a drink of her wine. "Durban getting married?"

"You'll have to ask him," I say around my mouthful.

"What's his fiancée's name again?"

"You'll have to ask him."

She snorts. "You don't know it?"

I set my slice of pizza down. "You know I'm just respecting their wishes. Anything to do with them, you have to go through them."

But I'm here. Ask about me. Ask if I've met anyone, and maybe I'll tell you about her. I'll tell you that she's amazing and thoughtful. I'll say she gives as good as she gets, and the balance is refreshing.

"I have grandkids I don't even know."

She has kids she doesn't know too. The little I've eaten sits like a stone in my gut. "I know, Mom."

She huffs out a breath and drops her food. Then she beams. "I got you a present."

Surprised, I look around, but there's no gift or brightly wrapped anything. "Oh?"

"Let me grab it." She gets up, and the silence of her place descends on me. It's not like how it was growing up, with her outbursts and her rants atop the noise of me and my brothers, but I wouldn't call it better either. Prescott would hate it.

When Prescott told me she hates the quiet, this is

what she's talking about. Yeah, I don't like it either. I like the life Meadow gives my place. The sound of Prescott's footsteps in my kitchen and our chatter at my table.

I'll get that tomorrow. And then I can forget about this.

Mom returns and plops a box labeled *Electric Wine Bottle Opener*.

"A wine kit?" I don't mean to sound confused, but I'm in the spirits industry. Wouldn't she think I have something like this already?

"It's electric. Beats the hell out of doing it by hand." She taps the box. "And it's got a stopper. Got it when I picked up the wine for dessert."

Is that my birthday cake, then? No. I'm not going to question it. "Thank you."

The war of being a good son rages inside me as I finish my slice of pizza. She got me a gift, and I'm not going to complain. Yet the disappointment won't lessen. It only grows and adds to the sense that I'm a shitty son. She can't afford much, and she did take the time to buy it. Why can't I just be grateful for the effort?

Maybe because she used my money for the purchase.

She finishes her slice and pours herself the last of the wine. My untouched glass is only half full.

If I eat one more bite, I might choke on it. This whole night has been...dismal. If my brothers find out that I drove here and then got treated like this, they'll give her an earful. Though she'd probably be happy that they contacted her. As long as it was about her.

One thing is certain—tonight is not about me.

I grab my present and rise. "I should get going. It's a long drive back."

Flipping open the lid of the pizza box, she studies the insides. "I hate to ask, but my gas light came on right when I parked in the garage."

"Okay?" I know damn well what she's asking. When will I learn? Not fucking today, apparently.

"You got enough cash on you to cover it? I had to pitch in for a going-away gift for a coworker, and payday isn't until next week."

Tell her no. Tell her no more.

I just want to leave and forget that I got my hopes up again. I work in the morning, and then a night with Prescott will help me forget all about today. With a sigh, I sit back down, drop my box on the table, and dig out my wallet. It's filled with twenties. I stare at them. Mom stays quiet, waiting.

If I do this, she'll just ask me for money again. And again. Next year, will she use my cash to buy me a gift that requires no thought? Will she even remember my birthday? Don't I deserve better?

I close my wallet and tuck it back into my pocket. "I'm sorry. I can't cover your bills anymore."

She laughs like I'm joking, then she catches my expression, and her smile extinguishes like a smothered candle. "What?"

I flinch at the whip-snap of her voice. Tension rides the back of my shoulders like a newbie on horseback—unsettled and clenching in all the wrong places. "No more money."

She draws back, confusion and disgust scrawled across her face. "Then what are you good for?"

"Wow, Mom." I take my gift because, dammit, tomorrow's my birthday, and I rise. "Have a good night," I say on my way to the door.

"You know, I never wanted you," she calls after me.

A burning ignites in my stomach. There are people in my life who want me. Two guys who helped raise me when she wouldn't. This is what my brothers warned me about. This is what I get for not listening to them. This is what I get for trying to celebrate my birthday.

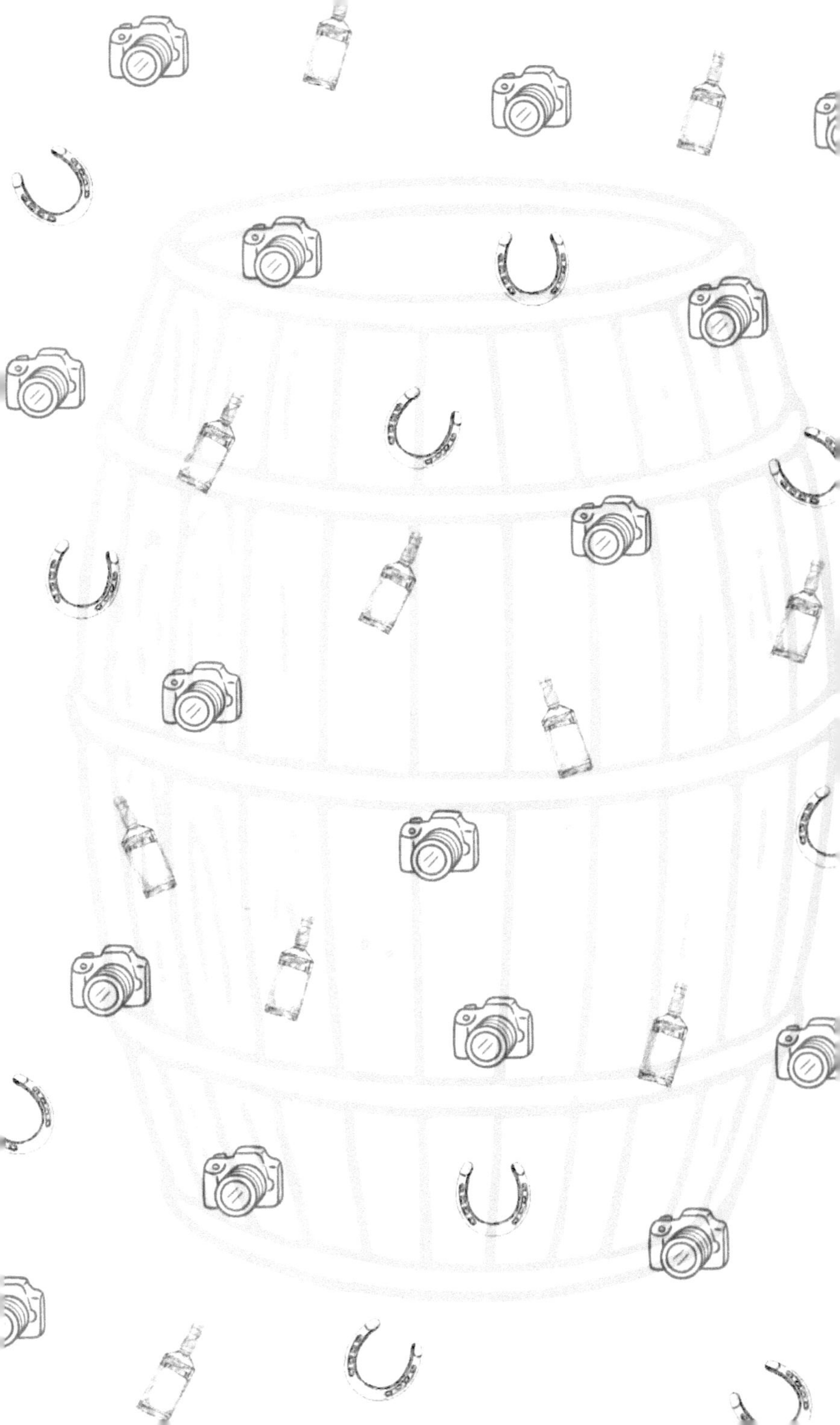

CHAPTER TWENTY-THREE

Haven

I finish putting away the shipment that came yesterday. All bags of grain are stacked, cases of bottles are stored away, and I'm walking out. Cruz jogs down the stairs.

"Happy birthday, man," he says. "Thanks for the muffins."

It's my birthday, but it's not happy. On the drive home last night, I tried to put my evening with Mom behind me. She uses people, and she was only trying to get to my brothers. She'd probably be abysmal to them too. I stood up for myself, and she swatted me down and let me leave.

I learned my lesson. Hard.

"Thank your girl," I say like nothing's bothering me. It's tradition that whoever's birthday it is brings a birthday treat. Mostly, we all go to Dee's Sweets, and that started even before Cruz and Elodie got together.

"Trust me, I will." His grin is shameless.

Irritation sweeps across the back of my neck. Excitement simmers inside me too, but it's like soured mash. A contaminant got inside me, and it's tainting this whole day. Prescott's making me a birthday dinner. She's at my house now. I can use the distraction. I can use looking forward to something, but I can't forget that she's got one foot out the door.

I can't forget that she never wanted me in the first place.

No. Today is not about me and her. Today is about our arrangement, and my anticipation needs to temper itself.

When I arrive home, her car's in the drive. She messaged me when she was coming over to start cooking, and I've been thinking all day about how she's in my house. A soothing warmth fills my chest and has only grown since I coasted down my driveway and saw her here. I inhale, and my chest is raw. Just an arrangement.

I park next to her car and rush inside. Meadow runs up to me from where she must've been sleeping on her mat. "Is my girl inside, Meadow?"

Meadow trots toward the chickens, and I smile, beelining into the house. The chickens are her binge-watching.

"Hey," she calls in a singsong voice.

"Smells great." I inhale the savory BBQ flavor. Today is about food, and her enthusiasm about birthdays. I don't have to see into it more than that. My stomach growls as I turn into the kitchen and skid to a stop.

The counters are clear, and the dishwasher's going, but it's not the way she cleaned the kitchen or set the table with a candle in the middle that she must've brought. I've only got candles for emergency kits.

The only thing on her full, curvy body is an apron.

That's the distraction I'm craving. Blood swells in my veins, plowing through my body like a giant tidal wave. My temples pound, but not as strongly as my heartbeat in my dick. "Fuck me, Red."

Her cheeks are flaming red, and she's shifting from foot to foot. "Is this okay? I mean— Oh."

I chew up the floor crossing to her. Her eyes are wide when I reach her. I don't stop, backing her into the counter.

"Hell yes, it's okay. If I could—" I cut that sentence off before she thinks this small-town cowboy is getting serious.

If I could come home to this every day, I'd think I won the biggest lottery in the world.

I need to forget those words before I start thinking I'm getting serious. Prescott is going to leave. She loves birthdays, and she's using mine to spread the joy. It's not a bad thing. It's just not for me.

Her lips are the prettiest pink as she blinks up at me.

"If I could see through that apron, it'd be even better," I murmur against her lips. Good save.

"I didn't know what you'd think." She stares at my shoulder like she's afraid to say what she really wants to. "Seems arrogant to think that me naked is a birthday present."

"It's good sense. Why wouldn't I want you naked in my kitchen? I'm a hungry man."

She giggles, and the way her body quivers in my hold only amps up the lust boiling inside me.

"I like this," I say honestly. "A lot."

"I think I'd like it if I came home from work, and you were naked."

"Your dad might have an issue with it."

"He'd have an issue with a lot if he knew."

"Like the way you come against my tongue?"

"Most definitely," she says hoarsely.

"What about how deep you took me in your mouth? How you swallowed me down like you were a starving kitten?"

She swallows. "That seems like it should stay between us."

"I want very little between us." When her lips part, I brush a kiss over them, not wanting her to think deeper about that comment. "I want to be in you."

Her eyelids flutter. "Yes. I want that."

I dig my wallet out before my brain goes offline from the noise of my dick. "Hope the ribs won't burn because I'm taking you now."

"Everything's ready when we are."

I find the condom, toss the wallet on the counter. It lands by the wine opener I got last night. I glare at it. Fuck wine, and fuck that opener. I rip my zipper down. She reaches behind her for the apron strings, but I yank her to me.

"Leave it. I'm fucking you with this apron on."

A sultry smile curves her lips. "So that whenever you wear it, you remember this?"

"Yes," I say roughly. I still owe her the red underwear, but I've been too busy getting into the pairs she's been wearing.

I claim her mouth, and a whimper leaves her immediately. The sweet taste of lemonade is on her tongue. I demand everything, dominating her mouth and shoving my knee between her legs. She grips my shoulders.

With a growl, I break the kiss. My lips wet, I drag my mouth along her jaw, pushing her head back. Once her neck is exposed, I take my time.

Another pool of warmth gathers in my gut. She

remembered the stories of drinking lemonade with my dad and brothers?

This woman is amazing. I should keep her.

And watch her walk out later?

She never wanted me, but she wants this. So do I. I move the apron aside to uncover a breast. She arches into my touch. The weight of her is pleasing in my hand, and I run a thumb over her nipple. I do the same to the other side.

Blood hammers through my erection. I won't keep my cock, her, or the dinner she worked on waiting any longer. "Turn around."

I stuff the condom on before she's completely turned.

The only things covering the back of her are the loop of the apron at the neck and the ties at her waist. Otherwise, she's open to me. The lush globes of her ass are on display. I carefully take the claw clip out of her hair.

She shakes out the tresses, and my only regret is that I missed seeing her tits jiggle.

"Are you ready for me, Red?" I touch the nape of her neck before skating my fingers down her spine. This is all mine. For tonight.

For how much longer?

Pushing that thought aside, it's sluggish, like I need to address these building emotions inside me. Desire. Need. Want. Hopes, dreams, and fantasies. Fear. Always anticipation of loss. They're strong, and it's probably because of that damn wine opener taunting me.

I give my head a shake. I have a naked goddess in front of me, and I'm wasting time. I continue my path down, but stop a moment at her round butt cheeks.

She looks over her shoulder at me. "Doesn't seem fair I can't touch you."

"I'm the birthday boy." My hand grazes downward until I get between her legs. Heat envelops my hand. She's ready. My patience runs out. I clamp a hand around my dick. "Put your hands on the counter and brace yourself."

When she does, I use my free hand to drag her hips back. She bends farther over, and yes, she's open for me. I slide the tip of my cock through her seam and push inside.

A low moan leaves her, and she drops her head. "Haven."

It feels like it's been for-fucking-ever, but that's how it always is with her. "The more I get of you, Prescott, the more I want."

The back of my throat burns. It's true. Truer than I can admit.

Her hair curtains over the side of her head as she looks back at me. I can't interpret her expression, but I don't have much intelligence at the moment.

I start thrusting. Pleasure swamps every other emotion. She's surrounding me, gripping and rippling around me so damn perfectly. I keep hold of her hip and grip her shoulder. I want to make this good for her too, but I'm indulging in my selfish side. I want to take and take and take. And I want to keep.

I punch into her harder. Her hands squeak against the counter, but she readjusts. My climax is bearing down on me like a hungry herd. I'm going to happily get trampled, but then she won't hit her peak. Can't have that.

"Touch yourself." It comes out a snarl.

She rests an elbow on the countertop and her other hand disappears between her and the countertop.

"Tell me what you feel." I keep plunging in and out of her.

"I'm wet," she says, breathless.

I tilt my head forward, hanging on every word. "I need to hear it all. I need you to come with me, but I need your help pushing you over the edge." Arousal gives me tunnel vision. I'm close. "I can't control myself around you."

"My clit," she pants, "is tight. Soaked."

I grunt for my reply.

"I feel you." She gasps. "In and out. In and out. So strong and..." A whimper. "Hard."

My world narrows to a pinhole. "Fuck. I can't—"

My orgasm smashes into me. Shit, shit, shit. I didn't get her off.

"Haven." My name on her exhale sounds pleased, but I didn't get her off.

I come long and hard, my body shaking. She takes it all, keeping both of us from collapsing on the counter.

She didn't climax. She needs to finish.

As soon as the last stream erupts from me, I pull out and sink to my knees. My zipper cuts into my balls, but I don't care.

"Haven?"

Her legs tilt like she's trying to turn around, but I put my hands on the inside of her thighs and nudge her legs farther apart. "Stay right there."

The angle might make my neck angry at me for a month, but I don't care. She tips her hips enough that I nail her clit with my tongue, lapping and sucking. In seconds, she's exploding and shuddering against my face.

Pure, crystalline satisfaction fills every facet of me. Tremors still rack my body. My brain is mush, my body is spent, and I'm tired. I'm tired of wanting more. But last night showed me that when I go after what I think I deserve, I end up with nothing but a wine opener. At least she'll leave satisfied.

Prescott

I light the candles on the cake. We're on his back deck facing a tidy yard that ends with hills gradually thickening with trees. *Happy Birthday Haven* is spread across the white buttercream frosting, written in the same navy blue as the trim I put on. Not bad for a rookie. This whole day has been nice. The cooking and baking. Being in Haven's house, where there's no stench of strong coffee. And the rest, of course.

My stomach is pleasantly full, and my body is humming from the quickie in the kitchen. I was prepared to be humiliated, but instead, my clit was annihilated. Yet the amazing sex can't hide that Haven's more subdued than normal. Is this all too hokey for him?

Well, I've committed. Standing back, I clap my hands. "Okay, time to blow out the candles."

"Did you really have to put all of them on the cake?"

"Yes." Every. Single. One. This is a mild birthday compared to what I got when I was younger, but loud and boisterous wouldn't be special for Haven. He's used to crowds and parties. This is intimate. "Let me get my camera."

"Are you doing a photo shoot?"

"We need to commemorate the experience. How long has it been since you've blown candles on a cake?"

He screws up his face, thinking. "Thirty-three years."

Damn, that's sad. I take a deep breath. The next part is going to be as embarrassing as I feared wearing nothing but an apron would be. "I'm going to sing the birthday song really awkwardly while I take pictures. When I'm done, you blow."

He arches a suggestive brow, but I roll my eyes at him and launch into the song. Since I'm not a singer, I add extra warble. He grins, and I capture the images.

I linger on the last *yoooouuu,* and he sucks in a breath. With a gusty exhale, all the candles puff out.

"Ha! No candles left. No girlfriends." At his perplexed look, I clarify. "You know, that old tale or whatever? However many candles you don't blow out is how many girlfriends or boyfriends you have?"

"Interesting." He laughs and clears his throat, his gaze flickering over the smoking remnants. "Yeah. Not a one."

"Did you make a wish?"

"No. I don't believe in those." He grimaces and covers it with an apologetic smile. "Sorry. That came out harsh. I prefer hard work to make things happen."

Hard work and no attachments. Okay.

I tuck my camera back in my bag and cut the cake. "I marbled it as best I could, and the buttercream frosting is what I grew up on."

"Just like Mama used to make?"

"Yes." I grin and dole out a big slice for each of us. "Exactly what she used to make."

He slides a forkful into his mouth, and his eyes roll back. "Mmmm, Red. This is amazing."

Pride surges in my chest and blooms outward. Was I imagining his dour demeanor before? Maybe he had a hard day at work. "Thank you."

He digs in, so I do the same.

When he's done, he pushes his plate away. "I'm going to have this for breakfast."

Me, too, almost slips out of my mouth. "There are worse things to have."

I take my last bite. A twinge zings through my neck. I tip my head to one side and then to another and roll a shoulder.

"Stiff neck?" He slides out of his chair and stands behind me.

My eyelids drift shut when his strong hands land on my shoulders. This is nice. He treats me so well. The cake and dinner are far out of his element, but he let me do it, and now I get a kink in my neck worked out. "I'm not used to being on the computer that long anymore. I worked at the kitchen table, but Papa's chairs aren't exactly ergonomic."

They're old, they've forgotten what cushion is, and they creak when they rock. A career on the rodeo circuit didn't come with a padded retirement plan. But neither did being an influencer.

I'll do things differently this time. If that's what I decide on.

I relax into Haven's massage. Nimble fingers dig into just the right places. "It was a long night, but it was nice. You're all so photogenic, it made edits easy."

He chuckles and his strokes slow. "Your Friday night still sounds a lot better than mine."

"Something happen at the tasting room?"

"No." His tone is as sluggish as his hands on me. "Nothing worth mentioning. Nothing worth a whole lot."

He digs back into my flesh, working away knots. I should be melting into him, but a warning bell rings in my head. No, I'm being foolish. "You know, I debated what to get to drink."

"Lemonade was perfect."

I beam inside. "Thanks. I knew I'd never pick a spirit

better than what you've got. But I saw that new wine opener and worried I should've gotten a good moscato or something to go with the birthday cake."

His hands stop. "Oh. That. It's a present from my mom."

"She sent you a present?"

"Nope."

I open my eyes right onto the empty plate. Dread fills my stomach. "If she didn't mail it, then did you see her?"

"Yep." He skates his hands up my neck and makes circles with his thumbs. "It was a shit show."

That must've hurt, but he didn't let on. Then again, I was naked in his kitchen. But still, he could've said something over dinner. "You want to talk about it?"

His laugh comes out scornful. "No. Not at all."

My jaw falls open. I snap it shut before he can see. Details fall into place. Looking at his watch. His brief weirdness about last night. "Is she still in town?"

"No. I went to Gillette."

Hurt echoes inside me so loud it drowns out the sounds of nature. I twist in my seat to look at him. His features are neutral, giving away nothing about how he felt. "Oh. You didn't say anything yesterday."

"Nope."

"Why didn't you talk to me?"

"What's there to say?" he snaps, and I flinch. I've never heard that hard tone come from him.

The pain in my chest is for him, but a large portion of it is for me too. He'd rather marinate in it than open up to me? This isn't good for either of us.

I made him a birthday dinner. We had sex.

But the dinner was just part of an arrangement. I owed him. And the sex was...just that. "I got pizza. She said it gave her heartburn, she asked about my brothers, and she got me that wine opener. Probably bought it right before I got to town."

"But you don't drink wine."

Disbelief flashes in his eyes, then hurt, then that distance returns. That space he puts between himself and anyone but his brothers. "It's fine."

I can't be left outside of that protective bubble. Because then that would mean… It would mean that I was right all along. "You should've said something—"

"I said it's fine." The muscles on either side of his jaw pop.

I snap my mouth shut.

"I'll get these." He gathers our dirty plates and silverware. The silence is so cutting it's like even the insects and frogs have fled. He uses his elbow to slide open the door to the house.

I'm left alone on the deck. Each breath struggles against a weight on my chest. A weight the exact size of one Haven Hennessy.

He let me into his house, and maybe not many, if any, women can say that. But where does that leave me?

Alone on the deck.

He's not serious about us. He's the best man I know, but he's built a wall to protect himself. Or a distillery to hide himself. And when things start getting serious, he won't let me in.

I shake my head and gaze at the cake. It grows fuzzy as tears gather in my eyes. Blinking them away, I draw in a calming breath. I was so excited to make that damn thing for him. So thrilled to give him this experience. But that's all it is. That cowboy is not giving his heart away.

I knew that when I met him. Yet I lit the match. Then

the whole box caught fire and took my heart with it. The cats and Meadow. Pleasure rides on his land. Movies, photo shoots, and lasagna. All of it morphed into the perfect package. A life I wanted. And in a town smaller than the one I grew up in.

Mom would've loved this, but she didn't have the partner she needed. And neither do I.

If I stay, I will always be chasing the man—or watching him walk away. I'd pretend I was happy to carve a place for myself in Huckleberry Springs, but then what?

My time in Huckleberry Springs rolls through my mind. We talked. We connected. But he didn't invite me to his brother's wedding. I feel like I busted him on his trip to Gillette. Do I wait to get kicked out of his house before he has to share his bed?

He'll probably have an excuse. There's always a reason we can't be closer. I've run out of them, but he hasn't. He doesn't need one.

This isn't going to change. We're going to keep fucking, and I'll nose-dive deeper and harder for him, and he'll...never change. He's Papa on the rodeo circuit, happy to keep doing what he's doing.

I had a plan when I arrived in town. It's time to remember what it was. I pick up the cake and go inside.

"I got an email from Toe Beans, the cat supply company." I set the cake on the counter, staring at the remaining half of *Happy* on the top. The damn wine opener is a foot away, taunting me in my periphery. "They want to meet with me."

"Really?" He leans against the counter, crossing his arms. His voice is light, like he didn't just incinerate my feelings. "Sponsorship?"

I nod, my heart breaking at the thought of packing all

my stuff. Of never working at Bootleg again. Goddammit, I enjoyed my shifts there. People were getting to know me, and...I felt like I belonged. But that's the lure of a small place. You feel like you're a part of town until everyone's getting on with their lives and you're on the outside, looking in. "A sponsorship and possibly a position with them."

His brows lift, but he doesn't smile. "They offered you a job?"

"In their marketing department. In Chicago."

His expression still doesn't crack. My hopes rise. Will the thought of me moving be enough to spur him on, to take a sledgehammer to those walls? What if he asks me to stay? What if he tells me he's also fallen for me, and that his birthday today has shown him it's time to settle down?

I chew on my lower lip, waiting. *Ask me. Please.* "They want to meet with me." Online or in person. My decision is so close to being made.

"Lots of strays in Chicago." He pushes off the counter and grabs a rag at the sink. That damn neutral expression is firmly in place.

I can't help a choking noise and cover it with a cough. "Yeah. Lots. A lot more places to foster. I, um..." God, why is this so hard? I knew how this would end. I just thought I was stronger than my mom. "I have a meeting with them. In person."

He rinses off the cloth. "Sounds like a solid plan. When do you go?"

I don't know. "The interview slot they gave me is next Monday." An exhale leaks out of me. Did I really do that? Maybe Toe Beans has a spot that day. "I'll leave on Friday."

The day of the wedding.

He scowls out of the window. "When will you be back?"

Drawing in air is a struggle. My chest has an ever-tightening band around it. *Just ask me to stay.* "I won't. I might as well make it my launching point."

A muscle in his jaw jumps again, the only sign that he's feeling *something*. "You'll drive, then."

Whatever he's feeling inside of him isn't enough.

"Yeah. I'll give myself a couple of days. I'll find a rental or something before I get there." It'd be a short flight there and back from Billings, but there's no reason to come back. I can see that now. Even Papa wants me to go.

I have the pay from the library, and with what Foster House gave me plus the gratuity, I'm set up for a while. Not long, but if I don't land the job, I can...keep going. Far away from Huckleberry Springs.

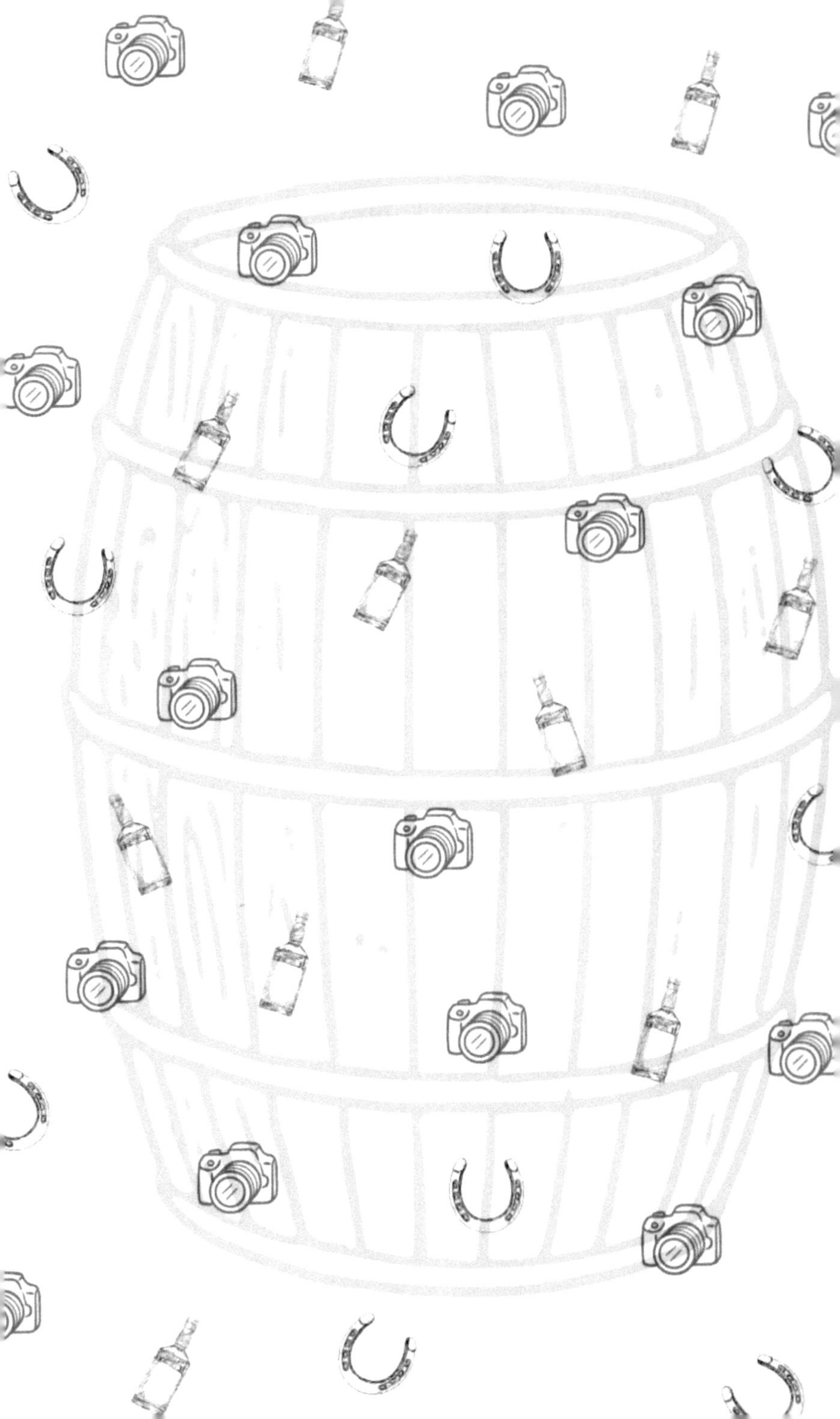

CHAPTER TWENTY-FOUR

Haven

Gravy walks through the rolling pastures surrounding Hawthorne Ranch. We're close to the big house and riding through the guest part of the ranch, which isn't crowded by the Beartooth Mountains. We stick to the trails the cattle have worn into the land over the years, and if any guests spy our procession, they think we're just other guests.

Campbell arranged the whole ride for the Monday before the wedding. Clem and Edna are holding down the distillery, but the guys and I caught up on work yesterday, so we could all take today off.

Ahead of me, Durban rides even with Lane. Behind him, Campbell chats with Jamison, and they chatter over their shoulders with Avery and Thea. Cruz and Elodie are next in line. Elodie isn't the most comfortable on horseback, but Campbell planned a mellow route, and Cruz isn't leaving her side.

As we leave a wide expanse, the crunching steps of another horse announce Iverson coming up beside me. He rides quietly for a few moments.

"Something going on?" he finally asks, keeping his voice low.

"Nope." Nothing. Including Prescott's stiff goodbye after mind-blowing sex and an amazing meal and the fact that she hasn't returned my message from yesterday about saying goodbye to the wildflower bunch she rescued.

"Sure about that?"

My shoulders are knotted from how tense I am. I slammed my thumb loading Gravy in the horse trailer to come out here. If a horse could call me a dumbass, he did with his eyes. Then I called myself one after I unloaded him and tied him off.

I haven't felt like talking all day, and apparently, it's been noticed.

"Did you ask Prescott to come out with us today?" He looks around as if he missed her in our small group of people.

No, goddammit. I didn't ask her to join in on prewedding festivities. I didn't ask her to the actual wedding. I didn't open up to her about the trip to see my mom. Coincidentally, after I shut down any further conversation on that topic, she hit me with the news she's leaving on Friday.

Fucking Friday.

Iverson's waiting for an answer.

"She wants to stay far away from weddings." I know how she feels now. Happy couples surround me. I wanted to be here, but I didn't. I wanted to go home, but I didn't. I'd lie on the couch like I did last night and wonder if I should spend my free time hanging out with Prescott, or if I should leave my birthday as the last bittersweet memory of us together. Only tonight, I can add the question of why she hasn't replied yet.

A sour taste stains my tongue. Last memory. My last memory is her walking out my front door, giving me a sad smile and one more birthday kiss. I grind my teeth together.

"I thought she might be different," he says. "You like to be with her."

"Well, she's leaving." There. I said it out loud. The weight doesn't lift from my chest. "She might land a gig with a cat supply company that'll combine her business and influencer skills. It's in Chicago."

"Ah."

The way he says it like that answers everything bristles hot across the back of my neck. "What?"

"You like her."

"Of course I like her."

"And you're pissed she's leaving."

"I'm happy for her," I say woodenly, and I am. This is what she wants. She gets to help animals without getting attached to one that'll leave her brokenhearted again, and she might get a full-time job.

He lets out a low whistle. Gravy's ears swivel. I give him a pat along his withers.

We reach a spot in the trail that winds through trees, and we have to ride single file. When we come out the other side, the path widens. We're in one of the main winter pastures close to the barn and shops. Durban pulls off to the side and circles around toward us. Iverson returns to my right side and Durban falls in on my left. A throbbing starts behind my eyes.

"You find out who spilled his beer?" Durban asks Iverson.

I sigh. "Leave it alone."

"Prescott's leaving town," Iverson answers.

I keep looking ahead, forcing myself to keep from clenching the reins. Everyone else is giving us a wide berth.

"Shit." Durban's gaze burns into the side of my face. "Why?"

I repeat the same information to him. Still no lightness in my chest.

Durban skims his fingers along the brim of his cowboy hat. "You don't want her to go."

"It's an excellent opportunity. It's what she wants." I've repeated those phrases so much in my head they come out robotic.

"But you don't want her to go," he repeats.

I scowl. "It doesn't matter. She's a friend. I want what's best for her."

Both of my brothers chuckle, and my shoulders tense to my ears. Gravy snorts like he senses the thundercloud building over my head.

Iverson scoffs. "You two aren't just friends. Why can't you admit that?"

"We messed around. That was it." The bitterness is back in my mouth.

Iverson scratches his chin. "Durban, you recall any of the girls Haven messed around with keeping a bunch of rescues at his house?"

My teeth are clenched so hard they should be cracking.

"Can't say I do," Durban says placidly. "What about taking any of the girls he messed around with fishing?"

Assholes, both of them.

"Also no." Iverson leans over so he can see Durban on the other side of me. "Any girls that he let into his house to cook to her heart's desire?"

"It's what friends do," I say tightly. Good thing they don't know about her wearing nothing but an apron to greet me. And it's only the tip of the iceberg of everything Prescott and I have done together.

Iverson's gaze weighs on me, but I refuse to look at him. "Remember how we didn't sell that portion of the property to Foster House so we wouldn't lose access to that trail?"

"We don't even go fishing with friends," Durban says. "That's *our* spot."

"It's not happening," I snap. "Fuck off."

We ride in silence, getting closer to the barn. If I didn't think a scene would invite more incessant questions, I'd spur Gravy toward my truck and trailer. I'd skip the dinner Campbell and Durban have planned for all of us.

"Listen, Haven." The gravity in Iverson's voice hits me hard in the solar plexus. I'm not going to like what he has to say. "We're allowed to be happy."

Not this again.

"I am." I was perfectly happy before I found a redhead with a nice ass in the ditch.

Durban grunts. "What we went through, it can fuck anyone up. But Iverson's right. We're allowed to be happy. We're allowed to be loved."

A chasm opens in my chest, black and yawning. Dad died, and Mom doesn't love me. Prescott's leaving. But I am loved. By my brothers. They've always watched out for me. And that's gotta be good enough.

Prescott

I gather up empty glasses from a table in the corner and pick a napkin off the floor. Bootleg is busy, and I've been running from table to table filling orders. I'll sleep well tonight. Then tomorrow, I'll leave. Toe Beans was thrilled to fit me into their schedule for a meeting on Monday, and I'm looking forward to it.

Liar.

I bite back a yawn and shove the napkin into a glass so I can grab another empty. I haven't slept well all week. Haven hasn't texted, called, or stopped in since I left his message from last Sunday on read. Maybe that's not the why behind the radio silence. He said he'd be busy this week with wedding plans.

When I close my eyes at night, the memories of him rise in my mind, and my lungs seize. I can't draw a breath, and everything just...hurts. He taught me how to fly-fish, he reinvigorated my love for horseback riding, and he took in my strays—after he helped me rescue them. He took pictures of me I would've never taken myself—or let anyone else take. He taught me about whiskey and, dammit, about myself.

There are so many things he did from his big, generous heart, but then there's the stuff he didn't do.

He didn't invite me to the wedding.

He didn't tell me about his visit to his mom's.

He hasn't reached out all week.

Is he going to let me leave town without a goodbye?

The front door cracks open, spearing the dim seating area with light. An older woman enters, looking around. Her salt-and-pepper hair is pulled back into a low bun.

"Welcome to Bootleg," I say, breezing past her. "I'll be right with you."

"No rush at all." She chooses a spot at the bar.

I return behind the bar with an armful of empties. I dump them on the counter by the sink. Those can wait until I have a moment. Papa's leaning against the wall by a table of older women in town for river fun, ever the charmer.

If I'd taken after Papa, life would be easier. I glance at him. Would it? He flits from group to group, never staying long. He lives alone, and... He's Haven in twenty-five years. Isolated and taking care of everyone around him.

I have got to get that charming cowboy off my mind. I'm not on his. Turning to the new arrival, I force a smile. "What can I get you?"

"Original Summit. Neat." She has her hands folded primly on the table. Nothing about her says dive bar, but she's relaxed, like this type of environment is as familiar as breathing.

I grab the bottle from one of the higher shelves. "Nice choice. Quality bourbon."

The corners of her eyes crinkle. "It most certainly is. What's your favorite drink?"

"I like to try different cocktails. I don't stick to just one." I pour her bourbon and set it in front of her. "A friend of mine is—" My voice catches, and the pain in my chest amplifies. "He *was* trying to get me to like whiskey."

"It can be an acquired taste." She holds up her glass to inspect the liquid inside. "I didn't like bourbon when I first tried it, but my husband came from a family of avid bourbon lovers."

"How long did it take you to get a taste for it?"

She takes a sip, seeming to consider my question.

"After all these years, I can say that I've acquired a taste, but I can't say that I *love* it." She lifts the glass to the light again. "I appreciate it. I respect the art and science that goes into it. The hard work. I enjoy it, and I'm grateful for it. So much more so than I could've ever imagined."

"Makes sense." That's pretty deep for bourbon, but I've seen how much Haven, his brothers, and the Fosters pour into their jobs. I might not like parsnips, but if I grew them, I'd damn sure eat some and appreciate them all the more. "I'll be right back."

I quickly wash the dirty glasses and clean off two empty tables. When I return, I take a breather and prop my hands on the prep counter.

"It's busy. Must be the wedding." Technically, I'm still invited. If I went, I'd get the whole night with Haven. I'd watch him laugh and witness his enjoyment as his brother secures a happily ever after. Or he wouldn't have time for me.

She sets her glass down. "Are you from Huckleberry Springs? If you don't mind me asking."

I shake my head. I don't mind. "My dad runs the place, and he's originally from here. I'm leaving tomorrow, actually."

"Oh, exciting."

It should be. I should want to hit the road and be in Chicago with plenty of time to get my shit together for the biggest pitch of my life. Yet I've left all the packing for when I wake up tomorrow, which won't be early. I need to be rested if I'm going to stare at the open road for hours.

"Yeah. It is. I'm a, uh, a pet influencer. Well, I used to be, but I'm working with a rescue, and it might've opened another door." I don't know why, but I dig out my phone and show her the images of the little wildflower rescues I posted last night. They're already starting to gain traction.

She might not be interested, but I hold my phone out like *Look! Look at it.* This is something I would've told Haven about, and he would've cheered me on.

She digs out a pair of readers from her purse and puts them on. "Oh my. How sweet are they?"

"They're the best. I found them, but I couldn't keep them. A...friend...did." I tuck the phone away before the memories start hammering at my brain once again. "A cat company wants to partner with me."

"You must be good at what you do."

"I can be." I was a good photographer, and I left that. Then I was a good pet influencer, and in a way, I left that. And now I'm leaving Huckleberry Springs and Haven.

There's nothing here for me. There's never been anything anywhere for me.

"Where are you from?" I ask to turn the conversation around. Another few tables empty, but I don't jump to clear them. I don't want to be lost in the thoughts banging around my head.

"Bourbon Canyon."

I frown, mulling over the name. Why is it so familiar? My gaze lands on the bottle of Copper Summit bourbon I poured. Bourbon Canyon. Why is that—

Haven. His brothers. They'll have friends and anyone they consider family in town. A weird spark ignites in my chest. "Are you Mae?"

Interest lights her eyes. "Have we met before? I'm so sorry. I'm usually better with faces."

Oh. The minuscule flame extinguishes. Haven hasn't gushed about me to Mae? What did I expect? She'd walk in here, snap her fingers, and think, that's right, there's the tall redhead that Haven gushed about? "I know you, but you don't know me. I got to know Haven while I was here."

"Oh!" Delight spreads across her face. "I adore Haven. All the Hennessy brothers mean a lot to me. And now their families too."

It's still hard to breathe.

She gestures vaguely toward the door. "We're staying out at Hawthorne Ranch, but I snuck away. I don't get a chance to roam a lot on my own when I'm in town." She winks. "I like to see Copper Summit on the shelf."

She's a bourbon distiller matriarch. Haven hasn't seemed to mention me. Would he have introduced me, or is Mae kept at arm's length too? The only woman he's ever tried with is his mom, and she doesn't know what she's throwing away.

I have to speak before I cry. "I'm relieved Papa carries Copper Summit. He can be"—cheap—"limited in his selection."

"I also enjoy a good Foster House spirit, but my appreciation for bourbon is unlimited." Her kind smile blankets me in warmth, and she lifts her drink. "A salute to your new adventure."

Tears stab the backs of my eyes hard and fast. I blink and rub at an eye like I have something in it. "Thank you."

But the truth is, I don't want to salute my new start. I don't want a new beginning. I want what I've had for the last two months. I want a cowboy distiller to tell me that it's me he wants. That he wants me and only me.

My mom taught me a long time ago to be enough for myself. Yet it doesn't change that I still want to be that one person for someone else. It's just my bad luck that person is Haven.

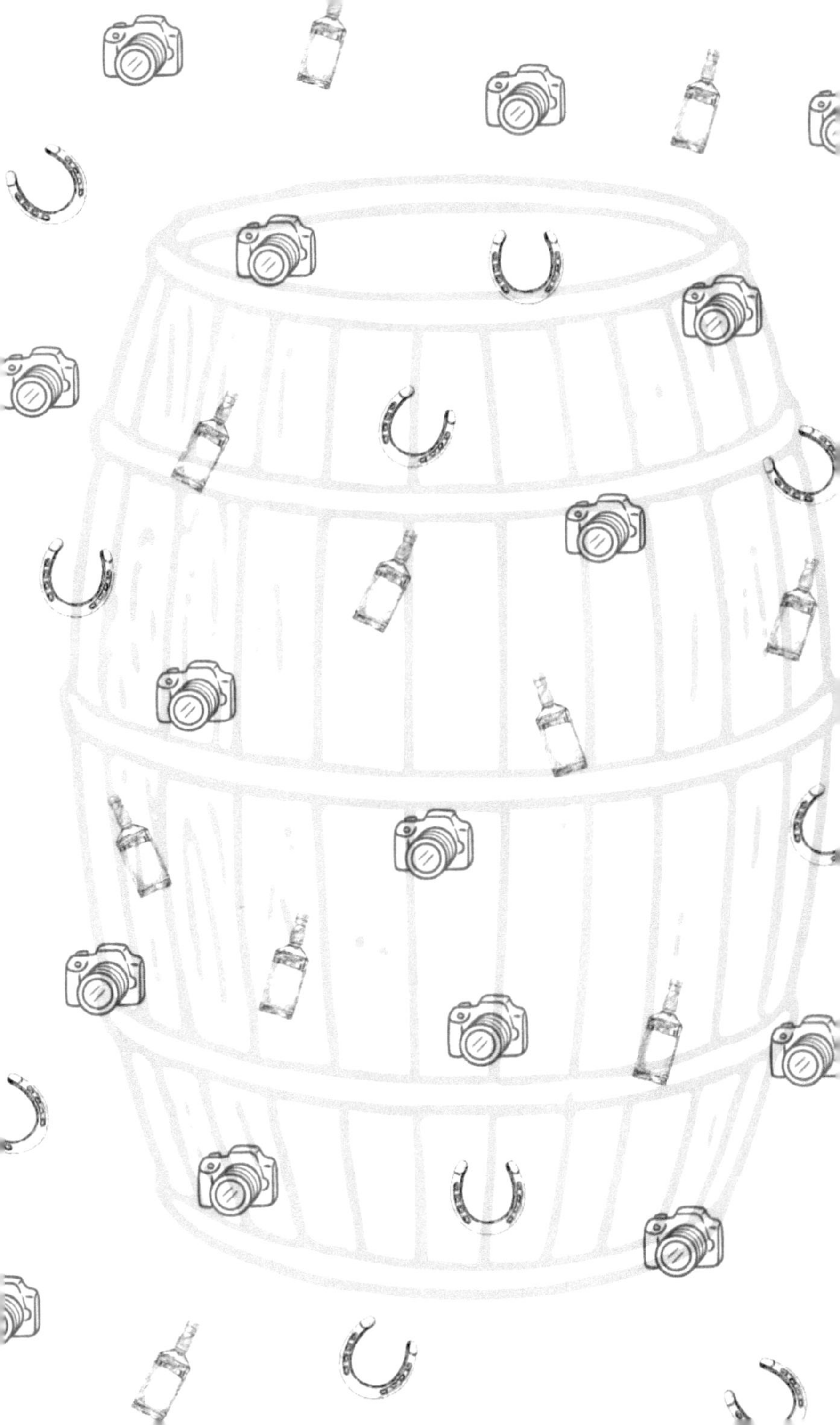

CHAPTER TWENTY-FIVE

Haven

Wedding guests mill around the pavilion. It's a gorgeous August day for my brother's wedding, and I don't have to rush around making sure it's all going to plan. Campbell's adept at her job, and everything's running smoothly. Iverson and Jamison are making sure of it. That leaves me with nothing to do. I've made idle chitchat for days, and I'm exhausted.

I can't get lost in my work like normal. I have to be personable, professional, and, most of all, happy.

I'm not fucking happy.

Is Prescott gone? She must be by now. Did she go to my place to say goodbye to the kittens and Meadow? What does it mean if she didn't?

We weren't anything official. I made sure of it. Yet when she gently disappears out of my life, I'm rudderless. What the hell am I going to do with this giant hole in my chest?

There's nothing for me at the pavilion but more aimless questions that have no answers. I cross the expansive lawn to the sprawling lodge, nodding at people from the community as I pass. Ned and Isadora Blake from the gas station both wave at me while they chat with Nellie Huang from Wok and Roll. Maya Reyes, one of the owners of the Mexican restaurant, approaches them. We exchange smiles. If it's a place that serves food in town, they'll have connections with Campbell, thanks to the food fair she holds every other year.

Cruz pushes out the door and holds it open for Elodie. She's not in her usual baggy shirt and leggings, instead in a gauzy pale-blue dress and sandals. Her long hair is braided with loose tendrils framing her face. The appreciation in Cruz's gaze deepens when his attention dips down to her ass. He lets go of the door and trots to her side, cocking an elbow out. They both smile as they pass.

"Lookin' good, Haven," Cruz says.

"Thanks, man." I'm in starched black jeans and a white shirt. The black suspenders are taking some getting used to, but it's too hot for a sport coat and Campbell wanted something a step up from our normal dress wear. I look better than I feel.

When I step inside the lodge, I have to decide where I'm going. The wedding starts in an hour. Pictures are done, and that was torture. Smiling for a photographer who isn't Prescott dulls the idea that I would've enjoyed my own senior pictures when I was a teen. *She's* what I enjoyed about that day.

I take the hallway that leads to the bar. I'm not getting wasted, but maybe a drink will calm the churning in my head.

I'm rubbing between my eyes when I enter. Damn. It's

not a big space, so it doesn't take many people to fill it up. More chatter sounds like the worst thing in the world right now. I'm about to turn when the middle Hawthorne sister spots me.

Avery snaps her fingers and beckons me to the table. Her brown hair is tied back, and she's wearing her blush-colored bridesmaid dress. She and her partner, Thea, have a small bottle of the wedding favors in front of them.

When I get near, Avery points to the whiskey. "Good stuff. Durban said you made it."

"I infused and double-aged it."

Thea pushes out an old-fashioned half-back chair with her foot. She's freshly shaved the sides of her dark hair and pushed the rest off her forehead. Her dress resembles Elodie's, but it's the color of iron-rich dirt—brownish red. "Sit. We have time."

I don't have an excuse other than I don't want to talk to anyone. Dropping into the chair, I grab the extra unopened favor. The blush label on it has the yellow outline of the Foster House logo. Durban and Campbell and the date form a circle around it. I crack the top and down half of it.

The flavor only propels me back in time. I'm between Prescott's legs in the rickhouse. Her moans are in my ear, and I finally have her.

"Fuck." I slam the tiny bottle down.

Avery and Thea exchange a glance.

"So," Avery says hesitantly, "I'm just going to be blunt."

I bark out a laugh. "Avery, I've known you for years now. That's your middle name."

"It's actually Marie, and I'm going to spare you the rant about how the middle kid got the generic middle name."

Thea's brows pinch together. "I thought your mom said it was her grandma's name."

"That doesn't sound as sad." Avery pins me with her direct gaze. "You've been out of sorts all week, and I've heard about a Bootleg bartender that you've been seen with a lot." She puts her hands up and looks around. "Yet... you're alone."

"She doesn't like weddings," I utter, empty, sick of repeating the excuse. Would she have made an exception for me? I didn't give her a chance to decide. Besides, she would've been a guest. *My* plus-one.

"Fair." Thea crosses her arms. "They aren't all relaxed soirées like the Hawthorne girls' weddings are."

Avery punctuates the statement with a knowing nod. "So where is the mystery woman who's got you all bound up?"

"Gone." I stare at the table filled with wedding favors. The words pile on my tongue, and for once, I don't want to keep them in. Avery and Thea are removed from the drama. It's why I talked to Prescott about things like my mom.

No. That's not why. It's because I wanted to talk with her. Emotions weren't crowded so fiercely inside me that I was ready to burst like now. I wanted Prescott, and I wanted her to want all of me.

"She left town," I say. "Today."

"Why?" Avery draws out the word.

I smack my lips. "Because she doesn't want this kind of life with a guy like me."

"Okay, a guy like you. But what about with *you*?" Thea shrugs. "I know the Hennessys aren't just normal dudes or Avery's sisters wouldn't keep marrying them."

"Well, no one's marrying me," I say.

"Did you ask?" Avery counters.

"Why would I? It wasn't that serious." She doesn't want me.

Avery narrows her eyes at me. "You've been moping around for a week like your puppy kicked you, yet you're all, 'it wasn't that serious?'" She makes her voice low when she mimics me. I scowl at her.

Thea fans herself. "Be still, my heart. A guy wants me, but doesn't want to chase me and just lets me go. Oh my god. I'm never going to recover from the romance."

I frown at each of them. Since they're on either side of the table, I have to switch back and forth. "What the hell are you two getting at?"

My stomach cramps and starts to free-fall. Because I know.

Avery smacks my arm. "Iverson gave up his entire career for his Sunny. And he dragged you two with him to do it. Durban rode off with Campbell from someone else's wedding."

"And he's doing it again tonight," Thea says and thinks a moment. "I mean, it's *their* wedding this time."

"But the point stands," Avery continues. "You want your woman, you're gonna have to work for it."

"What about her?"

"Again, the romance," Thea says flatly. "It's killing me."

A ding sounds faintly from nearby.

Thea waves her phone in the air. "Avery, you're on." She squeezes my biceps. "That means you are too." There's concern in her eyes. "I really think that if you like this girl, you should put yourself out there. I get the feeling you didn't."

"She gets that because she was the same way." Avery

pats my other arm, the same worry in her eyes. "I thought, whelp, this chick isn't into me. And then I planned to go on a big backpacking trip in Italy. I was going to be gone for months, and when I came back, I'd find a new town to start over in again."

"What happened?" I ask as if they aren't a united pair right in front of me.

"I packed my shit and went with her." Thea smacks her teeth against her lips and shudders. She takes my wedding favor and downs the rest. "I hate hiking, bugs, and not showering every day. Yet I had the time of my life."

They both give me a hug, sandwiching me for a second before disappearing.

I glower at the empty single-serving bottles of whiskey. Prescott didn't throw herself at me. She tried to resist. And then she kept making plans for her future.

I didn't ask her to stay. I couldn't do that to her.

What if I went with her?

I stand up, like I'm ready to run, but I don't know where to.

"Excuse me," a growly voice says behind me. "Oh, Haven. Hi." Silas takes the seat Thea was in. He sniffs and looks around. He's got a Busch Light in his hand, condensation gathered around the outside. "Been wanting to see this place firsthand."

"How's Prescott?" I blurt it out like I don't care about small talk. I don't.

"Good. She's probably taking off about now."

I lean closer to him. "She didn't leave this morning?"

He screws his face up. "Nope. Wanted to sleep in and take her time packing. She's only going to get as far as Rapid City tonight, and it's going to be late."

She could still be here? She could still be in town? I

scan the room as if she followed her dad to Hawthorne Ranch.

Silas sniffs, and a cloud passes over his features. I stop, ready to run, but caught by his expression. There's a sadness in his eyes I've never seen before. Silas has only one setting—cantankerous.

"You miss her?"

His mustache twitches. "The heck. I think I do. Kind of nice having her close and seeing her at the bar. Makes a guy think about some things he should've done differently."

Am I going to be that guy? Looking back and wishing I'd put myself out there? Because she's become so important to me that I treasure each day I got with her.

No. I'm not going to be the guy telling old stories in the tasting room in thirty years. I want to create new ones—with Prescott. "Which route is she taking?"

He rolls a shoulder. "Probably through Billings. Roads are better."

Probably. Good enough. I know she's going to Chicago, and I know it's a cat company. Without saying a word to Silas, I rush out the door.

Iverson and Durban are standing by the front door talking to Mae. They give me quizzical looks. I don't want to stop, but they're talking to Mae.

She smiles at me. "It's almost time. I'd better go take my seat."

She gives me a hug, and when she goes outside, there's a sense of loss. I wish she could've met Prescott. She could've met the girl I can't get enough of. Instead of going to my mom's the day before my birthday, I should've taken Prescott to Bourbon Canyon.

"She didn't leave this morning." My heart hammers against my ribs.

Iverson's brows draw together. "Prescott?"

"She might still be here. Or she might be gone by now." My mouth goes dry. "But she's only going as far as Rapid City tonight." My brothers exchange a heavy look, but I don't interpret it. I'm running highway calculus equations in my head. "Fuck. Will Silas know where she's staying? What if she's still in town? I've got to go after her."

The words are out of my mouth. They don't make sense, but they make perfect sense.

"I don't know if you noticed," Iverson says wryly, "but Durban's getting married in less than an hour."

"I know." *Fuck*. I can't let them down, but the pull between me and Prescott is going to tear me in two.

"Wait a sec." Durban holds his hand up. "You're finally ready to admit you like her?"

"I more than like her." I'm obsessed with her. I have been since I first saw her.

"Sounds like you've got to go," Durban says simply.

"I can't ditch your wedding. I can't be like Mom." But it's not fair for him to have me standing there with nothing but Prescott on my mind. "But Prescott means *everything* to me."

A smile stretches Durban's lips. "Then you're not like Mom, and it's the best reason to miss my wedding."

Iverson scratches the back of his neck. "You had the whole goddamn summer, but shit. You gotta go."

My gaze jumps between him and Durban, waiting for them to tell me I'm a loser for abandoning them.

Durban grips me by the shoulders, his gaze boring into me. "This wedding is a celebration, but I have Campbell no matter what. If I think back on this day and remember you're not here, I'm also going to remember how proud I was that you got over your fear. That you weren't too scared to go after your woman and be as happy as me and Iverson."

Emotion spills over. I yank him into a quick bear hug. I'm about to skirt around them to get out the door, but then a bride appears at my side. Campbell's in a gauzy white, off-the-shoulder dress that falls short enough to reveal her white-and-blush cowboy boots, and Jamison is in a dress just like what Avery's wearing next to her.

"Hey, Haven," she says, her gray eyes glittering with nothing but happiness.

"I'm sorry," is all I say.

Her brow creases. "For what?"

"He's gotta go after his girl," Durban says without censure.

Campbell gasps. "Oh. Go. *Go*."

Iverson opens the door and makes an ushering motion outside.

"I'm sorry. I don't want to be dramatic like Mom."

Iverson shakes his head, and Durban scoffs.

"This is nothing like her drama," Iverson says. "You're running to the people you love, not away from them."

"We'll delay as long as we can," Campbell says, her voice crackling with wedding planner authority. "Go get her and bring her back with you."

"If she'll come. Otherwise, I'm following her wherever she's going."

Prescott

. . .

Tears stream down my face. "Kitty, kitty, kitty."

Come on. I'm running out of time. I'm trying not to barge into the wedding of someone I barely know, but there's a groomsman I need to accost.

"Kitty?" Grasses tickle my legs, and I hold down my skirt. The last time it blew up and flashed a passerby, it didn't turn out so bad—until last weekend.

A tiny mew reaches me.

"Kitty? Don't run," I mutter to myself as I pick my way through the ditch. A furry little ball darts under the barbed-wire fence. "Not the fence."

I've crawled over more than a few in my day, and I've done it in dresses before, but not when I want to go win the man of my heart.

"I'll get him."

I whip around. My heart's in my throat—because I *know* that voice. My gaze lands on Haven. He's more handsome than ever in pristine black jeans with black suspenders. His scruff is trimmed, and his hair's combed to the side, but a lock's falling over his forehead.

His long legs eat up the space between us until he's right in front of me. He's not real. He can't be. How many times can a guy find a girl in a ditch?

"What are you doing here?" I ask, breathless.

"Looking for you." He squints at my car. "What are you doing here?"

"A kitten darted across the road."

The corner of his mouth cocks up. "Again?"

I swallow. He's so close. I could reach out and touch him, but that might burst the fantasy. "Seems they've heard about my new profile and one hundred percent success rate for rescue placement.”

“I get the cat. I wouldn’t expect anything less.” He crowds even closer, his gaze intense. “What are *you* doing here? This isn’t the way to Chicago.”

“No. It’s not.” It’s the way back to him. Wait— Isn’t he supposed to be somewhere? “What about the wedding? Is everything okay?”

“The wedding is fine.” He runs a tendril of my hair between his fingers. “I’m not. There’s this girl. I can’t quit thinking about her. I can’t quit wanting her. I can’t quit thinking that maybe…I could have something special with her.”

Oh my god, it’s too much. The sun shining on him. The way his dark eyes sparkle. This cannot be real. “She sounds hideous.”

He laughs, his breath laced with whiskey.

A small part of me shrivels. I cup his face with my hand. Did he need liquid courage for this? “Have you been drinking, Hennessy?”

“No, Red. Just a swallow as I was pouring out my woes to Avery and Thea. They asked the damnedest thing.” He grips my wrist and turns his face into my hand. His whiskers tickle my palm. “You wanna know what it was? Sure as hell got me thinking.”

I can barely nod. Yes, I want to know. Just like I have to know the reason why he’s here, on the side of the road with me, instead of at his brother’s wedding.

He strokes his thumb along my wrist. “They wanted to know if I asked you to stay.”

A small gasp escapes. If this is all in my imagination, I’m going to turn to dust and blow away. My emotions can’t take this. “No. You didn’t ask.”

"No," he echoes softly. His knuckles brush along my jaw. "I told myself it's what you want. You never wanted to fall for some whiskey cowboy."

"You're more than that, Haven."

"So much more that you'd let me make all your dreams come true from Huckleberry Springs, Montana?"

"You want me to stay?"

"I want you with me, in my house, in my bed, Prescott Keys. I want to come home to you wearing nothing but an apron in the kitchen. I want to build you your own studio. I want to travel with you to work with rescues. I want to help you track down strays." He points toward the pasture. "That little guy is watching us. He ain't going nowhere but in your arms. I just gotta say some stuff first."

I'm soaring, but my feet are on the ground. "You've said a lot, and I like what I'm hearing."

"Will you like hearing that I've fallen in love with you?"

I make a choking sound trying to get my "yes" out. "You have?"

"So much. I love you, Red."

He's putting himself out there, and it's something he's never done. I've heard enough about his childhood and his mom to know why. So before I can throw myself into his arms, I have to give him something in return. "This isn't the way to Chicago because I kept stalling. I couldn't leave."

"Why couldn't you leave?" Our faces are inches apart.

"You." I lift my chin, but a tremor runs through my body. Fear. Excitement. Despite what he's said, the anxiety that this is just a lucid dream won't go away. "I was hurt that you didn't tell me about your visit with your mom, and instead of giving you grace, I used it as an excuse. All week, I felt like I failed. Because I did. You needed space, but mostly, you needed someone there for you, and I want to be that person."

"You already are." He wraps his arms around my waist. "I've already been sharing my home and my secrets with you, and I should've trusted you about last weekend. I knew it was a bad idea, and I guess I was afraid to be told again that it was. When all along, I should've known you are the one person I can talk to about her."

"I love you, Hennessy."

His grin deepens. "You do, Red?"

"I've been miserable the whole week. I like this town. I like being close to my dad even if he doesn't want me around. I like your friends and family. I like your cowboy boots—the whole package. I love you."

He places a gentle kiss on my lips. "I love when you call me Hennessy. Like I stand out in a trio of Hennessys."

"That's because you're special—to your brothers, to everyone who knows you, to me."

He kisses me again, a longer, lingering one this time. "You might be surprised about your dad. But you're still going to Chicago."

The stab to my heart hits so fast I can't draw in a breath. He asked me to stay, and now he's telling me to go?

"Quit worrying, my little rescue influencer." He traces my lips with a finger. "I'm telling you that if you want to go to Chicago, I'm going with you."

"I don't want to move back to Chicago."

"Then we won't stay. But we're getting you there for that interview. The animals need it."

"Oh, Haven. You showed me that it's not the size of the town that matters, it's what I do in it, and I very much want to do you."

He cups my face and plants his mouth on mine, delving

deep. I meet each stroke of his tongue with a needy one of my own. Twining my arms around him is like securing my future. This man is mine, and I'm his.

"Mew."

Haven breaks the kiss with a soft chuckle. "Let's get your cat and get to the wedding so I can show you off."

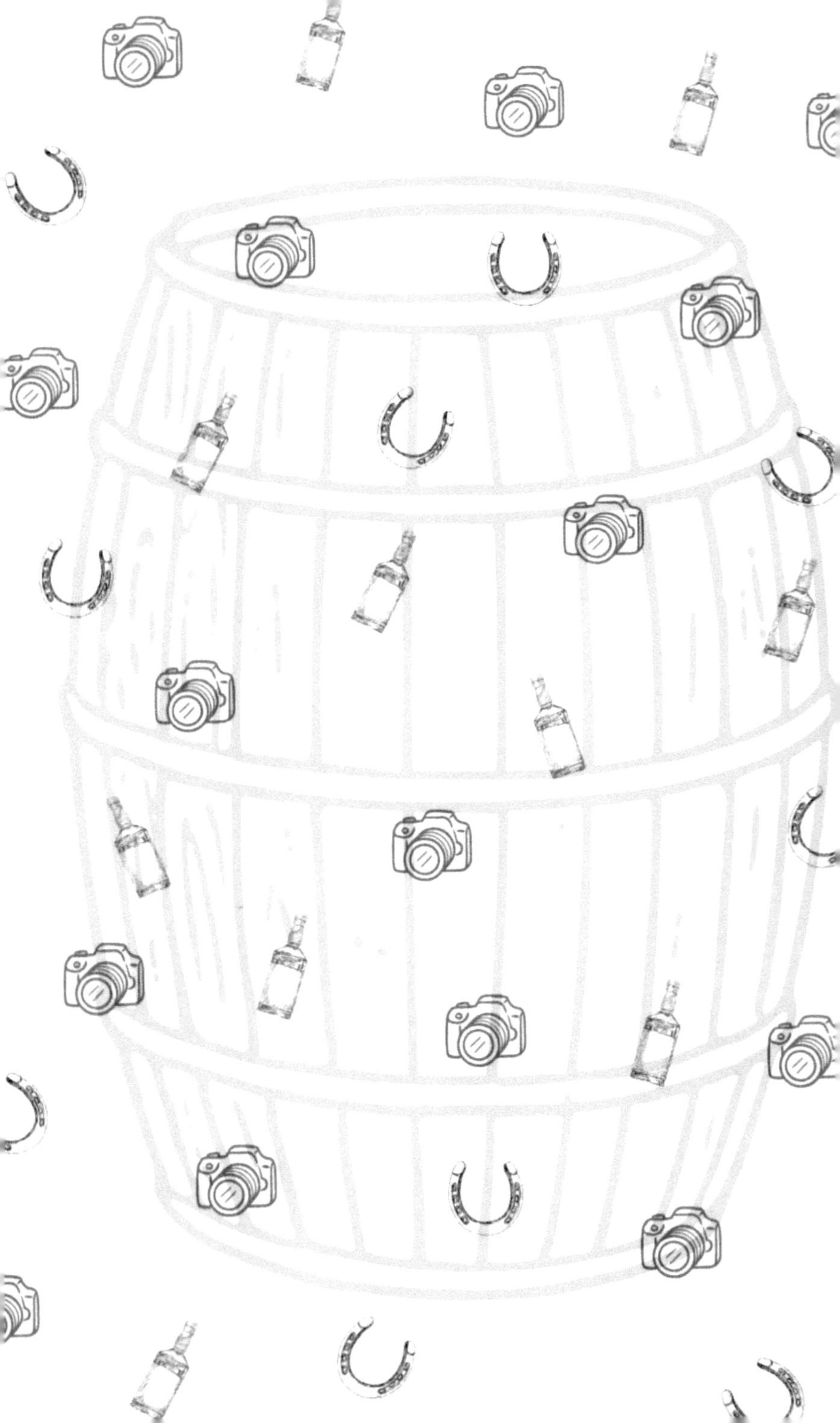

CHAPTER TWENTY-SIX

Haven

I haven't taken my arm from around Prescott since we arrived. We charged back to the wedding, driving separately so her car wasn't stuck on the side of the road all night. The ceremony hadn't started yet when we arrived. The cheers that went up when I pulled into the parking lot and ran to the lodge with Prescott were a good clue that they were waiting, just like Campbell said.

We found a ranch employee to watch over the kitten for us and procure some food for it while the wedding was going on. Prescott already named it Windy, for Chicago, the Windy City. Then we dusted ourselves off and went out to the pavilion.

Prescott sat next to her dad for the ceremony. I was at the front with my brothers, but I couldn't take my eyes off her. Her fiery hair made her easy to pick out, but I'd find her anywhere. I'll make sure that I don't need to.

Now we're milling around, but there's something I

have to tell her. The two of us are a small island amid the other guests. The food has been served and the dancing will start soon. Before the sun sets, Durban will ride off with his wife, and the rest of us will return to our lives. Prescott and I will head out to Chicago in the morning. After I take her home.

"About the night before my birthday," I start, my words halting. She's quiet and waits. "Mom asked for more money, and instead of giving in, I cut her off. She reminded me that she never wanted me."

Prescott's lips part, and she puts her hands on each side of my face. "You are the most wanted man. Your brothers love you. All the Baileys love you. This town loves you. *I* love you. I'm not even counting all the animals who eat out of your literal hand."

My nose burns and heat pricks the backs of my eyes. Fuck, I needed to hear that. "Maybe I can get you eating out of my hand."

She rises to put her mouth close to my ear. "I have a better idea of where to put the food."

Hell yeah.

But before I can carry her off caveman-style, her dad stops by us.

Silas scratches the side of his neck. He oscillates between scowling at me and looking delighted to have his daughter around. "You moving back in?"

I hug Prescott closer to me. "She's staying with me. When we get back from Chicago, I'm not letting her go." His eyes narrow. "Unless she wants me to."

"No," she says, smiling at both of us. "I'm not going anywhere."

His bushy brows rise. "You're both going to Chicago?"

"I don't want to live there again." Prescott puts her

hand on my chest. "This guy said he'd build me a studio, but I might only need really good Wi-Fi."

"So you're staying?" he asks gruffly. "Here in Huckleberry Springs?"

"Yeah, Papa. I am. I've got some bartending shifts to cover."

"Good. Good." He sniffs. "Maybe we can hire someone. So you can run that rescue thing. I might need you to look at the books too. You know, if you're not too busy."

She bites back a smile. "I'll make it work."

"Glad you're back." He nods once and shuffles to the wet bar.

"Wow," she says on an exhale. "That's the most I've ever gotten out of him."

"He loves you." I tip her chin up. "He might not know how to show it, but I'm going to spend a lot of time doing just that."

Mae leaves the circle of Foster brothers and crosses to us. Her kind smile heals old wounds inside me. From now on, I'm only going to surround myself with those who want to be with me. "Nice to see you again, Prescott."

I glance at Prescott, surprised. "You two have met?"

"She came into Bootleg last night." Prescott's expression says the encounter gave her some things to think about.

"I had my suspicions she was the girl you kept mentioning." Mae beams at me, then at Prescott.

I'd be embarrassed, but not with Prescott's astonished expression. "That was me trying not to talk about her all the time," I grumble.

Mae chuckles. "But I didn't realize Prescott is also the photographer who did the new shots for Foster House

Gold. They're amazing. Teller wants to hire you for a Copper Summit overhaul."

Prescott's eyes go wide. "Oh my—that would be an honor."

"Afterward," Mae says, "we'll have a get-together at my place. It's too quiet with all the kids gone. I'll supply the food as long as I get to see all the shots you take."

"You should see the ones she took of me." I'm digging out my phone when Prescott stiffens.

"Um, maybe send her one later," she whispers.

The alarm shining in her eyes makes me pause. "I have the gallery—"

"I added some," she blurts, her gaze darting to Mae and back to me. "From the bar." Her eyes are pleading with me to remember.

Oh. I clear my throat to cover the lust taking root inside me and growing, whispering exactly how long it's been since I've been inside Prescott. "Gotcha. I'll send you one, Mae."

A knowing glint lights Mae's eyes. "Can't wait." She gives Prescott's arm a squeeze. "I'm looking forward to getting to know you." Then she grabs me in a big hug.

I close my eyes and soak it in. This is the type of embrace a mom gives. It's the type of love I deserve. This pavilion is full of everyone who matters to me in the world. Anyone else doesn't deserve my time.

After Mae leaves, I spin Prescott in my arms. "Red, I'm gonna need to see those pictures ASAP."

"I can't believe I did that."

"I can't believe I didn't know. I would've been jacking off to them every night."

"Haven." She glances around to make sure no one's within earshot. "First, my underwear—"

"You mean this underwear?" I dig in my back pocket and withdraw the neatly folded wad of satiny material.

Her eyes fly wide. "Haven!" she whispers.

"I couldn't stand the thought of you leaving today, so I kept these with me." I grin and tuck them into her hand. "I told you when I gave them back, you'd know everything I did with them, but I want to drag you home and show you."

Her eyes simmer with affection. "As much as I want that, as much as I want to be under you and screaming your name, this is a big day for you. Your brothers are important."

"But you're coming home with me?" I might ask her five more times before the night is over.

She pulls me toward the makeshift dance floor. "I'm not going anywhere. Think of the rest of the night as foreplay."

"As long as it ends with you in my bed." I keep an arm around her waist and clasp her right hand in mine. "And me waking up to you in the morning."

The alarm goes off, and I crack an eye open. Half the blankets are kicked off, and I have an armful of warm woman. Prescott's ass is pressed into my groin. We're both naked from the shower we took together after a sex fest last night, and her hair is spread across the pillow and under my cheek.

She lets out a little moan. "It's early."

"We'll be able to stop and see some sights on our drive." I nestle my nose into the crook of her neck and shift my hips enough that my dick notches between her butt cheeks. Fucking perfect.

She rocks just enough to tease the hell out of me. "How was last night? And this morning?"

"You mean, do I like bringing a sexy woman home to fuck all night long?" I push my erection between her legs and let her ride it without pushing inside. "And then waking up to her in the morning to devour her again?"

"Is that what's going to happen?"

I nip her shoulder and cup her breast when she giggles. "It's going to happen once. I can't be in a car with you for hours with a hard-on. It's not safe driving."

She rocks her hips, slicking her wet heat across my cock. "We've gotta be safe."

"Yeah, we do." I push her legs apart with my knee and position my dick at her entrance. "As for your question— last night? This morning? You, in my bed? It's what I've been waiting for." I thrust inside. She groans and undulates. "You, in my house. You and the cats you come with. I've been waiting for you."

"*Haven*." She reaches behind her, pulling my hips closer.

I pump in and out, stroking us both higher. She's so wet and ready. This woman was made for me. "You're mine, Red. You're my person."

"You're mine," she says on an exhale, writhing against me.

"All mine." I slip my hand down her abdomen and slide my fingertip onto her clit. "This pussy is only mine."

"Yes." She bucks against me. The sensations coursing through me swell into an intensity I've never experienced before. She's hotter, wetter, and—

I freeze, and she gasps, looking back at me.

"I'm not wearing a condom." After last night, do I have any left? "I thought you were leaving, so I didn't replenish my stock."

She melts against me. "You're still saying sweet things."

Lust hammers into me, but I don't move. I'll pull out if she tells me to. I can't deny how right this feels. How... significant. "I love you, Prescott. I want you in my life for forever, but we'll go at your pace."

"What if my pace has waited a long time for you?"

My hips twitch, and I groan at the ecstasy slipping and sliding through my veins. I withdraw and thrust inside—hard. "Then I'm gonna make sure I keep up."

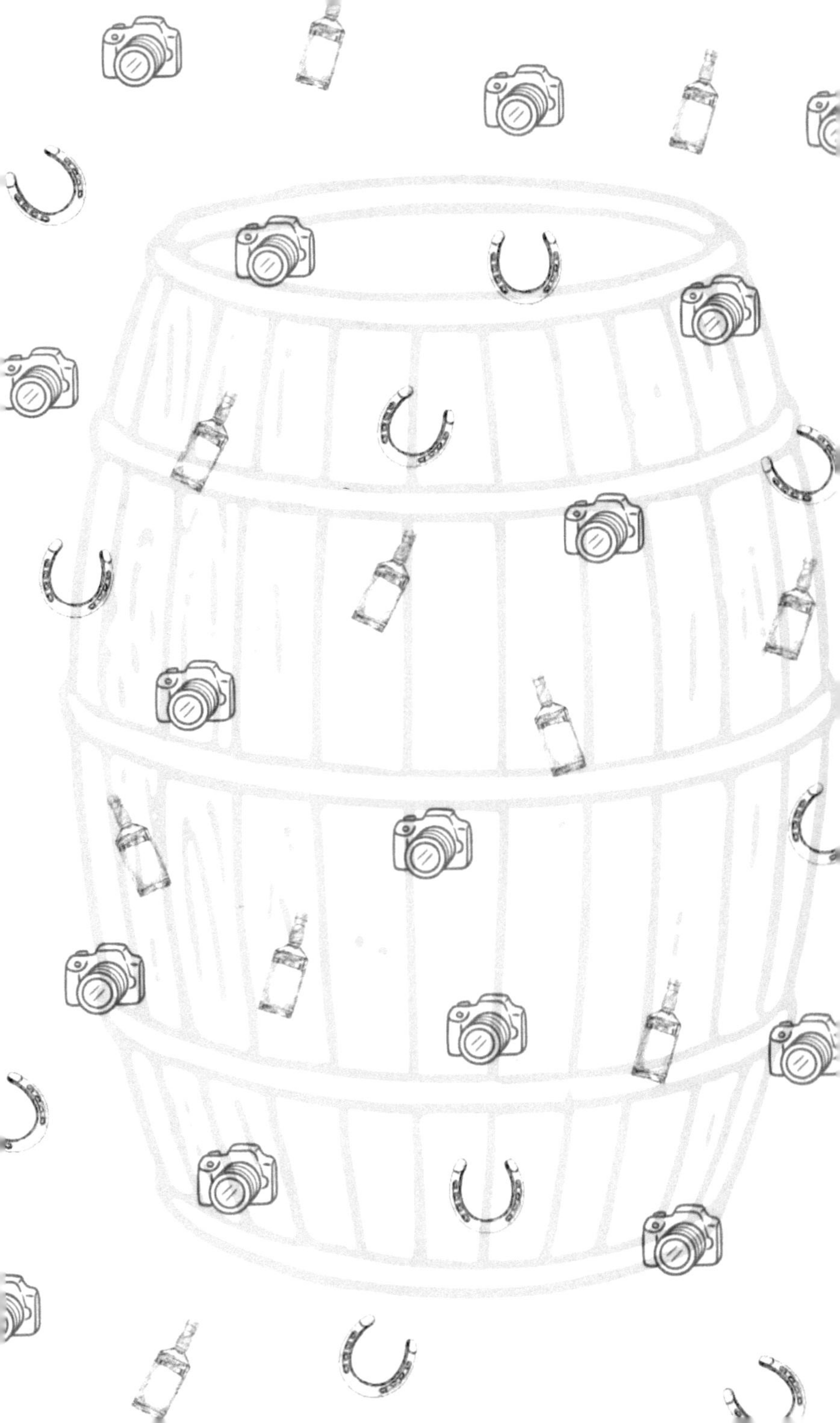

EPILOGUE

Prescott

I pull into my usual spot outside the new shop with my studio. I made better time coming home than I thought. Haven's probably still at the distillery. Meadow greets me instead, her tail wagging hard enough it could leave dents in my car.

"Hey, girl. I missed you." I give her a big hug and let her sniff me. I'm filled with the scents of the many cat and dog rescues from Miles City. The donkey is probably throwing her the most. Most photogenic one of my life. Not something I thought I'd ever say, but thanks to the last year of working with rescues to post their animals on my amazingly successful account, yeah. I have a photogenic donkey.

Before I unload my equipment, I cross to the barn. The kittens I rescued last spring are no longer tiny fluff balls. It's October, and they're getting their winter coats. Two of them run up to greet me. I crouch to pet them.

Meadow crowds to get more love too. Tan finally runs over to me, but he's probably after treats.

Boots crunch on the ground behind me. "I've had to peel Windy off my face every morning since you've been gone."

I straighten, grinning at the image that puts into my head. "You have to do that when I'm home."

He grins. "True, but then you're my reward for making her cranky."

Gah, this guy. I'm his, wrapped around his little finger and, honestly, whatever else I can access, but he still says sweet things more than ever. I drink him in.

He looks better than ever. He's still in a plain black T-shirt and jeans, but I'm so attuned to him he could be in a garbage bag, and I'd be drooling.

He yanks me to him and plasters a kiss on me. I tangle my hands in his hair. I was only gone a few days, but whenever I return, he greets me like he's missed me for years. This man wants me around and loves telling me—and showing me—how much.

When he breaks the kiss, he gives me a heavy-lidded smile. "The donkey pics were my favorite. Can't wait to see the rest. There are a ton of packages in your studio from Toe Beans."

"They have a new line of wet cat food and catnip toys. I told the rescue in Miles City that I'd bring them for the shoot next week."

"Need an assistant?"

"I can always put you to work." I take his hand. "They also would like some after-adoption videos. You know, showing how blissfully happy owners and rescues are—of course while using their products."

"Of course. They are happier with Toe Bean treats. Go ahead, get the stand."

"I can just toss the newest catnip toy and film them chasing it."

"Nah, Red. You're getting in this one. You said owners and pets."

A nervous laugh leaves me. I'm not afraid of being in front of the camera, but old feelings come roaring back. "I want to get views. That doesn't happen with me. The kittens get views."

He tugs me into him and plants a kiss on me. "Just this once."

"Fine." I give him a playful shove. "I'll prove it to you." And then he'll cheer me up by getting me naked, definitely not on camera.

I set up the camera stand and the light, adjusting it to catch me playing with the kittens. Haven digs out the fishing pole toy that has feathers and catnip fish on the end.

"I'm just going to make it short and then get more content when I'm done rambling."

His boots scrape on the floor of the barn as he moves out of the way.

I run my fingers through my hair. It doesn't matter. This will be a quick shot. I don't even have to talk. I hit record, take the toy from Haven, shoot him a smirk, and face the camera. Tansy jumps out of the shadows to grab at the feathers. Windy dances sideways. My laughter fills the barn. That will be genuine.

Meadow trots around us, and I spin in a circle, trying to get Windy to attack. I finish the rotation and gasp. I drop the toy, and my hands fly to my mouth.

Haven's on one knee, Meadow sitting beside him,

holding out a little velvet box. Mountains in the backdrop on the other side of the barn, just like I pictured so many months ago. But his home—our home—is also in view, and our rescues surround us. "Prescott, I've been waiting for this day. Will you marry me?"

Elation sweeps through me. This is it. What I've wanted for so long, but I'm so glad I didn't get it until Haven. "Yes, Haven. Absolutely yes."

He rises, a big, handsome grin in place. "You've made me the happiest damn man."

My hand's trembling when I hold it out. He slides the ring on my finger. A perfect fit. "I'm going to love seeing this on you for the rest of my life."

"I'm yours, Haven. I've wanted you since I met you."

He cups my chin and kisses me. "You rescued me that day."

If I'm not already a puddle for this guy, that does it. He's put himself out there for me in a way he's never done for anyone. "I'm going to marry you, Haven, and I'm going to love you forever. We're going to live in this house and rescue animals and raise kids someday, and we're going to be happy. Together."

His grin widens. "Because you're my person, Red."

I'm vibrating with giddiness. "I'm so going to post this."

"You're going to get a lot of rescues adopted if guys think they'll get a sexy redhead out of it."

"I'm thinking girls will go ditch diving if it makes cowboys show up." I glance at the camera. "I'll edit that part out."

He pulls me closer. "You're going to have a lot more to edit out."

"Can we watch it first?" I whisper.

"Hell yes. Now let me make you mine."

"I already am."

———

Thank you for reading Haven and Prescott's story!

Lane Foster will do anything for the people he cares about, even if it means marrying the daughter of his neighbor so she can inherit her father's house. Emerson Langley doesn't want to play wife when she's got a business to run, but to help her brother and her niece, she'll suck it up in Whiskey Proposal.

Join Haven and Prescott at the surprise birthday party he throws her in a special bonus epilogue.

ABOUT THE AUTHOR

I live the dream in my own slice of paradise where I get to enjoy colorful sunsets from my rocking chair while I'm working. I have my very own romance hero with Mr. Rose and there's more than a few little rose buds running around. A couple aren't so little anymore! We keep things interesting with cats and a dog and the critters that roam though the yard (fingers crossed the mountain lions stay away).

walkerrosebooks.com

ALSO BY WALKER ROSE

Foster House Series

Whiskey Cowboy

Whiskey Bargain

Whiskey Flirt

Whiskey Charm

Whiskey Proposal

Bourbon Canyon Series

Bourbon Bachelor

Bourbon Lullaby

Bourbon Runaway

Bourbon Promises

Bourbon Harmony

Bourbon Summer

Bourbon Sunset

9 781951 067861